# HONOR

# EMMA RENSHAW

# DEDICATION

*For Michelle and Suzanne,*
*The first readers to reach out to me.*
*I adore both of you so much. I'll never be able to thank y'all*
*enough for being a big part in my dreams coming true. Every*
*message, comment, and share makes me grin like a maniac.*
*Thank you for loving my stories and characters! Y'all are*
*wonderful!*


*As always, for my husband,*
*You're the reason I can chase my dreams fearlessly.*
*I love you with everything I am and everything I have.*

# PROLOGUE

## James
*Ten Years Ago*

'VE NEVER HAD MUCH IN MY LIFE. NOT A PENNY TO MY name. Don't think I've ever owned a new shirt; it's all been hand-me-downs from my foster "siblings." I've never been outside the Chicago city limits. I've never had a holiday meal that's shown on TV.

Tonight is the most destitute I've ever been, though.

No home.

No city.

No name.

Nothing.

I ran with just the ratty sneakers on my feet, a borrowed shirt under my dark gray hoodie, and jeans so tattered and worn, there's a tiny hole on my ass right above the left pocket.

That's all I have.

Those clothes.

And the duffle bag of stolen cash. My hand grips the bag so tightly, my tendons ache. I can't stop flashing my eyes down to the bag every other second, making sure it's still there. It's a conscious effort not to look around at the people like a crazed maniac.

*Play it cool* runs through my mind on a loop. I squeeze my thigh to stop my leg from bouncing up and down as I sit by the window of an old Greyhound, the ripped vinyl of the seat biting into my leg.

The hood of my sweatshirt conceals my face as I step off the bus, keeping my head down. The duffle bag and ratty clothes help. No one pays attention to a punk kid on a cheap-ass Greyhound headed to nowhere.

I'm being as careful as I can, even though I know no one looks for a dead man.

# CHAPTER
## ONE

## James
*Present Day*

LATE. AGAIN.

Waiting. Something I've spent my life doing. Something I hate.

First month of my life was spent in a hospital waiting for a vacancy in a foster home that accepted newborns born with an addiction.

My youth was spent waiting for a family. Waiting for food.

My life now is spent going day to day waiting for the world I've built to come crashing down.

I fucking hate waiting.

My eyes are glued to the clock above the door, watching the seconds ticking away. One after another, passing time, erasing precious minutes of my appointment. Every damn time, my physical therapist has come late but doesn't extend the hour I should be here. I'm over it. Done with it. This changes today. If the PT was helping, I could overlook his tardiness. Maybe. But there hasn't been any improvement since the first appointment. I'm half-way through the ordered six weeks and nothing to show for it.

Simon Lambert, worst physical therapist in the damn world, and of course I land him.

The surgeon assured me that the recovery after being shot should be simple enough. He only enforced physical therapy because of the extensive exercises I do on a normal basis. I chose the therapist with the most openings to get this done and over with, so I can get my ass back in the gym and not just watch.

Simon finally appears in the doorway, twenty-six minutes late, looking around until his eyes fall on me propped against the wall. The displeasure on my face must be evident because he backs up a tiny step before swallowing and straightening his spine. His eyes cast down to his shoes, he slowly walks toward me. I track him with my glare, waiting for him to look me in the eye like a man.

He doesn't.

Fuckin' dick.

The spineless prick doesn't even look my way when he finally reaches me. Doesn't even give me that courtesy.

When he finally looks up, his eyes wander around the room, snagging on every female in here, leering at them with his beady eyes. My patience is paper thin after continuously catching him staring at patients and other therapists. He watches them, running his tongue over his teeth, looking like a damn predator.

My fingers snap in front of his face. "Late," I clip through clenched teeth.

"Won't happen again," Simon says, holding his hands in front of him trying to placate me with a smile. My scowl deepens, my lip curls, and the smile slides from his face.

"Been hearin' that for weeks."

"Shall we get started?" he asks, changing the subject and expecting me to fall in line like I have been. Yes, I'm desperate to get out of here and done with this, but not with this guy. Not anymore.

I didn't have a damn person to teach me manners growing up, and I have more than this clown. Not even an apology. Every little thing is getting to me since I got shot near my shoulder and lower chest. I feel like a wounded animal trapped in someone else's clutches. Unable to find release my normal way, my anger is faster to rise to the surface.

Turning and striding toward our area, I wait for him to follow. His steps are slow and would be faster if he wasn't constantly distracted by every girl in the room. Won't lie, there are some beautiful women in here, but the way this man gawks, you'd think he's never seen a woman before in his life.

"Start with a shoulder roll."

I roll my eyes instead. He's been having me do light stretches and shit they do in an elementary school gym. An exasperated sigh passes my lips as I start my shoulder rolls, counting at a rapid pace. If I have to do this shit, I'll push myself any way I can.

"Take it easy, James."

A growl erupts from my chest, my glare locking on his eyes. "Done takin' it easy."

Simon Lambert excels at being a pain in my ass. He's excelled at this since the moment I met him. Fuck. Dealing with him and his constant need to move my progress along at the speed of a fuckin' snail is worse than the pain of the bullets that tore through my body several weeks ago.

Two bullets. One in the shoulder, one in the chest. Surgery was required for both, but it's the shoulder wound that needs physical therapy. The bullet ripped through my muscle, limiting my range of motion after surgery. I own a damn gym, and I can't do shit while I'm there. My body aches to get back in front of a bag or under a bench press.

"Let's start with the two-pound medicine ball, it's the lightest," Simon says lifting the ball from the rack.

"He looks like he can handle more," a female voice says from the side. I turn toward the voice to find a blonde nurse in hot pink scrubs. I've never seen scrubs so tight, they're perfectly molded to her body. Her eyes are slowly moving over every inch of me.

*What the hell is wrong with this place?*

"Kimmie," Simon greets with his usual leer.

"I came to drop this off," Kimmie says handing Simon a folder without breaking her gaze from me. "What happened to you?"

I know she's asking me this question, but I stay silent grabbing the puny ball from Simon's hands and turning my back on the pair of them.

"He was shot. Twice," Simon boasts as if he's the surgeon that saved my life.

"Oh my god," Kimmie breathes placing a hand on my arm. Her small hand has long pointed nails painted the same pink as her scrubs. I shake it off, take a step to the side, and proceed to mimic a shoulder press with the medicine ball resting in my palm. A two-pound medicine ball. I could lift this damn thing with my pinky finger.

My fingers curl into the ball, pressing in the rubber when Simon starts speaking again.

"He was shot by a police officer who was working with a gang," Simon brags. I see him move closer to a riveted Kimmie out of the corner of my eye.

The dirty cop was in a drug cartel's pocket. If this motherfucker is going to share my story, he could at least get it right.

"He was shot twice," Simon repeats. "He totally saved one of his friends though."

"You're so brave," Kimmie says, placing her hand on

my arm again. I shake it off. Again. "What else happened?"

I don't answer. I don't tell her my friend, Harper, and her man, Roman, were in a bind with a ruthless cartel president. I don't tell her I was shot by a dirty cop.

I clear my thoughts before the anger creeps in. That's what I feel every time I think about the situation. Story of my life. I told Harper to dial 9-1-1. First time I trusted the authorities to handle anything, and only told her to do it because that's what Roman would have wanted her to do. He was trusting me to do right by Harper and protect her until he could be back at her side. Trust is something I take seriously. I don't give it freely, but I aim to earn it from the people in my life. If I earn it, I'll do damn near anything to keep it. Out of respect for Roman, I played it his way—I told her to call the cops. Dirty fuckin' cop showed up and pushed Harper out of the way to drill two holes in my body, taking out her only protection.

Making sure Harper was safe from that lunatic was worth it though, and Roman has become a fast friend, even if I still want to kick his ass from time to time. I'm thankful as fuck those bullets hit me and not her. They've both been dealing with the fallout and the high body count of that night. Only thing I'm dealing with is this worthless physical therapist who sets off everything on my radar. The events from that day have had little effect on me otherwise. I've seen worse carnage. I've done worse carnage.

It's been a long time since I ran away from that life. Now I just try to live my life as honorably as I can and protecting the trust I've earned.

"Hey, asshole," I call when Simon continues to embellish my story. Kimmie and Simon look my way. "Does HIPPA ring any bells? Doctor-patient confidentiality? If I want someone to know my business. *I* tell them."

Simon's jaw snaps closed and he gives me a curt nod.

My eyes move to Kimmie. She scurries out of the room without a word. My tongue runs across my front teeth as I slowly inhale through my nose to calm myself. After another beat, I start raising the ball into the air again.

"You have to give your shoulder time to heal," Simon says, putting his hand on my shoulder, trying to slow me down.

I throw his hand off me as I whip around to face him. "It's a fucking two-pound ball," I growl. "I could lift you over my head with my one hand."

Simon sighs and pinches the bridge of his nose. We've been doing this back and forth since my first appointment. I've seen no improvements in my shoulder, and I've been as patient as I can. Six weeks of therapy, that's what they promised. At this point, I'll be here for the rest of my damn life.

"We have a plan, James," Simon says with his hands up in front of him, trying to calm me down.

I cock an eyebrow, challenging him to admit that his plan isn't fucking working. Not even a little bit. It's time for a new plan.

His lips roll between his teeth as he takes a step away from me, his hands still slightly raised. "Let's stick to the plan."

"Fuck the plan," I mutter.

"If you don't follow the plan, I'll have to move you to someone else's service," Simon threatens, placing his fists on his hips.

This could be the best news I've had in a long time. I raise my eyebrows. "That an option?"

"Well—"

I cut him off with an order. "Make it happen."

"James—"

"Make. It. Happen," I repeat in a low, thick tone. My

jaw hurts from clenching my teeth so hard.

Simon stares at me, waiting for me to change my mind. "Now."

With a shaky jerk of his head, Simon turns on his heel, rushing out of the room.

# CHAPTER
## TWO

*Tatum*

M Y BODY SHIVERS AS I HUM, HAPPILY SLURPING MY vanilla iced coffee. Heaven in a cup. Not one thing could take away from my good mood today. I woke up before my alarm, feeling fully rested instead of needing to drag myself out of bed. My hair dried fast, and for once my natural waves don't look frizzy after the hair dryer. That is enough to consider this a good day—no, a great day.

It's just kept going up from there, though. The cool, crisp fall air decided to make an appearance overnight. This is my absolute favorite time of year. I left on time to stop at my favorite Starbucks where the best barista works. When I arrived, there wasn't a single person in line. Usually it's so busy, I have to allow a good chunk of time before I'm supposed to be into work. This morning I waltzed in and ordered my delicious coffee and a croissant, just to celebrate the day.

The absolute best part about the empty Starbucks? No Simon. Simon Lambert, creepiest creeper on the planet. Most mornings I run into my weird coworker. Seeing the guy that makes my skin crawl before I've had coffee? Not the greatest thing in the world. Unfortunately, there's no other Starbucks on my drive to work.

Not one red light was hit on my drive from Starbucks to the hospital, just smooth sailing with my windows cracked open enough to let the fall breeze through, but not enough to mess up my hair. Now, here I am sipping on the best drink in the world, with the perfect amount of vanilla and the perfect amount of cream, while eating a soft, warm croissant. My shift hasn't even started yet, and I'm in blissful heaven.

Nothing can bring me down today.

A throat clearing on my left makes me doubt my declaration. Slowly, I turn my head to the man I know will be standing next to me. Skeevy vibes are already rolling off him, and I'm not even facing him yet. I take in his beady eyes and disgusting leer. My lips purse as I force myself not to grimace.

"Tatum," he says slowly, stepping closer.

I turn fully toward him, taking two steps back. I bite the inside of my cheek to keep from making a disgusted face. Even the way he says my name sets me on edge. Most of the other girls I work with steer clear of him as well, but I'm the only unlucky one he asks out, blatantly ignoring my outright rejections. He's never said anything overtly lewd, but it's everything else about him. His tone of voice, his endearments, the way he stares and licks his lips. The silent stare after I reject his date requests are the worst.

"Simon," I return dryly, barely hiding my grimace.

"I need a favor, babe." He steps closer again, speaking softly in a conspiratorial whisper.

I step back, not bothering to hide my annoyance. Taking a large sip of my now-watered-down coffee—just a symbol my day is going down the gutter—I wish the start of my great day stayed that way. "Can't wait to hear this."

I can tell he doesn't get the sarcasm when he grins at me, eyes lighting up and sweeping over my face before dipping down to my chest.

"Don't call me babe." Rolling my eyes, I angle my body

so it's half hidden behind the counter. He gives a little shrug as if to say he can't help it and his sheepish eyes snap back to mine. I can't hide my disgust, even if I wanted to.

"I need you to take over my patient."

Oh boy, this could be ugly. We typically don't make a habit of switching patients. Each of us have different philosophies when it comes to our therapy regimens, so switching can set a patient back. Simon has passed a patient off on me in the past, though. A pretty girl in her early thirties hated working with him so much, she asked for a trade. It wasn't until she'd been working with me for a while that she was honest about it. He creeped her out. *Same, girl. Same.*

"I don't think that's a good idea," I say carefully, thinking of any way I can get out of this without getting our boss involved. Simon is his nephew, and in our boss's eyes, the shining star amongst all the therapists.

"One of my long-term patients needs to change when they're coming in. Their schedule is so tight. Otherwise I wouldn't even ask. The patient I'm asking you to take has only been coming for a few weeks and only needs an additional few. Basic muscle movement type stuff. Please, I'll owe you one." He reaches out his hand to brush over my arm.

I masterfully step out of the way just in time to avoid contact. "When?"

"Right now," he says, grinning, trying—and failing—to be charming. "I owe you."

Holding up a hand, I stop him. "Right now? Why are you just asking now? And I haven't agreed yet."

"It's the end of his session, just thought you could meet him right now, walk through the chart with him. He's great. You'll like him."

I don't have a patient for another hour, so I could run through his chart, find out from him what he's done and how he feels. I've seen Simon work with his patients. I don't understand his philosophy when it comes to physical therapy and attaining a patient's goals and needs. If I needed to come to a therapist, he wouldn't be my choice, so I don't trust his assessment. Learning from the patient is the best way to go.

"Fine," I mutter, reaching past him to grab the rest of my croissant and iced coffee. The day started out so well, but conversing with Simon and having an unexpected patient that I'll need to work into my already rigorous schedule definitely dims my happy mood a bit. Hopefully Simon is the worst that will happen today. At least he didn't ask me out.

"Great," Simon says, pulling his tablet from the large pocket on his white coat. "I'll share the file with you now."

I don't respond as I walk toward the locker room to grab my tablet.

"Tatum?"

I stop, not bothering to face him.

"Ready for that date?"

"No," I spit out icily, resuming my trek to my locker and picking up the pace. An alert sounds from my cubby as soon as I step into the locker room. I reach for it and my notepad, getting ready to meet this new patient.

*A file has been shared with you.*

I swipe open the file and glance at the name while walking toward the physical therapy room. James Harris. Thirty. I lock the screen before reading any further, preferring to gather the information from the patient before forming an opinion about the treatment needed.

My eyes sweep over the large area. Everyone is with a therapist except for one man—one extremely large and good-looking man. He's leaning against the wall with a scowl on his face, staring at the door I just walked through, looking right through me like he doesn't even see me. His frame is huge, with broad shoulders that look like they're about to burst out of his shirt. The thin material leaves nothing to the imagination; every defined muscle can be seen clearly, all the way down to his tapered waist. His thigh muscles are like tree trunks, so strong, he has to have an ass just as strong.

I'm average height for a girl, but this man towers over me, making it seem like I'm short. Having the hots for a patient is frowned upon, but I can't help the immediate reaction I have upon seeing him.

"James?" I ask, smiling and extending my hand. "I'm—"

"No," he snarls.

I glance over my shoulder, looking around the room again, confused. Simon said James would be waiting for me to speak with him before he took off. Maybe I took too long getting here, and he left? "You're not James?" I ask.

"Yep."

Okay, now I'm officially confused. My eyes search his face, but the only emotion I see is annoyance.

"You *are* James?"

His jaw ticks as he grinds his molars and glares at me. His incredibly handsome face deepens its scowl as he looks me over from head to toe. Twice. "Incompetent prick. He really sent you?"

"Simon?" I ask, utterly confused by what is happening. If Simon didn't already repulse me, I'd surely dislike him now. He lied. He said this would be an easy patient. Nothing about this giant who can't stop glowering is going to be easy. No wonder my morning was so great, the universe was preparing me for this. Giving me just a bit a sunshine before sending this thundercloud my way.

"Yeah, Simon." James's tone is clipped and frustrated.

"He asked me to take over your therapy because your schedule conflicts with another patient of his."

James shakes his head, still glaring. "Played you."

"I'm getting that," I murmur.

James and I continue to stare each other down. I curl my

hair behind my ear and flick my gaze to the wall behind him, trying to compose myself before I speak. The longer I stand in front of this silent giant, the more annoyed I'm getting.

"Let's start over. I'm Tatum Rothschild. Call me Tate. Why don't you tell me why you're here for physical therapy?"

"Are you as incompetent as the other one?"

I bite my tongue. "Simon is not incompetent, but we definitely handle patients in a different manner."

"Everything is on the chart."

I run my free hand down the soft material of my scrubs covering my thighs. Once my hand stops shaking, I plant it on my hips, mustering up every ounce of attitude I have. "I prefer to hear it straight from the patient. No one knows your body better than you."

James's eyes rove over me from head to toe, twice, just like earlier. His jaw hasn't stopped ticking since I walked over here. When his steely eyes meet mine, a tiny flicker of annoyance flutters away.

"Got shot."

I suck in a sharp breath, looking over his form as if I could see the holes through his clothes. *Woah.* I've treated patients with a wide range of injuries, but I've never actually met someone who's been shot. I want to ask so many questions, none of which are necessary for our sessions.

"Chest and shoulder. Range of motion issue in the shoulder. Been here three weeks, no improvement. Simon *is* incompetent. Constantly late, having me do nothing but bullshit exercises while his eyes stay glued to all the tits and ass in the room."

"Ew," I mutter before I can stop myself.

James doesn't respond, just watching me, waiting for me to speak. His lips are shut tight. I wonder if he's ever spoken that much before. He gave me all the information as quickly and efficiently as possible.

"How limited would you describe your range of motion?"

"Not too much, but enough that I can't do my normal routine. That's unacceptable."

"Do you mind spending a few extra minutes here so I can see your baseline and map out a strategy for our next session?"

"If you ask me to do a shoulder roll, I'm walkin' out that fuckin' door," James warns in a tone that invites no arguments.

My lips twitch as I rein in my laughter. He is definitely not a fan of Simon. He's not really a fan of mine, either, but I will make sure by the end of all our appointments he's seeing improvements and getting to where he wants. I love watching a patient transform, gaining even the slightest movement back.

"Duly noted," I say, flashing him a smile, hoping we're going to start to form a bond to make these sessions easier. His scowl turns into a sneer as he motions for me to walk in front of him. Most of the other appointments have cleared out, so the room is almost empty.

"Is there anyone else?" he asks in a gruff tone.

I bristle and turn on my heel to face him, cutting his long stride short. He stares down at me as I step even closer, glaring up at him, poking a finger into his chest. There's not even a little bit of give, it's hard as a slab of granite. "You don't have to like me, but you will respect me. I'm the best. You want someone else? Sure, I'll get them. You won't get what you want from them, though." I raise an eyebrow, daring him to ask for someone else.

His eyes move slowly over my face before he leans down, getting into my personal space, my finger that's still pressed into his shoulder bending back at an uncomfortable angle, and growls, "Prove it."

# CHAPTER
# THREE

*James*

ARRIVE EARLY AT THE CELLAR. I NEED A DRINK. MY fuse has been close to blowing all day. No one has set me off like my new physical therapist, Tatum, in a long damn time. My control is usually better—evidence being the jackass Simon. Tatum, though, she sets me on edge. The moment she walked into that room, hips swaying, a tiny, knowing smile on her face, she pissed me off. Her mass of dark, red hair contrasting against her creamy, white skin, a fuckin' sight to behold—just like when I saw the anger flash in her eyes when she tried to put me in my place.

Not gonna happen.

Tatum. Asking to be called Tate. That ain't going to happen, either. It's rare I'll call someone by a nickname. Just use your damn name. It ain't that hard, and names fucking mean something.

Tate. The insistence on that nickname was just another check in the column for reasons she annoys me.

If she is the one Simon approached, I'm not real hopeful about her skills. I didn't get to see much today. She took notes and asked me question after question while babbling in between throwing jabs when she thought necessary.

I'm surprised my molars aren't dust by now after grinding them so much. Usually, when this much extra energy is pumping through me, I get rid of it by beating the shit out of a bag or working my muscles until I'm close to collapsing. Middle of the night, when the gym is closed, is my favorite time—just me, my music, and the sweet echo of my fists hitting the leather.

With the fucking wounds in my shoulder and chest, I can't do that, though. Being shot hurts, but it's afterward that's the worst. Takin' it easy. I'm not a man who likes to take anything easy.

The only way I can find release tonight is beer and sex. I scan the bar while sipping on my beer, my eyes darting past any redhead in the place. Not goin' there. Not tonight.

"What's going on, man?" Hudson asks, taking the seat next to me and raising his hand to get the bartender's attention. "Three fingers of whiskey and whatever local beer you have on draft tonight."

I raise an eyebrow at him.

He grins, shrugging. "Feel like getting a little wild tonight."

I shake my head. Hudson gets wild almost every night. I spend my time with plenty of women, but Hudson makes me look like a damn monk. He's also more showy about it. I like to be discreet with the women I bed, often waiting for my friends to leave the bar before finding the woman I'll spend the next few hours with. Just hours, never the night, and never at my place. Tonight will be one of those nights.

Hudson swirls the whiskey in his glass before taking a large gulp and turning his head toward me. "How's physical therapy?"

"Shit," I mutter.

Hudson chuckles. "Going that well?"

"Ditched Simon."

Hudson grins, laughing harder. "You aren't going to get back in the gym if you ditch your physical therapist."

I shake my head and take a gulp of beer. Three wasted weeks. I hate wasting time. Every moment needs to count; it could all end at any second. Sitting on my ass for weeks while I heal isn't my idea of a good time.

"What happened?" Hudson asked.

"He was too busy checking out the women in the room to help me. He threatened to find another therapist if I didn't follow his bullshit plan. I made him find me someone else."

Hudson throws his head back, laughing. "Of course, you did. Probably scared the piss out of the fucker, too. And you can't blame a guy for being distracted by a beautiful woman."

My head shakes slowly. "Not normal. He's the kind of guy that if you saw him on the news being described as a predator, you wouldn't be surprised."

"Damn," Hudson says with a disgusted look. "I'm shocked it took you three weeks to be rid of him."

I grunt. "If I'd known it was an option, it would have happened after the first session."

"Is this dude better?"

My jaw clenches as I think about Simon's replacement. I don't know why he picked her. Tiny little thing with delicate curves that could entice any man. Not sure what she's going to be able to do for me. If Simon and Tatum are friends, or their methods are similar, I'm done. She annoyed me the second I knew she was there for me. She's too small. Too beautiful. Too happy. Too everything.

"It's a chick," I state dryly.

Hudson raises his eyebrows and smirks. "Oh, yeah?"

Rolling my eyes and popping him on the back of the head, I firmly eliminate any ideas he's getting. "No."

"You're not fun."

I ignore that and steer the conversation back on track. "Not sure she's better. If she's who he recommends, my hopes aren't high."

"Don't count her out before she even tries," Hudson says, clapping me on the back.

If Tatum can help me toward my goal, I can ignore the overly chipper attitude she has. A few weeks with an immensely annoying, excessively sunny, too beautiful girl who talks too much will be easy. I clear my head of her, clinking my bottle against Hudson's. "What's going on?"

A crease forms between Hudson's eyebrows as he looks away. "Same as usual. Work, women, whiskey."

"How's your mom takin' Harper's engagement and pregnancy?" Hudson and Harper were never together—not even close, just friends. Hudson used Harper, though, to keep his mom off his back about settling down. He let her think they were together. She has five boys, none are married or seriously dating and she's chomping at the bit for grandkids, trying to marry her sons off to anyone who will take them. All his cousins are married with kids; her boys are the last in their big family to settle down. It ain't going to happen to Hudson anytime soon, if he has any say in the matter.

"She's sad. Wants me to make sure it's not mine."

The edges of my lips twitch. "Still won't admit to her that y'all were never a thing?"

"Nah, man. Don't want to break her heart. She's already hard at work setting me up with someone for some event. My attendance is mandatory, apparently." Hudson's hand jerks through his hair as he blows out a breath. "Damn, Harper was a good cover."

"I was a good cover for what?"

Hudson and I turn toward Harper who is standing

behind us with Roman, his arm wrapped around her stomach.

"My mom. You broke her heart when you got pregnant by another man. You little harlot, you." Hudson and I laugh as Roman growls, pulling Harper closer.

Harper shakes her head and licks her lips to control her amusement. "Well, her heart wouldn't have to be broken if you would meet a nice girl, instead of only bringing home girls from the bar."

"Where's the fun in that, Harp?" Hudson asks, cocky smile in place. "It'd be a disservice to take myself off the market. The ladies would riot."

Harper's lips press together before she bursts out laughing, her head falling back on Roman's shoulder. "Right," she replies sarcastically, her laugh turning into softer chuckles. "Please give your mother my condolences."

Hudson lifts his gaze to Roman's. "Wanna share Harper? Have split custody with the baby?"

"Fuck you," Roman says wrapping his other arm around Harper's chest and molding her to him even more. Harper giggles quietly. "No one would believe the kid would be yours, anyway. He's going to be handsome and badass, two things you aren't." Roman spins Harper with a smug smile before they walk away to the table where we normally sit.

"Shut up," Hudson says, looking at me, picking up his beer as he gets up from the barstool.

"Didn't say anything," I say, raising my hands in front of me before doing the same.

"You don't have to. You may not laugh out loud, but I know when you're cracking up on the inside."

"I like Roman," I state. "Nice addition to the group. Keeps your head from getting too big."

I walk away, leaving Hudson to trail behind.

Hudson sits next to me, glaring at Roman across the table. "Should y'all even be here? Harper is pregnant."

"I'm not drinking, dork," Harper says, smiling and running a hand over her belly. Watching the gorgeous smile stretch across Harper's face every time Roman looks down at her makes these physical therapy sessions bearable.

Just then, the rest of the group arrive—Savannah and Liam come rolling in, hand in hand, Gabe, with his arm around Valerie, and Kiernan brings up the rear.

I lapse into my normal quiet mode, listening to our group chatter about everything. My comfort zone is to sit and listen. Listening is how I survived my childhood. Talking too much resulted in a lot of different things, none of them good. When I escaped my past, talking meant exposing too much. Silence is safer. Staying mostly silent has kept me safe for over a decade.

One slip, one inconsequential detail about my life could mean the difference between me sitting here breathing, listening to my friends talking or me six feet under in a pine box.

"How's PT?" Kiernan asks from across the table, forcing me to join in the conversation.

"Pain in my ass," I mutter. Kiernan was shot the same night I was, but his wound didn't require physical therapy. He healed and recovered quickly, and was back in the field providing security for Roman's company, while I'm still battling for my shoulder not to twinge any time I lift something.

Hudson chuckles, slapping me on the back. "Our boy here has the hots for his therapist."

I groan as I watch the girls at the table perk up and watch me with hopeful eyes. "No, I don't."

"He won't admit it," Hudson says before he whispers conspiratorially, "He's shy about it."

"Shut the fuck up," I grumble.

"I thought it was a guy," Roman says, confused.

"Got rid of him today."

"He has a new one," Hudson informs everyone. "This one's a girl."

"Is she pretty, puddin' pop?" Savannah asks, smiling at me. Savannah is the only family I have. It may not be by blood, but she's family. She's like my sister and the only one I will allow to call me any sort of endearment. I know she changes them up and makes them as cute as possible because she finds it funny. The first time she did it was also the first time I saw her smile. I couldn't ask her to stop and make that smile go away. With a past as dark as hers, she needed anything to bring her back to the light.

Sister or not, I shoot a glare in her direction. "Nope," I lie.

She settles back in her chair, placing her hand in Liam's lap while watching me intently. I stare at her, not breaking eye contact, making my lie believable.

"Give the guy a break," Roman says. "He was shot, owns and runs a gym for a living, and can't work out. He's probably on the verge of exploding. James doesn't need to complicate things with his physical therapist."

"But what if something good can come out of it?" Harper retorts.

"The good thing that came out of that shit, sugar, is that you're alive. Don't need anything else."

I nod in agreement. Her sitting across from me with a kid on the way and a beating heart is the only thing that matters.

"If she's hot, show her your scars," Kiernan says, smiling. "Chicks love it."

Hudson claps his hand on the table, laughing hard. The two of them together are a force of nature, each of them taking on the role of wingman for the other.

Savannah, Harper, and Valerie are still watching me and assessing every expression to cross my face like hawks, so I do the only thing I can—throw Hudson under the bus. "Hudson's mom wants to set him up for some event, y'all know anyone available?"

All the females' eyes swing to Hudson as I relax back in my chair, taking a long pull of my beer.

"Fucker," Hudson mutters under his breath.

The edge of my lips twitch once.

# CHAPTER
## FOUR

*Tatum*

**P**ATHETIC.

Absolutely pathetic.

My fingers skim over the necklace around my neck and I wish I chose something else. Absolutely anything else. The half-heart, best-friends-forever necklace Isabella and I split in the fourth grade would be better than the jewelry I'm wearing. The necklace or the earrings, one or other, I could probably get away with; together they're overkill. I close my eyes, taking a sip of champagne, remembering how clever I felt putting on the jewelry Patrick gave me, a subtle reminder of how much I mean to him—meant to him.

Patrick Kensiger, love of my life, high school and college sweetheart, dumped me eight months ago. He gave me the pieces I'm wearing on different anniversaries, each with a promise that one day they would be paired with a ring. A ring that would take me from girlfriend to fiancée and eventually to wife. When he took me to dinner eight months ago after we celebrated his latest case win with our families, I thought he was going to drop to a knee and propose. We'd been together for twelve years, since the beginning of our sophomore year in high school. To be honest, I thought the proposal would've happened a long time ago. We're twenty-seven now and have married friends that haven't been in relationships as long. I fooled myself into thinking Patrick had a plan. Cold feet never crossed my mind. He was my first kiss, my first everything. My *only* everything. What better way to celebrate his first huge win than with an engagement? Winning that case was going to be the change of everything. It officially set him on the long path to partner.

The proposal didn't happen. We sat in that quiet, romantic restaurant with a 360-degree view of the city, sipping champagne and laughing through our high of being done with his late nights and hardly seeing each other. Bile rises in my throat when I remember how I thought we were a power couple on the rise. *Pathetic.* We'd been living together for three years. Our families ran in the same circles. It was a matter of time.

Then some of the most humiliating moments of my life happened. Patrick stared at me across the table, looking nervous before he pulled a red leather box from his jacket, setting it on the table between us before he grabbed my hand. The tears rushed to my eyes as I prepared to hear the most romantic words I'd ever hear.

Only they didn't come.

Not even close.

"I've had this for a while. It was always going to be after we graduated then after we landed jobs then after I got my feet under me at the firm. I can't give it to you, though."

*I can't give it to you, though.*

The happy tears dried up immediately as I stared at him in shock. "Patrick?" I whispered.

"We have to break up, Tate." He stated this firmly, grabbing the box before tucking it back into his suit pocket.

My mouth fell open and I could feel my lips begin to quiver as I asked my question shakily. "What?"

"I love you so much, and I do want to marry you one day, but we've been together so long, all we know is each other."

"I know. I love that," I whispered. And it's true. I did love that. I thought it was romantic that we would only know each other, learning everything from each other.

"I need to explore. I need to be sure. I want us to date other people."

"Date other people," I repeated quietly, in utter shock, the burn of hot, fresh tears coming back. Only this time they were anything but happy.

"Yes," he emphasized, squeezing my hand. "I love you. I want to marry you."

"You love me. You want to marry me," I repeated again, unable to do anything except repeat his every word. Staring at him, searching his face for answers, I willed myself to do something. Say something. *Anything.* The city lights and murmuring in the restaurant faded completely to the background. The only thing I can see and hear was Patrick sitting across from me taking my world apart piece by piece and tossing the remains of my heart carelessly. I wasn't sure if I should keep crying or laugh at the absurdity of this whole conversation. If this was a joke, it wasn't funny.

"I want us to be sure, Tate. We'll come back together soon."

I shake my head. "What if you want to be with someone else you 'explore' with?" I made sure he understood that the word *explore* came with air quotes.

"We'll be honest if that ever happens," he said quietly. "We'll come out stronger for this."

"I don't want this," I warn him. "I am sure. I don't need to 'explore.'"

"Please," Patrick said, squeezing my hand again.

While I couldn't even summon the energy to push the

food around my plate, he ate the rest of his meal in near silence while his words played on repeat through my head. The man I've loved for almost half of my life was a stranger sitting across from me. He's become even more of a stranger in the eight months since the break up, morphing into someone I hardly recognize. It's the rare glimpses I get of who I knew that keep me wishing he'll come back.

His words have been playing on repeat for eight months. The repeated rejection playing through my mind still hasn't been enough to change my feelings for him. *Pathetic. Pitiful. Third-rate. Third-rate Tate.*

What's even more pathetic is I've been lying to my family since we broke up. I told them it was mutual, that we wanted a chance to be young before we settled down together to start a family. We'd be back together in no time. We're still friends, I said. Every time someone in my family brings him up, I smile, playing along. If they knew even an ounce of my heartbreak, he'd be on their blacklist forever. I want them to still love him when we get back together though, so I stay silent.

Our first date in high school was a double date. His best friend with my best friend. Now I'm standing at their engagement party, sipping on champagne, wearing jewelry my ex-boyfriend gave me in hopes that he'll notice and realize it's been long enough, realize we belong together. I thought the jewelry would be a subtle reminder. I didn't expect to walk into my best friend's expansive backyard to see Patrick with his arm around another girl.

My heart squeezes painfully as I watch him smile down at her while she presses herself even closer to his side.

Patrick and I grew up together, going to the same private school. Our fathers are partners at the law firm. Our friends are the same; it's inevitable that we'll run into each other. It hasn't been the easiest eight months of my life. He never brings a date to a function he knows I will be at. Until now.

I stop dead in my tracks when I see him graze his hand over her ass. I've never seen her before, and I hope I never see her again. My worst fear is he'll show up with a date and inform me in front of our friends that he's met someone. A real someone. I haven't been with anyone since Patrick.

Patrick is still my only. We've hooked up a couple of times over the past year. Many times it felt like we were dating again without the official label until I'd run into him at a bar and see his tongue down someone else's throat. Each time I told myself I wouldn't let him back in again. The pain isn't worth it, but each time he mutters how much he loves me in my ear, I crumble. I've prided myself on being strong my entire life, but he's my weakness.

Austin is a big city, but sometimes it feels like the smallest town. As eyes start to swing my way, I feel the pity rolling off them and hitting me. My stomach turns as I push away feelings of inadequacy and plaster on a fake, confident smile and stride toward the friends I've known my entire life.

My best friend, Isabella, works her way around the crowd to hug me first. "I didn't know he'd bring a date, babe. I'm sorry. I tried to call and warn you," she whispers in my ear.

I clutch her tighter, loving her for worrying about me at her own damn party—a party she's been waiting to have since we were in high school. "It's okay. I'm okay, promise."

Isabella's hands rub up and down my back before breaking our hug and wrapping them around my shoulders. "Now the party can really start." She smiles at the gathering of people around the firepit. "My best girl is here."

Before I walk in the opposite direction of Patrick, planning to avoid him as much as possible, I smile and wave, pretending as if I'm totally fine on the inside. It's hurt each time I've seen him with another girl, but this is worse. This is his best friend's engagement party. Hookups don't belong at your best friend's engagement party.

Patrick smiles his perfect, charming smile, showing his straight, white teeth, and winks. I look away, focusing on some friends I haven't seen in a while. As I make my way around the group chatting, I force myself to keep my gaze on the people in front of me, not directed at the man I want to watch.

Is he still touching her?

Have they kissed?

Who is she?

She's nothing like me, which causes my gut to turn even more. If I went out to handpick a guy I wanted to date, he'd almost be a carbon copy of Patrick. His expertly coiffed blond hair, bright blue eyes, and classically handsome features are exactly my type. I don't know if they're my type because he's all I've ever known or if it's simply what I'm attracted to no matter what.

Every girl I've seen him with couldn't be more different from me. They're either far thinner or curvier. Blondes and brunettes, never a girl with the same shade as my hair. Every possibility of why he's needed to explore others has crossed my mind. Is he not attracted to me? Did I do something wrong? Am I too loud?

But every couple of months, when he approaches me whispering sweet nothings, just as I'm about to force myself to move on, I'm back in his iron grip, and he makes me believe his pretty words.

Each person I talk to pities me; I either see it in their eyes or know it when they try to set me up. I hear the whispers that they thought this would be us, too. Patrick and Tatum, I once thought that was a sure thing. One lesson I've learned, nothing is a sure thing.

"Tate."

I swallow when I hear his deep voice behind me. Plastering on my best smile, I turn toward him.

"Hey, Patrick," I say, gripping my champagne flute tighter in one hand and tucking my shaking hand behind my back. It's shaking so hard the chains on the front of my clutch quietly rattle. My gaze falls to the stunning, tall, leggy blonde standing next to him with her arm wrapped around his waist. "Hi, I'm Tatum."

I stick out my hand. She shakes it once before dropping it. "Hi, I'm Farrah."

"Nice to meet you," I manage to say through my smile without gagging. "How are y'all? Enjoying the party?"

Farrah rolls her eyes. "It's pretty boring."

My smile falls into a tight line. "That's too bad. I'm having a great time celebrating our best friends."

"We're having a nice time," Patrick says, making my eyes fall on him. He grins, looking down at Farrah then back to me as he rolls his eyes, making her a joke between us. He's joking with me about his date. I give him a tight smile in return. When we dated he was kind to everyone.

"I should—" I begin before Patrick cuts me off.

"Farrah, can you grab me a beer, please?"

"Fine. Also going to find a bathroom where I can cry tears of boredom," she mutters before taking off toward the house. I watch her walk all the way inside before turning back to Patrick. His eyes are burning a hole in the side of my face, but I want as much time as I can before I have to look him in the eye and hear what I fear will break my heart.

When my eyes move back to him, he's staring down at me with a small smile before taking a step toward me. His hand rests on my shoulder with his thumb brushing along my neck, hitting the chain of my necklace.

"I love this necklace on you," he whispers.

I don't respond, only close my eyes, wishing his

compliment didn't warm my entire body.

"You shouldn't have worn it though," he says. "Or the earrings."

The warmth spreading through my body turns to ice as I open my eyes to stare at him.

"I know what you're trying to do by wearing those," he says, still whispering. Of course, he knows. That was my intention, I just didn't think he'd have a date glued to his side.

"I didn't wear them for you," I lie.

His hand squeezes my shoulder as his expression turns mocking. Twelve years and never once have I seen his face so ugly. "Tate," he says in his placating way. He can make me feel really small in the space of a couple of words or with the tone in which he says my name. As much as I love him, he always needs to have every conversation or situation go his way. During our relationship, that wasn't the easiest part of his personality, for sure. He chose everything. It had to be his way, but he's never treated me maliciously and never made me feel worthless. After the night he ripped my heart from my chest, he turned into someone I barely recognize.

"I didn't," I insist. "They're classic and beautiful. It'd be a shame to toss them in a jewelry box never to be worn again just because they're from my ex."

"They're Cartier, darling," Patrick says with a smug smile. "You don't toss Cartier anywhere. They're meant to be treasured, just like the girl wearing them."

"Don't be an asshole," I hiss.

"I'm sorry, darling. I didn't mean anything by bringing her here. I've been excited to see you. I've missed you."

"Is she your girlfriend?" I ask, unable to hide the anger in my tone. This is what he does, says words that hurt but also soothe my soul.

"No, Tate. I'm single," he says, his smug grin only growing.

We stare at each other in silence, his hand still caressing my shoulder and neck. He finally breaks our stare-off, leaving on a parting blow, one that does its job—leave me wanting more of him.

"You look beautiful in the jewelry I gave you. One day, my ring will be on your finger, and this will be our party." He leans in, kissing my cheek. "I can't wait for that day." Patrick walks away before I can say anything, never being the one to let anyone else have the last word.

# CHAPTER
## FIVE

## James

THROWING MY SUV INTO PARK, I STARE AT THE entrance of the hospital. My appointment is in fifteen minutes. If she's late, I'm done. If she asks for a shoulder roll, I'm done. My patience is on a short fuse this morning. If one thing lights it up, I'll be blowing like a fucking stick of dynamite.

I keep a pulse on everything in my life, any threat that could become something more. Savannah's ex-boyfriend stalked her and used one of his friends, while he was in prison, to keep an eye on Savannah. When all that went down, I took care of it. I watch, keep my ear to the ground, and make damn sure none of what I did to make sure that friend never surfaces again blows back on Savannah and Liam.

Roman and Harper's trouble with the cartel recently got added to my extensive list. They only had trouble with two men, and I'm makin' sure it fuckin' stays that way. All good on both of those fronts, bringing the type of quiet that eases the mind.

The trouble from my past that I spend hours of my week checking into, checking from every angle? That shit is the wrong kind of quiet and has been that way for weeks.

Incessant chatter doesn't stop unless it knows it's being watched. This is the silence that eats at your soul, the silence that happens right before a storm. The eerie quiet that falls when the serial killer has its target in sight and the prey doesn't know it's about to die.

I have a few minutes before I need to head inside so I boot up my laptop, connect to the hotspot on the prepaid phone I keep specifically for this and connect the virtual private network. My private browser, Tor, finally opens up and I check through the usual sites but nothing. Nothing I can use, nothing that gives me any hint of what's going on in the world I left behind.

There's not a damn thing I can do to release my frustration. Instead, I'm here about to walk into a place that has done nothing but annoy me and meet a girl who is going to make it even worse.

I blow past the reception desk, not bothering to check in. The receptionist knows who I am and can check me in. It's pointless; she'll tell me to wait in the physical therapy room, so that's where I go instead of wasting time on needless small talk. I walk into the room, expecting a wait, but Tatum is there. Her back is to me as she sets up an area with equipment. She's the only person in here, which doesn't surprise me; she asked if I could take the earliest appointment. It's just the two of us, and with that knowledge alone, the tension threatens to suffocate me.

She hasn't even turned around. The door clicks closed behind me, and she doesn't acknowledge my presence.

"Tatum," I say.

She still doesn't turn around. Instead, she starts to sing and shimmy her hips, weaving her head from side to side. When I catch a view of her profile, I see the earbuds. This pisses me off. She's in a room alone, completely unaware of her surroundings. Shit can happen anywhere. I stalk toward her, already feeling my short fuse spark before I rip the bud away from her ear.

Tatum flinches and lets out a small yelp, dropping the eight-pound medicine ball as I grind my teeth. One hand comes to her chest and the other rests on my forearm. The moment her skin touched mine it felt like an electric minefield coming to life. I stare down at her hand battling with the want to rip it off my arm and the need to feel every inch of her skin pressed against mine.

"Oh, my god, James, you scared me," she says, breathing hard with a small smile and her other hand pressed to her chest.

My glare leaves her hand and shoots to her eyes. "Pay attention to your surroundings," I bark out as an order.

The tiny smile shuts down as a scowl takes over. Her hand leaves my arm, pointing a finger in my face. "Don't give me that shit, bucko. I'm perfectly fine and safe. You startled me."

"Bucko?" I ask, my annoyance racking up another notch.

"Yeah, bucko, I can take care of myself."

"What would you have done if I wanted to attack you?" My question comes out harsh and demanding. No victim is ever to blame, but it's smart to take notice of your surroundings and exits at all times.

"Attack me?" she asks, a hint of fear seeping in her voice as she takes a tiny step away from me.

My fists settle on my hips as I release a frustrated sigh. "I'm not going to attack you. I'm asking what you would have done since you can take such great care of yourself."

She watches me for a moment, a deep crease forming between her eyebrows. "I'd throw a medicine ball at you."

I don't answer, only stare at her. She gets my message.

"What? They're heavy. If I nailed you in the head, you'd definitely go down."

"It'd take a lot more than that to take me down."

"Not everyone is ginormous like you are," she sneers, propping a hand on her hip, mimicking my position.

"If you threw a medicine ball at me, I'd deflect it. I'm standing between you and the exit. Your back was turned with headphones in. Just be more fuckin' aware."

Her breaths are coming out in heavy pants while she stares at me with anger. It's taking everything in me not to look down at her chest. She annoys me, but there's no denying that this girl is gorgeous.

"Whatever," she finally mutters.

"Yeah, whatever." I survey the equipment she's been setting up. "What's the plan?"

"Shoulder rolls," she says sweetly.

My gaze pins her to the spot, impatience coursing through me.

"Ten forward, ten back, each shoulder."

She picks her clipboard up off the floor, watching me, waiting for me to start the shoulder rolls. My jaw is clenching so tightly, I swear I hear my molars cracking. Tatum snorts then slaps a hand over her mouth, trying hold in the laughter, causing my body to tense up even more. Her shoulders are shaking and her eyes become glassy before the laughter finally bursts out of her.

"You turn so red. It's hilarious," she says through her laughter. "If the Hulk turned red instead of green, I'd swear y'all are twins. You and the green Hulk could go as the Dynamic Christmas Duo."

"Hilarious," I mumble.

"You're not doing shoulder rolls, but we are taking it easier than you'd probably like. I know the original therapy with Simon suggested six weeks, but your progress isn't there. We'll need more than the remaining three weeks. I'm adding three additional weeks. We *will* go easy in the beginning and advance more later."

I open my mouth to object, but she holds up a hand, staring at me hard. "Please, let me finish."

After a beat, I reluctantly nod.

"Less is sometimes more," Tatum says with a smile. "I can tell by looking at you that you enjoy working out. I'll get you back in that gym with your old routine in no time, but you have to trust me. I'm going to ask you to do movements so tiny, you're going to doubt me, but don't. Eventually, you'll feel it. When truly focusing on a muscle, the slightest movement can be the difference between comfortable and pain so fierce you fall on the floor. How often do you normally go to the gym?"

"Every day," I answer.

"Every day? No rest days?"

"I own the place. No such thing as a rest day."

She nods. "Fair enough. Think you can trust me?"

I watch her watching me, waiting for me to determine my response. There's hopefulness pouring out her eyes. That alone makes her different than Simon.

"Fine," I answer.

Tatum guides me through stretching to warm up my body for our session. It's still just the two of us, her soft voice is the only noise in the room. She does the stretches next to me while keeping a close eye on my form, which irritates me.

"Good," she says. "We're going to start with something called framing the door."

My eyes move to her. "Seriously?"

"Yes." Her lips twitch. "That's what it's called."

Tatum steps in front of me, placing her small hands on my shoulders while looking up at me. "I'm not sure how useful the mental part of this exercise will be for you. You have to imagine you're in a doorway. Do you even fit in a doorway?"

A growl erupts from my chest as I roll my shoulders, shaking off her hands.

"I swear you move through shades of red so quickly." She cracks up at her own joke while wrapping an arm around her stomach. When she finally settles down, Tatum rests her hands on my shoulders again.

"Get on with it, Tatum," I snarl.

"Tate," she says. "Call me Tate."

"Tatum," I respond.

"You're kind of a jackass." Her smile is gone, her irritation starting to match my own. "It's Tate."

"Tatum," I growl. "I'll call you by your damn name. I don't do nicknames unless I like you."

She rolls her eyes and shakes her head softly before placing a fake smile on her lips. "Imagine you're in a doorway."

She waits for me, knowing I ain't picturing standing in a doorway.

"James," she says, mocking, the smile returning. "Before you turn red, just do what I say."

My chest rumbles before I stand straighter, imagining myself in a doorway.

"Okay, raise your arms," she says, taking her hands from my shoulders. "Turn your palms out and pretend you're pressing against the doorframe."

I do as she instructs, but my eyes catch on the man entering the room. Fucking Simon. He stops when he spots Tatum, his gaze losing focus. What the hell.

"Good." She brings her hands to my arms, slowly guiding her palms over my skin and slightly pushing my arms higher. Tatum walks around me under my arm and runs her hand down my spine between my shoulder blades. "You want to feel this right here. Slowly bring your hands down as if you're feeling the frame of the door, I'll tell you when to hold."

*Is she dating him?* I don't think I could work with anyone that stupid. My gaze moves over my shoulder to Tatum; she's watching my arms and back closely, completely unaware Simon is here and ogling at her.

"James?" she prompts when I don't answer or move my hands.

I nod, my eyes still cast over my shoulder looking at Tatum's face, and I bring my hands down. With her hand still resting between my shoulder blades, she says, "Stop and hold. Do you feel this right here?" *She's not with him, right?*

"Yeah," I say, focusing on the muscles surrounding her hand. *No, definitely not with him.* He's still standing in the same spot. I don't think he's blinked at all. My muscles tense thinking about her alone in this room, dancing around with earbuds in her ears, completely oblivious to the world. She hasn't even acknowledged that she knows he's there.

"What happened? Did something twinge your shoulder?" Tatum asks, kneading my back muscles. "Your muscles tensed up."

"Does he always watch you like that?"

"Who?" she asks, looking around and stopping when her gaze finds Simon. A weary look crosses her face. "He likes looking at all the girls."

I grunt. He's still staring at her with possessiveness in his eyes.

"Relax," Tatum whispers.

I tear my eyes away from Simon just as he finally breaks his concentration on Tatum and focuses it on another female in the room. Christ. My muscles slowly ease back into a more relaxed state.

"Good, slowly release. We'll do this for three sets of ten."

After Tatum maneuvers me through several exercises, she faces me with a triumphant grin. "Trust me yet?"

"Nope." I ignore the slight shift in my chest when her

face falls for a second before attitude replaces it.

"You'll be singing my praises one day, James."

I huff and shake my head in denial, aggravated that her new plan adds a few weeks to the original six. "Doubt that. You're a slight step up from Simon."

"I can send you back to him, if you like," she tosses back.

"Nope, but if there's someone better who understands strength, you can send me to them."

"Jackass," she mutters.

"Probably shouldn't call your client a jackass," I say seriously, relishing that it's her turning red and not me.

"Call it like I see it, James."

"Next Monday. 6:00 a.m. Tatum," I say, nodding once.

"Tate," she bites out between her teeth.

I turn away and walk to the door, calling over my shoulder in a grunt, "Later, *Tatum*."

# CHAPTER
## SIX

*Tatum*

MY MOM IS JUST AS EXCITED ABOUT FALL AS I AM, IF the pumpkins decorating the ground near the mailbox are any indication. Any holiday, event, or season, my mom pulls out all the stops, but fall—fall is her favorite time of year. We don't get the same beautiful foliage as the northeast, but my mom sure likes to pretend we do.

Our white, tin mailbox is now painted with colorful falling leaves with our last name, Rothschild, through the center. My mom grew up dreaming of a gorgeous house filled with family behind a white picket fence and a fun mailbox with her last name. When my parents built this house and planted a standard-looking mailbox at the edge of street, the white tin among the stone and brick mailboxes looked like a game of *what doesn't belong?* The neighborhood homeowners' association came knocking not even two days later, demanding they replace it.

My mom fought tooth and nail to keep her mailbox and constantly paints it. Sometimes a solid color—her favorite is navy. Sometimes a theme, such as a reindeer for Christmas, a field of clovers for St. Patty's Day, and fireworks for the Fourth of July. And my Pop Pop's favorite, dirty jokes. She only does this when the HOA really makes her angry, and it never lasts long.

Her most recent—what's the difference between the HOA and a dead lady of the night?

The HOA still blows.

My mom and Pop Pop took pictures standing in front of the mailbox when my mom finished painting it, both smiling wide and proud.

While my family is well-known in Austin society, we're not the typical blue-blood bunch. Hence, my mom and grandpa's willingness to paint dirty jokes on the mailbox for all to see. My dad isn't as free-spirited as they are, but he never stops their fun. He says that when he brought my mom home to meet Pop Pop and Grams, my mom and Pop Pop immediately bonded, becoming thick as thieves and partners in crime.

I pull into the circular drive, parking behind my brother's car. Running up the steps and letting myself inside, I call out into the massive entryway. "Hello? I'm here!"

"No one cares," I hear my brother, Hammond, shout back. It sounds like he's in the den, probably playing pool with Pop Pop.

"Come on in, sweetheart," Pop Pop calls from the same area. I smile, heading toward the den. The soft slap of the balls lets me know I'm right, they're playing pool.

Pop Pop is standing just inside the archway, leaning against the wall and rubbing the blue chalk on the end of his cue while my brother is bent over the table in front of me. I slowly sneak up behind him, waiting as he lines up his shot, and glace over my shoulder at a grinning Pop Pop. Right before Hammond pulls back to hit the ball, I whisper in his ear. "Boo."

His arm flinches as he moves the cue to forward, making him miss the ball completely. Hammond's head turns slowly toward me, glaring.

"Hey, big brother," I say, giving him my sweetest smile.

He moves quickly, wrapping me in a headlock and giving me a noogie. Pop Pop laughs as I wrestle to get out of Hammond's grip. When he finally lets me go, he playfully pushes me. "Thanks a lot, sis. I missed you so much," he says sarcastically.

I walk over to Pop Pop, wrapping my arms around his waist and lifting on my toes to kiss his cheek. "Sorry, I want Pop Pop to win."

"No loyalty," my brother says, trying to conceal his smile with a hand over his wounded heart.

"I only have loyalty for my favorite family members," I say as Pop Pop hugs me tighter and squeezes my shoulder.

"That's my girl." Pop Pop kisses the top of my head in a loud smacking kiss. "Good to see you, kid. I have to take my shot now."

"It's going to be the winning shot," Hammond says. "Thanks to you." His arm slings over my shoulder as we watch Pop Pop sink all the balls, including the eight, ending the game.

"That's how it's done, kids." Pop Pop grins, swaggering toward us. He may be getting up there in age, but he's still the absolute coolest person I know. "Let's go find your parents."

We find them in the kitchen, my dad at the stove listening to my mom chatter with a tiny, happy smile, and my mom sitting on a barstool sipping a mimosa and nibbling on a piece of fruit and her arms waving wildly in the air as she speaks.

"My babies," my mom sighs happily. "When did y'all get here?"

Hammond and I walk over to my mom, giving her a hug. She takes each of our faces in her hands, giving us a loud, smacking kiss on the cheek, just like Pop Pop.

"Most handsome boy in the world," she says to my brother. He grins, eating up the attention, reverting to his twelve-year-old-self and not acting like his real age—thirty. I snort in disagreement, smiling when my brother glowers at me.

"Most beautiful girl in the world," she whispers to me. I roll my eyes.

"Pop Pop wrangled me into a game of pool before we came in here," Hammond says, taking the barstool next to her and pouring a mimosa before handing it to me.

I accept it graciously. "I caught the end of the game."

"Do you wait for them by the door to be sure that you'll be the first they see, old man?" my mom asks my grandpa.

"People usually save the best for last, but I figure I should let the kids spend time with their favorite before looking for you two," Pop Pop says, leaning around my mom to grab a grape before popping it in his mouth.

I make my way around the island to give my dad a hug. "Hey, Dad," I say quietly, watching him cook our brunch.

"Hey, kiddo." He kisses the top of my head as I keep my arms wrapped around his middle. I lean my head against his shoulder and he keeps one around me as he continues cooking with one hand.

A bar stool scoots across the polished tile a few seconds before Hammond appears on the other side of my dad. He tugs the ends of my hair. "Move out of the way so he can say hello to his favorite."

"You're so not the favorite."

"Keep telling yourself that, little sis."

I give my dad one more tight squeeze before letting go.

"Hey, Dad," Hammond says picking up a spoon and stirring the boiling pot behind the skillet my dad is focusing on.

"Hey, bud," my dad greets happily.

My family gets together for a meal as often as we can.

Since Patrick and I broke up, I've spent a lot of nights at their dinner table. Hammond doesn't join as often, but he makes sure to come whenever possible. He's a lawyer at Dad's firm, working his way to becoming a partner, but right now his workload is insane.

Hammond and I make our way back to the barstools at the island after we talk with our dad. We wait for him to finish cooking. As he plates everything, Hammond and I set the table, still in the habit from when we were kids. Pop Pop and Mom happily chatter away about the latest neighborhood gossip—Mrs. Perkins dumped her husband's belongings on the front lawn and had the locks changed.

Sitting amongst my family as my dad prepares the meal and my mom and Pop Pop talk or argue, I feel content and settled. Coming home always brings me peace.

Once we've sat down, my dad waits at the head of the table with a smile on his face for all of us to take a bite. As a partner of the firm, he was always busy as we were growing up, but he made sure that when he could make it home, he'd cook dinner. This was partially due to the fact that my mom can't cook. At all. It's best to keep her out of the kitchen entirely. My dad takes pride in his cooking and feeding his family, never touching his plate until everyone at the table is happy and has taken their first bite. He always takes his first bite with a smile on his face.

"How was Isabella's engagement party?" my mom asks after we've sat down to eat.

My body tenses, remembering every word Patrick said to me. Slowly chewing my food, I give myself time to compose my thoughts before I answer. "It was great." I muster all the cheer I can.

"Was Patrick there?" my dad asks softly and kindly as he pats the top of my hand with his, giving it a tiny squeeze. Dad sees Patrick every day at work which is another reason

I've kept my mouth shut about the changes I've seen in Patrick. I don't want there to be any tension in their law firm.

"That boy is a schmuck," Pop Pop states, shaking his head and shoveling another bite of food into his mouth.

Hammond snorts, smiling at me before wiping his hand over his mouth to erase the smile—his way of telling me to ignore it. I grin back before answering my dad. "Yeah, he was there."

I don't mention his date; it'd shock everyone at this table, and they would ask questions I couldn't answer. Questions I'm still asking myself. Since our very first date and probably even before that, our families have been planning our wedding. How perfect would it be if two kids of one of the most successful law firms in Austin ended together?

Again, another reason why I've kept so quiet about our break up and Patrick turning into someone unrecognizable. I keep my eyes glued to my plate and focus on my shoulders staying in a relaxed position. I can feel my mom's questioning gaze burning into me.

"How's work, Hammond?" I ask, changing the subject.

A tiny smirk crosses his face—he knows exactly what I'm doing. He answers anyway, telling us about his current caseload and work hours as I release a relieved sigh.

My mom frowns, staring at him. "You're so busy. You need time to be young and have fun."

"If I work hard now, I can play hard later," Hammond states. This has always been his way.

"You hardly have time to go out. How will you meet a girl?" my mom asks, on the same mission as many mothers across the world—Mission Grandbaby.

"I do just fine," Hammond says with a cocky smile.

"Ew," I whisper, curling my lip and pushing my plate away from me. Hammond chuckles taking another croissant from the basket in front of him.

"You'll need to make time for the charity gala in a couple of months. I expect you both to be there with a date. I've already RSVP'd for you both." My mom's plate is forgotten in front of her as she stares at Hammond with her hands steepled under her chin.

Hammond drops his fork, looking slightly queasy. "Mom—"

I roll my lips between my teeth to keep from laughing, completely delighted the attention has been turned away from me. I pull my plate back in front of me, scooping up a forkful of fluffy scrambled eggs.

"Nope," she says firmly. "It's important. You'll be there with a date. End of story."

Pop Pop laughs, smiling as he shovels more food in his mouth and nudging my side with his elbow, enjoying the show just as much as I am.

My mom twists her authoritative gaze toward him. "That goes for you, too, Walter."

His laughter dies as his head comes up slowly, staring at my mom. "Come again?"

"You will be there with a date," my mom says, her eyes daring him to argue with her. My dad has stayed silent through this entire conversation, smiling and enjoying the meal he made for his family. He's a shark in the courtroom, but home is my mom's domain. She's judge, jury, and executioner. My dad has always let her take this role and usually just sits back to enjoy the show. It's only when Hammond, Pop Pop, or I got too angry and started to yell at her that my dad would step in to cut off any disrespect toward her.

Hammond cracks up as Pop Pop mutters, "For fuck's sake."

"I'll find a date for you and Hammond myself if I have to."

Hammond stops laughing again, pinching the bridge of

his nose and taking a deep breath. When he looks back up, he has on his most charming smile. "Mom, believe me, I got girls I can call," he says.

My mom raises her brows and purses her lips before turning to face me. I brace for what she's about to say as I wipe my mouth with the napkin.

"You can ask Patrick, honey," my mom says. "I imagine he'll be there, anyway, but he can count as your date."

I crush the napkin into a ball in my fist. "We'll see," I say quietly before biting the inside of my cheek.

"Or I can find you a date. My friends are always begging me to set you up with their sons." She takes a sip of her mimosa watching my reaction to her bringing up other men. This is the first time she's brought up setting me up with someone that isn't Patrick. Panic clogs my throat. She's figuring it out. That this break up just may be permanent, that he's probably not coming back to me.

I clear my throat and rub my hand over my heart. "No thanks, Mom. If I need a date, I can do that on my own."

"Just let me know. Some of these boys are cute." She winks as she picks up her mimosa to take a hearty sip.

I hold back my groan, wondering if I should take the plunge and ask Patrick. I could suggest going as friends, a night of fun. He's the one who brought up marriage last weekend at Isabella's party.

I'm debating the pros and cons of asking him, but at the same time, I'm picturing myself in a sexy dress I know he couldn't refuse. I sigh wistfully when the thought of reuniting just before the holidays crosses my mind. I shouldn't get my hopes up, but maybe it's time. If we're back together, this new asshole side of him will have to take a hike.

# CHAPTER
## SEVEN

*James*

WHEN HUDSON WALKED INTO THE GYM FOR THE first time, this cavernous space looked completely different. I bought the building from an old man in a private sale in cash, opening my gym with as little of a paper trail as I could manage. Hudson was my first customer.

I'd been in Texas a few years at this point, laying as low as a person could and still function in a normal society. Finding jobs that paid cash was essential. There are a lot of people out there willing to pay under the table, but most of the time it's for a pittance. I needed more than that. I needed to make more of myself and stop using the money I had; I wanted to use money I earned, money that no one but Uncle Sam could take from me. My entire life, I didn't own shit. Nothing to my name, ever. Not even to any of my names.

Derek. Preston. Michael. Connor. By the time I reached kindergarten, I could read small chapter books, but I didn't know my name. I didn't respond to any name. Four foster homes in my first five years, all of them calling me whatever the hell they wanted to call me, whatever name they could remember between their benders.

Preston was the worst. The parents lost their son in an accident. I was the only kid in that foster house and they tried to make me into their dead son Preston. At the age of five, if I couldn't anticipate the way they wanted me to act, they'd lock me in a closet. Eventually I learned silence was easier. The punishments fewer and farther between when I was silent.

James. My name, chosen for myself by myself, is the first true thing that belonged to me. My land is second. The house I built with my own two hands is the third. This gym is the fourth. The big SUV parked out front with every modification I could make to ensure my safety is the fifth. Every possession important that is mine can be counted on one hand. When I make something mine, I make damn sure it stays that way.

I had cash when I settled in Texas—cash I didn't want to spend, cash I had to use to survive, but never using more than necessary. There's one thing in this world I'm afraid of—the day the owners of that money come after me.

After bouncing from motel to motel, deciding if I wanted to stay in Austin, I found a gym similar to this one, bought a guest pass for the day, and worked out for the first time using real equipment. I was in shape, even back then, but I'd never been in a gym or used real, solid equipment. The closest I came was my high school gym, but all that metal was covered in rust or mostly broken machines.

That gym started an obsession for me. I floated from gym to gym, only getting guest passes until I found a place that I could pay for my membership in cash. As my muscles and bulk grew, so did my dreams. I'd never had dreams—kids like me weren't allowed to dream. Without the owner knowing, I listened to him and gained knowledge and motivation, then made my move to the other side of Austin so my gym wouldn't be close to his.

When I opened the gym doors, Hudson came in on the second day, looked around the huge space that had me at a folding table with a clunky laptop and one treadmill, one punching bag, a bench press, and a set of weights. Most people who walked in those first few months while I filled the space turned on their heel and walked right back out.

Of course, Hudson was a different story. He walked in, looked around, and burst out laughing, which only served to piss me off. He laughed so hard he doubled over, slapping his knee. I'd launched myself from the folding chair, set on kicking his ass. Walking in and deciding it's not for you, fine. Laughing at one of the only things I've ever owned, fuck no. His eyes settled on me as I stomped toward him with my hands balled in fists and my jaw clenched. And then his words stopped me in my tracks.

"This is kind of like heaven," Hudson said, looking between me and the space with his shit-eating grin. "I've been looking for a place to work out without having to wait in a long line to use a damn machine or listen to men grunt while they stare at themselves. Don't think I'd have to wait around in here. It's like you set it up just for me."

My lip curled as I continued to watch him.

"Not much for chitchat?"

I shook my head.

"That's perfect, too." Hudson grinned. "How much?"

When I responded with the price, those were the only words I spoke to him for a week. He came in and worked out, always stopping by my little folding table to talk, even though I didn't answer. I don't think he cared. He can talk without an audience and not get bored.

The second week, I added a brand new leg press. Hudson stopped when he walked in, staring at me. "You didn't have to get me a gift," he said jokingly.

"Your legs look like chicken legs," I responded, holding

back a smirk.

Hudson laughed with a hand resting on his shaking chest. "I'll get you to crack, just wait."

I shook my head, going back to the catalog in front of me, deciding what would be best to order for the gym. He never stopped, and somehow, he conned me into becoming his friend. Hudson, Savannah, and the rest of the group is the sixth thing I owned. I didn't buy them or pick them out or even go searching for them, but they're mine all the same. They're one of the few things that would gut me to leave behind.

I've left a friend in the past. A friend I never should've left. The guilt has eaten alive since I did. I'm not sure I could leave people I care about behind for the second time in my life.

The sounds of clinking metal and gloves hitting the bag fill my ears as I sit at the front desk watching everything in my gym. It's a slow form of torture not being able to participate in anything more than admin work. Every time I lift weights, hit the bag, or use the cardio machines, a sense of pride fills me. I did this. I accomplished this. I own this.

Hudson comes strolling through the door with his gym bag slung over his shoulder, smiling at each person he passes. He removes his sunglasses the farther into the gym he walks, looking around. When his eyes land on me at the reception desk in the center of the gym, he changes direction, heading toward me.

Most places keep the reception desk at the front of the house, but I prefer the middle; it provides a better 360 of everything. It allows me to face one way and be able to see what's going on behind me with the help of the large mirrors framing the walls.

Hudson walks behind the desk, taking a seat in the rolling chair in front of the computer, leaning back before he props his feet on the counter and brings his hands behind his head. My hand reaches out, swiping his feet off the counter, which makes him laugh before he props them back up in the same spot.

I heave a sigh and I leave him be. For now. "Didn't you come here to work out?" I ask dryly.

"I did." Hudson grins. "Thought I'd hang out with you first. Wouldn't want to miss out on any James time or your bright, sunny disposition."

I stare at him blankly.

Hudson has been talking this entire time I've been lost in thought, but I don't know what he's saying. Still, years later, he doesn't need an audience.

"Is that how it is now? If I eat the girl's pancakes the next morning, it means I want more? I told her before we left the grocery store that it would be a one-time thing. She said she was down."

This isn't the conversation I wanted to tune back into, but I find myself rolling my eyes and responding. "Told you, it's easier if you don't stay."

Hudson frowns. "I can't do that. I like cuddling."

"Christ," I mutter.

"Cuddling leads to more sex; plus, it's just…nice."

I shake my head, trying to go back to ignoring him, even as he continues.

"Is it my fault I thought the pancakes were a thank you for the several orgasms I gave her and not a commitment to see each other again?"

"Yes," I respond, once again tuning out as I survey all the patrons, hoping someone needs my help. I may not be able to lift like I normally do, but I can still help people with their form and get the fuck out of the conversation with Hudson. I'm about to resign myself to the fate of listening to Hudson when I spot a kid in the corner of the gym lifting dumbbells.

Lifting them incorrectly. Lifting a weight that looks like it could snap his twiggy arms as they bend at an uncomfortable angle.

I leave Hudson behind, not bothering with his outrage that I walked away while he was lamenting about sex and pancakes. The kid doesn't clock me as I approach him. He's tall and just on the side of thin. His form is solid, and with the right diet to fuel his growing body, he could be lean and athletic. I look around the area, seeing if there's a parent watching him. Underage kids aren't supposed to be in here unmonitored. It's not a family gym with a daycare, but if parents want to bring their teenager who will behave and use equipment properly, then I don't care. I offer day passes for situations like that, if they don't want to buy another membership. This kid didn't come to the desk and snuck in without getting a pass.

"Hey, kid," I call.

He jerks up, looking at me in fear before dropping the weight and taking off. Luckily, I'm faster. I catch him in a couple strides, grabbing the back of his T-shirt.

"I wasn't takin' anything," he spits out as the fear turns to white-hot anger flaring in his eyes.

"Slow down," I say, releasing his shirt but keeping a heavy hand on his shoulder. "You aren't in trouble."

His chin lifts defiantly. Biting the inside of my cheek to keep from snapping at him, I go for honesty. "Your form is slightly off when you're lifting the weight."

"You don't know shit," he responds, trying to jerk my hand off his shoulder.

"I do know my shit, and you have two options. You can either let me correct your form and give you the right weight to use, or you can leave. Won't allow you to work out here if you're intent on hurting yourself."

"I ain't gonna hurt myself." He tries to shake off my hand

again. I don't let it move, knowing he'll take off if he's not under my grip.

"You will," I insist, looking at him again. His clothes are ratty, and his jeans are slightly too small. He's probably growing too fast to stay in anything long. Judging by his clothes and the backpack he was about to abandon, his family doesn't have a lot of money. I hide my cringe when I look at his shoes, shoes that shouldn't have been anywhere near a gym. His threadbare shirt has the local high school football logo across the front. I point at his chest. "You play?"

"What's it to you?"

"You keep lifting the way you're lifting, it's only a matter of time before you cause too much damage to your shoulder, and the closest you'd ever get to a field is being the water boy."

"Fuck you," he grunts, not losing an ounce of the fire burning inside of him.

"What's it going to be? I teach you, help that strength that helps you on the field, or you're out of here. It's one or the other." I've kept our conversation as quiet as possible so no one hears us.

The kid stays silent, looking around the gym, keeping his focus on anything that isn't me. His eyes swing back to me. There's so much anger and pain swirling around him, my chest catches. His clothes, attitude, and pain remind me of myself when I was a kid. If he stays, which I hope he does, I will work my ass off not to let him down like I'm sure he's used to.

"Fine," he mutters, looking down at his shoes. "I'll stay."

"Good man."

His eyes pop back to mine, showing the barest hint of pride at the praise.

"I'm assuming your parents aren't here?"

He stiffens, the shields slamming back down. I hold up my hand before he can get snarky and take off. "Don't care, either way. Don't allow kids in the gym without supervision. You aren't here working out unless I'm here, yeah? Lucky for you, I'm always here. Got me?"

"Yeah," he mutters, his shoulders falling a bit as his gaze moves to his ratty shoes. "I ain't got parents. I can't pay. My fosters won't pay for this."

Yeah, this kid is just like me. "Don't need your money, kid. As long as you let me help with your form, listen to me when I tell you about workouts, and don't show up unless I'm here, then you're good."

The kid nods, looking at me with renewed hope. "My coach told me I could go places if I put in the effort."

"Imagine that's true," I say, finally releasing the hand from his shoulder. "Let's get you there. I'll bring you some clothes."

He opens his mouth to argue with me, but I hold up a hand. "My fosters wouldn't pay for shit. You need gym clothes. Shoes, shorts, and shirts. I have tons, don't argue. You won't like what happens if you wear jeans to work out."

His eyes flash in surprise looking down at his legs. "Chaffing hurts. Take the shorts."

The kid nods his head once.

"And the shoes," I state firmly leaving no room for arguments.

He licks his lips looking around the gym to avoid eye contact with me. "I'll make sure what you do in here makes your body star material for a football field, but you need shoes to do that."

His nod this time is much more enthusiastic. I hold back my smile as I stick my hand out for him to shake like a man. I can only assume he's never been given this kind of respect when he stares at my hand in awe.

"James," I say, giving his hand a firm shake.

"Corbin."

# CHAPTER
## EIGHT

*Tatum*

THE LINE AT THE COFFEE SHOP INCHES FORWARD slowly. I'm dead on my feet. Sleepless nights and long work hours landed me here at a coffee shop on a Friday afternoon craving for some serious caffeine. I'd love to go home and crash early, but if I do my entire sleeping schedule will be completely out of wack.

Isabella asked me to come over for dinner tonight, but I turned her down. My thoughts are consumed with Patrick. Since my mom brought up the two of us going to the gala together, it's been on mind as I replay every word he said a couple weeks ago. I haven't seen or heard from him since, which isn't weird. We can go a while without running into each other, but I can't deny—hope blossomed. I thought he would call.

Or text.

Or e-mail.

Something to let me know what he said wasn't a fluke. He hasn't brought up marriage as point-blank as he did since we broke up. There's been hinting around with promises of one day. One day has yet to happen.

I want to ask him to the gala. After hours of thinking,

I've decided I'll be nonchalant when I ask. If I'm casual, he might be more inclined to go with me. I just know that if we go together, we'll be together again and he won't act like he is now. Everything will go back to normal.

A voice, several people ahead of me at the cash register, shocks me to my core. Perfect. A grin stretches across my face as I watch Patrick walk down to the edge of the bar and wait for his coffee. He's in a navy suit, but he's lost the tie and has a button undone at the top of his light blue shirt. The blue matches his eyes perfectly, and I know when I see them, they'll practically be glowing.

He hasn't looked up at all, his attention entirely on his phone, my attention entirely on him. The barista has to try grabbing my attention twice before I turn to her and place my order as quickly as possible, then hustle down the bar toward Patrick. He's still waiting on his drink and looking at his phone, rubbing one hand along his angular jawline.

"Patrick," I say softly when I reach him.

His eyes lift from his phone, landing right on mine. A sexy, lopsided grin takes over his face as his eyes light up with happiness. "Tate."

"Hi." I bite my lip, suddenly nervous about asking him.

His gaze drops to my mouth before sliding back to my eyes. With heat filling his eyes, Patrick leans forward, lightly taking my chin between his thumb and finger and lifting my face toward his. "Hi," he whispers before his lips come down, meeting mine in a soft kiss that breaks all too quickly. "What's up?"

"Long week," I reply. "I needed a little pick-me-up."

"I know the feeling," he says, glancing back at his phone as he types a message. The smile slips from my face. When we were together, he'd never look at his phone when it was the two of us.

Unease swirls in my gut making me doubt myself and

my feelings. If this goes poorly, that's it. I'm done, I won't wait around anymore than I already have. I push away the doubt and stand taller with determination.

"That's my order," Patrick says when the barista calls his drink out. He picks up the cup, leans down to kiss me, and whispers against my lips. "Bye, Tate."

"Wait," I say, fisting my hand in his shirt and keeping him close to my lips. "Can you hang around for a minute? I want to talk to you."

Patrick pulls away, sighing and looking down at his phone. "I guess I have a few minutes. I'll grab a table."

"Be there in a second," I say. "I promise it won't take long."

I watch Patrick walk away, hoping my order arrives quickly. Thankfully, it does. I smile as I take the seat across from him. He glances up at me from his phone, but his gaze quickly returns back to the screen, talking to me while he continues swiping. How can a person change so quickly? Or did I just miss this? "What's up?" Patrick's tone is bordering on bored.

"Um," I hesitate, wanting his full attention. "I'll wait for you to finish emailing."

Patrick sighs, putting down his phone, and finally looks at me. "Tate, I really do have to be somewhere and need to get going. What's up?"

"Would you like to go to the charity gala together?" I ask in a rush before quickly adding the disclaimer, "As friends, of course."

Patrick gives me a sympathetic and placating smile. "Tate," he says slowly. "I—"

"I thought it could be fun, for old times' sake. We'll both be there, anyway. It could be fun." I take a deep breath, biting my lower lip. "I already said that."

"Yeah, I'm sure we'd have fun," he says.

"Yeah," I respond, my smiling growing and hope filling my chest.

"But I don't know who I want to go with. I kind of want to keep my options open. Alana and Todd just broke off their engagement, I thought about asking her."

"Oh." My tightly clasped hands fall into my lap facing the defeat.

He spreads his hands in front of him and shrugs. "If not, maybe we could go together. As friends, though."

"Of course," I whisper, fighting to keep my smile in place and the burn of tears out of my eyes.

"If we went as friends, you'd have to be cool if I went home with someone else."

I swallow, unable to respond. I try to force a laugh, but it sounds like I'm choking instead. I force a lie from my lips. The sadness completely leaves me and anger, irritation, and fury set in. I feel all of those feelings toward him, but mostly toward myself. My tongue runs over my teeth before I take a deep breath and respond as normally as possible. "No big deal. Thought it would be fun, and it'd take the pressure from needing to find a date. Greg is a good-looking guy, maybe I'll see what he's up to."

"Tate," Patrick says in a mocking tone. "Greg wouldn't go there with you."

"Why not?"

"He knows you're mine."

"Yours?" I ask on a disbelieving whisper. A small, shocked laugh leaves my lips.

"Yes, mine. This is all temporary. Everyone knows that. No guy is going to go there with you when they know who you belong to."

I'm stunned into silence. Has he kept men away from me? He thinks it's okay that he can date but still considers me his? Before I can say another word, he gets up from his chair, leans down for a light kiss to my lips, but I pull back and turn my face away. The kiss lands on my cheek and he departs quickly without saying another word.

"He's joking," I quietly say out loud to no one. "He's got to be joking."

I hate the way my heart is breaking for someone I realize I truly didn't know. Every side of him that's he's shown me since our break up has been awful. I wanted to believe that was the façade, but it wasn't. The guy I spent over a decade with was the façade. I look around at the other tables, shocked that no one is paying attention to my life imploding. My eyes close as the tears start to form out of frustration. Taking a deep breath, I wipe under my eyes, stand up, and head out into the crisp fall evening. Tears are coming, but I don't want to do it in public. The tears are inevitable. I hate that I'm crying for someone who doesn't deserve it. For a life—a future—I wouldn't have been happy with.

###

I'm surrounded by tissues from my crying jag. Since I got home, I've been watching sappy movies, allowing myself to cry during every sad and happy scene. Watching sappy movies is my favorite way to release pent up emotions. I don't truly have to think about what's burning inside my chest or clogging my throat, but I can let it all go while getting lost in another reality. Of course I didn't have any junk food in the house, so I've been waiting until it's late to go to the store. I don't want to run into anyone.

My cart is full of the best junk food in the world—food I'll probably hate myself for eating by the end of the weekend, but it will taste wonderful. Chips, dips, cookies, and cakes. When Patrick broke up with me, I mourned for one day, but then I convinced myself he'd do what he said—come back. I never thought this separation would last eight months. I thought a couple weeks tops. I never thought I'd become the girl who sat around waiting for him while he said awful things and made me feel incredibly small and worthless.

As much as I'm mourning for what I thought would be, I'm mostly crying for the small part of myself I lost during these eight months I sat around waiting.

Eight months of seeing him and getting mixed signals. Eight months of berating myself to move on but letting it fly out the window the moment he showed me any attention. Dreams and plans are hard to let go when it's everything I ever wanted. I refuse to keep doing this to myself and vow to never let it happen again.

The tears start flowing again as I picture all my dreams of a happy marriage with Patrick washing down the drain. That was all a lie. Eventually I would've seen this side of him, eventually I would've felt trapped. I look around to see if anyone is near me. There's not. It's empty here tonight except for a few workers restocking the shelves. I open one of the tissue packs in my cart to wipe my eyes and blow my nose. The tissue comes away from my face streaked with mascara. Groaning, I drop my head down to the cart handle. I forgot to check in the mirror before I left. My mascara is probably all over my face, which makes my eyes start to water again.

I pop up when I hear a mumbled curse behind me.

Oh, no.

This isn't happening.

Slowly, I turn around to face the last person I want to see. James. Okay, maybe second to last. I want to see Patrick even less than him.

"What are you doing here?" he growls, looking at me from head to toe, his lip curling slightly into a sneer.

I can't stop my eyes from rolling and a groan releasing past my lips. His attitude is one thing I don't need right now.

"Picking strawberries," I retort. "What does it look like I'm doing?"

His eyes have dropped to my pajamas. If it were any other guy, I'd say he's looking at my chest, but I'm pretty sure I repel James. Every time we've had a physical therapy session, we argue almost the entire time. Personally, I have a great time seeing how red I can make him.

It's too bad I repel him, because he's insanely sexy. Even now, way past midnight in the middle of the frozen treats aisle, he looks like he's about to pose for a magazine ad. His gray eyes are bright and sparkling, even through the annoyance. The muscles that make his shirt look close to popping only enhance the tattoos down his arms. I'm not sure what's so sexy about seeing a man in a plain, white T-shirt and well-worn jeans, but wow, James wears it well.

"What in the hell are you wearing?" He's still staring at my pajamas with confusion written all over his face.

I look down at my outfit and notice the buttons are misaligned, so a tiny patch of my stomach is showing. I shrug. "Pajamas."

"Are those cats?"

"Kittens," I answer, sniffing and trying to sound superior, like this is the next 'it' item in high fashion. "Kittens chasing little balls of yarn. It's cute."

"It's childish," he responds dryly before making a choking noise. His eyes go from my feet to my face and back again. "Fuck. I didn't notice your shoes."

I look down at my slippered feet, wiggling my toes and giggling when I hear James curse again.

"Polar bears are my favorite animal." I wiggle my toes again, making the bear claws dance and tap against the floor. "They're bear claws."

"Christ."

I finally look back up at him, meeting his eyes. His head cocks slightly, a frown taking over his beautiful face. "Are you okay?"

The soft whisper and earnest question bring on a fresh wave of tears. Before they fall, I clear my throat and blink quickly to get rid of the moisture. He isn't asking because he thinks he has to; he's asking because, for some odd reason, he actually wants to know the answer.

My mouth pulls up on one side, the only smile I can muster at the moment. "Bad night," I say, looking down at my white and fuzzy polar bear paw slippers to compose myself.

When my eyes meet his, the regular annoyance is gone, and sympathy is in its place. His eyes flit all over my face, the frown growing deeper by the second. I'm uncomfortable under his scrutiny, needing to change the look in his eyes or I'll melt right here into a puddle.

"Why are you here?" I ask, even though I gave him attitude just minutes before for the same question.

"Shopping," James grunts.

"Do they only allow you to come at this time so you don't scare away the customers?" I ask seriously with a little bit of concern in my voice.

Bingo! His scowl is back, the annoyance pouring quickly back into his eyes, and his face is moving through his shades of red at a rapid rate. "Surprised they even let you in without supervision. You look like you're twelve."

"My pajamas are cute," I say, placing my hand on my hip, my heart kicking into a gallop. This is what I needed. Familiar. Arguing with James is becoming second nature.

"For a twelve-year-old," he responds gruffly. "Don't even get me started on the shoes."

"The shoes are the best part," I argue, trying to keep my smile from breaking loose.

"And the hair." His hand flies in my direction, motioning around the top of my head. "Do you own a mirror?"

"It's not that bad," I say, curling my fingers into a fist

to keep myself from running my hand over my hair. James takes his phone out of his pants, looking down a second before holding it up in front of my face.

"What are you doing?" I ask in surprise staring at his phone in front of my face.

He looks down at the screen before turning his phone around to show me and cocks an eyebrow. On the screen is a picture of me. It's not a great picture. In fact, it's a terrible picture of me. I'm not sure I've ever looked so bad in a picture.

I look up at him in horror. My hair is piled on top of my head with frizzy fly-aways sticking out in every direction. Albert Einstein would be having a better hair day. The mascara I feared being around my eyes is there, and faint black lines travel down my cheeks, only more highlighted by the flush underneath them.

"Told you." James tucks his phone back in his pocket. "Your hair looks like a bird's nest. Something could be living in there." James's hand reaches out patting my hair with an eyebrow raised.

"Delete that," I hiss.

His big shoulder shrugs as he crosses his arms over his chest. "Insurance," he responds.

"Insurance?"

"Yep."

"I can't believe I ran into someone this late," I grumble to rows of ice cream, rocking back on my slippers.

"Why are you here this late? Without shoes?"

"These are shoes," I argue, lifting up my foot and showing him the bottom of my slipper. "They have soles."

"They're slippers. Those aren't soles. You step on something, there's no protection. Then my physical therapist will need a physical therapist, and I'll be shit out of luck."

"I won't step on anything," I protest, lowering my foot

back down to the scuffed floor.

"Why are you here so late?"

I stick my tongue in my cheek, avoiding his eyes, while pointing to the ice cream. "Ice cream."

"Christ. I've never seen you before, and now you're everywhere." My gaze flashes back to him. This is the first time I've seen him outside of our sessions, where I have to see him.

"What are you talking about?"

"You're my therapist. You're here. You're at the cafe. You're at the post office."

I think back to the last time I went to the cafe and the post office. I went to the cafe on Wednesday, but I didn't see James there. I didn't see him at the post office on Thursday, either. "I didn't see you," I respond.

"That's because I saw you and left." His hand falls to the metal cart in front of him gripping it hard.

"That's rude," I snap. "I'm not that bad. And how do you know you've never seen me? We could have passed each other a thousand times before we met and not known."

I don't actually think that's true. Even if Patrick and I didn't break up, I'd notice James walking down the street. He is so far from my usual classically handsome, straight-laced type, but James turns heads. Everyone's head. He's impossible not to notice.

"Believe me, I'd remember seeing you," he says.

I can't tell by his tone if that's a compliment or not. Would he remember because he thinks I'm nice to look at, or because he finds me so repulsive, I'd be hard to forget?

# CHAPTER
## NINE

*James*

CHRIST.

I can't believe fucking Tatum is here. Even with black shit all around her eyes and her hair looking like something is living in it, she's still fucking beautiful. The thin silk of pajamas with fucking cats chasing fucking yarn hides nothing. Her slim body and full curves are on perfect display. She should seriously look in a mirror before she leaves the house.

The stocker at the end of the aisle has been staring at her ass and long legs for several minutes. He doesn't seem to mind that those long legs end in polar bear slippers. Polar bear slippers. Who is this girl?

Her blue eyes are so round and huge, and the pain in them is gutting me, which only pisses me off more. Why do I care if she's been crying? She's been the bane of my existence since I met her, grinding my gears in every way she can think of. It pisses me off watching her smile when she says something she knows will make me angry.

And here she is, standing in front of me in silk cat pajamas looking fucking cute, even if she's been crying and filling her cart with enough processed shit to last through the damn apocalypse. A small, protective instinct wants to demand to know why she's out alone so late and carry her to her car so she won't step on anything that could hurt her. I don't know why I care.

She keeps popping up everywhere I go. Both times I saw her outside of PT this week, I got out of there before she saw me. Today she heard my muttered curse because it's just the two of us in this grocery store besides the employees.

I'm usually so careful with my words, but my stupid mouth just opened and let the words slip before I could control it, telling her I'd remembered seeing her. Fuck. She's my physical therapist, I can't flirt with her. Now she's looking at me in confusion.

"I'm not sure if I should take that in a good way or a bad way," she finally responds.

I grunt instead of responding, keeping my mouth closed. Seems to be safer that way. My words flow too easily around her, and I don't like it. Just another reason she irritates me.

"What are you doing in this aisle?" she asks, looking down at my cart with a frown. It's filled with fruits and vegetables and packs of lean meats.

"Picking strawberries," I say, slinging her earlier retort back to her. Her eyes pop up, glaring at me. My words may flow too easily, but at least I still have control over my facial expressions. I prevent the smile wanting to break across my face and make my lips stay in a flat line. "Want me to show you the produce section?" I ask sarcastically.

She huffs, turning toward the ice cream and scanning the flavors before opening the door, grabbing three, and tossing them in her cart. "I should go," she says quietly. "Don't want my ice cream to melt."

"Yep," I reply before watching her walk down the aisle. Right before she turns the corner, she glances at me over her shoulder. When she finds me staring at her, she gives a little wave before taking off.

I groan, turning back toward the desserts and finding my favorite sugar-free chocolate treats.

###

"Hold that stretch," Tatum says, running her small hand along my shoulder blade and down my arm. "Do you feel any pain?"

"Yes."

Tatum steps in front of me with a crease between her brows and a frown pulling down her lips. "Where?"

"My ass."

"What?" Tatum squeaks, her eyes darting down to my ass.

"It's you. You're the pain in my ass."

She scoffs. "You're a pain in *my* ass."

"Good one," I mutter, shaking my head.

The loud cackle that rings out behind me can't be mistaken. I release the stretch Tatum told me to hold and turn to find Savannah, her eyes flicking back and forth between Tatum and me.

*Shit.*

"What are you doing here?" I ask as I step toward her, worried something has happened and also hoping she didn't notice I lied about my physical therapist being pretty. She'd get too many ideas in that head of hers. My eyes flash behind her, but Liam isn't there which causes the uncertainty to sky rocket.

"That's not a nice greeting, sugar pop," Savannah says, curling her hair behind her ear, looking down at her shoes. I don't miss the smirk that slides across her face before vanishing. When she looks up at me there's a sheen of tears in her eyes, but they don't look sad. Only mischievous.

I release a frustrated breath.

"I'm pregnant," she says into the silence.

"What?" I croak, looking down at her still-flat stomach where her hand is resting.

"It's yours," she says, her lip quirking up on the side, completely giving her away. "You said you would always love me, shortcake."

"Oh, my," I hear whispered from behind me as a heavy thud hits the floor. Tatum must've dropped a medicine ball.

"Christ," I groan, my heated face signaling my embarrassment. I run my palm over my head and squeeze my neck when it lands there.

"I'll step out for a second," Tatum whispers, scooting around us as her eyes fly back and forth between Savannah, me, and the floor. Her cheeks are pink. My hand flies out, latching onto her arm, not letting her move even an inch more. I don't like her, but for some reason, I don't want her to think I'm the one who knocked Savannah up.

"Savannah," I growl.

"Fine," she says, smiling, her eyes flicking to Tatum and happiness takes over her features. "I'm only joking. I just like to make him mad."

"It's fun to make him mad," Tatum says, grinning back at Savannah.

I drop my hand from Tatum's arm, and she glances down at that spot with a little frown. My hand clenches in a fist and opens back up, trying to release the feeling of her skin on mine. It feels like pinpricks moving along the skin that was touching Tatum. Savannah's eyes are bright and excited as she flicks them back and forth between Tatum and me.

"I like her," Savannah states.

"Yippee," I mumble while scratching my abdomen just to give my hands something to do besides touching Tatum. "What are you doing here, Sav?"

"Sav?" Tatum asks. "So you will use nicknames, just won't call me by my preferred name."

"Don't know you," I state firmly, angling my body toward Savannah and away from Tatum.

"I'm your physical therapist." Her hands fall onto her hips as she faces me completely, squaring off with me.

"She's my friend," I bite out.

"I'm Savannah." Savannah sticks out her hand toward Tatum with a smile splitting her face. It wasn't too long ago that it was much harder to make Savannah smile. That nightmare is completely behind her, and she's on cloud nine with her new husband.

"Tatum. Call me Tate," Tatum says, shaking Savannah's hand while smirking at me. She thinks she's getting the upper hand by meeting one of my friends.

"Tate." Savannah scrunches her nose as her smile grows even larger. "That's cute. I like that name. Do you know what it means?"

"It means happy," Tatum replies with her bright grin.

"Fitting," I say out loud without meaning to, but brush it off quickly by turning to Savannah.

I raise an eyebrow at her. That's kind of a weird question to ask someone. Savannah's hand drops to my forearm, squeezing lightly. "I really am pregnant."

"Really?" I ask.

A hand drops to her flat stomach. "Yeah." Tears shimmer in her eyes. "So, now I'm really interested in names." My arms shoot out, wrapping around her and hugging tightly, bringing her flush to my chest as my hand cradles the back of her head. Her hands clutch my back as she whispers, "Thank you. I'm alive and here because of you."

"It was all you, Savannah." I drop a kiss to the top of her head as pride swells through my chest.

"Told him the happy news?"

I look up, seeing Liam striding toward us with a broad grin.

One of my hands leaves Savannah's back, extending toward Liam. "Congrats, man."

Liam takes Savannah from my arms, encasing her in his and kissing her cheek. "Thanks, James. I—"

"Don't," I say. I didn't do anything besides befriend Savannah and teach her some self-defense moves to help her protect herself. The rest of it was all her.

"James—"

I wave my hand to cut him off. "What are y'all doing here?"

"My OB is close to here. I remembered that you had your appointment today. Just stopping by to say hi," Savannah informs me.

"I can't believe you have two friends," Tatum says, chuckling at her own joke. My glare sharpens, pinning her to the spot. She shrugs and grins when Liam lets out a shocked noise that quickly turns into a howl of laughter.

"Turning on the charm, James?" he asks with his hand on his shaking chest.

"Fuck off," I order, leveling him with a glare.

"Liam, this is Tate, James's physical therapist. Tate, this is my husband, Liam." Savannah's making unnecessary introductions. She and Liam will be out of here in a minute, and they'll never see Tatum again.

"Can we get back to our session?" I ask, interrupting the greeting and trying to halt any further conversation.

"Tate, we're going out tonight to The Cellar; we hang out there a few nights a week. You should come," Savannah says, clutching Tatum's arm as if they're old friends.

"That's a great idea, gorgeous," Liam says, smiling at his wife.

"She's busy," I growl.

"I'd love to come join y'all," Tatum replies at the same time.

"No, you wouldn't," I insist.

"Yeah, I think I would," she says, smirking at me before turning back to Savannah. "Can y'all give me some more pointers tonight about how to annoy this guy?"

"Love to." Liam grins, and I make a note to not go so easy the next time we spar in the ring at my gym. If I have to, I'll order some shitty pads, just to make sure he feels every hit.

"Can't wait," Tatum says.

"Ride in an Uber. Us girls usually drink too much, and with Harper and I not being able to drink, our friend Valerie is going to need someone to sip on wine with."

I walk away, knowing I lost this and Tatum is coming tonight. Maybe I shouldn't go. I could stay home and not torture myself with Tatum's incessant chatter. Savannah and Tatum keep talking while I go through my own series of stretches, working my muscles.

I keep my back to the group so I don't have to see them together. What the hell is Savannah up to? She's never invited someone before, and Liam looked way too delighted to bask in my torture. If they get Tatum close to Hudson, I'll never hear the end of it.

I should stay home.

I'm definitely going to stay home.

As much as I don't want her there, a small part of me is curious about what Tatum is like away from the hospital. Seeing her in her crazy pajamas in the middle of the night at the grocery store piqued my interest.

"How's that feel?"

I turn my head, and Tatum is looking over the position I'm holding. "Good," I grumble. If I have to see her tonight, I'm going to ignore her as much as possible now or it will be way too much of her in one day.

"Your friends left," she says.

I grunt, changing positions, relishing in the burn I feel pulling through the muscle over my shoulder blade.

"I won't come if you really don't want me to," Tatum says softly, and something I don't want to acknowledge pulls in my chest, clutching my heart tight.

I want to tell her that I don't want her there, she shouldn't be there, but instead, I find myself saying something entirely different. "You should come."

# CHAPTER
## TEN

*Tatum*

WHEN SAVANNAH ASKED ME TO GO OUT WITH them, my first instinct was to say no. It's not necessarily inappropriate to hang out with a patient, but it's also not encouraged. I said yes for two reasons. One, I really need some new friends that don't know Patrick. Our entangled lives are becoming too much for me to handle. Every time I go out with my friends, I'm reduced to a ball of anxiety, wondering if he'll be there. Will he be alone? Will he notice me? I'm done being that pathetic girl. He's made it clear that he'll keep me around as plan B. I'm done being plan B. As a girlfriend and as a friend. Savannah is lovely and funny. She could definitely be a friend. Her husband seems just as wonderful, and it's a bonus that he's fun to look at.

Reason number two that I said yes? The shade of James's face was priceless. I couldn't resist. We've been at each other's throats since meeting, always trying to one-up the other. Each session I try to make him admit that my plan for him is working. Slow and steady. That's my motto. Being offered the chance to go out to make new friends and annoy James, there's no way in hell I'd say no.

I'm not sure what to expect tonight. I've never been to The Cellar. There's a menu online, but I don't want to be the only one eating or turn into *that girl*—the only stumbling drunk because I didn't eat. Probably wouldn't be the way to make friends. I like to be prepared, which is why I'm now in my kitchen cooking pasta with roasted tomatoes.

A grin takes over my face when Isabella's ringtone cuts off my music. I turn to my phone, propping it against the back of the bar, and swipe across the screen to answer her video call. "Hey, girlie," I call over my shoulder as I turn back to grab the bowl I just finished preparing.

"Come entertain me," Isabella whines.

I sit at the bar with my bowl of pasta, adjusting the phone so it's focused on me. Isabella is lying on her bed with her arm stretched in front of her to hold her phone while the other hand is holding up her head Her full lips are turned down in a pout.

"Where's Spencer?" I ask before taking my first bite.

She rolls to her back, sighing dramatically. "Working. As usual. He's in New York."

"Bummer," I respond. Spencer works for his father's hotel business, which requires a lot of travel to their properties around the world. Isabella is left alone in their monstrosity of a house often. She hates it. She works from home as a web designer, so it's not unusual that I get a call from her like this when she's desperate for some human interaction.

"I offered to go with him, but he said I would be bored. I'm bored here, though, and isn't half the fun of working from home that I get to work from anywhere?"

"But sitting in a hotel room working, unable to explore wherever you are is completely different."

She shrugs, still pouting, staring off into a corner of her room. I know spending so much time apart from Spencer is hard on her, but I feel like something else is going on.

"How long is he gone?" I ask.

Her eyes flick to the screen. "Stop worrying. You have that wrinkle between your eyebrows you get when you're worried. He's only gone for a few days. I'm fine."

She doesn't seem fine, though. "Are you okay?" I ask softly.

Her chest rises as she takes a deep breath before smiling a brilliant smile. It's not her genuine happy smile, but it's the one that tells me she wants to change the subject. "I'm fine. I just miss my fiancé. It's a good excuse to hang out with my bestie, though. Come over. Cook me dinner."

I laugh, taking a sip of my water before I choke on the bite of pasta. "You'll have to make your own dinner. I have plans."

Isabella gasps, sitting up, her eyes becoming so big and round she looks like a cartoon character. "A date? With who? Patrick? Someone new? Tell me everything!"

Covering my mouth with my hand as I chuckle, I shake my head before answering. "Not a date. With some friends."

"Who? I'll meet up with y'all. No one called me."

"Some new friends," I answer vaguely. Can you call someone a friend after talking to them for five minutes? Can I call a patient who I love to annoy a friend? I don't know, but I was invited and I'm going.

"Who?" she asks again with a tiny, adorable scowl on her face. Her tone is laced with skepticism and curiosity.

I bite my lip to stop myself from laughing as I get up from the bar, placing my empty bowl in the dishwasher. Isabella is waiting for me to answer. "One of my patients had a friend stop by today during our session. We hit it off and she invited me out with her."

"Are you sure she wasn't asking you on a date?"

"Yeah." I laugh. "I'm sure. She was with her sexy-as-sin husband and they have a bun in the oven."

"Is your patient going to be there?"

"Yes," I say slowly, looking at the wall as I walk down the hallway toward my bedroom and into my closet.

"Is he hot?"

"He's…." I trail off, thinking about James. He's huge. Intimidating. Frustrating. Silent. Broody. Annoying. And so undeniably sexy. I shiver thinking of his eyes. "Good looking," I finish, hoping she'll drop it, but I know she won't.

"Really?" she asks, waggling her eyebrows.

"He's more frustrating than he is hot."

"Frustrating?" Isabella rolls to stomach, repositioning the phone against some pillows.

"Yes, everything about him sets me on edge." I take a dress and a top from the rod and toss them onto my bed as options.

"Then why are you going tonight?"

"His friend Savannah and her husband, Liam, seem great. I need new friends."

Isabella is silent for a moment. I stop scanning my clothes and look at my phone to see her raise an eyebrow. "New friends?"

"Yes," I answer. "Our entire friends circle—hell, our entire world is too intertwined with Patrick. I can't… I just need space from it."

"I get that," Isabella says quietly, looking down while worrying her lip.

I go back to scanning my clothes, searching for the right outfit. I haven't filled Isabella in on my latest embarrassing "Get Patrick To Notice Me" attempt. She's been begging for me to forget about him since he dumped me. It's hard to move on, though, when I see him around frequently, when he's thrown in my face constantly. It's time to change that, hence the new friends.

"I'm not sure what to wear," I say, breaking our silence.

"Where are y'all going?"

"Some bar called The Cellar. Have you been?"

"Yeah," she answers, smiling. "Spence and I went for happy hour once. It's a cool place."

"What should I wear?" Isabella knows my closet almost as well as I do. She could pinpoint an outfit without me having to show her what's in it.

"Any of these friends single?"

I glare at my phone as she winks with a flirtatious smile on her face. I shake my head, unable to stop my smile. "Not sure," I answer honestly. "I'm not interested, though."

A flash of James's intense gray eyes appear in my mind before I clear that image. He is the last person I'm interested in. A small, snorting laugh escapes as I think of what a disaster that would be. We'd kill each other ten minutes into a first date. Guaranteed.

Even with that knowledge, a small piece of me—that I'm trying to ignore—wants to look good tonight and wants him to notice.

"You can't say you're not interested if you haven't even met them. You could meet the love of your life."

"The love of my life recently asked me to keep waiting for him while he continues to fuck everything in Texas."

Isabella groans, flipping to her back again dramatically. "He's not the love of your life."

"I've been in love with him for almost half my life. If that's not the love of my life, then I don't know what is. I need him to be the love of my life because if I wasted that amount of time on him and he isn't the love of my life? What the hell does that say about me? How could I waste that much time? I don't even want to be with him anymore, but I can't even think about the time I wasted on...on...on some guy because that's all he is now. Just some freaking guy." I slam the drawer where I just pulled a new pair of panties from.

"Tate," Isabella whispers, trying to get me to look at her.

A fresh wave of unwanted tears floods my eyes. My pink polished toes are becoming blurry. I suck in a giant breath, blinking rapidly. "Help me pick an outfit," I say, finally looking into the camera again.

There're tears in her eyes, too. We've been so close most of our lives, that we feel each other's pain. Every time she cries, so do I. And vice versa.

She looks like she's about to say something, but I cut her off before she has the chance. "Please, Iz. When you look good, you feel good. Help me look good."

After a moment, she nods once before a slow smirk slides across her face and excitement lights up her eyes. Isabella tells me exactly what to change into. It's sexier than I would have picked for myself, but it gives me the confidence boost I'm looking for.

As I'm swiping on the last touch of lipstick, Isabella speaks. "Have fun tonight. Be safe. Make new friends. Just don't make a new best friend."

"Thanks," I say, smiling and fluffing my auburn hair.

"I mean it, you can't replace me. I'm your best friend. I'll tackle a bitch that tries to take my spot."

"Noted," I say, chuckling. I couldn't ever replace Isabella. We hang up, and I take a few steadying breaths before I head out to what I'm hoping will be a great night.

# CHAPTER
# ELEVEN

## James

M Y HANDS CURL INTO FISTS AND RELEASE SEVERAL times before I fling the door of The Cellar open. I don't know what kind of car Tatum drives, so I don't know if she's here yet, or if she followed Savannah's advice and took an Uber. I'm not quite prepared to see her. Annoyance bristles in my gut when I spot Savannah and Liam sitting with Harper and Roman.

Our group has grown a lot in the past year or so, and it's about all I can handle. Throw Tatum into that mix? I know it's not going to be a good night for me. Keeping a stoic face is usually the easiest thing in the world, but Tatum grates on every last nerve, making me want to explode.

My ass lands hard in the seat across from Savannah. She turns her face away from Liam's to smile at me, a smile I don't return. Not even a glimpse of a smile.

"Puddin' pop," Savannah says brightly, squeezing my hand resting on the table. I slide it out from beneath hers, bringing my hands to my lap and continuing to glower at her.

Savannah's smile widens when I remain silent. Liam chuckles, looking at her like she's the cutest thing in the fucking world. Usually, I agree with him about Savannah, but right now she's the meddling little sister I definitely don't need. Growing up without a family means I missed out on a lot. Having a meddling little sister is one aspect I could keep going without. Every wish I dared to make as a kid was about having a family. I eventually stopped making those wishes.

"Don't be mad," Savannah urges.

"Why would he be mad at you?" Harper asks.

My gaze swings to her and Roman, whose eyebrow is quirked.

"I invited James's physical therapist to come out with us. I met her today. She's great," Savannah says.

"The one who annoys you? The one you want to strangle?" Roman asks.

"Yep." My one answer doesn't hide the irritation I'm feeling.

"Like a setup?" Harper asks, watching me with a slight smile. Christ. These women.

"Better not be a fuckin' setup," I hiss at Savannah.

"Not a setup," Savannah raises her hands in front of her, trying to calm me down.

"Wouldn't be a bad thing," Liam chimes in. "She's cute."

"She's more than cute," Savannah says, looking at Harper. "She is hot. You'll love her. She's fun and feisty."

I roll my eyes. Tatum is feisty, but unless you'd call getting pricked by a porcupine fun, that's the last adjective I'd use for her.

"Better not be a setup," I mutter again.

"It's not. Would that really be so bad, though?" Savannah asks.

"Yes."

"Why?"

"She's my PT. And I like not having attachments."

Savannah's smile curves down into a frown.

My hard resolve to stay angry at her slips away. "Didn't mean it like that."

Savannah nods as Liam leans over to kiss her shoulder. "I didn't do it to set you up, James. I just like her. She seems fun."

Right. Lots of fun.

The front door of the bar swings open, the sun pouring inside. It's still so bright out, even though it's late evening. I can't see anything but a silhouette, but I know it's her. It's like we're in some goddamn romantic comedy and the spotlight is shining just for her. As the door swings closed behind her, I curse under my breath.

"There she is," Savannah says, waving her arm above her head.

"That's a shirt from my boutique," Harper says excitedly. "I like her already. She is freaking gorgeous."

The fact that she is so beautiful only makes her more annoying. The hold on my beer bottle tightens to a white-knuckled grip as she walks closer to our table. I have to clench my teeth so hard to keep my jaw shut, otherwise it would fall to the floor watching her hips sway as she walks toward us. Tatum's long auburn hair is curled and a little wild around her face, and her piercing blue eyes land on each person at our table, bouncing back to me each time. Long, slender legs are in dark jeans that hug her small curves perfectly. Her breasts are perfectly framed in the low-cut V with cutouts along the edge showcasing more of her skin. There isn't anything obscene about her outfit, but she looks like temptation.

I bring my beer bottle to my lips, guzzling down the almost full bottle. She stops next to our table with a shy smile. As much as I tell myself to look away from her, I can't.

Savannah stands, giving Tatum a tight hug. "Glad you made it."

Tatum's gaze lands on me over Savannah's shoulder, giving me a small, timid smile. I incline my head in return.

Liam stands next, giving Tatum a hug, as well, before Savannah introduces her to Roman and Harper. Roman smirks at me over his beer bottle, chuckling to himself while shaking his head.

Tatum awkwardly glances around the table at the empty seats, trying to decide where to sit. The couples are on one side as I sit across from them. Since the others aren't here yet, it'd be awkward as fuck if she sat anywhere except on either side of me. I kick out the chair on my left, indicating to it with my now empty beer bottle.

She hesitates, staring into my eyes while chewing on her bottom lip. Finally, she sits next to me, clutching her purse in her lap. "Hi," she says quietly, looking at me with those glacier blue eyes through her long lashes. Fuck.

"Hey," I say, almost as softly.

Owen, our usual waiter, appears. He doesn't look at anyone at the table except for Tatum. She orders a glass of wine, and I order another beer and a bourbon.

After Owen walks away, Tatum launches into a conversation, never one to be quiet for long. She murmurs to herself throughout our physical therapy appointments, trying to get me to talk to her. When I don't, she just talks to herself.

"Harper, you look really familiar," Tatum says.

"Your top is from my boutique, Harper Avenue," Harper responds, beaming.

"That's your store? I love it! Are you moving locations? I drove by the other week and it was closed."

Roman tenses next to Harper. It's only been a couple months since their entire worlds were turned upside down by a half brother Roman never knew existed. Harper's store was collateral in the fallout of that shitstorm. She's been operating business online but hasn't found a space to rent.

"Long story," Harper hedges.

Tatum's back straightens as she starts shaking her head softly. "I'm sorry. I didn't mean to pry. That's none of my business."

Harper smiles. "No, it's okay, really. I'm looking for a new place, but everything is online now. I love that top on you. The flared sleeves and details along the neckline are perfect!"

Perfectly tempting.

Perfectly inviting.

"Thank you. That's great to hear about your store," Tatum says, but she is still clutching the purse in her lap, and when Owen drops off her wine, her small hand shakes slightly as she reaches for the glass.

Tatum doesn't seem like a person who gets nervous, and I don't know why she's nervous right now. Or if it's me who's making her uncomfortable. I've barely looked anywhere else but at her profile since she sat down.

Hudson's voice as he approaches makes me break my stare so I can glare at him. "It's not my birthday yet, guys. This pretty lady sure is a great present, though," he says, winking at Tatum. He sits on the other side of her. I reach around, popping him on the back of his head.

"Quit being an ass," I grumble.

"Touchy, touchy," Hudson says, grinning. "I'm Hudson." He sticks out his hand for Tatum to shake, but brings it to his lips while looking at me. I know he's trying to get a rise out of me, but I won't take the bait. I also know that it will only get worse when he finds out who she is.

"Tatum," she replies softly.

"And how did we get so lucky to be graced by your presence?"

Savannah answers. "She's James's physical therapist. I met her today and invited her out."

Hudson's grin widens, and his eyes fucking sparkle when he looks at me over her shoulder. I know he's replaying our conversation about Tatum in his head. "Lucky us."

Tatum's head cocks while tugging her hand back to her lap. "Are you always like this?"

"Irresistible?" Hudson asks, tearing his gaze away from me and winking at Tatum.

"Arrogant," Tatum replies.

The entire table (except for me) erupts in peals of laughter. Even Hudson has his head thrown back laughing. I'm too busy staring into Tatum's eyes to laugh.

She turns back toward me, gauging my reaction. "Sorry," she murmurs quietly enough that only I can hear while everyone else is still laughing and giving Hudson shit.

"For what?"

"For being rude to your friend."

I shake my head. "Not rude. He needed to be knocked down a few pegs. Probably needs a few more."

She chuckles. "Good."

"If you didn't do that, he'd probably keep hitting on you." The words tumble past my lips before I can stop them. Normally I wouldn't continue the conversation.

"And now he won't."

I shake my head. "No, now he respects you and probably will want to be your friend. He's a one-night-only kind of guy. He'd never jeopardize a friendship for that."

"Good to know. Though I may turn into a one-night kind of girl," she says wryly.

My chest clenches. "Not looking for a boyfriend?"

"Nope."

I wonder if I read the situation wrong and if her remark was banter with Hudson. Maybe she's actually interested. It makes me uncomfortable to think about, but I have no claim on her. "While he won't make you uncomfortable, I'm sure he wouldn't deny you if that's what you want."

"It's not," she says firmly. "I don't want to hook up with your friends. I like them. I could use some new friends."

I nod, unsure of what else to say, and frustrated that the uneasiness left my gut when she admitted she didn't want to hook up with Hudson.

"Are you upset I'm here?" she asks.

"No," I answer honestly. "I'm not."

# CHAPTER
# TWELVE

*Tatum*

I'M SANDWICHED BETWEEN TWO OF THE MOST GORGEOUS men I've ever seen. Neither one is quite my type. This whole group is something I'm not exactly used to being around, but I'm loving every single second—especially the heat radiating off both men on either side of me.

I could also be drunk.

Possibly.

Maybe.

Which was not the plan. I decided not to use Uber and take my own car. I hoped that would keep my in line, but no such luck. My face is tingling and I can't feel my lips or nose.

Yes, I could be drunk.

Maybe just slightly.

James's words earlier were right. Hudson is a shameless flirt, but he's not hitting on me. I got up to go to the bathroom after James admitted he didn't mind that I was here. When I returned, James was leaning over my chair whispering furiously to Hudson.

Hudson frowned when I sat down looking contrite, immediately filling me in, much to James's dismay. "James said that I can't mess around with his PT." Hudson rolls his eyes before winking at me.

And just like that, he becomes one of my favorite people. Making James turn red could quite possibly be my new favorite hobby.

"If a night with you will piss this big guy off," I say, pointing over my shoulder toward James, "then you may just be worth it."

Hudson grins wickedly. "It would definitely make him mad. Have you ever seen him mad? Give me a kiss, let's test it."

I giggle and think about if I've ever seen James mad. I don't think so. I've seen him frustrated and irritated, but not mad. The level of heat that comes to his cheeks is how I measure his irritation with me. I glance over my shoulder, finding those stone-gray eyes glaring at me, which only makes this more fun. "What shade of red does he turn?"

"I think you just became my favorite person," Hudson says.

I wink at him. "Likewise."

At that moment, another insanely attractive guy plops down at our table. He pushes his dark blond hair back with a large hand before his mossy green eyes land on me. Savannah introduces him as Kiernan. The last two seats at the table are filled by another couple—Valerie and Gabe.

Each of them is so wonderful, and I'm so happy I met Savannah. This group feels like they could truly become my friends. I could have friends that don't even know Patrick exists. I won't see pity in any of their eyes or get the sad head tilts asking if I'm okay. I've been stuck in a rut for so long, it's nice to be somewhere new.

The table is filled with food and empty drink glasses. Valerie and I are drinking enough for Savannah and Harper since they're pregnant. James switched to water not long ago, earning him some heckling from Hudson and me.

"Are you always so growly?" I ask him, crinkling my nose.

"Someone's going to have to drive you home," he responds dryly.

A shock zaps through my system, imagining myself alone in a tightly enclosed space with James. He overwhelms me in a large room, which means he'll decimate me in a car when we're alone.

"I'll take her home," Kiernan says, leaning around Hudson to wink at me. With all these men winking at me, they could really make me dizzy.

James huffs. There's a slight undertone of pink in his cheeks. A grin slides over my face, wondering how much worse I can make it.

"Don't even think about it," James growls in a low tone, only meant for me to hear.

"Jealous?" I taunt quietly, swaying toward him.

He sucks in a deep breath before blowing it out and leans toward me, giving me as good as I give him. "Never."

One word and my frustration level rises through the roof. It's not even like I want to make him jealous, but for him to rub my face in the fact that he's clearly out of my league stings.

As red as I can make him, I know he can match it on me. It's like this when we're trying to one-up the other.

"If it's not one of your friends, I'm sure I can find another guy in the bar to take me home."

"I'd rather make sure you get home safely."

"Why?" I ask.

"I really don't want to be with that other idiot PT again."

I roll my eyes, turning back to the group and immersing myself in the conversation. James stays mostly silent except when we're verbally sparring back and forth. I can feel every eye at the table on us when that happens. And when I turn back toward them, each of them is sporting a grin.

James hasn't smiled or laughed once. I've seen his lips twitch and his eyes light up in amusement, but mostly he keeps his stoic mask on the entire time.

When Owen comes around, dropping off the checks, I'm confused when he doesn't place one in front of me.

"It's been taken care of, sweetheart," Owen replies after I ask him.

In my drunken state, I immediately turn toward James. His cheeks are slightly pink, giving himself away, but he's avoiding my eyes.

"James," I say, hoping it sounds clear, but could be coming out a slurred mess.

He glances up at me then back at the receipt in front of him, placing cash on top of it.

"Did you pay for me?" I ask.

He shrugs, refusing to look my way.

"Why?"

"My shoulder is feeling good. No big deal, Tatum."

"Tate," I correct automatically. "I really wish you would call me Tate."

Everyone stands from the table. James walks around, hugging the girls and tapping fists with the guys. "Let's go, Tatum. I'll bring you home. You can't drive."

He's right. I can't drive. I'll have to figure out a way to get my car home tomorrow, but for tonight, I'll be in the passenger seat of James's car.

I say goodbye to everyone and quietly follow James out to a black SUV. He opens the passenger door for me. I climb in, buckling my seatbelt as he silently stands there until it's clicked before shutting the door and walking around to the driver's side.

The air is crisp and slightly chilly for an early fall night. Goosebumps break out along my arms as he starts the car and points the vents with warm air toward me.

"Where am I going?" he asks.

I guide him to my house, but other than that, it's a silent drive. When he pulls up to the curb, I expect him to stay in the car, but he surprises me when he turns it off and meets me around the side.

"You don't need to walk me to the door," I say, looking up at the side of his face.

His eyes flick down to me before looking at the house again as we slowly walk up the driveway. "You're drunk. I'm not just going to dump you on the sidewalk."

"I'm not that drunk."

He shrugs and continues walking toward my door. Our arms brush slightly, making electricity course through my body. Just a small brush of skin, and I'm electrified. *It's not James, Tate. It's his muscles. Patrick is in good shape, but he's no James.*

When we reach my door, James leans against the jamb, waiting for me to unlock it. I pull my keys out of my purse, flipping slowly through each one before landing on my house key.

I don't know why, but I don't want to walk away from him quite yet. I look up into his eyes that, for once, aren't glaring at me. They're just watching me. My eyes move down to the keys in my hands as I take a deep breath, my shoulders rising and falling dramatically.

A rush of gratitude floods my system for James. Tonight has been perfect. I need this. I need new friends, and his group of friends is amazing. "Thanks for letting me come tonight."

"Free country," he replies quietly before clearing his throat. "It wasn't as torturous as I thought it would be." He's not smiling, but I can see the amusement in his eyes. The gray is sparkling like crystal.

"Your company wasn't horrible, either," I say, unable to stop the smile from taking over my face. He doesn't know what tonight meant to me. I rush him, hugging him around his waist and squeezing him tightly.

His arms stay at his side for a long moment before wrapping me in a tight, warm hug. James's nose and mouth come down to the top of my head.

"Really, thank you."

"Nothing to thank me for, Tatum," he says softly against my hair.

He's so wrong about that. If I weren't drunk, I wouldn't be touching him right now. I'm sure he's only placating me because I'm wasted and obviously in need of friends.

I lean back, not letting go of his waist. He's staring down at me. My eyes move to his full lips, watching them open and close. Twice. Before I find myself leaning in toward him, something I would never do under normal circumstances.

James's hands come down on my shoulders, gently removing me from his hard body. Mortification sets in, but I'm determined to play it off as if I wasn't about to launch myself at him and kiss him. This is James. He annoys me. I annoy him. Nope. It's the alcohol.

"Goodnight, Tatum," he says, stepping away from me and down the sidewalk, waiting there until I let myself inside.

# CHAPTER
# THIRTEEN

## James

**"I**F YOU'RE SO TOUGH, THEN WHY DON'T YOU DO IT?"
Corbin barks out, his chest heaving up and down. It's
been a delicate balance of showing him the correct
way to move his body with the weights. Each time I tweak
his form, he takes it personally.

"Can't," I mutter.

His jaw clenches. "Then why are you teaching me? You
don't know what you're talking about."

"I do know," I insist. "Doctors orders. Can't lift weights
until my PT is over."

Corbin scans me from head to toe, looking for an injury.
But my scars are beneath my shirt. He won't be able to see
them.

"What happened?"

I open my mouth to tell him it's none of his business, but
I'm trying to get him to trust me. So far, I'm failing. No one
would accuse me of being a people person, but working with
him is important. To get him to trust me and listen to me, I'll
have to be more open than I'd like with this kid.

"Took a couple bullets," I respond.

His eyes get huge. "No shit?"

I nod.

"Did it hurt?" he asks quietly, still scanning my body, looking for the wounds.

"Yeah, it fuckin' hurt," I answer honestly. "That's why you need to listen to me. You say you got talent on the field. I believe it, kid. If you fuck up in a gym, you'll ruin your muscles and ligaments and your chances of playing. Most kids at your school end up in gangs, right?"

Corbin looks down at his tattered shoes, not giving him nearly the support his feet need. I wouldn't be surprised if his toes are curled, just so he can wear them. I'd dig through the lost-and-found at school and local churches for clothes. I was a paycheck to every foster parent I had. Not a doubt in my mind that it's the same for Corbin. When I hit my growth spurt and started to gain muscle mass, I grew out of my clothes quickly. I couldn't button my jeans, so I'd duct tape them to my body so they wouldn't fall. I did that until I stole clothes from a clothing drive.

I bought him new shoes, but today he's not wearing them. He said he lost them, but avoided eye contact with me when he said that. I told him I'd have another pair for him next time he shows up. I don't know if they were stolen, taken by his foster parents, or he sold them for extra money, but it's clear he doesn't have them anymore.

"Yeah, there's gangs," he answers with utmost honesty. I have a feeling he's only rewarding me with this honesty because I was honest with him.

"We're going to make sure you don't end up in that, and you're going to get your chance to get yourself out," I say, putting my hand on his neck and squeezing. "Things don't happen to you. You make them fuckin' happen. You make it happen. You're in charge of your destiny. Fuck fate. Make it yours."

"All right," he mutters, taking a deep breath. I release his neck, waiting for him to gather himself. He shakes his head once before looking up at me, square in the eye. "I'm not stupid, though."

"Kid, I never said you were stupid. If I need to tweak your position, it doesn't mean you're stupid. Just like everything else in life, you have to learn the best way, the right way. You are not stupid, Corbin."

His chest expands, and his shoulders roll back as he stands at his full height, taking more pride in himself than I've seen. Satisfaction swells in my chest. I'd have done anything to have one adult care when I was his age. The only person I had was my best friend. We met when we were foster brothers. When I was his age, I thought I'd end up dead or in jail at some point, I didn't know that I would own something of my own that I'd take pride in. I will make damn sure I help as many kids like me as I can, show them they can have whatever they want if they work for it and keep their nose to the grindstone, ignoring outside influences.

"James," I hear Savannah call out. I turn my head, watching her walk across the gym toward me.

"Damn," Corbin mutters under his breath. I cut him a glare. He just shrugs.

"Hi, gummy bear," Savannah says, wrapping her arms around my waist. I roll my eyes, bringing her into a tight hug.

"Savannah."

"Gummy bear?" Corbin asks, laughing. "You let your girl call you gummy bear?"

"Not my girl," I say.

"Like he could control me," Savannah says sassily, cocking her hip and smiling at Corbin.

"You single?" Corbin asks.

I turn toward him. "Kid, you're fourteen."

"Doesn't hurt to try," Corbin says, grinning playfully,

looking like a real kid for the first time. His expression is young, goofy, and carefree.

"Sorry," Savannah says, resting a hand on his shoulder. "I'm married and pregnant. Also, way too old for you."

"Again, doesn't hurt to try."

Savannah pulls her hand away, and Corbin's hand immediately covers the spot hers just left. He's staring at her with big, round eyes and a happy smile. Leave it to a pretty girl to make this surly kid happy.

"What's up?" I ask Savannah.

She turns fully toward me, beaming. Her smile is so wide that I know she's about to ask for something. My intuition is confirmed when she opens her mouth. "I need a favor."

I stare at her as her smile grows impossibly wider. She knows she has me. I don't think I've ever told this girl no.

"This has been the first week that my morning sickness hasn't knocked me on my ass. Liam just finished a huge project at work and wants to take me on a date night. The last time we went out was over a week ago when Tate met us at the bar."

"Okay," I say, wondering why she's filling me in on date nights with her husband.

"I'm teaching the women's self-defense class tonight, remember?"

Shit. I completely forgot that Savannah asked to teach a beginner's self-defense class for women. It's something I host every few weeks, but Savannah wanted to get involved with the teaching aspect of it. I never forget about anything that's happening at my gym; I can't believe this slipped my mind.

"Can you take it over? Just this once?"

"Isn't this your first class tonight?"

"Yes, but I wanted you there, in case I needed help. I couldn't do much by myself anyway since I'm pregnant.

Please. I miss my husband. He's been working so hard." Her eyes grow huge and round.

I look away before she asks for anything else. "Sure," I mutter. "What time?"

"Seven," she says, rising on her toes to kiss my cheek. "You're the best surrogate brother a girl could ask for, lollipop."

A snort escapes Corbin when Savannah utters her ridiculous nickname for me. She tries to outdo herself every time she sees me. Savannah is the only person on this planet that I would let get away with it. When she started, I didn't stop her because she was broken from her past. The first time I saw her smile was when she called me a stupid name. Who am I to deny a broken girl something so small? Now that she's this badass chick standing in front of me, she's refused to break the habit.

"Have fun," I say, squeezing her once before she hustles out of the gym. I pull my phone from my pocket to check the time. I have a little over an hour before women will start arriving for the class.

One good thing about taking over this class, I won't have to fight with Corbin today about food. He came in last week with his stomach growling. He hadn't eaten all day but didn't want to accept a handout from me. I've been thinking of ways to help him without making it seem like a handout.

"Can you help me out?" I say.

"With what?" he asks. "I don't know how to teach self-defense."

"I need to get ready for the class, so won't have time to grab dinner. Will you go pick something up for me? Grab yourself something, too, for your trouble."

He rolls his lips between his teeth. "You don't need to buy me dinner."

"I would pay you for the errand, anyway. You said your

foster were working the night shift. Now you don't have to cook something for yourself, and you'd be doing me a solid."

I watch him think it over carefully before he nods. "Sure."

---

I'm throwing padded mats on the floor in one of the back rooms when I hear her voice.

"James," Tatum says from behind me. I turn around to find her standing in the doorway. She has a tight tank top on paired with yoga pants that are perfectly molded to her body. A gym bag is slung over her shoulder, and her grip is so tight around the handle, I can see her knuckles turning white.

"Tatum," I greet before turning back to the mats, straightening them even though they don't need it. I just need something to do with my hands before I either strangle Tatum for continually encroaching my space or run my hands up and down her curves. It will be one or the other.

She stands there silently without entering the room. She hasn't signed up for a gym membership, so I'm not really sure why she's here. I glance at her in the mirrors on the walls. If I'm not mistaken, her eyes are glued to my ass.

"What are you doing here, Tatum?"

Her eyes fly up, meeting mine in the mirror, her cheeks turning red. I hold my smirk at bay. "Meeting Savannah. She talked me into a self-defense class."

"Christ," I mutter. "I'm teaching the class."

Tatum shakes her head. "No, Savannah is. I'm in her class. Is that somewhere else?" She looks over her shoulder as if she is in the wrong place.

"Sav asked me to take it over."

"Oh," she says quietly, her hand gripping the strap on the bag flung over her shoulder as she rocks back on her heels. The last time I saw her do that was at the grocery store in those crazy slippers.

"She'll be teaching another one in a couple of weeks."

I wait for her to turn around and walk away. That night after the bar, I know she would have kissed me if I didn't step away. I'm just not sure if she was doing it to keep getting under my skin or if she actually wanted it. Each time I see her, I feel like she's taunting me and testing my will.

"I'll...I'll stay."

I turn my head over my shoulder. "Why?"

She shrugs. "Could be fun."

Yep, she's definitely here to torture me.

I start the class a few minutes after seven, running through basic drills, only touching the women when it's necessary. Unfortunately, when I task everyone to find a partner, Tatum is the only one left without one. She didn't even look for one; the class knew that one woman would be left without since there's eleven women here. Tatum stands in the center of the room, meeting my stare.

I stride toward her, positioning myself behind her, but not touching her yet.

"Many attackers will attack from behind," I say to the class. "Decide who is playing the attacker first and that person needs to come up from behind wrapping their arm over the neck of your partner."

Tatum's light scent fills my nostrils as I wrap my arm around her tiny neck. Our cheeks are right next to each other, her heavy breaths making my arm rise and fall quickly.

"If you are trapped in this position, you'll want to hit a few areas to make a fast getaway. Once you break free, run. Run like hell. First, mimic stomping on his foot with the heel of yours as hard as possible." Tatum lifts her leg which pushes her butt back into me. I hold back a groan. I run through the rest of the maneuvers, trying my hardest not to focus on

Tatum's body against me. Tatum freezes feeling our position and where she's landing on me. She leans into me more making our bodies flush to each other.

"You're doing this on purpose, aren't you?" I quietly growl in her ear.

# CHAPTER
# FOURTEEN

*Tatum*

J AMES'S GRUFF VOICE HISSES IN MY EAR. THE STUBBLE on his cheek scrapes against my cheek, causing a small shiver to run up my spine. What the hell is wrong with me?

I'm learning how to get away from an attacker. He's pretending to be an attacker, and somehow I'm feeling turned on. *Only slightly, though. Slightly turned on…*

That's a major lie. I'm majorly fucking turned on. His massive, muscular chest is against my back while his clean, masculine scent invades my nose. And the stubble. Oh my. I mean, I've read about the stubble scrapes between a woman's thighs in romance novels. I always thought that sounded like it would hurt, but right now with him against my cheek, I want to feel that.

*Feel it in general. Not from James. The growly, grouchy, burly man behind me isn't actually who I want. This is just a generalization. It's just been too long. Yeah, that's it. I'd feel this way with any attractive guy behind me. And, for the record, I wasn't checking out his ass, earlier.*

"Doing what on purpose?" I whisper.

"Torturing me." His voice is husky, and I feel his breath

caress my skin as he rubs his nose along my cheek.

"I don't know what you're talking about," I say, my hands sliding up to his arm around my neck. All the other women in the class are practicing the moves he taught us while we're standing here in this hold, whispering to each other.

"Bullshit," he mutters in my ear. "You're doing all this to annoy me."

Annoy him? If he would have acted like a considerate human being the first time we met, I wouldn't enjoy getting a rise out of him. He's so silent and hard to crack, I can't help that I find it fun to try. I don't try to annoy him, though, or torture him. He's torturing me by never speaking, only growling in our PT sessions unless he's lobbing an insult my way.

We both breathe deeply. I don't know what's going through his head, but I'm lost in his touch and heady scent. My nipples are puckered beneath my sports bra, and the more turned on I get, the more irritated I become with myself. With him.

"Get out of the hold," he whispers furiously. That's when I know he's feeling the same thing. There's something completely captivating about being this close to him, surrounded by everything that is him. His scent fills my nose, his warm body is pressed against mine, and his deep and rich voice is intoxicating. I need to stop forgetting that I don't like him.

My foot comes down hard on top of his. Satisfaction rolls through me when I hear him grunt. I'm careful of his shoulder with the rest of my moves. When he releases me, we stare at each other. His eyes are smoldering with heat and hate.

He rakes a hand through his hair, muttering curses while glaring at me. "Get out of my head."

*Get out of his head?* He needs to get out of *my* head. There's no way he's thinking the same things about me.

James marches to the front of the room, instructing the class on the next exercise and insisting everyone change partners. When I end up alone again, he asks one of the women to break up their duo and pair with him. I stumble my way through the different holds and scenarios, unable to take my eyes off him. Jealously flares through my belly every time he gets close to someone else in the class. I want him to look my way once. That's it. I want to feel like I'm not alone in this insane situation we've gotten ourselves into.

He doesn't.

As the class continues, he walks around correcting stances and postures, but avoids me the entire time. I even know I'm messing things up because I'm too distracted by his deep voice floating through the room and watching the way other women react when he's near. My eyes scan his facial features and body language, wondering if he's aware of any of them.

His easy command of the room excites me in a completely foreign way. In PT he throws verbal jabs at me, but easily listens to each of my commands, but in this room, he's in charge. Even at The Cellar as he sat there mostly silent, his presence couldn't be ignored. Every woman in this room is hanging on his every word working as hard as they can to prove their worth through the maneuvers he's teaching.

His husky voice is even deeper the louder he talks, but he's not intimidating to anyone in here. I'm completely at ease in his hulking presence and I know every other woman in here is, too.

*Dammit. He's captivating me again.*

At one point, I'm so desperate for a tiny sliver of his attention, I call out his name. His shoulders tighten when he hears me. Slowly turning around, he walks toward me, only glancing my way for a second before stopping in front of me, but looking at the wall behind me. He's close enough to touch, if I went on my tippy-toes, I could land my lips on his, although it feels like he's a million miles away.

"James," I whisper. I'm unsure of what I want to say, I just needed to say something, have his attention for a minute. My mind is racing. Should I apologize? Ask for a truce? Finally, I land on a lame attempt. "Can you show me the maneuvers to escape the chokehold?"

James's eyes finally rest on mine before flickering over my face and down my body. I start to ramble, wanting to keep him here. "To be honest, Savannah insisted that I take this class. I kind of wish she told me she wouldn't be teaching it tonight, but I'm sure she got busy. And she's pregnant. Pregnant. I bet that takes up a lot of energy. And I've heard women say something about pregnancy brain. Maybe she just forgot. Do you know why she's not here? I don't know why I need to take this class. I carry mace with me. I'll just spray it and run if I'm ever in a situation. I do live in a pretty safe area, though. I'm sure I'll be okay. I try to be aware of my surroundings. I don't know how good I am at actually keeping track of that. Maybe this class is a good idea, but in the moment, I might—"

"Tatum."

The one word is a warning to stop speaking immediately.

"You talk. A lot." His hands are on his trim hips and his chest is rising and falling slowly. There's a deep crease between his brows.

"I know."

One of his large hands scrubs down his face before resting on his neck, squeezing. There's a tick in his jaw from clenching his teeth. "This is good information to have. Next time, you should wait for Savannah to teach the class."

I open my mouth to speak, to say I didn't know she wouldn't be here, but he shakes his head, walking away. His eyes don't meet mine for the rest of the class. He dismisses us without glancing at me. I'm not in his head.

Rage ignites in my system. I asked him if he wanted me to skip going to the bar. He said it was okay. I'm friends with them now. I need these new friends. I'll avoid him when I can, but I'm not going to stop hanging out with Savannah, Harper, and Valerie. It's not easy making friends as an adult. I'm not letting him scare me away.

I let one man control my thoughts for too long, I won't allow myself to fall down that rabbit hole with James.

I rush out of the gym, feeling like I can't properly breathe until I'm in my car. My breaths sound wheezy and weak. From this moment on, things will remain strictly professional between us. If he's there when I'm with the girls, I'll ignore him. During PT, I won't say anything except instructions. This will work. If I take another class and he's teaching, I'll come a different day. Easy-peasy. Definitely don't let him touch me again. My brain doesn't function properly when that happens.

I'll stop thinking about him. I have just over a day before our next appointment to get my ass in gear and on board with this new plan.

# CHAPTER
# FIFTEEN

## James

T HE SWEET THWACKING SOUND OF GLOVES HITTING pads surrounds me. Liam and Hudson are in one ring, and Kiernan and Roman are in the other. They're lightly sparring while I'm standing between the rings, wishing I was in the middle, pounding into something.

"Thought you had PT on Thursdays," Hudson says, dodging a punch from Liam.

"Nope," I mutter. It's a lie. I do have PT today. I'm not going. There're only a few weeks left, I'll do it on my own. Use YouTube or some shit. Being around Tatum in that capacity is not working. She's infiltrated my life on too many different levels. Something's got to give.

Tatum may disagree, but I'm not a complete asshole. I noticed how much she needed the new friendships she formed with my friends. If I have to tolerate her there, that's about my limit. I've never been so attracted to someone that I also don't really like.

"Yeah, Mondays and Thursdays are your days, right?" Kiernan says.

"Nope," I say again, pulling my phone from my pocket. I have several missed calls from the clinic since I'm a no-show.

I'll pay for the sessions, but I'm done going there and being in that close to her. Using someone else isn't an option, either. I'm so close to the finish line I can taste it.

"I wouldn't mind Tate being my physical therapist," Hudson says, smirking. "Oof." A grin crosses my face when Liam decks him and he lands on his back. That's what he gets for losing focus in the ring and for trying to bait me.

"I wouldn't mind, either," Kiernan says, laughing.

The growl of frustration leaves my lips before I can stop it. I roll my shoulders while wiping my face of any expression. Letting these guys know how Tatum is affecting me is not my idea of a good time. Especially when I can't hop in the ring and settle it that way.

Tatum hasn't left my mind since the other night's self-defense class. That's when I made my decision to create a distance between us. When we go out, she can sit with the girls, and I'll sit with Hudson and Kiernan. Or I won't go sometimes. I don't mind the solitude. Even though I'm quiet and observe, I enjoy the fuck out of my friends. Hanging with them is great, but I can't get caught up in what is happening with Tatum.

She's everywhere. All the time. In just a matter of weeks, I've gone from never seeing her to seeing her everywhere. Even the grocery store in the middle of the night. Tatum in her kitten pajamas and crazy polar bear slippers appears in my mind. Fuck. She's cute. I've created a calm life for myself here. And here she comes, like a talkative hurricane shaking everything up.

"Something is going on with you two," Roman says, resting against the ropes with Kiernan at his side. My head swings the other way, finding Liam and Hudson also leaning against the ropes. I thought men weren't supposed to gossip, but here they are waiting for any damn morsel of information I'm willing to share.

"Nope," I say, walking toward the extra boxing equipment. I pick up the disinfectant bottle and a roll of paper towels, wiping it all down, even though it's already clean. I need my back to them, and I need to do something with my hands. Sitting idle for weeks is slowly killing me. I wonder if, while I do my own PT, I can start working in some light weights, just something to take the edge off.

"I think our boy likes her," Hudson says. I can hear the smile in his voice. I don't turn around. Turning around would only confirm that she's in my head. Like. Like is not what I feel for Tatum. An intense irritation that I want to scratch off like a bad rash? That's more accurate. An insane desire to lay her out on my bed, in the boxing ring, any fucking flat surface, and explore her gorgeous body? Unfortunately, that's accurate, too.

"Hate to break it to you, man, but I think Savannah is set on getting you two together. As soon as we walked out of the physical therapy room, she was plotting and planning. She probably has your wedding planned," Liam says.

That does get me to look over my shoulder at him. He shrugs with a small smile that says, *What are you going to do? My wife is cute.*

My mouth tightens in irritation and I bite my tongue, forcing myself to be silent. Liam thinks anything Savannah does is cute.

Having a relationship will not work with my life. A short, sexual fling or a one-night stand is the only thing I can offer. I can't do feelings.

I've been in Texas for a long time now, but I'm always prepared to run at a moment's notice. I have go-bags everywhere. I could pick up my life and leave from anywhere if I need to. It's been quiet for years, but that doesn't mean my safety is ensured. That could change in a minute. Entering into a relationship would jeopardize everything.

"I'll talk to her," I mutter.

"Good luck with that," Roman says. "Harper and Val have joined in on Savannah's crusade."

"Fuck," I hiss, squeezing the back of my neck. It feels like a slab of concrete from the tension I have residing there. "Dammit."

"I tried to tell Savannah to leave it alone, but she ignored me," Liam says.

"Same with Harper," Roman says.

I turn around, glaring at Hudson and Kiernan. "They're single. Get them to find someone for them."

Hudson and Kiernan look at each other before cracking up. Neither one is ready to settle down, but they eventually want to. That makes them a better candidate than me. That's not a possibility with my life. Even if it were, it's not something I want.

"Looks like someone's here for you," Roman says, tilting his head toward the door. I swing around to see Tatum stomping into the gym with a scowl, scanning the area until her angry eyes land on me.

I release a breath, once again squeezing the tension in my neck and leaning my head toward my shoulder to stretch those muscles. Her hands are balled into little fists at her sides as she storms toward me. I finally walk toward her. "Tatum," I greet.

"Tatum? Seriously? That's it?" she shrieks. "That's all you're going to say? What the hell, James? You freaking no-show on me?"

Everyone in the gym stops what they're doing to turn and stare at us.

"Come on," I murmur, walking toward my office. I don't want an audience for this conversation. When I reach my office, I swing open the door, gesturing her inside. She glares while she passes me.

"What the hell, James?" Her arms are held out to her sides as she stares at me.

I close the door, leaning against it with my ankles crossed and my arms crossed over my chest. "I don't know what you want me to say."

She laughs maniacally. "I've been fighting with you for weeks about your treatment plan. I've worked my ass off for our plan to get you back to where you want to be."

"I know," I murmur, watching her pace from the couch on one end of the office to the desk on the other. One hand is on her forehead and the other is propped against a hip.

"You can't do that, James. They're going to charge you for the appointment."

"I don't care about that."

She glances at me, shaking her head. "So, what? You're just done?"

"I'm going to finish it myself."

"Did you get a degree in physical therapy since the other day?"

I shrug. I know my next answer will piss her off, but I just can't resist. "I'll YouTube it."

"YouTube?"

I lift my shoulder carelessly, keeping my smile in check.

"YouTube?" she shrieks. "I thought you cared about what happens to your body."

"I do," I say uncrossing my arms and bringing them up behind my head.

"Can you give me something besides these freaking short sentences?"

I sigh, scrubbing a hand over the stubble on my jaw. She continues to talk.

"A sigh? That's what you're going to give me? No. You know what? You can't do this, James. We had an agreement, and you're just going to stop showing up? You've worked too hard to get here. I don't even get why. What happened?"

I can't believe she asked what happened. We both damn well know what happened. She's taking over my fucking life. She's everywhere.

"I'm making a new plan, and we're going to stick to that. You want to do therapy here, we'll do it, but you're not watching freaking YouTube. How could you suggest that?"

"Tatum," I say, but she keeps storming on, her pacing picking up speed. She hasn't stopped talking. I'm not even sure she's taken a breath since she started on this tirade. I try again. "Tatum."

"You didn't show up. I worried about you. I didn't know if you got in an accident on the way or what happened. I waited and waited, just watching the freaking clock like a loser. I got stood up by my patient. I was seriously worried, James."

I don't hear anything else after that. Her worry and care float through my head, filling my veins with adrenaline as I launch myself to her, catching her midstride and turning her to me. One of my hands weaves in her silky red hair, and the other uses her lower back to anchor her to me. My lips crash down on hers, as I walk her backward until she hits the wall.

When I break our kiss, both of us are panting. We're panting and there wasn't even fucking tongue. Her hand comes up to her lips, and her wide blue eyes stare at me in shock.

I pull my face away from her, my hands anchored on her body. "You never stop talking."

# CHAPTER
## SIXTEEN

*Tatum*

H E KISSED ME.
        He *kissed* me.
        James kissed *me. James.*
    I'm staring up at him, watching his eyes move across my face as he waits for me to respond. Did he just say he kissed me to shut me up? I feel like I should be offended. But I'm not. His hand slowly starts to move out of my hair.

I don't want it to move, though.

He only kissed me to shut me up. That kind of makes me mad.

Oh, fuck it.

I launch myself at him, wrapping my arms around his neck as my lips land on his. His hand slides back into my hair, gripping the roots hard, almost in a painful way, but it all feels too good to be painful.

I breathe in through my nose, inhaling the woodsy scent that's intoxicated me since our first physical therapy session. A small moan escapes me, and James uses the opportunity to slip his tongue into my mouth. My nails scrape along the back of his head, causing him to groan.

I break our kiss to glare up at him. "I don't like you," I

say. His eyes move all around my face. As I feel him start to pull away, I make my demands. "Kiss me. Don't fucking stop."

His melted steel gray eyes pool with lust and amusement. Desire burns in my veins, aching to get closer to him. "I don't like you much, either," he growls before we crash together again. His lips break away from mine to kiss down my neck, biting at my pulse point, keeping it just shy of painful. It's definitely going to leave a mark.

"Yes," I hiss as his hand slides down to my ass, lifting me so I can wrap my legs around his waist. He crashes us even harder into the wall. I bite his lip in response, fury and lust mixing together, taking over every rational thought.

Our kisses turn into bites as we rip at the other's clothes. His hand tugs at my hair, turning my head so he can control our kiss. His tongue plunders my mouth, and I use mine to battle with his, trying to take control from the angle he has me in.

We break apart, staring at each other and breathing heavily. I don't think I've ever been this turned on. I feel his long, hard length pushing against the seam of my pants. He pulls on my hair again, making me moan, as he bucks his hips forward, rolling into me. My tongue slides along his neck. When he releases a deep rumble from his chest, I shiver from the sound. There's a small rip on the edge of his shirt where I've been tugging it at his neck. His T-shirt feels smooth under my hands as I slide them down his torso to reach the hem. I rip the shirt off over his head, leaning back into the wall to marvel at his expanse of muscle.

"Take off your top," he demands, looking down at my puckered nipples showing through my shirt. I yank it over my head, flinging my bra off right after it, desperate to feel his hard chest against my soft one. Before I can make that contact and slide my nipples over his skin, he ducks his head, pulling one taut nipple into his mouth, sucking hard and running his teeth over the point.

Weaving my fingers through his short hair, I tug and bring his lips back to mine. I suck hard on his lower lip, causing his hips to jerk. I quiver and grind my hips toward his, seeking the friction.

"You're beautiful," he admits as he stares at my chest, his hand sliding from my hair and along the side of my neck, pressing the area where he bit me. His eyes land on mine again, possession evident, which sends a thrill through me straight to my core. I arch my back offering more of myself to him. When his eyes leave mine to look at my chest arched for him, a deep groan fills the room. I rake my finger nails down his abs watching each one contract under my touch.

"Shut up," I groan, gliding my hand down his abs and pushing his shorts down as much as I can in this position. Before I can free him, James drops me to my feet, sinking to his knees in front of me. He looks up at me, watching me as he takes my shoes off my feet. One of his hands slides up the inside of my thigh, cupping my sex.

"I can feel your heat through your pants, Tatum," he grumbles, leaning in toward the apex of my thighs. James rips my pants and panties down my legs, flinging them behind him. His fingers skim up my naked leg, pulling it over his shoulder. I moan when his lips are centimeters from where I'm aching for him.

His breath brushes over my heated skin when he asks, "Is this okay?"

I nod, shamelessly tilting my hips toward his mouth, but he backs away. "Say it, Tatum."

"Yes."

Before the word even escapes my lips, he nips the inside of my thigh, bringing a hand to my hip, pressing me into the wall at my back. I whimper with the sting of his bite, rocking my hips forward, searching for contact. He doesn't make me wait long before he starts devouring my pussy, furiously licking me, bringing me to the edge of orgasm in record time.

Two of his fingers plunge into me as he sucks my clit into his mouth. His fingers fuck me fast, tapping the spot inside that drives me crazy. I look down at him, meeting his eyes. James pulls his fingers out and fucks me with his tongue while rubbing his thumb over my clit in slow circles. His hand caresses my skin as he moves around my waist to the back, squeezing my ass hard enough to leave a mark—he's not letting me forget that this isn't making love. This isn't sex. It's not even regular fucking. It's hate fucking.

And it's the best damn thing I've ever felt.

My fingers wrap into his short hair, pulling hard and holding his face where I need him most. I can feel myself dripping all over him as I move my hips in sync with his tongue. My body fills with need each time his pleasure filled noises send vibrations through my body.

I tumble over into an orgasm when he slaps my ass while sucking on my clit. His hands caress my body as he stands. I pull his shorts down, freeing his cock so I can wrap my hand around it. He growls, his head falling back and hips moving, fucking my fist. I lean forward, not stopping the momentum of my fist as I kiss and bite along his chest. His hand weaves into my hair and tugs when I bite along the edge of his nipple, regaining control.

James steps away and snags his wallet from his desk, pulling out a condom and quickly rolling it down his length before coming back at me. He picks me up, wrapping my legs around his hips.

"Tatum?" he asks. The head of his cock is against my entrance, waiting to make sure I'm good with what's happening. I know he wants to hear the word yes. I give him better.

"Fuck me, James."

He rams his dick inside of me, both of us groaning in pleasure before we attack each other's mouths. Our tongues sweep along each other's, battling, fighting for dominance, wanting to win the war waging between us. My nails scrape down his back, leaving marks as he pulls on my hair. We're both making unintelligible noises as we slap against each other.

"Fuck," James hisses as my pussy starts to flutter around his dick. I'm so close to falling over the edge, but I need…

"More," I whisper.

James ducks his head, pulling a nipple into his mouth and propping me better against the wall while his hand leaves my hair, drifting down my body.

His thumb flicks my clit lightly.

"Yes. More. I…I…"

My words trail off as I moan when his thumb starts circling with more pressure and I explode, quivering in his arms as he continues to fuck me through my orgasm. My back claps against the wall over and over. His lips crash into mine, giving me another soul-searing kiss as he slams into me one final time, growling as he comes, sending me over the edge again.

James pulls his lips away from mine. We're both shaking as we hold onto each other, breathing heavily. Our slick skin feels fused together. We're polar magnets, clashing and fighting until finally we fall against each other, unable to break apart.

His eyes don't leave mine as he slips out of me and lightly kisses my lips. He takes off the condom, tying it off before tossing it in the trash. I'm surprised when he takes a clean towel from a storage unit behind his desk and kneels in front of me.

"I can—"

"Let me." He places my foot on his knee and slowly slides

the towel up my leg before cleaning me softly.

"Thanks," I whisper, unsure what else to say about this gentle act. A moment ago he was fucking me so hard there might be a Tate-shaped hole in the wall and knowing he's kneeling down in front of me, showing me kindness through an act more intimate than the sex we just had. He nods, not looking away from me, but I can hardly look at him. A rush of emotions is filling me, and I don't know what to think right now. It feels like it was bound to happen, but I barely even like him. I don't hesitate—"I still don't like you."

"Feeling's mutual," he mutters, picking up my clothes and handing them to me before getting dressed himself.

Once we're both dressed, we face each other a little awkwardly. "I need to go," I say.

"I'll walk you out."

I nod; an argument isn't worth it. As we exit his office, I keep my head down, but I can feel the stares from his friends and see them in the peripheral vision. When light laughter comes from that area, James turns quickly.

"Fucking quiet. Now."

Their laughter dies immediately, I don't stop my strides to the front. I know they weren't laughing at me, just the absurdity of the situation and I pray they didn't hear me from James's office. James catches up to me, walking closely without touching me muttering under his breath. "Assholes."

I take a deep breath shaking my head.

"They don't mean anything by it."

"I know," I mutter. When we reach my car, I turn toward him. "I expect you to show up to the next session."

"I'll be there," he says, opening my car door for me. Then he stands in the entry of his gym, watching me drive away.

# CHAPTER
# SEVENTEEN

## James

TATUM AND I TOOK THINGS TOO FAR THE OTHER DAY. Neither of us planned for that to happen. It shouldn't have happened. End of story.

She's my fucking physical therapist. And I fucked her. Christ. She's friends with the girls now, too, so I will be seeing her. This is exactly why I set the boundaries I do, so shit like this doesn't happen. I don't want complications in my life. Every facet of my life is complicated enough without adding in a pretty girl.

It won't happen again.

It can't happen again.

Even if I can still feel her silky-smooth skin under my palm. Even if every time I breathe, I smell her jasmine scent. I didn't even know I knew what jasmine smelled like, but that's what comes to mind when I step close to her. Tatum's face. Tatum's body. Tatum's hair. Tatum's smile. Every single part of her is burned into my mind. I don't only see it when I close my eyes. It's all the damn time, playing like a movie on loop through my mind.

By the time I pull into the clinic's parking lot, I'm completely hard, aching to be inside her again. But that won't happen. It can't.

I also can't walk inside there like this.

Stench of a locker room. Spoiled milk. Every nasty thing I can think of runs through my mind until I no longer have the hard issue in my pants. I need to pretend we're normal. Uneasiness settles in my gut. I don't know what she'll expect or think. When she left the other day, she was hardly able to look at me, which fucking gutted me. I don't want our relationship to change or for things to be weird. We'll go back to how it was before.

I can't believe I'm thinking so much about this.

I'll gauge my reaction by how she acts when she sees me. We only have a couple weeks left of sessions. After that, I can keep as much distance between us when we're out. We won't be alone. This will be easy. *Liar*, my mind roars as an image of a naked Tatum stays front and center.

There's no way I can erase that from my mind. I could be ninety-four-years-old, completely senile, but every detail of Tatum will be remembered. Every single inch of her skin is branded on my brain.

I groan, hopping out of my SUV and heading toward what I'm sure will be the longest session yet.

Tatum isn't in the room when I enter. I head for the corner we usually start in. She's late. Tatum is never late. Fuck. This is going to be awkward. She's probably in the hallway gathering enough courage to come in here. Pacing like she does and talking to herself.

I push off from the wall when Simon comes into the room. He smiles as he strides toward me with false confidence. My head turns to either side of me. He must be here for someone else.

"James," he says, sticking out his hand. "I'm going to take over the remainder of your sessions, following Tate's plan."

"No," I growl. "Tatum is my PT. That's it."

"She asked me to take you back on as a patient."

"Where is she?"

"I'm not sure how that's any of your concern," he says hesitantly. Simon takes a step back bringing his tablet to his front and crossing his arms in a protective manner.

I step toward him, looking down at him. He shrinks away slightly. "Tell me where she is."

"I'm not sure," he says quietly. "Tate and I had lunch together. I don't know where she is now."

She had lunch with this clown? Not that I'm jealous. That's not what the swirling in my gut is about. I just don't like this guy. I shove past him, stalking into the hall. I'm going to find her.

This is bullshit.

She came storming into my office when I didn't show. When she left the other night, she told me I needed to be here. Well, here I am, and now she ditches out and gives me back that fucking clown? Hell, no.

I open every door I pass, knowing she'll be behind one of them. I'm nearing the end of the last hall, frustrated I haven't located her yet.

I swing open the door to the break room, a group of women at one table turn their heads my way, and two guys look up from their food.

"Tatum," I bark.

Each of them blinks in surprise. I growl, the impatience eating me alive. "Tell me where she is."

Nothing.

Fucking Christ.

"Have you seen Tatum?" My tone demands an answer. After a moment I finally get a silent answer from all of them.

They shake their heads slowly continuing to watch me. I stomp out of the room into the hallway. Security is probably on their way to haul me out of here for acting like an insane person. If they spend five minutes with Tatum, though, they'd get it. That crazy, infuriating, gorgeous girl has me wrapped up so fucking tight, I don't know which way is up. Security would let me go after just a few minutes with her.

I reach the end of the hall; there's a door on either side of me. One is the women's restroom and the other is a supply closet. Obvious choice is the women's restroom. She's hiding and probably thinks I won't go in there. I will. I don't give a shit, but I really hope it's the supply closet. I try that door first.

Tatum yelps as I yank open the supply closet door. Her hand comes over her mouth, and medical supplies fly from her grasp. I prop my fist on my hip and pinch the bridge of my nose before glowering at her. "The supply closet?"

She's silent, looking around like she's waiting for something to pop out and save her from this conversation. Finally, her eyes meet mine as her arms cross over her chest, and she raises her chin slightly—a rich girl attitude taking over her normal persona. "I needed supplies."

"You need to get your ass to our session. I don't have all day."

"I traded you to Simon's shift."

"Simon," I spit out his name. "Simon is not my guy. I already fired Simon. Get your ass in check and come do the session."

"I'll find you someone else," she says, flinging her hair over her shoulder and avoiding eye contact.

"You're the one who showed up the other day demanding I be here and finish this. You. That's it. It's you or it's no one."

"I thought about it, and…" She trails off, worrying her plump lip between her teeth.

Her taste fills my mouth. I want to bite that lip before soothing it with my tongue. I shake my head to clear those thoughts. "And?"

"It's not a good idea for us to work together."

"Because we fucked?"

Tatum flinches, sucking in a sharp breath. Her stunning eyes meet mine, her brows pulled down. The next words spoken are hiss through her teeth. "Keep it down. James, I don't normally do things like that. I acted inappropriately."

I like the way she acted. I rub a hand over my mouth to stop my smirk. "Tatum, it was a one-time thing. It happened. Let's pretend it didn't and go back to how things were."

"Just like that?" she asks hesitantly.

"Just like that."

"Don't tell anyone what happened."

I grunt. I don't go around informing my friends of the women I've been with, but I have to admit, it stings a tiny bit. Shouldn't be surprised, though, she's a girl from a well-to-do family with buckets of money and a higher education, and I'm just me. I've been the dirty secret for a lot of women.

"Didn't plan on it," I finally mutter.

"It's not going to be weird?"

"Not on my end."

"Are you sure?"

"Look, Tatum, it happened, okay? Can't change that fact. It's not going to happen again. It was just…"

"What was it?" she asks quietly, taking a small step toward me. I can smell her enticing jasmine scent. That smell alone is enough to drive me wild and makes me want to pounce on her and keep her under me for the rest of eternity.

"A release of anger or something."

"Yeah," she says, taking another step closer. She looks down at her feet before craning her neck back to look into my eyes. "It'd been awhile for me, so it was probably just that."

"Yeah," I breathe. The urge to ask her just how long it'd

been overwhelms me, but I keep a lid on my curiosity. It's none of my damn business, and I have a feeling the answer would make me feel more possessive than I already do. It's a feeling I need to fucking shake, so I don't ask. Nothing good would come from having that knowledge.

"Sorry I paired you with Simon," she says, her lips twitching.

I glare at her, scrutinizing her face. "No, you're not. It's just another way you're trying to torture me. I suspect you asked him on purpose."

A tiny shrug and the hint of a smile makes me want to laugh, but I hold it in. "You knew I would come looking for you."

"Only because it was Simon," she says, coming next to me as we start down the hall toward the physical therapy room.

As if he's been summoned, Simon appears at the end of the hall, watching Tatum before moving his glower to me. His eyes snag on the limited space between Tatum and me before spinning on his heel and marching in the other direction.

"No," I say. "It's because of you. I only want your help."

# CHAPTER
# EIGHTEEN

*Tatum*

J AMES AND I WALK INTO THE PHYSIO ROOM TO START
our session. Deep down, I knew he'd try to find me, but
I hoped he would accept Simon as his fate. If I truly
wanted it to work, though, I should have picked anyone
besides Simon. I knew he would piss James off the most, and
I couldn't resist that.

Simon is standing just inside the door with his long,
lanky arms crossed over his chest. Compared to James's
strong, brawny arms in the same position, Simon's look like
spaghetti noodles—pale with no definition. James is glaring
at Simon in his usual broody manner.

Simon's hands come down on my shoulders, softly
squeezing. James takes a slight step closer, his menacing
shadow falling over us. Simon's Adam's apple bobs as he
swallows, but a wave of relief and comfort sweeps through
me. "I can stay," Simon says quietly.

"Not necessary," James growls.

"Tate?" Simon asks.

"I'm good, Simon. It was a misunderstanding," I reply,
backing away from his hold. My back hits James's strong
chest, but he doesn't move; He just stands there, his body

searing mine through our clothes.

Simon huffs before glancing at James and returning his eyes to mine. "Call me if you need me," he says. He sweeps a finger down my cheek. I jerk my head back breaking the contact. Simon has been a little creepy since I met him, but this is the most forward he's ever been.

"Please don't touch me," I say before turning into James and pushing him so he'll start walking in another direction.

"I don't like him," James says as soon as we're a foot away.

"Shh, he'll hear you."

"Like I give a shit."

Rolling my eyes, I ignore him and walk to our usual area. "Let's get started."

James snags a sixteen-pound medicine ball from the floor with one hand and starts swinging his shoulder around while keeping a firm grip on the ball. I've been testing his strength lately, getting his motion and movement much closer to what it was before he was shot. He's improving rapidly, and I know we'll be able to finish by our target date, even with the one session setback from a few days ago.

"You had lunch with him?" James asks in the middle of an exercise without looking at me. The feeling I get is exactly why having sex with him is a bad idea. The idea that he could be jealous fills me with a sense of elation.

"With Simon?" I ask.

"Yeah." He glances up at me from his position.

"Not unless you count being in the same building as eating lunch together."

James gives a slight nod before falling back into silence. There's tension between us, even though we agreed there wouldn't be. I'm not exactly good at pretending nothing happened.

"Why?" I ask after the silence extends for too long.

"That's what he said," James replies.

"What do you mean?"

James sighs, reluctantly giving more than a few words. "He implied that y'all were eating together when you asked him to save you from me." James finishes with a grunt, like it's ridiculous that I could possibly need to be saved from him. He's exactly who I need to be saved from. How is it possible to truly not like a person but want them naked at the same time?

A naked James is a good James.

His scowls and broody nature turn into something else completely. His face while he fucked me against his office wall was carnal desire. He became even more beautiful in those moments. It's really not fair to look that good. It's probably why he's so moody. You can't look like him and have a good personality. It'd be too much; women of the world couldn't handle something like that.

James would have a trail of women following him everywhere if every woman got a glimpse at what's under his clothes. If they got the chance to run their fingers over the intricate tattoos on his arms. If they all got to feel his hot skin beneath their touch, see his face when he…

My breath shakes when I inhale deeply, wiping away the image of naked James from my mind to turn back to our conversation. "I didn't eat with Simon," I finally say.

"Good," James grunts.

"Why is that good?"

"I can tell you don't like him. He's a creep. You shouldn't be around him."

"Instead I should be around you?"

James turns his big head, astounding me with the heartbreaking confusion and agony on his face. "No, Tatum, you shouldn't be around me, either."

Dammit. That soft voice with a warning against him only makes me want him more.

⚜

When I leave work it's with one goal in mind—get to my best friend's house. I need to unload on her. James is slowly taking over every thought in my head. Today after our session, I was thinking about his facial expression while showing a client how to use the resistance bands. I snapped myself in the face because I lost focus. Thoughts of him are becoming dangerous. I jog to my car. It's been an insanely long day—a long week, and I need my best friend.

My fist rapidly beats on the huge wooden door while ringing the doorbell with my other hand. "Answer, answer, answer," I chant to myself.

Isabella swings open the door with a scowl on her face that quickly wipes away when she sees that it's me. "What on earth?" she asks. "Are you okay?"

"I slept with someone."

Her eyes round comically as she chokes, her mouth gaping like a fish. "Someone as in not Patrick?"

"Yes."

"Oh, my God," she breathes, clutching the door. "How was it?"

"Best I've ever had," I answer honestly.

"Oh, my God." Isabella's hand comes up to cover her mouth.

I sigh before bringing a hand to my forehead. "I know."

"Come in, come in." She grabs my arm and pulls me into her white marble entryway. "I need to know everything."

I follow her through the long and wide hallways, our footsteps echoing around the quiet house. She rushes over to the bar in the living room as I plop down on the white sofa. "White wine," I say. I'm always terrified to spill something in her immaculate space. It's huge, cavernous, and very cold. Almost unwelcoming, but Spencer loves it. And, Isabella loves Spencer. "Where's Spencer?"

She sighs, uncorking a bottle of wine. "Working. Where else?"

I study her face, noticing the dark circles under her eyes and the tiny lines around her frowning mouth. Before Spencer started working and trying to keep up with everyone by showcasing his insane wealth, they were happy. I truly hope this is a rough patch and that things will settle down for the two of them. "Y'all should plan a trip, just the two of you, to reconnect."

Her hand grips the bottle tightly, her lips curling into her mouth. Her shoulders shake slightly as she releases a shuddering breath. "I think it would take more than a getaway," she says softly.

"Oh, Iz. What's going on?"

She shakes her head, a sad smile crossing her face. "I don't want to talk about it. Let's talk about you and sex. Sex is so much more fun than my issues."

I laugh, taking the glass of wine she extends to me before she sits next to me, curling her legs underneath her.

"Okay, tell me everything. Don't you dare leave out a dirty detail." She takes a large sip of wine, waiting for me to dish it all.

After I finish telling her about James—from the moment we met to the intense physical therapy session we just had—I'm still reeling from everything I'm feeling.

"I really like his friends, and I don't want to stop hanging out with them because I messed up and slept with him."

"Did he tell you to go away?"

"No," I admit. "He said let's pretend like it didn't happen. I can't forget that it happened. He may be able to, but I can't. He's obviously more experienced than me, so maybe this is his usual. I don't know. How do I act around someone I've slept with?"

"You manage to be around Patrick," she says, taking a sip of her wine and running her fingers through her long hair.

"That's different."

"How?"

"We were together for years. I still wanted to be with him, and I thought it was just a matter of time before we got back together."

I cringe, thinking of all the sleepless nights and countless times I cried myself to sleep worrying over Patrick. I thought if I could just change something, do something different, make him notice me again, that he'd come back. He's never coming back, though. And more importantly, I don't want him to come back.

"Babe," Isabella says slowly and hesitantly.

"What?" I ask on a whisper.

"I saw him with Alana. Did you know her and Todd broke off their engagement?"

"I heard," I say, not mentioning that I heard this from Patrick, who told me he planned to ask her out. That conversation truly sealed that door shut. All the windows, too. He'll never get back in. I won't be the girl who comes in second. I just won't do it. I won't be the girl who pines for the boy.

"Do you want to sleep with James again?"

*Yes.* My core clenches, as if remembering the rippling orgasms. "No," I mutter.

Isabella smirks and chuckles while patting my arm placatingly. "Liar."

"I don't even like him," I insist. That's not quite true. His grumpiness is growing on me. It's almost…charming.

"Treat him like a stranger," Isabella says. "Go out, have fun with these new friends, but focus on the girls. Try to let him fade into the background."

Right. As if a man like James could ever fade into the background.

# CHAPTER
## NINETEEN

*Tatum*

"IGNORE HIM. I CAN DO THAT. IGNORE. IGNORE. Ignore," I chant. My hand taps my knee with each word. My stomach is rolling with nerves. I'm minutes away from seeing James again where I will have to act cool and like our one-time-thing didn't happen. How do people do this? I'm so not cut out for this.

"I'm sorry, did you say something?" the Uber driver asks, looking at me through the rearview mirror like I'm a crazy person.

"Sorry, talking to myself," I say, smiling brightly. I watch him roll his eyes and mutter something under his breath. Okay then. *One-star for you, buddy.*

The driver pulls up in front of the restaurant where I'm meeting James and the rest of the group—I mean, Savannah and the rest of the group. I'm not meeting James here. He'll be here, but he's not the reason I'm showing up.

"Um…," I say, staring at the front door, clutching my turning stomach. A quick glance at the clock lets me know I'm a little early. Most of them are never early, except the one I'm too nervous to sit alone with. I'm not ready to go in. What if he's already there, but no one else is? "Can you drive around the block again?"

He turns toward me, staring at me with a look of pure annoyance and a raised eyebrow. I smile and shrug, making my voice sound impossibly sweet. "Please?"

The driver stares at me for another moment before turning around and shifting the gear into Drive. At that moment, James walks in front of the car, doing a double take when he sees me in the backseat.

Shit.

"Never mind." I sigh. "It's too late."

"Do you want to go around the block or not?" the driver asks rudely. James hasn't moved a muscle; he's stalled in front of the car, staring at me through the windshield.

"No, I'm getting out."

James walks around the car as I open the door and meet him on the sidewalk.

"Uber?" he asks, his eyes grazing down my body quickly before they meet mine again.

"Yeah." I shrug. "Thought it would be best. That Valerie sure can talk a girl into a lot of things."

James's lips roll into his teeth like he's biting back a smile. I wish he'd just release it. I've never seen him smile or laugh. His face will light up with amusement, but other than that, he doesn't show much emotion.

"She's good at that," he finally says with so much affection in his voice. James walks to the door, holding it open for me and following me inside with his hand hovering over my lower back. He isn't touching me, but I feel the heat of his palm radiating just above my skin.

I'm lost in a mental debate about whether I should act nonchalant or if I should take a step back to make that palm connect with me. A shiver rolls up my spine when I remember how good his large, rough, calloused hands felt on my skin. James's gruff voice breaks my reverie.

"We're meeting people here. Think they're already here," he says to the hostess before motioning me forward. As soon as we step into the dining area, I spot Valerie, Harper, and Savannah. James and I head toward them, and I try to ignore the smiles the girls are wearing.

"Pick a spot," James murmurs when we reach the table. There are two open seats on the other side of Valerie. I sit in one of them, and for some reason, I expect James to sit next to me. So I'm surprised when he sits next to Liam, far away from me.

That's okay. I'm supposed to ignore him, anyway. I'm here to be friends with the girls, not to get caught up in him, I remind myself. I paste a smile on my face, turning toward the girls.

Valerie launches straight into questioning. "Did y'all come together?"

I cringe. "Oh, no. Definitely not," I state firmly. "Just happened to arrive at the same time."

"Do you have a boyfriend we don't know about?"

My lips twitch. I've only been around these girls a few times, but Valerie is already acting offended, like I've kept something from her.

"Nope," I say, smiling. Heat creeps up my neck when I feel the weight of a stare. I know it's impossible to feel some-one staring at you, but I swear I feel his eyes burning holes into the side of my face. I force my smile to stay put and keep looking at the girls. "Why? Know anyone I'd like?"

My hand curls into a fist underneath the table while I replay the same sentence over and over in my head. *Don't look, don't look, don't look.*

"I might know someone," Savannah says with a sly smile.

"Do you have a fuck buddy?" Valerie asks.

I flush in embarrassment, but I'll keep the smile plas-tered on my face if it's the last thing I do. I clear my throat to answer Valerie's question, but I'm interrupted by someone else speaking.

"Hey, Harper," James calls from the other end of the table. "Are you and Roman getting married before or after the baby?"

We turn our heads toward him. His eyes are on mine even though he's speaking to Harper. I glance at her; her mouth is open in shock over his blunt question. If I didn't know for sure that he's not interested in me, I'd think he's trying to steer the conversation away from my love life.

Harper smiles and says, "We haven't decided," at the same time Roman voices, "Definitely before." She turns toward him, leveling him with a scowl. His face splits into a wide grin before he winks at her. Harper's nose crinkles before the scowl slides off her face and she matches his grin.

James is still staring at me, but I'm focusing at the table, trying to be fascinated by the design of the tablecloth.

"I still want to know if you have a fuck buddy," Valerie says, causing me to look up.

Hudson and Kiernan walk up to the table at that moment, taking the last two seats. "I'd like to know that, too," Hudson says, winking at me.

"No, I don't," I say nervously. My gaze accidentally turning to James before turning back to everyone else. I hope no one caught that look. In the second my eyes were on James, I noticed his features were strained.

And, finally, the man looks away from me, and I feel like I can take my first deep breath since sitting down.

Happiness overwhelms me throughout dinner while I enjoy the company of each person at the table—except James. I continue to ignore him throughout the night, but I am thankful that he brought Savannah into my life. As we're finishing up dinner, none of us quite ready to go home, we decide to head toward The Cellar.

Harper walks out hand-in-hand with Roman, her other hand on Hudson's arm as she talks quietly to him. Valerie is whispering in Gabe's ear, and Savannah is making Liam chuckle as she murmurs to him and Kiernan. James is in the front of our pack as we head out, and I'm in the back. The friendship I felt toward Savannah, Valerie, and Harper a moment ago vanishes when we stand in front of the restaurant.

"James said you Ubered, Tate?" Savannah asks.

"Yes, can I—"

"Liam and I have a quick stop to make, so we'll meet everyone there," she says, rushing off with Liam following behind her.

"I want to get frisky with Gabe in the car." Valerie laughs, pulling him toward their car before I can ask for a ride. Kiernan and Hudson take off after them without uttering a word.

My eyes fall on Harper, anticipating her excuse. Savannah's words from earlier ring through my head. She might know someone for me. Right. Funny how James is about to be the only one left while the rest of them just took off.

"I really need to talk to Roman," Harper says. "Privately."

Roman shoots me a wink before wrapping an arm around Harper. They're both laughing as they walk toward their car.

I lick my lips before turning to James. "I can always request an Uber." My voice sounds quiet and unsure. I know he wants us to act normal around each other, but if we're going to be thrown together over and over again, that could get really difficult.

"Don't do that," James says gruffly. "Let's go."

I sigh and follow behind to his SUV. He opens the passenger door for me, patiently waiting for me to get inside and buckle up. When he closes the door, James's scent overwhelms me. I close my eyes and breathe it in deeply, opening my eyes once he hops inside the car.

"Thanks for the ride," I say.

He nods. The vibration of my phone echoes loudly in the silence of the car. We've been on the road for a couple of miles and neither one of us has tried to start a conversation.

James glances at me when my phone vibrates loudly again. "You can take that."

I grab my phone out of my purse, surprised to see a text message from Patrick.

**Patrick:** Hey
**Me:** Hey

Nerves flutter in my belly as I wonder why he's texting me. It's been a while since Patrick has sought me out.

**Patrick:** Pretty girl like you shouldn't be home alone on a Saturday night.

I roll my eyes. Booty call. That's where this is going.

**Me:** I'm not alone.
**Patrick:** Yes, you are.

I look over at James.

**Me:** I'm sitting next to someone right now, pretty sure that means I'm not alone.

**Patrick:** LOL. I meant you should be with friends. Where are you? Sitting at a coffee shop?

**Me:** I'm with friends, going to a bar.

**Patrick:** Everyone is here tonight. You're not here, so I know you're lying.

**Me:** Yeah, Isabella invited me, but I already had plans with some friends.

**Patrick:** Come here instead. I miss you.

I laugh at the absurdity of this situation. It's as if he has alarm bells signaling him for when I'm ready to move on. This time he's too late.

**Patrick:** I've been thinking...

**Me:** What?

**Patrick:** Since you'll be bored out of your mind with whoever your mom sets you up with for the gala, let's make plans to go home together if I don't like my date.

Heat creeps up my neck, making my face feel like it's on fire. I know James can't see my screen, but I'm embarrassed to even be having this conversation next to him. Does he really think I'm that pathetic? Why does he assume that I can't get my own date and that I won't go home with them? How did I not see this before?

**Me:** My mom isn't setting me up.

**Patrick:** Doesn't matter. I don't know who I'm taking yet, but ending the night with you sounds fun.

**Me:** We won't be starting or ending that night together.

**Patrick:** Babe, we've been through this, keeping our options open. Don't get in a hissy fit.

By "our" options he means his options. I ignore his message and don't respond and am surprised when he doesn't take the hint and sends another message.

**Patrick:** Come meet us tonight. I want to see you.

# CHAPTER
## TWENTY

*James*

TATUM IS FURIOUSLY TYPING ON HER PHONE THE ENTIRE way to the bar. Her mouth is turned down and her cheeks are bright red. She clears her throat a few times and blinks rapidly before slipping her phone into her purse as we pull into the parking lot.

I meet her at the tailgate, and we walk inside together in silence. She has a pained look on her face. I open my mouth to ask if she's okay, but she beats me to speaking.

"I'll meet y'all at the table in a minute."

I watch her walk to the bar and flag down the bartender before tearing my gaze away to look for everyone. They're not here. I expected to be first, since they all gave us lame excuses why they couldn't take Tatum. I knew their game the moment Savannah gave the first excuse.

I plop down at our usual table and search out Tatum at the bar again. She tosses back a shot, cringing as she swallows. Worry eats my gut, wondering if it's something to do with the text messages she received in the car.

She turns around, her eyes landing on me, and walks toward the table, never breaking eye contact. My dick hardens behind my zipper as I watch her hips sway with each step.

Her bright blue heavy-lidded eyes roaming my face and down my body. She is so fucking fascinating to watch. Every thought that goes through her head flashes across her face. I could spend hours, days, years watching her and never get tired of it. I've never been a guy who can lounge around watching hours of mindless TV, but I'd happily spend my life looking at nothing else but Tatum.

Her walk slows as she gets closer to the table, looking at the nine empty chairs. Indecision and fear is at war on her face, amusing the shit out of me. My amusement turns to delight when I see her eyes land on a chair, nodding slightly to herself. Of course, it's the chair farthest from me.

"Tatum," I say in a slight warning. Her eyes widen as I pull out the chair next to me, indicating to it with my hand. I don't know when I decided that I need her next to me, but right now it feels fucking crucial that she's within touching distance.

Her eyes jump back to the other chair. She takes a step toward it, but I stop her with one word. "Tate."

Her nickname, something I swore I'd never use. She sucks in a sharp breath, whipping around to face me with large, shocked eyes. I shocked myself by uttering that word, but after watching her in the car and then throwing back a shot as soon as we got in here. I need to know she's okay more than I need to keep my distance.

The honesty of that one word is as much as I can give. That word says everything I can't say.

"You called me Tate."

"Sit down." I point to the chair next to me again. "Please."

Her blue eyes widen even more as she sits down next to me, staring at me the entire time, doing exactly what I knew she would do if I called her by her nickname, giving her even that tiny glimpse into my thoughts. I told her I never would. I told her only people I like will get called by their nicknames.

I'm completely unsure how I feel about her, I'm unsure of our whole situation. There's one thing I'm damn sure of though. I need to make sure she's okay and that's only going to happen if she's next to me.

"Thank you." I incline my head just a bit.

"Uh…you're welcome?"

She turns toward the table, her hands fidgeting in her lap. Her long, slender fingers with nails painted the same shade as her eyes tangle together as she looks around the room. When Owen comes over to the table, I order a beer and she orders a shot of tequila and a fruity cocktail.

She slams back the tequila shot the moment Owen drops our order at the table. My brows pull down in confusion. "Are you okay?" I ask softly, placing my hand on the back of her chair and leaning toward her.

Tatum's lips purse before she takes a deep breath. "Yep."

"Are you sure?"

"Yep." She takes a long drink of her cocktail, and I raise an eyebrow. "Why do you ask?"

"The slamming of the tequila shots," I answer honestly.

She bites her lip, running a hand through her long hair. "I'm fine."

I don't want to press. If she doesn't want to talk about it, that's her decision. I know more than anyone about keeping secrets and thoughts to yourself. My secrets are essential to my survival. Even if hers aren't, I won't push.

I switch topics, hoping to get answers to something else that has been on my mind tonight. "Why did you ignore me tonight?"

Her whole body jerks in surprise, nearly making her fall off her chair. I reach out, grabbing her arm to balance her. She looks down at my hand touching her bare skin and back up at me. And then she lies. "I didn't."

"You did," I say, widening my eyes in challenge.

She opens her mouth, no doubt to tell another lie, before she closes it again, staring at me. "Okay. Fine. I lied. I was ignoring you."

"Why?" It bothered me the entire night. Yes, I didn't sit by her, but I thought she'd want to sit with the girls, not with me. I tried to catch her eye throughout dinner and every time she laughed, but she avoided eye contact. She wouldn't engage with me.

She went so far as to ask Hudson for the bread basket that was next to me. Hudson had to ask me to pass the basket to him, which I did, and the smug smirk on his face made me want to fucking deck him in his pretty-boy face.

"Where are they?" she asks, changing the subject. It's been close to thirty minutes since we got here, and none of them are here. I don't have any messages on my phone, and I'd bet my gym that Tatum doesn't, either.

"Don't think they're coming, sunshine."

"What? Why?" she shrieks, looking around as if they're all going to pop out of nowhere.

"Think they want us together," I admit honestly. As soon as I heard the girls whispering behind me as we headed out of the restaurant and their blatant attempt to put Tatum in my passenger seat, I knew those girls were up to something.

Tatum sighs, muttering under her breath about meddling friends who are not helpful. "You could have told me, you know."

"Told you what?" I ask hesitantly.

"The day I met Savannah, you could have said, 'Tate, if you go out with us, they'll meddle in your life.'"

I grunt. "There was no stopping you when you saw it annoyed me."

"That's true," she says happily. "You make it so fun and way too easy."

I glare at her, which makes her smile brighten even more. Goddamn sunshine. She's the only person who gets under my skin the way she does. It irritates the hell out of me. Mostly. A small, dark part of me also finds it thrilling. And an even smaller, darker part of me breathes easier when she's near as that part is basking in her light.

Suddenly Tatum freezes.

"What?" I ask. "Are you okay?"

"Tate," she says slowly. "Sunshine."

I grunt again, looking away. I didn't mean to call her sunshine. It slipped out before I even thought about it. I did mean to call her Tate, but only to get her attention and to get her to sit next to me at a table I was suspecting would stay empty.

"That's two nicknames. I think you're starting to like me."

"I'm not," I say. I honestly can't decide if I do like her or if I find her fascinating yet irritating.

"Sunshine is a sweet nickname. Is it because I'm bright and happy?" she asks, giggling.

"Nope."

"Then why?" she challenges.

"You know when you're in the sun for too long and it makes you sick? It's kind of like that," I lie, trying not to smile.

She stares at me for a moment before starting to laugh. Her hand reaches out, pushing against my chest.

I lay my hand over hers and can feel the vibrations of her laugh; her whole body is shaking with it. I swear I can feel the warmth of it, too.

"No," she says, still laughing. "I don't think that's it."

"Believe what you want, Tatum." I reluctantly let her hand go.

She shakes her head, smiling, but it slips again a moment

later with my next question. "Why did you ignore me?"

She sighs. "Honestly?"

"Always."

"I don't know how to act around you now."

"Just like you are now," I say. "Nothing has changed. You still annoy me."

She smiles, rolling her eyes. "I'll try to be normal."

"Just don't ignore me. I don't like it," I admit.

We stare at each other for a moment. I take my wallet out of my pocket, throwing enough cash down on the table. Tatum opens her purse, grabbing her wallet, but I stop her.

"Let me pay," she says, standing at the same time I do.

"No. Ready to get out of here?"

"James," she says softly, looking up at me with her glassy eyes.

"Yeah?" I ask, my voice turning husky.

"When we got here, things were happening with me, and it could've been a really shitty night. Thank you for turning it around." She stands on her toes, laughing slightly. "I can't reach you." Her hand curls around my neck, bringing me toward her.

My entire body tenses, unsure of what is happening. When her lips land on my cheek, my hand curls around the back of her neck, bringing her lips to mine.

# CHAPTER
# TWENTY-ONE

*Tatum*

I GASP WHEN JAMES'S MOUTH CRASHES DOWN ON MINE. He takes the opportunity to explore my mouth with his tongue, making my toes curl. My eyes slide closed as I revel in the moment.

When James breaks our kiss, I try to bring him back to me, but he pulls away. "Tatum," he starts, releasing my hair and rubbing his hand over his face.

"I want to," I say, assuring him.

His hand leaves his face, and he looks down at me with serious eyes sweeping over every centimeter. "Yeah?" he asks gruffly.

"Yes." I lean into him. "Take me home."

His large hand cups my face as he kisses me once. Twice. Three times. His palm brushes over my skin, eliciting goosebumps in its wake before he grabs my hand and we walk out of The Cellar.

Looks like the girls are getting their wish.

At least for tonight.

James drives quickly to my place, the car filled with our sexual tension. His rough hand skates along my thigh the entire drive, sending me into a frenzy. My body is pressing deeply into the seat and my hands are curled over the edges, forcing them to stay put so I don't feel him as he drives. I'm ready to attack him by the time we pull up.

He shuts off the SUV, jumps out, and rushes to my side taking me from the car and up to my porch. As I'm trying to unlock the front door, he's standing flush against my back with one hand squeezing my hip and the other sweeping my hair off my neck.

James's head comes down, brushing his tongue along my shoulder and neck. The keys shake in my hand. He's distracted me so much, I haven't even reached for the door to unlock it. I'm motionless in front of the door, lost in the sensations he's causing.

He nips at the space where my neck meets my shoulder. When he whispers into my skin, his breath causes me to shiver. "Unlock it, Tatum." He nips again, urging me into action.

Finally the key lands in the slot and I unlock it, pushing the door open. James stays glued to my back as we tumble inside. He kicks the door closed and spins me toward him by my hip. His hands slide down my back to my ass, squeezing and kneading before lifting me. I collapse into him on a sigh, exhilarated from the feeling of his hands on me.

My lips find his neck, kissing up to his jaw and working my way toward his lips. "Bedroom," he growls, his throat vibrating under my lips. The deep timber of his voice makes my panties wet. I want him to whisper dirty, illicit things into my ear while pounding into me.

I've never felt this before. I thought sex with Patrick was out of this world, mind-blowing. It's nothing compared to this. I'm still fully clothed, and James's voice, touch, smell, and fucking everything are electrifying me, bringing me to life for the first time. This tall, sexy, broody man could probably make me come from dirty words.

"Down the hall," I say before tugging on his earlobe with my teeth. "Second door on the right. I need your touch, James. Everywhere, all over me."

He groans, clutching my ass tighter, moving me over his thick erection. The contact of his jeans over my underwear is just under enough pressure to send me racing toward the edge.

When we make it to my room, James spins to sit on my bed with me straddling him. His hands coast up my back to my shoulders, pulling down the straps of my dress. I slide my arms out of the straps and let it pool around my hips. James's tongue traces the line of my strapless bra before leaning back and gazing at me.

His finger comes up to follow along where his tongue did before falling and tugging on one of the nipples showing through the sheer lace. "So fucking pretty," he says. The roughness of his calloused hands makes my core clench.

I reach behind me, unsnapping my bra and letting the cups fall. He picks it up from his lap between our bodies and tosses it on the floor. I arch into him, moaning when his hot mouth comes down on one of my nipples, pulling hard on the bud. His hand squeezes my other breast before tugging on the peak.

My hips grind over him, searching for friction. I'm going to go insane if I don't feel his skin against mine soon. My hands start tugging at his shirt, ripping it over his head. His guttural moan fills my room as my nails scrape over his chest and down his impossibly defined abs.

James stands, lifting me, then placing me on the floor. My dress falls from my hips with the little tug that he gives. I step out of the fabric around my feet as my hands glide down to his belt. He's kicking off his shoes as I push down his pants. James bends down, ripping them off his legs along with his socks.

He's completely naked, and I'm standing in front of him in a lacy, barely-there thong. His large hand tucks into one side and yanks it from my body.

"Hey!"

"Just making it fair." He pulls me flush against him with a hand on my lower back. "You're beautiful, Tatum."

A blush spreads up my neck to my cheeks. His heated gray eyes turn absolutely molten as he gazes down at me. "Let's see how far I can make that spread. Christ. You're even prettier when you blush."

I squirm in his arms, aching to feel the hard cock that's pressed against my stomach inside of me. When James looks at me like this, his hands lightly skimming across my body, purposefully missing every place I want him to touch, I feel bold and brave. In the past, every dirty thought has stayed in my head during sex, but with James, I want to say everything.

"I want your cock inside me, James," I murmur, kissing across his chest and wrapping my hand around his dick.

He bites his lip, growling, his eyes closing. "Fuck," he says, opening his eyes. "I like that word coming from your delicious mouth." His thumb pushes against my chin, raising my head before skimming along my lips. I pull his thumb inside my mouth, curling my tongue around it and sucking once.

His breathing picks up speed, his chest rising and falling rapidly. His thumb slips from my mouth and he devours my lips with his. My hand is slowing jerking him, his hips meeting each stroke until he pushes my hand away, turning me and laying me gently on the bed.

"Spread your legs." His voice sends shivers through me. "Show me your pussy." A rush of desire floods my system.

"I want to record you saying dirty things to me so I can listen to it when I'm alone," I confess.

His hand comes down on my stomach, gliding down to

the apex of my thighs. I lift my hips, trying to meet his hand even a second sooner. "Would you touch your pussy while I told you how much I want to fuck you? While I told you I want to lick you until you're begging me to stop? While I told you I want to watch you ride me? While I told you I want to fuck you from behind while I play with your fucking delectable ass? Tell me. Is that what you'd like to hear?" His fingers are just outside my entrance, hovering, barely skimming my core. The touches are too light, too inconsistent. I need more. I moan, lost in my desperation.

"Answer."

"Yes," I admit. "Yes to it all."

He rewards me by slipping two fingers inside me.

"Already clamping down on me?" His voice is so gruff and filled with need. I open my eyes, watching him as I move my hips to fuck his hand. His fingers have been inside me for under a minute, and I'm hurdling toward my orgasm.

"So close," I whisper. "Never this fast."

He uses his thumb to rub tight circles on my clit with just the right amount of pressure. This man doesn't even know me, yet he's so in tune with my desires and my body. "Fuck," he grits out as my orgasm starts, making my pussy flutter around his fingers. He curls his fingers, hitting a blessedly sweet spot. My eyes slam closed as I mumble his name over and over. He works me through my orgasm before coming over me, kissing along my jaw to my lips. "I wanted to give you two orgasms before I sink inside you, but I can't wait."

"Fuck me, James. I want your cock."

"So sweet," he mumbles, kissing and nibbling my lips. "And so fucking dirty."

Only with him.

I hear the crinkle of a condom, and then I'm filled with his thick erection. We both sigh in pleasure when he's fully seated. "Fuck," he mutters, pumping slowly, bringing his mouth down to one of my nipples. My hands close around his head, shamelessly holding him against me. Each pleasure-filled groan he hums against my skin only makes me want more.

"More. Harder."

James's hips thrust into me harder and deeper. My head falls back, deeper into the mattress as I cry out. His hand leaves my hips to hold my shoulder in place.

"Oh, God," I yell as I'm about to orgasm around his cock.

"My name," he grunts, slamming into me as his hand coasts down my body to my clit. The pressure there is just enough to send me rocketing over.

"Yes," I whimper, rolling my hips.

"My name," he says gruffly increasing the speed and force with every thrust.

"James." I call out his name, arching my back, my toes curling, and fingernails digging into the skin along his shoulders. I burst around him, shaking and quivering, bursting at the seams. My eyes are locked on his. He growls watching me come apart for him, giving him more than I ever could've imagined. My entire body is shaking from the intensity. I've never had an orgasm like this. I call out his name again.

"Fuck yes," he says. "Tatum." He repeats my name over and over as he moves inside of me hard and fast before he stills, emptying himself. James collapses on top of me before sliding out and rolling to the side so his huge body doesn't crush me.

His arm reaches out, pulling me toward him. He kisses my forehead, both of us still trying to catch our breaths. "Stay here." He rolls off the bed and heads into the bathroom. I hear a couple cabinets opening and then running water. He comes back with a wet washcloth. I reach for it, but he stops me. "Let me."

I spread my legs and allow him to attend to me for the second time. He tosses the towel into the hamper before falling back into bed and wrapping me up.

He surprises me when he speaks. "I want to do this again."

"Okay," I say, not at all turned off by that idea. Two times with him isn't nearly enough.

"I can't do relationships."

I lift off him slightly, looking down into his eyes. "That's fine," I say honestly.

"If we do this, it's just sex." He looks at me like he's expecting me to say no. I'm not going to, though. I've spent the past two years pining for a boy who doesn't want me. It's amazing to feel wanted and to have some fun that I've never allowed myself before.

"That's fine," I say again. "It doesn't mean I like you, though. I just like your cock."

"That's fine, sunshine. I don't like you much, either. I just like your pussy."

The lies tumble out of each of our mouths. We're both so far past not liking each other. We're almost sort of friends, I think.

# CHAPTER
# TWENTY-TWO

## *James*

I<small>T'S BEEN A WEEK SINCE</small> T<small>ATUM AND</small> I <small>AGREED TO KEEP</small> things casual and sexual. It's been a great fuckin' week. Two days after that night at her house, I had a PT session. That session was awkward and uncomfortable. We both wanted to keep a level of professionalism while I finished physical therapy. It's a line I wouldn't cross; her job is not something I would risk.

I haven't seen Savannah since that night. I'm pretty sure she's avoiding me. Tatum and I haven't talked about how we will handle things in front of everyone else, but unless she pushes me away, my hands will be on her. This isn't going to last forever; it's just a fun fling, so I want to take advantage of every second I have with her. We've spent every night together, and I still haven't done all the things I want to do with her. The list is endless.

We'll see what happens tonight. Tonight is the monthly dinner I host at the gym for anyone in the area who needs it—for any reason. Everyone is welcome. All my friends come and help out, and tonight will be Tatum's first. I'm nervous as hell to see how she is with it, even though I shouldn't be. This is a casual relationship; it's only sex.

But I want her to care. I know she comes from a wealthy family, the type of wealth I can't even fathom. I'm not sure she's ever been around underprivileged youths before. Or how she'll be when she hears that some of these kids have barely eaten in days or don't have parents. Or their parents are in jail. Or worse, some of these kids have been arrested or are on the verge of joining gangs. That's one reason I do this, being involved in community activities can help kids stay far away from that life.

When you're from those types of neighborhoods, it's all too easy to fall into that lifestyle. I was never part of a gang, but once upon a time, I was an errand boy for one of the Italian mafia families in Chicago. I'll never forget the day a senior at my school helped me when some rich pricks stole the last of my lunch money—money I needed to last through the week. It happened on a Tuesday. This was before I went through a growth spurt and filled out.

I'd sat there, beaten to a bloody pulp with nothing but a fucking quarter to my name. Luca Mancini kicked all their asses without breaking a sweat. He took me and my only friend under his wing. He gave us so much. At first he didn't ask for anything, and then it was small favors. Small errands. When my friend's deadbeat mom had another baby, Luca gave him money to help out, to buy her things a baby needed. Next thing I knew, I'm out of the system, out of the fuckin' street, and I'm an errand boy for the Italian fucking mafia. We both owed Luca and Luca took everything we had to offer.

I had nothing to fall back on. That was my only way of making a living. The only way I could eat and not sleep outside. Now that I'm out of that life and away from it all, I want to show these kids there are options. Options I didn't know I had. Options I wish someone told me about. I wish just one good person cared. It was too late by the time I realized Luca fucking Mancini groomed me for a life of crime.

Since I walked away, I've lived a mostly clean life. I just have a few blips, some areas that I consider gray instead of black and white. Those things have been few and far between. If someone I care for is messed with, though, there isn't anything I wouldn't do.

"Muffin," I hear from behind me. I turn to watch Savannah walk cautiously toward me. I raise an eyebrow and my mouth flattens into a straight line. She sighs when she gets closer, grimacing. "Are you mad?"

"No, I'm used to you calling me by your ridiculous names," I say, wanting to throw her off and make her admit to her plan of forcing Tatum and I to be alone. She doesn't need to know that it worked out pretty damn well for the both of us. At least not yet.

Savannah winces right before Liam walks up, throwing an arm around her shoulders. "Not about that," she says.

"Why would I be mad, Savannah?" I ask, acting confused. "Please, tell me."

Liam's lips twitch. He shakes his head, his shoulders shaking as he laughs silently. I know the girls came up with the plan and the guys just played along because they can't say no to their women. And Hudson and Kiernan are wrapped around their fingers, even if they'll never admit it.

"Um," Savannah starts, looking around to avoid my unwavering gaze. "Well, you see, I don't know if you noticed or not, but none of us made it to The Cellar last weekend."

"No, Savannah," I say dryly, rolling my eyes. "I didn't notice as Tatum and I sat alone at a table meant for ten."

"Well, y'all didn't kill each other, so that's a step in the right direction."

"Yet," I say.

Savannah says something else, but I miss it because Tatum just walked in holding a platter. She stops in her tracks, turning her head left and right, before her eyes settle on me again. A couple steps after she resumes walking toward us, she stops again worrying her lush lip between her teeth. I wave slightly, hoping to ease some of her discomfort. Her shoulders rise and fall dramatically and she takes and releases a big breath before taking her final few steps toward us.

"Hey," Tatum says when she reaches us, lifting the platter slightly. "I brought some seven-layer dip."

I take it from her, hold it out to the side with one hand, and use my other hand to wrap around her neck. I guide her toward me and lower my mouth to hers, giving her a hard kiss. She's stiff underneath my lips, but melts against me after a second, sending my heart galloping in my chest. I break our kiss and press a light kiss to her nose, definitely not casual behavior, but whatever.

"Hi." I speak quietly, but I can still hear the gruffness in my voice. My eyes dart toward Savannah and Liam; both of them have their mouths hanging open, staring at us. I thrust the dip into Liam's hands. "Put that on a table, yeah?"

My arm goes over Tatum's shoulders as I turn her toward my office. She looks up at me. "Was that necessary?"

I shrug.

"I didn't know we were going to tell them," she says softly as I guide her into my office and onto the couch. I sit next to her, keeping an arm wrapped around her loosely.

"They'd find out eventually." My fingers trail up her arm, over her shoulder, and to her neck. When I reach the point behind her ear, I lightly caress her skin on the path back down.

"They'll think it's something it's not." Goosebumps are popping up in my fingers wake, making my chest swell.

"That's our business." Tatum leans closer to my side, plastering herself to me before tossing one of her long legs over mine and placing her head on my chest. Not a damn thing about this is casual, but I'd rip off my own arm before asking her to move.

She laughs once as her eyes roll to the ceiling. "Right."

"We know where we stand. We'll both walk away without hurt feelings. After this is done and we're normal around each other, you annoying me, et cetera, they'll see it's okay." Tatum smiles when I talk about her annoying me, nuzzling her head deeper into my chest.

"I hope you're right." My arm tightens around her shoulders and she slings her arm over my abs. Her fingers trace patterns making my muscles clench with her light touch.

"I am." I squeeze her shoulders again, keeping her tight against me.

"You know, you've become a little chattier," she says as one finger drags up the middle of my torso, past up my neck, settling on my lips. I stick my tongue out, flicking her finger with it.

"It's you." I hug her close before standing from the couch and leaving her sitting comfortably on the soft worn leather.

"Now you revert back to your old ways. Just a few words here and there, walking away without telling me where you're going."

"I knew you'd follow," I say, looking at her over my shoulder, shooting her a wink.

"What can I do to help?" She pops up and claps her hands in front of her once before rubbing them together.

The expression on her face melts some of the ice around my heart. She looks like she's ready to do anything I asked her to do. My fists clench. I know she's waiting for instruction of how she can help set up. I want to ask her to help me out. My fists clench at my sides to keep my distance, we need to walk out there.

"James?" The softness in her voice when she says my name snaps me into action. I take a giant step toward her, wrapping her tightly in my arms. My lips are so close to hers that when we breathe, they touch slightly.

I weave my head and dip it to her neck so I drag my tongue up her soft skin. Jasmine fills my nose, warming me from the inside out. Tatum's hands sneak under my shirt sliding against my skin making me want more, more, more. My arms tighten around her, pulling her closer to me. Her breasts are smashed against my chest and every soft, sweet inch of her is against me wreaking havoc on my control.

My lips leave her neck so I can kiss her. Her mouth immediately opens underneath mine, allowing me to taste, devour, and consume her. I don't know what I've done to deserve this, but Tatum feels like a reward. She's something to be cherished and worshipped. When she whimpers as I kiss her, it makes a guttural noise leave my chest.

Tatum pulls back panting staring at me with hooded eyes and her chest heaving from her deep breaths. I cup her cheeks as I kiss her lips, the tip of her nose, and her forehead. Tatum's hands fall away from me as I take a step back to gain back an ounce of my control.

"Most everything is set up. I did it earlier. I had barbecue catered tonight; that should be here any minute. You don't need to do anything but enjoy yourself, sunshine."

The door opens, and I expect it to be the caterers, but it's Corbin. I lift my chin in greeting. "You're early. You helping?"

He shakes his head. When he gets closer, I freeze. His eyes are bloodshot and red-rimmed. He looks like hell. Corbin glances at Tatum and hesitates.

"What's going on?" I ask.

He clenches his jaw and closes his eyes, pure anguish written all over his face. "I fucked up my knee. No surgery, but need physical therapy, and I'm out for fucking weeks."

"What happened?" I scan him from head to toe.

"Dirty tackle," he mumbles, looking down at his feet. When his eyes meet mine again, they're glassy. Fuck.

I place my hand on his shoulder. "After PT, you'll be good

as new."

"Can't afford it," he says, his jaw twitching as he looks off to the side.

"We'll figure it out." I squeeze his shoulder. Not a chance in hell I'm going to let this kid slip through the cracks. Injuries in sports happen; he can come back from this. If I have to pay for every session myself, then that's what I'll do. "We'll find someone who takes clients without insurance, and I'll pay for it."

"I can't—"

"Yes, you can." I squeeze his shoulder again.

He swallows. I can tell he wants to argue, but I guarantee this is a fight I can win. My eyes move to Tatum's when she pokes me in the arm. Her eyes are huge, and she's looking at me like I'm crazy. "Give us a minute, Corbin. Sit on the couch if you need a minute."

He nods, glancing at Tatum before walking off around us to the couch. Tatum leaves my office walking to an area that's clear of people before whipping around, planting her hands on her hips, and leaning toward me angrily.

"What the hell, James?" Tatum asks, sounding pissed.

My blood starts boiling, the irritation that always rises so quickly with her coming in hot and fast. "If I want to pay his way through PT, that's my fuckin' business," I growl.

"Not that," she hisses through her teeth. "I honestly can't even believe you right now."

"What?" I grind out.

"I'm a physical therapist," she whisper yells, jabbing a finger in my chest, twice. I catch it and hold on. I damn sure don't want to be poked again.

"I'm aware."

"I could help." She pulls her finger away from me, lifting her arms to her sides, silently asking me what the hell I'm thinking.

"Weren't you listening?" I ask, now looking at her like she's the crazy one.

"Uh, yeah, which is why I," she says, motioning to herself from head to toe, "a physical therapist, said I can help with his physical therapy needs."

"He doesn't have insurance and doesn't have money."

"Okay," she says slowly. "And?"

I scrub a hand over my face. "And? Do I really need to spell it out for you?"

"I guess you do." She crosses her arms over her chest and cocks her hip, flinging attitude all over the place.

"You're too expensive for him. I see my insurance bills; I know how much it is hourly. There's no way in hell he'd be able to go to your place."

Her eyes narrow and her lips roll between her teeth as her head tilts. She laughs humorlessly. "I know we're not the best of friends and really only have sex in common, but you honestly think that little of me?"

"What the hell are you talking about?"

"He's a kid," she seethes, leaning toward me.

"I fucking know that," I growl, leaning toward her.

"Even if he wasn't, I'd help. I'm allowed to take as many pro bono clients as I want as long as I schedule it during my off hours," she states. "Right now, I have eleven pro bono patients. That's enough to make a part-time job."

I stare at her, not saying a damn word. I didn't know.

"He," she says, pointing toward my office, "just became number twelve."

Tatum pulls her wallet out of her purse, shoving a card toward my chest. "Give that to him, will you? Tell him it's free, any time he can come. If transportation is an issue, I do home visits, as well." She walks away without looking back.

Shit.

# CHAPTER
# TWENTY-THREE

*Tatum*

THIS IS A MISTAKE. THIS ENTIRE THING WITH JAMES. It's not a relationship, but I won't be involved with a man who thinks so little of me. Been there, done that, have the wasted years to prove it.

My face is so hot from embarrassment. I don't look up from my shoes as I head out the door I walked in only minutes ago. Earlier I was nervous to come; I didn't know how James would handle things, but then he kissed me in front of Savannah and Liam. He claimed me. He chose me. At least that's the way it felt in my stupid heart.

My heart was freaking soaring. No, it shouldn't have been. I know where we stand, but I thought he had a little more respect for me. I am a physical therapist. Here's a kid practically in tears thinking his whole life is over because he needs one, and James doesn't even look at me. Ask my opinion. Nothing. Freaking nothing.

Right before I reach the exit, James's big hand latches onto my arm, spinning me to face him. "Yes?" I snap, trying to wiggle free from his grasp.

He doesn't let go. Instead, he grabs onto my other arm, as well, firmly holding me in place as he moves me backward until my back hits a wall, effectively caging me in.

"Please move," I say with all the courage I can muster. I hear the thick emotion in my voice. Fuck. I don't want to cry, at least not here.

His hands drop from my arms, framing my face. "Tatum," he says softly, curling my hair behind one ear. I turn my face away from his, finding a spot on the far wall to stare at. He sighs, bringing his head down to mine. "Don't leave."

"I think it's best if I go." I look him in the eye, forcing him to lift his head from resting against mine.

"Don't go," he repeats, cupping my cheek. "I'm sorry, Tatum."

It takes everything inside me not to lean into his palm.

James pulls me against him, hugging me tightly. My arms hang loosely at my sides. He squeezes me tighter, rubbing a large hand up and down my back. His scruff tickles my cheek as he whispers in my ear. "I'm sorry, sunshine."

My arms hesitantly wind around his hips. I don't squeeze him back, but I'm not completely ignoring the hug, either. His heartbeat underneath my ear calms me.

"Don't go because I acted like an ass," he says, running his fingers through my hair.

I look up at him, resting my chin against his chest. "James—"

"Please don't say you're leaving."

I shake my head. "James, I get that this thing between us is sex. I still need your respect outside of the bedroom, though. This is probably an overshare, but I've been this girl before."

"What girl?" His brow draws up in confusion.

"The one who allows the guy to treat her any way he wants to," I admit. "I don't like you or anyone else thinking so little of me."

James stiffens underneath my touch. "I don't," he insists.

I sigh in frustration. "You do on some level. You basically just told me that because my family has money, I wouldn't want to help people. That kid was breaking down in front of us, and you didn't even cast me a glance, when my job is the thing he needs."

"Fuck," James mutters, leaning his head back and looking at the ceiling. "You're right. I'm a dick."

A smile tugs at the corner of my mouth. "I'm what?" I ask, biting back my grin.

"You heard me." James shakes his head, amusement lighting up his eyes. He licks his lip, but I swear I just saw his lip twitch. I still haven't seen him smile. Can a miniscule lip twitch count as a smile?

"Say it again," I prod.

"I'm a dick." James's brows lift silently asking me if that's what I wanted to hear. It's not.

"Not that part." I try to tickle his sides. It does nothing. His rock-solid form doesn't even budge. Not even a flinch.

"You're right," James says seriously. "I shouldn't have done that. I do think better of you than that. I swear."

I nod while unleashing a huge smile. *You're right* are two words I never thought James would say to me. "Thank you."

"So, you'll stay?" His hands rest of my hips and his fingers dig into my skin as he asks his question. There's hope laced through his voice.

"Yeah, as long as you don't act like a dick again."

James closes his eyes for a second as a long breath leaves his lungs. When he opens his eyes and they connect with mine, I only see relief. "I won't be a dick," he promises.

"You're walking a fine line, Harris. I only tolerate you because I like your cock," I whisper as I poke him in the chest. I'm only joking. He apologized and meant it, I could feel how much he meant it. Therefore, I'm over it. I won't hold it against him.

James shakes his head, pulling me away from the wall, but keeping me planted against his body. "Tatum," he says in his growly voice and his features are set in stone. His lips morph into a frown as he swallows and a muscle pops along his jaw. The creases on his forehead deepen as he stares down at me.

"Yes?" My hands slide up his chest to his neck. I knead the muscles there as I wait for him to speak.

James's chest expands as he pulls in oxygen. When he releases his breath, it tickles along my skin and fills my nose with minty freshness. "There's a young guy I help out that really needs a physical therapist. He's a good kid, but he can't exactly afford to pay anything. He's in the foster system and is already struggling to keep food in his belly. His fosters are worthless, unfortunately if he's placed somewhere else, it could be even worse," he says. "Think you could help? I trust you to take care of him."

Pride and happiness radiates throughout my chest and fills my heart. I'm melting for this man and there's no way I could stop the wishes for a future of us filling my mind. As apologies go, this may be the best one I've ever received.

James takes me to his place for the first time tonight. The past week we've spent at mine, but from now on, we are definitely coming here. He lives just outside of Austin on a piece of property I can't wait to explore.

To say I'm shocked when we pulled up to his house is an understatement—a small, quintessential ranch-style home with a wraparound porch complete with a bench swing. It's painted a creamy white with black shutters and a black front door. An immediate smile breaks across my face as I step out

of the car, feeling like I'm on a movie set. His lawn is beauti-
fully manicured with flowers around the edges of the house.
A small garden sits off to the side. It's too late to tell what's
growing there, but it looks well cared for.

"I can't believe you bought something this cute," I say,
unable to look away from the modest, one-story home.

"I built it," James says.

"Did you use Hudson's company? Didn't he say he owns
a construction company?" My focus is on the two rocking
chairs just to the right of the front door. They're painted a
glossy black to match the door and shutters on the house. I'd
love to sit there reading for hours with a cold glass of iced tea
on the small wooden table between the chairs.

"Yeah, his family own it. Hadn't met Hudson yet," James
says. "When I say I built it, I mean that I built it myself."

My head whips around to stare at him. I point at the
house then to him and finally my finger settles on the house
again. "You built this?"

"Yep." James's hands tuck into his pockets and his eyes
are trained on his feet. He rocks back slightly, not offering
anything else besides the one word answer.

"By yourself?" I face the house again taking it all in in a
new light. James did this. By himself. My eyes take in every
detail, each piece of wood, the paint, the flowers, and the
garden. The chairs sitting on the front porch. James did this.
I turn to face him again resisting the urge to run into his
arms and kiss him all over.

"Yep." He coughs once, clearing his throat. His shoulders are up almost to his ears and every muscle in his body
is tensed. After a few moments of silence those gray orbs
finally settle on me again. I want to tell him how amazing I
think he is. I want to ask him a thousand questions so I can
get every minute detail of his build.

I don't.

I hold all that in. He's still standing there with his body strung so tight. Allowing me to see his house has to be a big step for him, I think that's all he can offer me right now. Instead I picture James in tight jeans, no shirt, and a tool belt.

His eyes melt with heat and every ounce of tension leaves his body as he heaves a sigh. "I love when you flush like that. Tell me what you're thinking," he demands.

So I do. I tell him every dirty detail in my construction worker James fantasy.

And now we're here, a tangled sweaty mess of limbs in James's large bed. I'm on my stomach, my body stuck against the cool, dark gray sheets. I collapsed after James finished taking me from behind.

"You okay?" he asks, standing to take care of the condom and me.

I grumble something unintelligible, even to me. He's exhausted me. I'm now just this boneless heap, unable to move, still trying to catch my breath. James's breathing has evened out. Bastard.

He gets back in bed, jostling me until I'm lying half on him and half on the bed. My cheek is pressed against his naked, muscular chest. It's really the best pillow. I always thought I wanted something soft and fluffy to sleep on, but that was before I found the expanse of James's rock-hard chest.

I crane my head to look at his face, keeping my cheek against his chest. "I don't think I'll ever move again."

"No?" he asks with a smug look.

"No, I'm like a barnacle now. Permanently attached. My limbs no longer work. I'm just a blob. You'll need to take care of me, feed me and all that."

James is silent, and I worry I took my joke too far. I open my mouth to tell him I'm joking, I'm not permanently attached, I know this is temporary with an expiration date, and the one way he's taking care of me during that time is with orgasms. But I'm stunned. Dumbfounded. Flabbergasted. And absolutely, completely dazed by his beauty.

James is smiling.

And laughing.

Not a small smile.

Not a chuckle.

He's grinning. Fucking grinning.

And laughing so hard he's clutching his stomach.

He was the most handsome man I've seen before he did that; now he's on the level of a god or something. A natural wonder of the world. No wonder he doesn't smile and laugh all the time. He'd have a gaggle of women following him constantly. Nuns giving up their virtue. People worshipping him.

Holy shit.

And his eyes have turned from a hard gray to a bright silver with happiness shining through. I don't know what to do with myself, outside of wishing my phone were closer so I could whip it out and record this, keep it forever, watching after he's gone. There's no way I would go looking for my phone right now, though. I wouldn't miss this show for anything.

His smile broadens even more when our eyes connect. My entire body tingles and everything in me is focused on him and only him.

"Don't worry, sunshine, I've got you," James says through his laughter. I know he's joking about taking care of me while I'm reduced to a mess after epic orgasms, but fireworks start popping in my belly, making my mind think about things it really shouldn't.

Slowly his laughter and smile die, but his gaze still holds amusement and joy. His lips tug into a sinful smirk, making me wet as he asks a question in his deep, rumbling voice. "Why are you staring at me like that?"

"You're beautiful."

His body goes rigid underneath me before relaxing a second later. A large hand cups my cheeks, bringing my face to his. His lips ghost across mine. "Tatum, there's nothing in this world as beautiful as you."

# CHAPTER
## TWENTY-FOUR

## James

TATUM'S PHONE RINGING STARTLES HER AWAKE. I'VE been awake, staring at the ceiling and skimming my fingers along her arms. She moves to get up, but I lock my arms around her, keeping her soft, warm body against mine. My nose skims along her neck, nuzzling and kissing her sensitive skin until she giggles. I murmur in her ear when she tries to move again. "Not yet."

She bites her lip, stopping the grin from forming across her face. "I always answer," she whispers.

"This is better." My legs tangle with hers, anchoring her against me even more.

We're both still naked, as I had woken up several times in the night with the need to sink into her. She buries her face in my neck, kissing me as I luxuriate in the feel of her silky skin against mine.

I groan when her phone starts ringing again, and she sighs. "I need to get it."

Grumbling, I stand from the bed with her. There's no reason to stay in bed if she's not against me. I walk out of the room toward the kitchen, calling over my shoulder. "Want coffee?"

"Sure," she replies happily. I turnaround watching her dig through her purse when she catches me staring at her.

She looks up at me, meeting my eyes. Her soft, sweet, sleepy smile goes straight to my dick. It's the same smile she wears when she's completely satisfied.

I release a breath and continue to the kitchen, turning on the coffee pot before digging in the refrigerator for some food. I'm preparing egg white omelets when Tatum wanders into the kitchen wearing my shirt and rubbing her eyes.

I walk toward her with a mug of coffee. "Want it?"

"Yes," she groans, reaching for the cup.

I set it on the counter before turning toward her adorable, confused face. My hands fall on her hips, sliding down her thighs to where the shirt ends, and slipping underneath. I take the shirt off her and grin. "That's better," I say, picking up the coffee cup and placing it in front of one of the barstools.

She chuckles, shaking her head, but stays naked—just the way I want her. She moans when she takes a sip of coffee.

"Everything okay?" I ask, gesturing to the phone in her hand. I turn my back to her to plate each omelet. Setting one in front of her and another in the space next to her, I hop onto the barstool and turn to look at her.

"Yeah, just my mom."

We dig into the food, eating mostly in silence. Tatum stares out the large picture window that faces the back of my property. It's nothing but tall grass and small hills for miles. Even though it's early fall, the grass is still a light green.

"Let's agree to something," she says, still staring out the window.

"What's that?"

"Every time we hang out, let's do it here. I'm obsessed with this place. The house, the land, your body."

The corners of my lips tug slightly, but I cover it with my

coffee cup and take a sip. "Deal."

"Oh, and one more thing." She takes a bite of her omelet while staring out the picture window.

"What is it?" Her face slowly rotates to mine and her cheeks turn pink as her lip quirks on one side.

"You fuck me right there on the bench seat. You can slip into me from behind, and I can watch the sunset." My fork clatters on my plate when I drop it. A tiny drop of coffee spills onto my hand after it spasms making the mug shake.

"I've got you," I say, winking at her. She grins, her nose crinkling just a bit before facing the window again.

"Really, I love it here. It's so quiet." Her eyes close as she turns her head so her ear is facing the window as if she's listening for any sound. During the day, the only thing she'll hear is the rustling of the tall grass. We're too far from the creek running through my property to hear that. At night, the occasional coyote can be heard. I decide not to mention that.

I wrap a strand of her hair around my finger tugging it until she gives me her attention. "Want to go for a walk?"

"Naked?" she asks, looking down at each of our bodies. I wouldn't mind walking with her naked, but I don't think she'd be up for that.

"No, we'll get dressed." I unwind my finger from her hair, gliding my hand under her hair up her spine until it settles at the nape of her neck. My thumb strokes along the edge until I feel heartbeat. I stop there, holding that spot, leaning toward her and feeling masculine pride when the beat starts drumming faster.

Her breath hitches slightly before she begins speaking. "I don't have any shoes for walking through grass, just my heels."

"Savannah has some clothes here," I say, my gaze dipping down to her puckered nipples. My omelet and coffee are completely forgotten as I focus on the heartbeat under my thumb as the knuckle of my other hand brushes over the tight bud.

I smile when her pulse starts racing wildly with one simple touch. My smile turns to a frown when she pulls away, placing a hand over her heart. "I can't think with you doing that."

I lean toward her, but her next question halts my movements. "Were y'all ever friends with benefits?"

I laugh, but cut it off when she raises an eyebrow waiting for my response. "God, no. She's like my little sister. Liam has to go out of town for work occasionally, though it's rare, but when he does, she stays with me."

"Why?"

"Gives Liam peace of mind," I say honestly. After Savannah's run-in with her ex that turned nasty and could've been deadly, Liam doesn't want her alone when he's out of town. Savannah feels safe, but doesn't want Liam to worry, so she comes here.

"He won't let her stay alone? My best friend, Isabella's, husband travels constantly, and she stays alone."

"Not that he won't let her, just makes him more comfortable to know she's with someone who will watch out for her."

"Why?" Tatum's arms cross over her chest, completely blocking my view of her still puckered nipples. I heave a sigh, turning back to my breakfast and picking up the fork again to take my last few bites.

"Not my story to tell. Ready for that walk?" I ask before she can question it anymore.

A few minutes later, I'm standing by the back door waiting for Tatum. When she comes out of the bathroom, I immediately want to strip her naked again. Her long hair is piled on top of her head, showcasing her long, elegant neck.

She's in the same dress as last night but has Converse on her feet. She looks perfect.

I hold out my hand so I can lace our fingers together. The first couple of minutes of our walk is in silence. The grass is tall, skimming along Tatum's thighs; she doesn't seem to mind, though. Her eyes scan the horizon of the endless blue sky.

"How many acres do you have?"

"Thirty-eight."

"Wow," she mumbles, her thumb rubbing circles on the back of my hand. "I wasn't expecting it to be that much. How long have you lived here?"

I shrug. "Pretty much since I moved to Texas about ten years ago."

She stops and stares at me, bringing her free hand up to shield her eyes from the sun. "You're what? Thirty?"

"Yeah, thirty-one pretty soon."

"You bought this place when you were twenty?"

"Yep," I reply, feeling my face flush with this unwanted conversation. I don't like anyone to examine my life too closely.

"Where did you move from?"

"Midwest." I scramble for a way to change the subject. I find myself wanting to be honest with her about everything. It scares me. My mind comes up blank for a new topic, though, but I'm saved when Tatum shrieks.

"What?" I ask, scanning her body. "What happened?"

"I heard rustling," she says with wide, panicked eyes, looking around her feet.

"Okay," I say slowly. We are in tall grass, there are going to be noises.

"Are…are there snakes out here?"

*Oh, shit.* I hesitate. "I've seen a couple. This is uninhabited land; I'm sure there's some stuff out here."

Tatum gets closer to me, scanning the ground around her. Her hands are clutched tightly in my shirt. "I don't like snakes."

"I can tell." I grin, wrapping an arm around her shoulders. "Don't worry, they're more scared of you than you are of them."

There's more rustling in the tall blades of grass. Her fingers claw into my chest. "It's a snake. That's a snake. It has to be," she says, whipping her head back and forth, trying to pinpoint the noise.

"I promise, there's nothing to worry about," I say, urging her to walk again, but she's frozen solid against me.

"Nothing to worry about?" she hisses, glaring at me. "There are snakes out here! That's something to worry about."

"Tatum, they are more scared of you."

"I don't think that's possible," she speaks quietly as her head continues to whip around looking in every direction. Her feet are now on top of mine and she's slightly shaking.

"It's not only possible, it's the truth." I keep my voice low and tone even. My hand rubs up and down her back in soothing circles.

"Nope."

"Yes," I say holding back a chuckle.

"James," she says, her eyes becoming glassy. "No."

"Sunshine," I say, softly cupping her face. "They are more scared of you, but I promise, if a snake jumps out, I'll protect you."

She bites her lip, looking up at me with her wide eyes. "Sometimes you make me like you for more than your body," she whispers.

She sways toward me, lifting on her tiptoes. I bend my head to steal a kiss when the noise gets closer and she shrieks. She climbs my body, her legs wrapping around my waist. Pulling her close, I secure her to me as her arms tighten around my head. She's freaking out as I struggle to breathe through her tight embrace.

I look down when the noise is right on top of us and am shocked at what's making the rustling noise.

# CHAPTER
# TWENTY-FIVE

*Tatum*

G ASPING, I SLIDE OFF JAMES'S BODY AND COLLAPSE to my knees in front of the tiny, black puppy.

"Hi," I coo to the puppy, and it wags its little tail so hard, it looks like it's trying to take flight. I pick up the puppy, confirming it's a boy, and bring him to my chest.

His tiny tongue happily sticks out of his mouth. The black fur is a bit matted in some areas, but curly and soft as silk in others. The paws and legs are so little, even for a puppy. He's definitely not going to be a big dog.

I'm already so in love with him. I smile, looking up at James. His eyes are big, and he looks confused. He's scanning the area, maybe looking for others. I don't hear anymore rustling, though. I think it's just this little guy.

"Where'd you come from?" I ask the puppy, raising his face to mine. He squirms excitedly in my hands.

"Don't think he's going to answer," James mutters.

"Don't you just love puppies?" I ask, nuzzling this little guy's neck.

"I don't know. I've never had one."

"What kind of pet did you have growing up?" I ask curiously. I lean back looking up his tall form and staring into his face.

"None," James replies, looking at the dog like it's an alien.

"We need to get him cleaned up," I say, standing, trying to balance while holding the puppy.

"We do?" James asks. "Shouldn't we go to the shelter or vet or something?"

"He doesn't have a collar," I say, looking around the land. "Do you have neighbors?"

"Not for miles," James replies, running a hand over his short hair.

"I think he's a stray." I can't stop petting the little guy and he hasn't stopped wagging his tail happily. By the looks of his fur and the dirt caked on to some areas, it looks like he's been out here alone for a while.

"So, what do we do?" James takes a step closer to me watching the pup struggling in my arms. It looks like he's trying to launch himself at James.

"First, we'll give him a bath. Then we'll need to go to the pet store for some supplies."

"Supplies?" James asks dryly.

"Yes. Dog bed, food, toys, treats, and a collar. There's a vet next door to the pet store. We'll go in, have him scanned for a microchip, but if he's a stray, then we'll need to buy all that stuff."

"You're going to keep him?"

I step into his personal space, taking one arm from the puppy and wrapping it around James. "No," I say sweetly, leaning my head against his chest. "My landlord doesn't allow pets of any kind. Even fish."

"What are you going to do with him, then?" He rubs his hand along my back.

"You're going to keep him."

His hand freezes and his entire frame tenses. "Me?" he asks incredulously. "No, not happening."

"Why not?"

"I don't know what to do for a dog." He starts to back away, but my fist clutches his shirt.

"This little guy will be easy." I try to reassure him and coax him into keeping the puppy. He's too cute and he needs a good home. James would definitely give that to him and I could visit him all the time.

"Tatum," he says, but stops when he looks at my face. "I don't know if this is a good idea."

"Let's just go get the poor little guy cleaned up, shall we?"

James turns around and starts walking back toward the house dragging me along with him by the elbow. There's a slight twitch happening below his eye that I'm choosing to ignore.

"What should we name him?" I ask, hoping if I bring him in on each aspect of this, he'll want to keep the puppy.

"Whatever you want," James grumbles. "I wish it was a snake."

"Prince Furrybutt," I declare, ignoring his grumbling.

James stops, turning toward me and raising an eyebrow as he scoffs. "If you actually want me to keep this dog, his name sure as fuck won't be Prince Furrybutt."

"Then what do you suggest?" I ask, hoping he'll crack and give me a semblance of a smile or even just amusement in his eyes. Something.

The only thing I get is a shrug.

"Bark Twain," I suggest, trying to keep my smile to myself.

"No," James says immediately with no lip twitch.

"Droolius Caesar," I try again. The small black puppy yaps once. I don't think he likes that one.

"No." Still no smile. The furball in my arms licks my hand as I'm petting his head making me giggle. James rolls his lips between his teeth, shaking his head.

"Dog McDoggins," I say, unable to stop my chuckle this time.

"Nope." Still nothing.

I grab his arm to stop him from walking. "You suggest something, then."

James's eyes slide from my face to the dog in my arms. One of his fingers reaches out, rubbing along its tiny head. Wow. James's finger is almost the size of this sweet baby.

"Sirius," James says.

"Serious?" I reply. "Yes, I'm serious. I want you to suggest something. Anything."

"No," James says. "Sirius, as in, Sirius Black."

I rear my head back. "Like from Harry Potter?" I thought James would suggest something like Tiny or Ace. I'd never in a million years think he'd suggest something from Harry Potter.

"Yeah," James says, scratching his chest. "Obviously he's smaller, but he has black fur, and it's a cool name." And, finally, there's a tiny smile on James's face as he continues to pet the newly appointed Sirius. He's graduated from his finger to using his entire hand. If it makes James smile, that's his name. I saw his full smile and laugh once, and I'm already hooked. I'll do just about anything to see it again.

"You're a Harry Potter fan?" I ask.

His gaze slides up to mine. A slow, charming, boyish grin slips across his face, and my heart goes tumbling over itself. His massive shoulder shrugs shyly. "Yeah."

"Books or movies?"

"Both," he replies automatically, his focus back on Sirius in my arms. He's wiggling so frantically under James's massive hand, I'm about to drop him.

"Really?" I ask, readjusting the squirming dog in my arms.

James stares at me, amusement lighting up his face. He

extends his left arm, pointing to a spot in the tattoo sleeve near the bend of his arm. And right there in the middle of the chaos of intricate artwork that I haven't had a chance to examine closely is the Deathly Hallows symbol.

I've wanted to explore his tattoos with my hands and tongue, but when he takes off his clothes, I'm distracted by other parts of his body, and by the time we're done, I'm boneless and falling asleep. I'm remedying that situation soon.

"Wow," I whisper, running my fingers over it. I turn my gaze from the tattoo and look at his face. "I didn't know you're a reader."

"I don't read much anymore. It was an escape as a kid."

The last part is spoken so quietly, and the look of surprise on his face makes me think he didn't mean to be that honest. I'm going to push in hopes to get more. He may shut me down, but I'm desperate to try.

I shuffle Sirius into the crook of one arm and grab James's hand with the other, taking off toward the house. "Was Harry Potter your favorite?"

"Yeah," he says softly. "It helped because it was so popular so some of the foster homes had a tattered set."

I didn't know he grew up in the foster system. My heart breaks for him. "I read Harry Potter so many times."

"I did, too," he admits. "It took me years to read the first few, though. I was shuffled around so much at that time. Not every home had it, and not every foster parent was willing to get me a library card."

My heart keeps cracking, and tears sting my eyes, but I blink them away quickly. I know if he sees them, he'll stop talking immediately and shut down. "How'd you finish them?"

"I'd sit in a library sometimes and read it off the shelf. It was really popular, so even if I had a chance to do that, they weren't always in stock."

"Why Harry Potter?"

The only noises are Sirius's panting and our feet scraping over the ground. "I think I identified. Unwanted kid who had no idea where he was from. Some of the truths he found weren't great. He still sacrificed for those he loved and tried to be honorable. That's all I try to be."

I halt, yanking James to a stop. His eyes roam over my face before settling on mine. "I think you're honorable," I whisper.

His cheeks turn pink. I wonder if he reacts to compliments with blushes because he wasn't shown affection as a kid. My heart is bursting with sadness and a fierce need to give him everything I can.

"Thank you," he whispers, running a finger down my cheek. "I promise that as long as we're doing what we're doing, I'll do my best to honor you in every way I know how."

I fill with pride that I know this man, and that he's giving me something I don't think he freely gives others. I wonder if his friends even know this much about him.

"What was it like in the foster system?" I ask hesitantly.

He sighs, turning us to keep trudging back to the house that just came into view. "Another day. Okay?"

I simply nod. His voice is rough and uncertain when he stuns me with his next question. "What was it like with a loving family?"

A grin breaks across my face. "It'll be better if I show you."

# CHAPTER
# TWENTY-SIX

## James

ATUM AND I HAVEN'T REACHED HER PARENTS' HOUSE yet, and I already feel like I don't belong in this neighborhood with these insane homes and luxury cars parked in the drive. "This isn't a good idea," I grumble.

"Sure it is," Tatum says happily. "Take a left at that stop sign. It's that house with the pumpkins on the mailbox."

"The one that says 'Fuck Yeah! Fall!'?" I ask skeptically.

"Yep, that's the one. That's new. I like it." Tatum pulls out her phone snapping a picture as we pass it turning into her driveway.

"The mailbox is new?" I ask, pulling into the driveway. Who buys mailboxes for every season?

"No," she answers, laying a hand on my bicep. Sirius is curled into her lap, softly snoring. "My mom paints the mailbox whenever she feels like it. Last time I was here, it was just leaves. When the HOA pisses her off, she usually paints something like that." She gestures toward the mailbox.

Huh. That's kind of cool. A tiny bit of relief courses through me, hoping that her family isn't awful. She says they're not, but how will they feel when she brings her new "friend" in to meet them? The tiny bit of relief dies a swift death when I look up at the house. I close my eyes and pinch the bridge of my nose after throwing it in park.

It would be the biggest house in the neighborhood.

Fuck. I've never done this before.

Met a girl's parents. This isn't even me meeting them as her boyfriend, which I'm not. The only parents I've met are Savannah's, and that doesn't count. She's like my sister. I didn't have a problem looking her father in the eye because I didn't want to touch his daughter.

"So," Tatum says, petting Sirius with a small smile. She's been happy since we found out that he's just a puppy and didn't have a chip. The vet suspects that someone dumped a litter on the side of the road and he wandered into my property.

I still don't think it's a good idea. I'll probably accidentally crush him, he's so tiny. He won't get much larger either.

"So," I supply, still waiting for Tatum to finish her thought.

"I'm guessing you want me to say you're my friend, not my boyfriend," she says.

I don't reply, just stare at her. She waits me out, not saying a word. Finally, I relent. "Do what you think is best."

"What are you comfortable with?" The hand petting Sirius freezes mid-stroke. Even Sirius has paused wagging his tail. They're both staring at me, not breathing, waiting for the answer.

"Going home," I reply automatically, somewhat joking, somewhat being honest.

"Hilarious," she says, rolling her eyes, resuming petting the fuzzy dog in her arms. "You wanted to know what my family is like, I'm giving you the answer."

"Friend," I say.

She nods. "Okay, let's do this."

Reluctantly, I step out of the car, going around to open the door for her. I take Sirius from her hands, cradling him in the nook of my elbow, holding my other hand out to help Tatum out of the car.

She leads me into the massive house, turning right through the entryway and walking down a long hallway. There's framed art and photos decorating the walls. She is walking too fast for me to take all of them in, but I do see school pictures of her and a boy—her brother, I'm assuming.

"That old bitch," I hear shouted from a room at the end of the hall.

Tatum turns her head toward me, lifting an eyebrow while smirking. "Welcome to this crazy mess."

She pushes open a door, sets Sirius on the floor, and calls out, "Who's an old bitch?"

I swallow, steeling myself for judgment before stepping into the room behind her. An old man is leaning against a barstool smoking a cigar with a pool stick resting between his legs. A guy about my age is leaned over the table, lining up a shot, and a middle-aged couple is standing behind the bar in the corner.

"Sweetheart," the old man on the stool calls out, holding open an arm. He sticks the cigar in an ashtray. Tatum walks over to him, giving him a big hug. I stand awkwardly in the entrance. The old man's eyes meet mine over Tatum's shoulder. I try my best to smile; it's not something that comes naturally at the drop of a hat for me. "Who's this?"

Tatum turns, keeping an arm around his shoulders and turning her radiant smile on me. "This is my friend, James."

I step forward, holding out my hand. "I'm James. It's nice to meet you, sir."

"Sir?" he asks. "Don't call me that shit. You'll make me feel old."

This comment pulls a genuine smile from me. He has to be in his late seventies, but I suppose as long as you don't feel old.

"Besides," her grandfather says, "I wasn't talking about him. I'm talking about the rat. Who's that rat?"

"He's not a rat." Tatum gasps, putting her hands on her hips. "That's Sirius, James's dog."

"That's your dog?" Tatum's brother asks with a smirk, looking at the tiny black dog trotting around the room happily and sniffing at every nook and cranny.

"According to Tatum," I reply dryly. "Didn't give me much choice in the matter."

Everyone in the room laughs. "That's my girl," her grandfather says proudly. "Hammond, remember this—any girl worth your time has gumption like your sister."

Tatum kisses her grandfather's cheek.

"Anyway, let me finish introductions. James, this is Pop Pop, my grandfather."

I'm not calling him Pop Pop. No fuckin' way.

Her grandfather grasps my hand, giving it a firm shake. "Call me Walt," he says, grinning. "I like your tattoos."

I can't tell if he's being sarcastic and letting me know I clearly don't belong with someone like Tatum, or if he's being genuine. The smile on his face feels genuine, but I don't trust this quite yet.

"Thank you," I manage.

Tatum unhooks her arm from her grandfather's neck, grabbing my hand to lead me toward the others.

"James, this is my brother, Hammond. Hammond, this is James."

"Hey, man," Hammond says, sticking out his hand.

I shake it once before dropping it and clearing my throat. "Hey."

"And these crazy people over here," Tatum says, gesturing

to the bar, "are my parents, Daniel and Eliza."

I shake hands with Tatum's dad and nod a simple greeting.

Tatum's mom comes around the bar and wraps me in an awkward hug. I have to bend my knees a little so she can reach my neck. Heat creeps up my neck, discomforted from being locked in an embrace with someone I don't know. I pat her back softly and awkwardly.

"It's great to meet you, James," Eliza says, breaking the hug. "Tatum speaks highly of you."

I turn toward Tatum, fucking thrilled when I find her blushing. When the red stains her cheeks, it makes her eyes look like blue flames. They burn brighter the closer I get to her and the more I touch her. Every time I see the heat creeping up her face, I want to make it spread and the flames dance.

I raise an eyebrow and smirk. "That's good to hear."

"Would you like a drink?" Daniel asks. I hesitate, looking around the room at the glasses in everyone's hands. It's early afternoon on a Sunday. I don't want to ask for a beer if it would be inappropriate. "Eliza ordered me some hard cider from a farm in Vermont, haven't had a chance to crack one open. Would you like one of those?"

"Sounds good," I say, opening the fist that was clenched at my side and exhaling a long breath.

"Pop Pop," Tatum says with her perfect lips twitching. "Who's the old bitch I heard you yelling about?"

"Did you see the mailbox?" he asks, his gaze shining on Tatum's mom.

"Sure did," Tatum says, grinning and leans back on the wall next to me crossing one ankle over the other.

"Those craggy old bitty bitches down the street really put a bee in your mom's bonnet." Walt picks up the cue from between his legs and slams it down to send his point home.

He rests his cigar on the edge of an ashtray and curses the women down the street under his breath.

"What'd they do, Mom?" Tatum's eyes swing to her mother and she's still controlling the smile begging to break through. Finally, she bites her lip to stop the twitching.

Eliza sighs. Daniel rolls his eyes, shaking his head while running his palm across his forehead. "This is my house," she says, placing a hand on her hip. I envision Tatum just like that, twenty years from now, looking just like her mom and throwing around her attitude.

"You signed a contract, Mom," Hammond says, leaning one head on the pool table and staring at his mom.

"You're such a lawyer," Eliza shoots back, clearly not thinking too highly of her son's profession. "It's my house. I should be able to do whatever I see fit. Some little HOA fine is not going to stop me!"

"It was a two-hundred dollar fine, my dear," Daniel says, resting a hand on her shoulder. "That's not a little fine."

"I love fall, so sue me." Eliza flips her hair over her shoulder and waves her hand in the air.

"What'd you do, Mom?" Tatum asks again.

Her mom turns toward her, smiling. "I found these cute little orange lights I thought would look really cute around the flowerbed where I put the pumpkins. The HOA ladies claim they're Christmas lights and reminded me we can't have Christmas lights until December seventh."

"Ridiculous," Tatum mutters.

"They fined me," Eliza says, waving her hand in the air like it's no big deal to be fined. "Your father asked me to take them down so we don't receive a weekly fine, so I did. There's nothing in the HOA rules about foul language, though."

I burst into laughter, along with the rest of the room. Eliza laughs until she catches my eye and stops. Her eyes go wide as she stares at me. My laughter cuts off, too, and I'm feeling uncomfortable under her gaze.

"Wow," she says softly. Tatum hooks her arm through mine. I look down at her with a slight frown.

"I know," she says to her mother. Her face turns toward mine; she's wearing the softest smile and her eyes are filled with tenderness. For me.

Fuck.

All the oxygen in my lungs ceases to circulate. I stop breathing. My heart stops beating. Everyone in the room falls away as I soak in the tenderness in Tatum's eyes. I've never felt anything like this.

I swallow, but I still can't tear my gaze from hers. When her hand skims down my arm and wraps around my hand, my heart restarts and my lungs fill with air. My eyes finally leave hers, I feel like I just went ten rounds in a boxing ring. One look from Tatum knocked me on my ass. It's a fight I want to lose, though.

"Friends," Hammond grunts. "Right."

I tense, remembering we aren't alone in a room. We're in a room filled with her family. I raise my head over Tatum, and my eyes meet his. I expect him to be scowling at me, but he's just wearing a knowing smile.

"Tatum," Hammond says. "Go help Mom with the food."

"Uh…" Tatum freezes. I feel every part of her body tense. "I think I'll stay here."

"It's going to happen, honey," Eliza says, pulling Tatum away from me. "None of us buy that friend act. Just let the men get their man chat over with."

"But…" Tatum reaches for me.

"Go," I say quietly, enough for only her to hear.

"But—"

"Sunshine, just go with your mom." I bend down, scooping Sirius up and passing him to her.

Once the women leave the room—Tatum practically

clawing her way to try and stay—I turn toward the men, expecting the inquisition immediately. Tatum and I aren't dating. That's not what we're doing. I'm not about to tell the men in her family that we're fuck buddies. While we're not dating, we're not exactly just friends, either.

None of them start in on any questioning. Her father hands me a bottle of cider before pulling one out for Hammond and Walt. Hammond racks the pool table, glancing up at me. "You play?"

I shrug. "A bit."

"Let's do this over a game," he says.

I lick my lips, nodding and readying myself for questions I don't want to answer, that I don't know how to answer. There isn't a way in hell I would've been able to get out of this. I knew when Tatum and I strolled into that room, something like this would come. We could claim friendship until we're blue in the face, and this still would've happened. I hoped it wouldn't, but still knew.

I grab a cue from the wall after Hammond tells me to break. I line up my shot, fully aware that every eye in the room is on me. Breaking these balls is a fucking test of some sort, and fuck me, I hope I pass.

We're only kind of friends who fuck occasionally. Okay, daily. But still, there's nothing else happening between us.

I still want to pass this little test of theirs more than I should.

I line up my shot from the corner, going for a solid break. Two solids land in the pockets. When I stand to my full height, each guy has a tiny smile on his face.

"Look," Hammond says, chalking his cue. "I'm not one of those brothers who looks into who their sister dates. Tate's smart, and I trust her judgment. I'm pretty sure if I did try to dictate anything in her life, she'd cut off my balls. I like my balls where they are, so her decisions are hers."

I chuckle. "She's something else," I say, my smile lingering. Since Tatum pulled a smile and a laugh from me—which I don't think I've experienced in years, maybe ever—each smile comes a bit easier, erasing the rust just a bit more.

Hammond returns my grin before sobering again. "I'm not going to tell you I can kick your ass, because shit, dude, you just might be the biggest motherfucker I've ever seen. But I won't hesitate to destroy you in other ways. I'd dismantle your life so quickly and thoroughly, you'd be standing on a street corner begging for change before you could wonder what happened. That's only if you hurt her, though."

"I think my son covered just about all of it," Daniel says. "She's my baby girl. If one hair on her head is harmed because of you, I'll use my money to find a guy bigger than you and have him kick your ass. Then Hammond can go about dismantling your life."

That makes me snicker. I open my mouth to speak, give them some honesty, it's the least they deserve. Being here in this house where there's so much warmth, light, and sunshine, I feel like an even bigger dick for judging Tatum as a spoiled rich girl.

Before I can speak, Walt pipes in. "I don't give a shit how big you are. I have enough guns to supply a Texas army. One of those is bound to take down something as big as you. Hell, I could bring you out to the woods, kill ya there, and claim I found Bigfoot."

I throw my head back laughing, Tatum's family laughing along with me. My expectations of today were totally off. I understand why Tatum is this bright spot in my dark life. I wonder who I would be right now if I had a family like this one.

Once my laughter dies down, I look at each of them. "I won't lie to you. My respect for Tatum and you guys—mostly Tatum, though—is too big for that. I don't know when the thing between us will end. I do know that I care for her, and we're honest with each other about where we stand. I also know that she deserves a much better man than me, but selfishly, right now, I really enjoy spending time with her. We're friends first before anything else. I do anything for the people in my life. She's one of them. The wedding bells in her future won't be with me, but I'm in her life now. My friends, who are my family, are in her life. While she's there, no matter where we stand, I'll do everything to protect her and care for her."

# CHAPTER
# TWENTY-SEVEN

*Tatum*

A HUGE BOOM OF LAUGHTER EXPLODES FROM THE room James is trapped in. I've been staring at the door, sliding my finger across my lower lip since my mom pulled me out of there, internally kicking and screaming.

"They're laughing," I say to my mom, not taking my eyes off the door. "That's a good thing, right?"

"Yes, honey," she says moving around the kitchen to gather things for our lunch. "Can you take this to the table?"

"In a minute," I reply, hoping if I stare hard enough, I'll gain superpowers and be able to see through the door. "Maybe they're killing him and laughing about it."

"Pretty sure I heard your sexy man's laugh in that group."

"He's not my man," I insist, sinking my teeth into my bottom lip. I'm starting to wish I could call him my man. My sexy man. My sweet man. My everything man. Just mine.

"Then, I'm pretty sure I heard that sexy man's laugh," she says, chuckling.

"Don't call him sexy. That's weird." My leg bounces on the footrest of the barstool making a slight clinking noise.

"Because you're sleeping with him?" If I could take my

eyes off the door I would turn around and glare at her, but I'm too anxious to look away from the white door.

"Mother." I sigh. She's really not helping my anxiety over this situation. "What do you think is happening in there?"

"I wouldn't blame you." She's still chuckling to herself as the noises of opening and closing drawers fill the room.

"Do you think they're killing him?" My mom closes a drawer and walks over to me, standing just to the side of me, but not blocking my view of the door.

"No, baby girl," my mom says, brushing my hair away from my face. "You know they respect anyone you choose to date. They'd never hurt anything that makes you smile like you do when you look at him."

This does break my gaze from the door. "How do I look at him?"

"Like he makes the sun rise each day, just for you. Like he's keeping a dog he obviously doesn't want, just to see you smile." I find Sirius drinking from a small water bowl my mom placed there. His bright red collar stands out against his black fur. A smile crosses my face thinking about James keeping Sirius.

Butterflies swarm my stomach. I don't look at him like that. I just decided I can even tolerate him as a human. I want to believe she's wrong and that she's just on a mission to get grandbabies. The alternative could lead to heartache.

The door opens down the hall, all the men spilling out. Hammond has his hand on James's shoulder. James has the tiniest of smiles on his face as his shoulders shake with quiet laughter while Hammond grins and gestures with his other hand.

I don't hear what he's saying until they approach, and I gasp in horror. "She's standing on stage, drunk, singing Carrie Underwood at the top of her lungs. Have you heard her sing?"

James shakes his head, his eyes finding mine and not wavering away as he listens to my brother. "No." He winks at me.

"Hammond, don't you dare." I move to jump off the barstool, but my dad wraps an arm around me.

"I love this story," he says, keeping me pinned to the spot and giving me an affectionate squeeze.

I groan, cursing the heavens for my family and covering my face with my hands.

"Good," Hammond says. "Don't let her sing around you; she'll bust your eardrum. Worst thing you've ever heard. Every cliché awful noise—nails on a chalkboard, screeching cats—she's worse than all of that. Our little Tate was a scorned woman at this time…" Hammond continues. I drop my hands from my face sucking in air through my nose. James's eyes cut to mine, raising an eyebrow, asking a silent question.

"She's wearing this dress and dancing all around the stage, acting out carving her name into some leather seats." Hammond howls with laughter. "She gets to the end of the song, finishing in style, raising her hand in the air like she's on a stage in an arena. And then, her underwear falls off, wrapping around her ankles. She bends quickly to pick them up but tumbles off the stage."

"I can't believe you told that story." I groan as my dad lets go of me, no longer needing to restrain me. Sirius is dancing around our feet, excited from all the noise.

James walks over to me and plants a kiss on my temple. I can feel his body vibrating from his laughter. "Wish I would have seen that."

"No, that would've made it worse." My hands come up to my cheeks feeling them burn beneath my palms.

"You're cute," James says, leaning over to lay another kiss against my temple.

My eyes widen, and I suck in a breath. He just showed me affection in front of my family. *Twice.* Hammond winks at me before he turns, helping to bring the food to the table.

That small touch of his lips against my skin makes the embarrassing story totally worth it.

---

The embarrassing stories haven't stopped. My family is taking turns regaling tales from my childhood to James who is eating up each of them. The plate in front of him is clear of food with the silverware lying on top of it. He's casually relaxed back in his chair, one big foot resting on his knee. His hands are clasped in his lap, and his gray eyes are shining with humor.

"Tate," my brother calls from across the table, grinning mischievously. "Try to do something at the gala in a couple of weeks? It'll make it much more entertaining."

I roll my eyes. "I'll see what I can do."

"Hammond, don't tease your sister." My mom's sly smile slides across her face. "At least she has a date, so her momma doesn't need to find one for her."

I jolt. Date? I don't have a date to the gala. Truthfully, it hasn't crossed my mind since getting shot down by Patrick. Is she thinking about James?

"Don't need you to find me a date, Mother," Hammond mutters.

"James, dear," my mom asks, turning a genuine smile toward him. "Has Tate told you what the gala is benefitting? Do you have all the details?"

James's big, round eyes slice to mine, his eyebrows shooting up to his hairline. I cough into my hand, clearing my throat. "That's not really James's thing. I don't have a date," I respond. Everyone at the table stares at me, including

James. There's a frown on his face as his eyes skim over me, searching.

"Oh," my mom says quietly.

James rubs his hand along the back of his neck. "What's it benefitting?"

My mom's eyes twinkle as a knowing smile takes over her face. "One of the nonprofits I volunteer with has a large gala every year; it's coming up in just a couple of weeks. Don't listen to Tate or Hammond, it is really a fun event. We raise money for scholarships for underprivileged youth. Not just scholarships for colleges, but private schools in the area, as well. Each individual who participates can donate to a scholarship that's already formed, or they can create their own with volunteers to cater the behind-the-scenes admin parts that go into it. For example, let's say Pop Pop wanted to donate ten-thousand dollars. He could decide he wants the recipient to be great at billiards. Maybe the child has learned math through billiards. Or he can put the money into something existing."

James nods, taking in everything my mom said as his finger runs absently over his lips. Those gray eyes that see too much of me find mine. He doesn't say anything, just gazes at me. Hammond starts a conversation with the rest of the table, leaving us in this bubble where everything else fades away.

My heartbeat picks up when James's features soften. "You don't have a date?"

"No." I shake my head without breaking eye contact.

"Do you need one?"

"I do." My voice is trembling and comes out so softly, he may not have even heard the words, but his eyes have moved to my lips.

"Your mom will set you up if you don't find one?"

I grimace, completely annoyed by the thought of my

mom finding me a date. It's almost as bad as taking your cousin to prom. I nod.

"I'll take you." The conviction in James's voice takes me by surprise.

"You will?" My hands stop fidgeting with the napkin in my lap, completely stunned by this turn of events.

"Yes," he replies firmly. Sirius licks my ankle as he weaves between my feet, but I don't look down. Nothing could take my eyes away from James's right now.

"It's not really your type of thing. You'll have to wear a tux." I don't know why I'm pointing this out. He said he'd take me, I should shut up and accept it.

He smirks, shrugging. "I'll manage."

"You'll be my date?" I ask for confirmation. My question comes out in a breathy whisper.

"Yes."

"Why?" His gray eyes drop down to my lips before meeting mine again and dropping his hand to my knee, softly stroking the skin there.

"Tatum, if you need something, ask. I've got you."

# CHAPTER
# TWENTY-EIGHT

*Tatum*

’M IN THE MIDDLE OF DOING MY MAKEUP WHEN THE doorbell rings. Crap. James is really early. I'm not even close to being ready, but that's okay. I'll give him a beer and he can wait while watching TV or something.

I'm about to run out of the room when I realize I'm still in my bra and panty set. The doorbell rings again as I'm shoving my arms through the armholes of my robe. "Coming," I yell and hustle down the hall to the door.

"I'm sorry," I say, adjusting the robe to cover myself completely. "I didn't expect you this early."

"I always loved watching you get ready."

At the sound of that voice, my head jerks up and my voice catches in my throat. I take a small step back which allows Patrick just enough space to enter. "Patrick," I whisper. "What are you doing here?"

"I'm saving you from being bored with whomever your mother set you up with. Call him and cancel. I've been missing you." I open my mouth, but snap it shut again. Wondering if this is a dream, I dig my fingernails into my palm until I feel a bite of pain. When my palm twinges, I realize this is indeed happening and I want to laugh.

Patrick steps forward, brings me into his arms, and nuzzles me, dragging his tongue along the crook of my neck. The urge to laugh flees quickly when I feel his mouth on my neck. My hands grip his biceps, firmly pushing him away. "My mom didn't set me up."

"Perfect," he says, grinning. "Let's go together. And leave together. No one is quite like you, Tate."

*Ugh.*

"I have a date," I say a little coldly, fisting the opening of my robe tightly together.

"You just said your mom didn't set you up." He's stalking toward me while I'm backing up, trying to keep some distance between us.

"She didn't. I'm...." I stop, not really sure how to describe James. I go for the easiest explanation. "I'm seeing someone."

Patrick stops dead in his tracks, raising his eyebrows. His mouth slowly opens, disbelief written all over his face. "You're seeing someone?"

"Yes." I curl a loose strand of hair behind my ear and bite the inside of my cheek.

"I... I don't like that," he says softly, almost to himself. He runs his hand across his smooth-shaven jaw, looking down at his dress shoes.

He doesn't like that. *He doesn't like that.* I roll my lip between my teeth trying not to explode. I don't have the time to yell at him or have this argument. I need him to leave. *Now.* "It's not really up to you," I respond, moving around him to the door and opening it. "I need to finish getting ready. He'll be here soon."

Patrick stares at me for several long moments, taking me in from the top of my head to the tips of my toes, then slowly nods. "Right." He walks to the door, but pauses, facing me. "Is it serious?"

I hesitate, looking down at my feet before meeting his

eyes again. "It's early."

Patrick gives me one last once-over before walking out the door. I breathe a sigh of relief, slamming it behind him and lock it when the doorbell rings again. My forehead rests against the door as I groan is frustration. I don't have time for this conversation with him.

I swing open the door, but it's not Patrick.

A delivery man in a green polo stands with a bouquet of flowers. "Tatum Rothschild?"

"Yes," I say, wrapping my fist around my robe to close it even tighter as the delivery man's eyes rake over my body.

"These are for you, beautiful."

"Thanks." I grab them and shut the door quickly, throwing the lock in place. Now that I'm not under the scrutiny of the delivery man, I truly look at the flowers. They're lovely—a mix of deep red and pristine white roses in a crystal vase. The scent brings a smile to my face as I pluck the card from the top.

*I'll see you tonight.*

*Save me a dance.*

A giddy feeling consumes me as I hold the card to my chest. I set the vase on the living room coffee table where James will see them when he walks in. Maybe this is something that could become serious.

I hustle back into my bedroom to finish getting ready before James arrives. I'm sliding the silk material of my dress up my body when the doorbell rings. Reaching behind my back to pull up the zipper, I can't get it all the way. I'm struggling when the doorbell rings again.

Softly holding the material to my chest, I go to the door, opening it to reveal James. In a tuxedo. Dear God. I inhale in a sharp breath, completely blown away by the sight of him. It fits him perfectly, framing every hard, solid inch of him.

"Tatum," he says, looking down at me with a cockiness

in his gaze. He knows I'm checking him out, and that I truly like what I see.

"James." I say his name on a breath.

He brings out a hand from behind his back. revealing a gorgeous bouquet with deep fall colors and a mix of flowers. I gasp putting my hand over my chest. "They're beautiful," I whisper. His hand extends a little farther, prompting me to take them. I chuckle. "I need some help with my dress. Can you put them down and help me?"

James walks past me, laying the flowers on the coffee table next to the other bouquet. I turn my back to him when he steps toward me. His breathing picks up, turning just a little heavier when his finger skims along my back, creating goosebumps in its wake.

He trails his finger down my spine to where the zipper starts just above my ass and slowly back up to my neck. His lips take the spot where his finger left off. His tongue caresses my skin as he slowly zips my zipper.

My nipples pebble through the fabric as I crane my neck to the side, giving him easier access. When he's done zipping me up, his large hand wraps around my hip, sliding up my body until his thumb brushes over my extended nipple. I moan, arching into his hand, silently pleading for more. He bites my neck before spinning me around.

James doesn't say anything, just stares at me standing before him. He drags his finger along the neckline of my dress. It's a sweetheart neckline with a small, sharp V showing off a hint of cleavage. The straps hang loosely around my arms, leaving my shoulders and neck bare.

"You look gorgeous. You are gorgeous, Tatum." James's voice is husky and thick as his hand wraps around the nape of my neck, forcing me to look into his eyes before he bends to kiss my lips.

"Not so bad yourself," I whisper, arching so my chest is

flush against his. "You didn't have to get me two bouquets."

James turns his head, gazing at the coffee table.

The smile on my face dies when he turns back to me with irritated eyes. "I didn't."

"But…" I step away from him to pick up the card on the first bouquet. "It says, 'See you tonight.' This really wasn't you?"

"No." James's voice is gruff as he rakes a frustrated hand through his hair. He's glaring at the roses. "Should've got a vase. Fuck." The curse is muttered so low I almost miss it.

"No," I say, squeezing his bicep. "I have the perfect vase for these. They're gorgeous. My favorite colors." I bring the blooms to my nose, inhaling deeply before walking to the kitchen to grab the vase. I'm not sure who the other flowers could be from. Patrick? My parents? I put it out of my mind as I open the cabinet door.

The vase is at the top of one of my cabinets. I try to reach it without my stepstool, but my fingers are just shy of the glass. James presses his body to my back, one hand firmly attached to my hip while he easily plucks the burgundy vase from the shelf.

"So tiny," James teases.

"Everyone is tiny compared to you. You're like the Jolly Green Giant, only not so jolly."

James's booming laugh echoes in my ears, sending a delighted shiver up my back. "Your grandfather called me Bigfoot."

I laugh along with James, spinning around in his arms and pressing my hands against his chest to feel every shake and echo of his laugh.

After taking care of the ends and filling the vase with water, I arrange the flowers neatly, smiling the entire time. "See? It's perfect."

"Know who it could be?"

"Who what could be?" I ask.

"The other flowers."

"Oh," I say, thinking while still arranging James's bouquet. I frown when I remember Patrick stopping by. It's not like him to not deliver them personally, but maybe they should have arrived sooner? "Patrick, maybe. Or my parents"

"Your ex?" James is stiff while watching me arrange the flowers. His focus is on the other room. When he turns back to me his mouth is in a flat line.

"Yeah," I say. I spent almost eight months trying to get over Patrick, but once I truly realized this other side of him is the real Patrick, it happened quickly. I don't want to think about him tonight.

James scans my face, stepping closer before landing a hard kiss against my forehead. "Ready?"

"Yeah. Let me grab my purse."

I walk into my room, grabbing the clutch that matches my ice blue dress perfectly before meeting James back at the door. He grabs my hand as he leads me to his SUV, opening the door for me.

The drive starts out quietly, but comfortably. When James and I met, every moment of silence was filled with thick tension. That's eased between us significantly, and I can't even pretend anymore that I don't like him. Every time he shows me another piece of himself, I treasure it, keeping it close to me. My irritation with him has turned into fascination, and my fascination has turned into obsession. Every caress, laugh, smile, I want to hold onto forever, and I'm willing to do anything to get more of him. He's a whole new brand of obsession.

"Thank you for taking me," I say, breaking our silence. His gray eyes cut to me before looking back at the road.

"Not a problem." He runs a finger under the collar of his tux.

"Are you uncomfortable?"

"Not used to wearing this," he admits sheepishly.

"Formal attire isn't the most comfortable. Thank you, James. I really mean it."

"It's not a big deal, Tatum."

"It is to me." I turn my head fully toward him, watching his hand wrap the wheel a little tighter.

"Tell me about Patrick." His is tone is low and intimidating. My focus swings to him. The glow from the lights on the dash are highlighting his scowling face.

I lean on the door, slightly facing James and cup my neck with my hand. My tongue slides over my teeth. This isn't a question I want to answer right now, but I'd rather get it out of the way and have a good night.

"My ex," I answer slowly with some hesitation.

"Got that part," he answers. "Is he the guy Hammond referred to in the drunk singing story?"

"Yeah," I admit while rubbing my fingers together, focusing on the friction it creates. "The summarized version is we dated for twelve years and broke up eight months ago."

"Longer version." It doesn't come out as a question, but as a demand.

"I thought we would get married. We talked about it since high school, our families our close, our fathers work together. It just seemed to make sense. Eight months ago, we went out to celebrate a milestone in his career. He pulled out an engagement ring box and then dumped me in the middle of a restaurant."

"Fucker," James grunts.

I close my eyes to center myself again. The pain I once felt when I thought about that night is now just a sore spot, something that isn't felt unless prodded. "He told me he still wanted to marry me, but not yet. Before you, he was the only guy I'd been with. I was the only girl he'd been with.

He wanted to experience other people. Patrick completely changed after we split. He wasn't the kind and considerate person I thought I knew. He said horrible things to me and made me feel about two inches tall. I admit I lost myself for a bit, but the night I ran into you at the grocery store, I decided I was done. To be honest, it's been easy to let him go."

James swings into a parking lot so suddenly I'm thrown towards him. He slams his SUV into park, unclicks both of our belts and faces me. His hands comes up to my face, cupping my cheeks. "I hate him," he states. "You may be tiny."

James's mouth tilts up on one side before he continues. "But, no one should ever make you feel small. Don't ever let that fucker make you feel that way again. You astound me. I've never met someone as beautiful as you. Not just your looks either. It's everything. It's just you. Fuck, Tatum. You're *my* sunshine. If he ever makes you feel that way again, I'll bury him."

James doesn't let me respond. He sends my pulse skyrocketing. His thumbs brush against the tears on my cheeks as his mouth slams down on mine. "I know I can't keep you, but you're the best part of my life."

I open my mouth, but he shakes his head. "Don't say anything. I shouldn't have brought him up. He doesn't get this night. I do. It's mine. And yours."

He kisses me again before instructing me to buckle up and starts heading toward the gala again.

After a few minutes of silence, James's mood is lighter than it was and I'm still stunned by his words. I want to reply. There's so much I want to say, but it'll wait. I force a question to my lips. It's not what I want to ask, but it will turn this completely away from Patrick. "Have you ever been to a black-tie event?"

He snorts. "Nope."

"They're a little stuffy, but not horrible. Lots of silverware, formal dancing."

"Okay," he says.

"I'll make it worth your while."

His eyes cut to me again, a smirk curling his lips. "Maybe I should complain a lot while we're there."

My hand grips his thigh before slowly sliding up with tantalizing fingers. His chest expands as he breathes deeply and adjusts himself in the seat. "Tatum," he growls.

"I'll make sure every time you complain, I'll give you something you want."

"Sounds promising," he says. "This bowtie is really tight. I don't like things around my neck like this."

"Solid complaint," I whisper, cupping his hardness through his pants. He hisses through his teeth, shifting his hips as much as he can beneath the restraint of the seat belt.

I take my hand away as James pulls into the hotel valet and mumbles about dirty gym socks under his breath. A valet worker opens my door, holding out a hand to help me step down.

James rushes around just as my feet touch the ground. "Should've been me," he grumbles, snagging my hand in his.

"Is that a complaint?" I ask, my lip quirking on one side.

"Nope. Just the truth."

The air in my lungs leaves in a whoosh. I'm completely dazed as I follow James inside the lobby. "Where do we go?" he asks, bending his head so his lips are close to my ear.

I gesture toward the grand ballroom. Our names are checked off a list, and we're guided toward our assigned table. I stumble when I notice Patrick standing next to my parents, chatting with them. He has one hand tucked into his pocket while the other rests casually on the back of a chair.

I wish he'd leave the table. I don't want to introduce James and Patrick. It's too uncomfortable, especially after his visit earlier. Unfortunately, he doesn't leave, but he does notice us approaching, and his eyes drag up and down my body as a slow smile breaks across his face.

James doesn't miss it. His hand grips mine tighter, and I can feel his eyes boring into the side of my face, but I don't look at him. I turn my attention to the band playing low music while the guests file in.

"Tate, James," my dad says happily, kissing my cheek and slapping a hand on James's shoulder.

My mom steps up beside him, smiling and kissing both our cheeks. "Y'all look wonderful together."

"Thank you," I say.

James lets go of my hand to wrap an arm around my waist. I bite back a grin, but look up at him when he squeezes my hip. He winks at me, and I swear I melt into a puddle right on the hotel floor.

"Tate," Patrick says. I hear the slight sharpness underneath the charm he's trying to emanate.

"Patrick," I reply, hesitating before doing what I know I have to do. "James, this is Patrick, an old family friend. Patrick, this is my date, James Harris."

Patrick walks around the circular table, placing his hand on my side a few inches above James's, and pulls me into a tight hug. I smell the whiskey on him, but he's not drunk yet.

James doesn't let go of my hip, and his grip tightens.

When Patrick lets go of me, James pulls me closer to his side. "We're a little more than old family friends, darling."

I stiffen at the pet name. James emits a growl low enough that only I hear it. I look up at him; his jaw is twitching and his eyes are blazing.

"James," I say. "Patrick, as you know, is my ex."

"Great to meet you," Patrick says, extending a hand toward James. After a moment, James takes it, and I can tell he's gripping it tightly. "Nice of you to accompany Tate as a friend."

"We're not here as friends," James says in a low, harsh tone, dropping his hand. I wrap my arm around James's waist, giving him a tight squeeze.

"We're going to go ahead and sit now," I say, hoping this will dismiss Patrick, and he'll walk away.

"I'm sitting at your table tonight," Patrick says. "My family is hosting some of their friends. It seems Hammond and I are the only two single men here."

"Great," I mutter, hoping to keep some of the sarcasm out of my tone. I walk with James around the table, hoping Patrick will sit where he's standing, but he comes around the other side, and now I'm sandwiched between the only two men who've been inside me.

Wonderful.

# CHAPTER
# TWENTY-NINE

## James

"YOU LOOK PRETTY, TATE. I DIDN'T GET TO SEE you dressed earlier." Patrick's words pack a punch. Did he deliver those damn flowers in person? Did she lie about that? My small gift to her looked cheap compared to that frivolous monstrosity.

Motherfucker. He said it that way on purpose. I see him watching me out of the corner of his eye, gauging my reaction as he leans in close to Tatum.

"She doesn't *look* pretty," I say. "She *is* gorgeous."

Tatum's hand falls to my thigh, gripping me tightly, and those damn blue eyes are shining at me like I put each star in the sky just for her. My chest expands under her tender gaze. Every time she looks at me like that, I feel like I've scaled a fucking mountain.

Slowly, she leans toward me, brushing her lips along mine and whispering, "Thank you."

When she leans back, I move my lips to her ear, speaking as softly as I can. "I'm complaining that he's here."

Her lips tilt up at the edges. "Each complaint gets you something you want. Tell me what you want, James." She pulls back slightly so she can look into my eyes. The blue fire of her gaze makes me feel alive.

"Tell me you're mine."

Tatum gasps. It's not what I was expecting to say, but I want her to say it. I need her to say it. Tatum is becoming as vital as my beating heart, blood running through my veins, and oxygen filling my lungs. I need to hear those words from her lips, even if that prick is sitting next to her paying way too close attention to us.

"I'm yours," she finally says on a breathy whisper.

When my attention turns back to the table, I find the rest of Tatum's family has arrived. Hammond is drinking a scotch, grimacing as he pulls at the collar of his tux. Her grandfather is chatting with her parents, and Patrick's eyes are glued to Tatum's cleavage.

"James, what do you do?" Patrick tears his eyes away from Tatum to meet mine. He has an arrogant smirk as he studies me, his eyes locking on the tattoos poking out of my sleeve.

"I own a gym," I respond flatly.

"How quaint," he says. "Keeping a small business open is no simple task. Where did you get your business degree?"

"Didn't."

Patrick clucks his tongue, shaking his head. It's taking every ounce of willpower to not launch myself over Tatum and send a fist flying through his skull. What the hell did Tatum ever see in this asshole? Is this really what she wants?

"It takes a lot to run a business. With so many business-es failing, it's really best to have a degree."

Tatum's small hand grabbing mine and making me un-curl my fist is the only thing that keeps me from shaking in rage.

"I manage," I spit out. Fuckin' prick doesn't need to know anything about my damn job.

"Idiot," Hammond mutters, just loud enough for

everyone at the table to hear. I tense further. Tatum opens her mouth to speak, but I squeeze her hand.

"It is a shame, isn't it, Hammond?" Patrick asks him. "James isn't—"

Hammond cuts him off. "Not him. You. You're the idiot."

My body relaxes and I release a low chuckle. I don't want to embarrass Tatum, but keeping my mouth shut and my fists in check around Patrick is going to be a test. I'm done listening to this. My eyes scan the ballroom, looking for any type of escape. I stand, and Tatum's eyes meet mine as she frowns. I offer her my hand. "Dance with me?"

Her frown slowly morphs into a brilliant smile as we leave Patrick and Hammond arguing behind us. I lead Tatum through other dancing couples until we reach an empty spot on the dance floor farthest from the table. My arm wraps around her, pulling her until she's flush against my body. Her satisfied hum goes straight to my cock. My hand clasps hers, putting us in position, and I lead us in a waltz around the dance floor.

Tatum's eyes are huge. "You know how to dance?"

"Yep."

"Where did you learn?"

"Taught myself," I reply, skimming my hand up and down her spine, eliciting the most delicious shivers from her.

"Why?"

I've never talked about my life. I had friends growing up, most in the same shitty situation as me, so there wasn't a need to talk about it. We all knew the fucking reality. Since I left that life behind, I've kept the tightest seal over it, not revealing a damn thing about myself. It's been easy; it's not hard to hide my past. My first instinct with Tatum, though, is complete honesty, to tell her everything, hold nothing back.

Her posture sags in my arms when she thinks I'm not

going to answer. Those blue eyes leave my face to look down at the nonexistent space between us.

"I was almost adopted once," I admit, gearing myself to tell this story for the first time in almost twenty years.

"Really?" Her gaze finds mine again.

"Yeah," I say gruffly, clearing my throat. "I was about eleven. An older couple with no children became interested in adoption. They thought an older kid might suit their lifestyle better. It's also more competitive to get a baby from the system."

I sigh, shaking my head. Always fucking hated the way that sounded, like it's a damn competition to acquire a kid that needs help. It's the truth, though. Tatum stays silent, waiting for me to continue.

"The couple was wealthy. I met them once and really liked them. I asked my social worker so many questions. I was determined to be the son they wanted."

"James," Tatum whispers, her eyes glassy with unshed tears.

I bring my hand up to her face, swiping along her cheek. "Don't do that for me, sunshine."

She bites her lips, pressing impossibly closer to me. My hand at her back tightens, welcoming every sliver of warmth she'll give me.

"I found out that he was the CEO of some major company, and she was on the board of just about everything in Chicago. Events like this were their bread and butter. I studied so hard."

"Studied what?"

"Etiquette. How to use the crazy number of utensils they give you at this kind of stuff. How to dance. I watched videos at the library and practiced any time I was alone. They had an old TV and VCR they let me use sometimes. I did everything I could to become the son I thought they would want.

They were my chance. My one fucking chance. I was getting older by the day. Each day that passed, it became more un-likely that a family would ever want me."

I've never been this honest with anyone in my life. I'm showing her so many dark pieces of myself, and she's still gazing at me like I'm her reason for everything, shining her light on every shadow I'm revealing.

"What happened?" she asks.

"A weekend visit was planned. I was going to stay at their house, and that would be pretty much the final step before I'd live with them permanently. I was in a group home at the time. The day they showed up, someone dumped a baby on the porch just a few minutes before they arrived. They took it as a sign. I didn't even see them that day. I learned this from my social worker after I'd been sitting on my bunk for hours waiting for them to come get me."

Tatum rests her forehead against my chest, breathing me in. I know she's hiding the tears sliding down her cheeks. I kiss the top of her head.

"No tears."

"I hate that that was your life."

"I got out." Barely, but I got out. Everything I worked for isn't any more stable than a house of cards. One wrong move or turn could send everything tumbling down.

"I wish you had a family," she admits sadly."

"I did," I say gruffly. "A foster brother who became my best friend. He had a little sister I loved like my own, too."

"Do you still talk to them?"

"We lost touch," I lie. "But, they were my family."

We both startle when a flash goes off next to us. My en-tire body freezes, stilling in the middle of the dance floor. My eyes are fixated on the photographer who snapped a pic-ture of us and walked away.

"James?" Tatum asks, looking around. "Are you okay?"

"I don't like my picture being taken," I say, unable to focus back on her. My photograph appearing anywhere wouldn't just send my house of cards crashing down, it'd decimate it, set it on fire until there's nothing but ash. Ash of everything in my life, including me. "Why are they taking pictures?"

"They do at events like this all the time."

"Are they posted somewhere?"

"Not that I know of," she says, confusion in her voice. "They'll print one in the paper; it's usually the keynote speaker."

"After this dance, I'm asking him to delete it."

"Why?"

"I don't like my picture being taken, Tatum." Part of me wonders how she'd react to everything I'm hiding; the other part knows if I tell her, she'd be in danger. I'm not willing to risk that.

We're silent for a long moment, tension moving between us. Tatum tries to lighten the mood. "Is that a complaint?" She tilts her face up to mine, fluttering her eyes lashes and biting her lower lip.

"Definitely," I mutter. "You'll have to do something really dirty to make up for this one."

She bites her lip, her pupils dilating as her breathing picks up.

"Fuck," I grumble, my cock rising to attention to press against her stomach. I know she feels it when she whimpers slightly.

"Is dancing with me a complaint?" she asks after another minute of silence.

"Not a damn thing to complain about with that."

She smiles before laying her head on my chest. "I think dinner is about to be served. Ready to head back?"

"If that prick stops staring at your tits, then yes."

Tatum laughs. "Remember what I said earlier?"

I raise an eyebrow.

"I said I'm yours. That means only you get to see them." She winks at me before walking off the dance floor, swaying her hips. She looks over her shoulder at me, still rooted to the spot. She gives me a saucy smile that finally gets me to chase after her, ready for my hands to be back on her.

# CHAPTER
## THIRTY

*Tatum*

J AMES FINALLY LEAVES THE DANCE FLOOR, REACHING me and immediately wrapping an arm around my waist. His hand slides down my hip, resting at the top of my ass.

"How long are we staying?" he asks, his lips tracing my ear.

"Only as long as we have to," I muse, ready to be back at his house with Sirius, curled up in his bed.

"Where did you learn to dance like that?" The voice coming from behind us sounds amused and curious. James and I turn toward the voice to see a grinning Hudson.

"Hudson," I greet, leaning over to give him a hug as I turn my cheek when he leans in to kiss it.

"You look gorgeous, Tatum. What are you doing here with this big lug?" Hudson shoves his thumb in James's direction.

James grunts. "What are you doing here?" James asks, clapping Hudson on the back.

"This is one of my mom's charities. Whole family is here. Stop by the table to say hi." Hudson points behind him where a table is filled with a stunning blonde family. Most of the table is filled with men, Hudson's brothers.

"We will," James says. "We need to get back to Tatum's family."

"Have fun, you two." Hudson grins, winking.

When we get back to the table, Patrick is beyond just having a drink; he's on the edge of drunk. Hammond's eyes meet James's over my shoulder, slightly shaking his head. James situates us so he's now sitting next to Patrick and I'm on the other side of him, blocked by his hulking frame.

Patrick chuckles darkly while the rest of my family tries to forget he's there. The courses are served as we chatter on, ignoring Patrick's remarks and grumbles.

James and I dance again after dinner, and I'm completely content being wrapped in his arms. We walk around the room hand in hand, both donating to scholarship organizations. Hudson keeps us entertained with his date and shenanigans.

James has found ways to touch me all night—gentle caresses, needy squeezes. I feel like I'm about to burst out of my skin if we don't leave soon.

I lean over to whisper in his ear, interrupting his conversation with Hammond. "I'm running to the ladies' room. Then let's leave."

He turns toward me, his eyes darkening as he nods. Patrick got up from the table after dinner and didn't return; it made the rest of the evening much more enjoyable.

Exiting the restroom, I'm putting my lipstick back in my bag when a hand reaches out, pulling me into a closet. A smile starts to stretch across my mouth when lips slam down on mine. I gasp, realizing this isn't James. It's Patrick.

My hands slam against his chest pushing him off with every ounce of strength I possess. I turn my head to the side forcing our lips to break apart.

"Tate," he mumbles against my skin, kissing just behind my ear.

"Get off me," I state firmly, futilely shoving against his chest and leaning as far away as I can, but my back is against a wall in this tiny closet.

"Tate, please." The alcohol on his breath is pungent and disgusting. It sends fear into my gut. I don't think Patrick would ever intentionally hurt me, but he seems out of his mind tonight.

"Patrick, get the fuck off me," I beg as I start to scratch against his neck, hoping to hurt him, so he gives me room to move away from him.

He backs up an inch, plucking the string hanging above him. A dim light comes on creating menacing shadows on his confused face. "Talk to me, Tate."

"No. Leave me alone." The inch of space he provided is just enough to shove my elbow into his gut, allowing me to make a break for it. I throw open the door, tumbling into the hallway.

Patrick recovers quickly, following me, grabbing my upper arm and spinning me so my back is against the wall and he's caging me in.

"Move," I hiss, pushing against him and lifting my foot to stomp down on his toes. Just like James taught me in the one self-defense class I took. Patrick's foot shifts to the side missing the contact. My bones quiver causing pain to shoot up my leg when my foot hits the hard tile floor.

"Talk to me," he says. "Just listen."

"What, Patrick? What?" My voice sounds shrill as I continue to push him. I've never felt this angry in my life.

I'm hoping the easiest way out of this will be to listen to his drunken ramble, and then I will make it clear that I have moved on and have no interest in any type of relationship with him—not even friendship. After that, I can forget about him. Every ounce of love I felt for him is gone. At this point, pinned against a wall and all the terrible things he's said over the past eight months running through my mind, I don't even wish him well. After this, he will no longer exist for me. He's destroyed me over the last two years, and I let him. The moment I meet someone and find my backbone he's back, and what? Interested again? *Bullshit.*

"I miss you," he says. "We belong together."

I laugh. I actually laugh like he's telling a joke. When I'm able to compose myself I speak clearly. "No, Patrick, we don't. You were right to end things before we got engaged or married. We're not right for each other."

"And he is?" Patrick growls. "That fucking lowlife is right for you?"

"Don't you dare speak about him like that." I lean forward, our noses an inch apart. My chest is heaving from the angry breaths. "Don't you fucking dare."

"He's uneducated. He can't take care of you." My head falls back to the wall.

"I don't need to be taken care of," I hiss, pushing against his chest once more. "This is done. We're over. I'm finally on board with it."

"No," Patrick growls, slamming his lips down on mine again. I push against him, beating on his chest, but he's stronger.

Suddenly he's ripped away from me. James is hovering over him with his hand around his throat. "Don't. Fucking. Touch. Her."

"Get off me," Patrick croaks, his hands pulling on James's hand that's still wrapped around his throat.

"Do not ever touch her," James repeats, his hand tightening. He pins Patrick against the wall so hard I hear Patrick's teeth smack together.

"James," I plead, putting my hand on his arm. He looks at me with so much rage in his eyes, but they soften when he takes me in, scanning me from head to toe.

"Are you okay?" All the ferocity has left his voice as he speaks to me. There's only concern and affection

I nod, rubbing my hand along his arm. "Let him go. I'm okay," I urge.

James lets up on his hold, but steps in front of me, effectively blocking me from Patrick's view. "I won't be so easy next time. If you touch her again, if you even fucking look her way—hell, if you even think about her, I will end you."

"She belongs with me," Patrick argues.

"Like hell she does," James barks, leaning into his space. I edge around James, wrapping my arm around his large bicep.

"Patrick, we will never get back together. You can't come over or send me flowers like you did today." I enunciate each word, making it as clear as I can that I have no interest in him.

"I didn't send flowers," he says. "But if I want to send flowers to my future wife, I will."

"I'm not your future anything, Patrick." I fold my hands in front of me as if I'm praying. "Please understand me, I don't want to be with you. This is over."

"This isn't over, Tate. You'll be mine again." Patrick pulls out a small red box, one I've seen before, from his pocket.

"Oh my god," I whisper, my eyes widening to the size of saucers. I back up a step, crashing into James, as Patrick sinks to the floor on one knee.

"Tatum, it's always been us. I was a fool. Marry me. Let's end this utterly stupid separation."

I start blinking fast, not even believing what is happening in front of me. Before I can answer James has hauled Patrick up to his feet and slams his fist into his face.

"You fucking propose to *my girl* in front of me? Are you serious?" James's fist connects with Patrick's gut and he falls against the wall from the force of it.

"James," I implore. "Stop. He's not worth it."

James's hand releases him, letting him fall to the floor. I step in front of Patrick, leaning over. "Don't ever speak to me again. I don't ever want to see you again. Unfortunately, I assume I will at our fathers' company parties. You no longer exist to me. You're nothing."

I stand back to my full height, my eyes still locked with Patrick's. He hasn't tried to say anything. He's only staring at me with countless emotions rolling across his face. I brush my hands over my dress. "In case that wasn't clear—my answer is no. My answer will always be no."

I turn on my heel and stride away. James falls into step next to me, wrapping his arm around my hips and pulling me tightly against him. His head bends down. "That was hot," he whispers.

My face turns toward him to see him smiling a brilliant smile.

When we reach the end of the hallway and turn the corner, James stops us, moving to stand in front of me and my face in his large hands. "Are you okay?"

"Yeah. I'm happy you showed up when you did." A broad grin takes over my face. "That felt so good. It felt *so* good to say that to him."

"Love that you got your chance, sunshine," he says matching my grin. "Wish I was there sooner. I can't believe he put his lips on you."

I shake my head and my lip curls in disgust. "I can't, either. I'm sorry that happened. I know it's not what we expected out of tonight or our arrangement."

"Our arrangement?" He asks taking a small step back as his hands fall to his sides.

"Yes, the just sex, nothing else." My eyes focus on my shoes while I say this.

James's finger tucks under my chin lifting my face to his.

"Tatum, we both know that it's more than that."

"Really?" I breathe, my chest expanding with newfound hope.

"Yes. It's so much more." James runs a hand through his hair. He closes his eyes, leaning his forehead against mine. "Come on. I want to get you home."

James makes it as simple as that, a few words and I'm irrevocably his.

As we're walking back to the table, Simon steps in front of me. James and I halt. Simon's eyes travel down my body until they lock on my hand in James's. His face flushes, and anger floods his features.

"Simon," I squeak while trying to pry my hand from James's strong grip, but he refuses to let go.

"Tate," he says, staring at our joined hands until a mask slips over his face. His lips are stretched into a fake smile. "Would you like to dance?"

"We're leaving," James says before I get a chance to respond.

"I asked you to save me a dance, Tate," Simon scolds.

"What? When?" I ask. "I didn't know you would be here."

"I sent you flowers," he says exasperatedly.

"Those were from you?" I ask nervously. This entire interaction is making my stomach turn.

"Who else would they be from?" Simon asks incredulously.

Did I walk into a different conversation? I feel like I'm missing something huge.

"Why are you sending my girl flowers?" James asks gruffly.

"She's not your girlfriend," Simon says, his fists balling at his sides.

"Pretty sure the fact that she's in my bed every night

implies differently."

"James," I hiss. I take a steadying breath before calmly speaking. "Simon, we're colleagues. That's all. I appreciate the flowers, they're beautiful, but inappropriate."

"You've been leading me on," Simon accuses.

"No, I haven't." I'm confused. Simon and I only interact when it's absolutely necessary.

James pulls me tighter to his side and moves us around Simon. I'm still in shock when I look over my shoulder to see Simon glaring at us.

"What the hell?" I murmur.

"He has a thing for you. Knew that from the second I saw him looking at you in the PT room."

"His behavior is still weird, though. He's asked me out a couple of times, but I've always said no. I avoid him as much as possible."

"Yeah," he says. "I thought you were sleeping with him, which was why he chose you."

"What?" I screech. "Yuck."

"Figured out you were too smart for that after about a minute." James smirks.

"He's never pressed when I've denied him," I remark.

"He stares at you constantly. I've seen him watching you in the room and in the halls."

I have noticed when he stares at me. It's not only me, though. It's every living, breathing female. So many images are flashing through my mind. Eating lunch in the breakroom with his eyes on me the entire time. Simon ignoring patients while trying to get my attention. Asking me for favors. A client switching to my service because he made them uncomfortable. A shudder rocks through me. He's a creep. "Yuck," I mutter.

"If he makes you uncomfortable at work, tell me," James says, coming to a stop and spinning me to face him. His hands come down on my arms, gently squeezing when I don't answer right away.

"He's harmless. Creepy, but harmless," I insist. "He stares at every girl."

"Just promise me."

"Fine," I groan, rolling my eyes. "I promise."

"This sounds fun," a voice laced with humor says. I glance toward it to find Hudson watching us in amusement. He steps forward, placing a kiss on my cheek. "What are you promising? Can I tell you again how lovely you look, Tate?"

I smile. "Thank you."

"Anytime, babe," he says, winking.

James squeezes my arms tighter, but nowhere near enough to hurt. "Go away," he growls at his best friend.

"James," I say, widening my eyes.

"Not until I know what she's promising," Hudson says. "Is it dirty? Please tell me it's dirty."

I lean my head into James's shoulder as I crack up. It's impossible not to find Hudson charming. He's a complete man-whore, but a lot of fun to be around.

"Never mind. I'll just imagine it's something dirty. Something really dirty with just me and Tate."

"Go away," James growls again. He doesn't wait for Hudson to walk away, he just pulls me after him, muttering to himself. "Three men in just a matter of minutes. Christ. Fuck."

He guides me out of the hotel after we say goodbye to my family. At James's insistence, the valet driver hands over James's keys and points us to where the car is parked. He backs me up against the door, leaning down and cupping my face in his hands.

"This is more," he says. He sucks in a breath and closes his eyes briefly before opening them and pinning me to the spot with a serious look, stopping the process of me turning into a puddle on the pavement. "This shouldn't go anywhere. My life is complicated. We should end this, but I can't. If I wasn't so damn selfish, I'd tell you to walk away now before this gets deeper, before you let me sink into your body again. I can't do that, though."

"I don't understand," I say wrapping my arms around his hips. My chin falling to the center of his chest.

"Not tonight," he says gliding his hands over my hair and down my back.

"I don't get why it shouldn't go somewhere. What we have is good, baby." I punctuate my words with my hands pressing into his back.

He smiles sadly. "Everything good slips away."

# CHAPTER
## THIRTY-ONE

*James*

MMM. BACON. THE DELICIOUS SCENT OF BACON sizzling in a pan wakes me up. My arm reaches over, feeling Tatum's empty spot before rubbing my hand over my face. Unable to keep my eyes open, I start to drift back to sleep when I feel a cool wetness against my cheek. The explosion of warmth in my chest surprises me. Smiling, I pop one eye open, expecting to see Tatum.

It's not.

Sirius's wet nose moves against my face as he sniffs me and tries to lick me. "No," I mumble. "Sorry, little man. No kisses for me." I pick him up and stand from the bed while keeping Sirius cradled against my chest. He wags his entire body happily. Sirius flops down on the bed when I place him there to pull on some shorts.

He jumps back into my hand when I lay it on the bed. At only a few pounds, he can fit in my palm. Every time I set my hand down, he hops into it like I'm his personal magic carpet ride. It's been over a month since we found him. I won't admit this to Tatum, but I actually enjoy having him here.

Tatum's in her scrubs with her hair piled on top of her head, standing in front of the stove. Her hips sway and she's singing along to the song playing from her phone. Her brother didn't lie. She's terrible, but still damn cute. I sneak up behind her, placing a hand on her hip and a kiss on her neck. The shriek that escapes her mouth makes my eardrums ring.

"Oh, my God," she breathes, spinning around to face me with her hand covering her heart. "You scared me."

I bend over, placing Sirius on the ground where he runs in circles around our feet. I give her a wry smile, which she barely catches when she leans over, petting the top of Sirius's fuzzy head and murmuring to him. "I had to get you to stop singing somehow."

"I sing like an angel," she says, standing and placing her hands on her hips.

"A fallen angel, maybe."

When she gasps, I take advantage of her open mouth. My hand wraps around the nape of her neck, holding her in place as I kiss her, my tongue sliding against hers. She reacts to me immediately, sinking against my chest, pressing up on her tiptoes, her hands wrapping around my back.

By the time our kiss breaks, we're both panting. Her eyes are dazed, still staring at my lips. I kiss her softly then step back, grabbing myself a cup of coffee while she turns back to the stove. "I'm making you breakfast," she says.

"Thanks. You didn't need to do that."

"We're celebrating." Tatum turns off the stove and starts to plate the food.

I grab silverware and our coffee cups, bringing them to the table. "We're celebrating?" I ask.

"Yes, it's your last day of PT." Tatum claps her hands together and bounces on the balls of her feet.

"And that's cause for a celebratory breakfast? For you, someone who hates waking up, to wake up early and cook me breakfast? It's worth that?" I rest my hand on the back of the chair staring at her, waiting for her answer.

"Yes," she says, grinning. "It's like getting a huge break-fast with pancakes, bacon, and all the good stuff on the first day of school. You know?"

I shake my head, taking a sip of my coffee as I sit down. "Nope."

Out of the corner of my eye, I see Tatum freeze. I glance up at her, wondering what's wrong. There's a pained expres-sion on her face as she stands there, holding our breakfast plates. I jump out of my seat, cupping her face. "What's wrong?"

She shakes her head as tears well in her eyes. "You never had that?"

I exhale a sigh of relief and brush my thumb along her cheek. "You're okay?"

She nods, staring into my eyes, breaking my heart with the tears that make the blue of her eyes even more crystal. "No, sunshine. I never had that."

"I should've realized that. I'm sorry I said anything." Her face turns toward the floor as she breathes deeply

"Don't." My finger tucks under her chin, lifting her face to mine.

"But—"

I cut her off with a quick kiss on her lips before sitting back down. "It's in the past."

She places the plates on the table, sitting in the chair next to me. Her lips are pursed, and her eyes are glued to her hands twisting in her lap. Tatum's fierce gaze meets mine, and her hand wraps around the back of my neck, trying to hold me in place so she can look in my eyes. "If I could, I'd give you everything you missed out on."

I push back from the table then snag her around the waist, bringing her to my lap and cupping her face. Her expression is so earnest. When it's time to walk away from this, I'm not going to want to let her go. I bring her forehead to mine then wrap her in a hug. Tatum's face nuzzles my neck, and mine is buried in hers, breathing in the jasmine scent. She's clutching me so tightly, as if she'll never let go. She leans back and presses her lips softly to mine.

"You don't need to worry about my childhood, Tatum," I whisper.

"I wish it was better," she says, fresh tears springing to her eyes. "It doesn't seem fair that I had an amazing childhood, and there are too many other kids like you out there who don't know some of the simplest pleasures."

I can't believe I ever thought this girl was anything but kind and generous. "It does suck that kids go through that, but don't be upset about my childhood. Not worth it. I'm here now. It wasn't all bad. My friend Callan made it better and when his little sister came along, we both tried to make hers better." My lips land on hers again. Disbelief swims in my gut. I haven't said Callan's name aloud in a long time. "Thank you for my celebratory breakfast."

"Maybe you should try getting in contact with Callan?" Tatum asks running her hand over the back of my head.

My hand spasms on her hip. "Can't."

"Why?"

"Let's just celebrate this morning," I request.

After a moment she smiles, kissing me before she slides back into her chair. The heaviness of the moment is slowly ebbing away as we eat in silence.

"I'm worried," Tatum says.

"About?" I ask, groaning around a mouth full of fluffy pancakes.

She wipes her mouth with her napkin, placing it on the table next to her plate before twisting in her seat and facing me. "Simon."

I stop chewing to look at her. "You think he's going to harass you?"

She twirls a loose strand of hair around her finger as her head tilts to the side as she thinks. "No. Not about that. I'm worried he's going to report me for seeing you."

"Is it against the rules?" I abandon the piece of bacon that I was about to eat and swing my torso around to face her completely.

"Not technically, but it's frowned upon."

"It's my last session today. I don't plan on being shot again anytime soon, so really, I won't be a patient anymore. It's a moot point."

"But—"

"Tatum, don't worry about it." I place my palms on her knees and slowly glide up to the top of her thighs. "We'll cross that bridge if it comes. We never did anything while you were at work. It was professional."

She nods. "Okay." She releases a huge sigh then glances at her phone. "I need to go or I'll be late." She starts to pick up her plate, but I stop her with a hand on her wrist.

"Go. I got this."

"Thanks. I'll see you soon." She leans over, kissing me. Before she can pull away, I slide my hand into hers, deepening our kiss.

"Thank you for breakfast, sunshine."

Her eyes melt as she bites her lip. "You're welcome."

"I'll see you soon. Go." I slap her ass as she bends down, scooping Sirius off the floor to nuzzle his neck, making her giggle. His bright pink tongue is sticking out just a bit, making him look like he's smiling while soaking up her attention.

After Tatum leaves, I take care of the dishes and Sirius before hopping in the shower to get ready for my appointment.

※

Tatum is already in the physical therapy room when I walk in a couple hours later. She's bent over, her ass high in the air, making my cock stir in my shorts. I grit my teeth, redirecting my mind so everyone doesn't get a show. I avert my eyes from her body. We're so close to the finish line of these sessions. They've been difficult to get through when she's that close to me and I can't touch her the way I want to.

As I'm looking around the room, anywhere but at Tatum, I notice Simon is in the corner, watching her. His focus is trained so hard on her ass, he isn't blinking at all. His features are filled with rage. My veins turn ice cold as dread sinks in my gut. Getting rid of him isn't going to be easy. Tatum thinks he's harmless, but I think he's toeing the line of insanity.

I quicken my steps, placing my body between Tatum and Simon. With my back to Tatum, I send a furious glower at Simon. His eyes break contact and slide up until they meet mine. I can't see, but I'm sure his jaw is ticking. Sucking in a huge breath and causing his chest to rise, he balls his hands into fists as he turns toward his patient.

"Hey," Tatum says from behind me. I turn toward her, still upset that Simon is even near her. "Ready for your last appointment?" She dances a little jig with a bright smile on her face.

"He was staring at you," I grumble.

"What?" she asks, looking around the room until her eyes land on Simon. "Oh."

"Yeah."

"Not here," she whispers.

"If he comes near you, call me right away."

"James." She sighs.

"If he comes near you, call me right away," I repeat.

"Fine," she says, rolling her eyes. "Let's start with some shoulder rolls."

"Hilarious," I mutter.

"I know," she says sweetly. "We're going to run through our normal routine. Then I'm going to have you lift some weights, just to make sure you're not feeling any pain."

"Let's get it over with."

"How do you feel?" Tatum asks after I drop a weight to the floor. We ran through our final routine and I've spent the last twenty minutes lifting weights.

I smile. "Great."

She sticks out her hand, beaming. "Congratulations! You've graduated Tatum Rothschild's school of physical therapy."

My hand slides into hers, letting her shake my hand. I use our joined hands to pull her closer to me—closer than a patient would normally stand to their therapist. "Does that mean I can kiss you now?"

"No," she says, shaking her head as she bites her lip trying not to grin.

"Celebratory kiss?" I coax, pulling her just a little bit closer until I can smell jasmine and her breath hitches.

"No," she repeats, laughing, pushing against my chest with her free hand.

"Come over when you get off," I whisper, leaning close to her.

Her breathing picks up as a saucy grin stretches across her face. "Will you get *me* off later?"

"Yes," I groan, desperately wanting to haul her against my body, sink into her warmth, and consume her.

"I'll see you tonight," she whispers with heated eyes.

# CHAPTER
## THIRTY-TWO

### James

L IKE A KID AT *CHRISTMAS* IS A CLICHÉ TERM I UNDERSTAND logically, but never experienced for myself. There wasn't ever a rush of anticipation of what would be waiting for me under the tree. The big guy in the red suit spreading his cheer for all to hear never came.

I finally get it. The thrill of knowing that something you've wanted and waited for is waiting for you, too. My lips are spread widely in an uncomfortable smile I'm not used to. My hands on the wheel are tapping out a steady beat while I stare at the last red light between me and the one thing I've been missing.

The force of slamming on the gas sends me jolting back into my seat when the light turns green. The bright white sign with red and black letters standing at the edge of the driveway to the gym is calling me home.

One hundred feet.

The same excitement I feel when Tatum is taking off her shirt rushes through my stomach.

Fifty feet.

When Tatum is naked in front of me, I never know where to caress first. Each part of her is as enticing as the next. I don't know where I'll go first or if I'll bounce around, tasting everything.

I pull into this parking lot every single day. As soon as I was released from the hospital, I was back here, manning my space, watching the equipment move and click was just a tease. No more. Today is the day.

The cold air hits me in the face the moment I step inside the gym. Everything from the huge, bright LEDs overhead to the faint smell of sweat from hard work is refreshing.

"Heads up," I call out as I throw my bag toward the reception desk, not even pausing to see if it hit Trevor, the guy working at the counter. He'll store it for me. My energy and focus are trained on what workout or machine I'll choose first.

An ear-splitting whistle breaks over the noise. Hudson is leaning against a pole near the boxing ring with a grin as big as mine. "Up for some celebratory sparring?" He tosses me my gloves.

"Fuck, yeah," I say, catching the gloves.

"Sure you're up for it? How're ya feeling?" Hudson pulls his own gloves from the bag at his feet, but keeps his eyes trained on me.

"I'm feeling like I want to kick your ass," I mutter as I drop into a stretch. I quietly add, "thanks for being here."

"Wouldn't miss it, brother. Let's get you back to work, you're looking a little soft around the edges. You're going from Incredible Hulk to Marshmallow Man." Hudson's shoulders are shaking with silent laughter as he laughs at his own joke. I grab a towel from the bench closest to me, ball it up, and toss it at his head.

A few minutes later Hudson and I are suited up and facing off in the ring, both of us grinning like fools. He bounces on the balls of his feet, shaking out his arms while glancing around the room—always loving an audience, no matter what he's doing.

I'm his opposite. I'll gladly hide in the shadows for the rest of my damn life.

Hudson and I circle each other, neither taking the first swing. My arms are up, ready to block, waiting him out. I'm bigger and I'm faster. If I want to really test if I'm truly ready to be back here, I need him to swing first and leave a tiny opening of weakness. Speed and power.

"Need me to go easy on you? I'd hate to hurt you. You haven't touched any weights in weeks. You're looking a little scrawny, like a delicate little flower," Hudson taunts.

I step closer, tightening our revolving circle. *Come on. Swing. I know you want to.* My shoulder drops slightly and my hand moves just a fraction of an inch, but I smirk knowing it's enough. He doesn't need to know I just lifted weights.

Hudson swings a split second before I do, and his body is open just enough for a solid punch to his side.

Victory.

"Oof," Hudson groans, but the tilt of his lips broadens. "That what you wanted?"

I cock an eyebrow, sending a jab toward him again. He blocks it, bouncing on his feet. "Stop taking it easy," I demand. His first and only punch wasn't easy, but his eyes have been falling to my shoulder every other second since my first swing. For as laid-back and easy-going as Hudson is, no one would suspect that he's actually annoyingly caring.

We circle each other three more times before a voice breaks our concentration.

"You're not any help to him if you keep babyin' him."

Roman stands with his arms crossed over his chest and Harper by his side. Two brown paper bags sit at their feet. Roman looks like he's ready to step into the ring, but Harper is in a dress and heels, looking perfectly put together, as usual.

I grunt, covering my stomach with my gloved hand and whipping my head back to Hudson. He grins, waggling his eyebrows. "Never take your eye off your opponent. Show me what you got." He claps his gloves together before motioning me forward with one.

Slowly, the rest of the group arrives to congratulate me, each man stepping into the ring with me. A peace settles in my chest each time I look over at my friends on the other side of the ropes and remember Tatum will be coming over tonight. Right at this moment, I have everything a man could ever need.

I made it through a couple rounds with Liam, Roman, Hudson, and Kiernan, but I know I need to work on my stamina and strength to get back to where I was. My muscles are burning, and it feels fucking fantastic.

Sweat soaks my shirt when I hop out of the ring, my feet landing firmly on the floor. My racing heart swells with pride knowing I can fucking do this shit again. In the grand scheme of things, it hasn't been that long, but each day dragged when I was here unable to workout.

Harper steps up to me with a sheen in her eyes while she rubs her belly. She's just started to really show, no denying that she is really pregnant. Every time I see her, guilt consumes me. She could've lost her baby easily that night. I should've had more of a guard up, maybe it would've turned out differently. Maybe I wouldn't have been shot.

But then I wouldn't have met Tatum.

I swallow, bringing up a dry patch of my shirt to wipe across my face, and force myself to refocus. Every moment spent with Tatum makes those two bullets worth it.

"I'm so happy you're back where you belong, James." Harper's tone is quiet and thoughtful.

"Thanks. Happy to be done with physical therapy."

She takes a deep breath before crashing into me,

hugging me around my waist, but retreating just as quickly, pinching her nose. "Make sure you shower if you're going to see Tatum tonight."

Hudson lets out a delighted laugh, loving anything that has to do with ribbing me.

"Hilarious," I mutter.

Harper bends down, reaching into the brown paper bag, and pulls out a food carrier before standing and grinning at me. "We really are so appreciative of everything you helped us with a few months ago and so happy that you're now fully healed. This is for you." She hands it to me.

When I take it and look down, my stomach grumbles. Cake. Harper makes the best desserts, especially cake. I open the lid to find a perfectly round cake with white frosting and sprinkles all over the top. It's small, meant for just one or two people. I won't have any issues finishing this off. I close the lid, looking back up at Roman and Harper. Roman's arm hangs over Harper's shoulders, and he's staring down at her with a sappy look on his face that makes me want to laugh.

"It's a protein cake," Harper says and hands me the other bag. "This is a normal, non-strong person cake for Tate."

A chuckle breaks free from my chest. "Thanks, Harper."

"Want to go get a beer?" Liam asks. "Or dinner? Our treat."

I shake my head, a smirk pulling at my lips. "Not tonight."

"Why?" Savannah asks.

"Have plans with Tatum," I say, turning away from them and snagging a water bottle from the nearby refrigerator.

"She can come," Hudson says, laughing to himself and enjoying his dirty mind.

"Fuck off," I say dryly.

"She's always welcome to join us," Savannah says sweetly.

"Not what he meant, gorgeous," Liam says quietly in her ear.

Savannah pushes Hudson's shoulder. "When you meet someone, I hope they knock you on your ass."

I glance at the large clock above the entrance of the gym. It's later than I thought. Tatum will get out of work soon, and I want to have dinner started by the time she shows up.

"See y'all later," I say waving to the guys and dropping a kiss on Savannah's and Harper's cheek.

"Have fun with your girlfriend," Hudson calls after me.

I flip him off over my shoulder.

# CHAPTER
# THIRTY-THREE

*Tatum*

B UTTERFLIES BUZZ AROUND IN MY STOMACH AS I PULL up James's long driveway to his house nestled in the center of his property. This isn't a relationship, that's fully established by both of us, but I can't deny that every time I even think of him, my stomach flips over itself and my heart takes off at a gallop.

The butterflies are worse right now because of what I have to tell him.

My knuckles tap on James's back door.

"Come in," he calls.

I walk through his mudroom into his kitchen and stop breathing, every thought flying out of my head. Right now, it doesn't matter what I need to tell him, right now the only thing that matters is what's in front of me.

Sirius is perched on James's broad shoulder, easily curled up there. I have no clue how he's balancing, but he is. My heart squeezes tightly when a tiny puppy snore escapes Sirius with his face pressed into James's neck.

The tight, white shirt hugging James's body showcases his muscles. The material is so thin I can see each muscle flex as he moves in front of the stove. His jeans are low on his hips, showing off his amazing ass. This image would be perfect for one of those Hot Guy With Dog pictures.

His head turns over his shoulder as he raises one eyebrow. I release my pent-up breath, my heart restarting before he turns around slowly, keeping a hand on Sirius. James crosses his arms over his chest, and the corner of his lips twitch. My eyes roll over every inch of him. The bright and bold tattoos on his arms look even bolder against the stark white of his shirt.

"Hi." My voice comes out squeaky and unsure as my twitching hand curls my hair behind my ear, and I bite down on my lower lip.

James takes three long strides toward me, pulling my lip from my teeth and raising my chin using one of his knuckles. His gray eyes are melting. I reach up, taking Sirius from James's shoulder and put him on the ground. My arms circle around James's hips as I press up on my tippy-toes and lean into him.

He doesn't hesitate. Full lips cover mine in a searing kiss. My hands fist in his shirt, trying to bring him closer to me, trying to mold my body into his impossibly hard one. James wraps one arm around my lower back, pressing me against him and lifting my feet slightly off the ground; his other hand tangles in my hair.

I gasp from the slight pull, and he takes the opportunity to plunge his tongue into my mouth. My feet fall back to the floor, and the hand anchored on my back slides down, cupping my ass as James leans into me. His clean, masculine scent surrounds me, every inch of me is touching some part of him, and I still need more.

Sirius's barking breaks our kiss. James places one more soft kiss against my lips before resting his forehead against mine, breathing heavily. My senses slowly come back to life, taking in everything that isn't James.

"Spaghetti?" I ask, smelling the marinara simmering and garlic bread baking.

"Yeah." James's voice is gruff. He steps back from me, coughing. "That okay?"

"Of course," I answer. "I love spaghetti. Or anything with carbs, really."

James shakes his head, bending down and scooping up Sirius to place him back on his shoulder as he turns to the pots on the stove.

I smirk, biting my tongue to keep from laughing. "I have some good news."

"Yeah?"

"Yeah. I talked to my landlord," I lie. "He'll make an exception since Sirius is so small. I can take him home with me."

James spins around with one hand holding Sirius in place. His face is a mask of outrage and confusion while Sirius's small, pink tongue is hanging out with his head tipped to the side and his tail wagging madly.

"No," James says.

"No?" I force a frown to my face.

He swallows, looking out the window over the sink before meeting my eyes again. "I just mean...I don't want to put you out. Your landlord doesn't want animals. What if he changes his mind? Best if he stays here."

"I'll take him. I know you didn't want a dog."

James brings Sirius from his shoulder to cradle him against his chest like a baby.

I roll my lips between my teeth, struggling to keep the laughter at bay, but my shoulders are shaking slightly. "I'll take him," I repeat.

I swear James clutches Sirius even tighter to his chest. "You don't have a yard."

"There's a dog park around almost every corner."

"That's dangerous at night."

"I have a small enough patch of grass for him to use at night."

"I read on the internet that dogs shouldn't be disrupted and moved from home to home. They could get sick."

"What else did you read on the internet?" I ask, covering my mouth with my hand to hide my twitching lips.

James is petting Sirius's head, his hand almost as big as Sirius's whole body. A spark lights in James's eyes and his lips tilt up. I've never seen him vibrate with this much energy.

"Watch this," he says, setting Sirius on the ground.

Sirius runs around James's feet, his whole body wiggling with excitement when James grabs a canister from his counter that I've never noticed before. He opens it and reaches inside. "Sirius. Sit."

Sirius plops down immediately, staring up at James with his mouth open. James tosses a treat from the canister in the air, and it lands perfectly in Sirius's waiting mouth.

"Do you want a treat?" James asks.

Sirius raises his front arms, balancing on his butt and waves his tiny arms in front of him. As soon as he drops his feet back on the ground, he opens his mouth with his face tilted up, and James tosses the treat in.

James looks at me out of the corner of his eye then focuses back on Sirius. He makes a gun with his fingers. James creates a shooting noise with his mouth, and Sirius shakes then spins in a circle before dropping dramatically to the ground with his eyes closed.

Sirius pops one eye open, looking up at James. "Up." He tosses two treats in the air that Sirius happily catches.

James faces me again with his eyebrows raised.

"You should probably keep him," I say with a broad smile and start clapping frantically. "That was fantastic."

I rush across the kitchen to James, reaching for his lips

on my tippy-toes. "You're something else." After a brief kiss, I bend down rubbing Sirius on his head cooing about what a good boy he is.

"If it helps you out, I'll keep him here," James says, shrugging. I don't miss the grin that he tries to hide by spinning back toward the stove. "Dinner's ready."

James picks up his fork once he sits down, ready to dig in. I take a deep breath, knowing I need to tell him about the rest of my day. His fork is halfway to his mouth when he pauses, glancing at me. The fork slowly lowers toward to the plate and hovers as he lifts his eyebrows and his jaw tightens.

"Tatum." The one word, my name, is a warning. One to which I heed.

"Simon reported me to his uncle, my boss. Well, reported us, I guess."

"What?" James half-shouts, his fork clattering to the plate. "Fuckin' prick. What happened?"

I rub a hand over my heart, feeling my chest rise and fall with my deep breath. "Thankfully, nothing *too* bad. It really freaked me out, though."

James cups my cheek in his large hand. I lean against his hand, closing my eyes for a moment before opening them and meeting his worried stare. "Sunshine," he whispers.

I give him a tight smile. "I was pulled into the director's office this afternoon. I've never been pulled into the principal's office or my boss's office."

James's lips twitch. "Of course, you haven't."

"They reminded me that a relationship with a patient is frowned upon, but since you're technically no longer a patient, they wrote me up instead of firing me."

James's body tightens, the hand still cupping my cheek twitches, and his eyes fill with anger. "That fucking weasel. I'll—"

"No," I interrupt. "You won't do anything. If you ever

need more physical therapy, you can't do it with me, but it's over. I'll continue to ignore Simon. After I was pulled into the office, he started to ignore me, anyway. He got what he wanted after I rejected him."

"He wanted to get back at you."

"I know."

"I'm sorry, sunshine," James says. "Really I think he wants to get back at me, but he has no opening for that."

"It's okay," I respond, releasing a shaky breath. "It sucks, but it's no longer an issue. It's done. Let's eat."

"If I need more physical therapy, we'll do it at home," James states, his thumb caressing my cheek one last time before dropping his hand. He picks up his fork and begins digging into his food as if he didn't just rock my world.

*We'll do it at home.*

*Home.*

# CHAPTER
# THIRTY-FOUR

*Tatum*

J AMES AND I ARE SITTING ON HIS HUGE, BROWN LEATHER sofa in front of the TV with steaming cups of coffee. Sirius is curled on James's shoulder, sleeping and snoring tiny little puppy snores. My side is fully molded to his with my head resting on his free shoulder. He has an arm wrapped around me with his hand on my hip, tracing tiny designs on the patch of skin showing.

"I can't believe Savannah is going to be on the news," I say.

"Yeah," James says with a tiny, proud smile.

"This is going to be huge for her company."

"It is," James says. "No one deserves it more."

James hasn't told me anything about their relationship, but I know they have an incredibly deep bond, and he helped her out with something from her past. I haven't wanted to pry, but I really want to know the story.

Savannah's stunning face appears on the screen. She looks fantastic in a dress that shows off her adorable baby bump. A startup tech company in Austin hired her to do all their marketing. When the company exploded and reached a high level of success, they accredited it all to Savannah's efforts. Her phones have been ringing off the hook with potential new clients.

James and I watch the entire segment. I'm almost jumping in my seat, I'm so excited for her. I know both of us will need to leave for work shortly, but I love that I've met this crazy group of people, and I get to share in their success. Savannah gives Harper's boutique a shout-out, which I know Harper will love. I'm so proud of these friends of mine.

When her segment is over and the news channel starts talking about breaking news out of Chicago, James tenses next to me. I reach for the remote on the coffee table, but he stops me. "Don't."

"Recently, Texas Congressman Phillip McKay's son, Phillip McKay Junior, was arrested, suspected of arson. While the police searched his home with a warrant, they found video evidence of six fires and explosions from around the country for which he is now being investigated. An explosion at a restaurant in Chicago several years ago is the first incident in the video evidence retrieved from McKay's home. As far as police have gathered, they suspect McKay set up video surveillance and then watched from somewhere remotely. In each fire, a state representative died."

"Oh my gosh. We just saw him. He was at the gala, do you remember?" I ask James, but he doesn't answer. His entire body has turned to stone as he stares at the screen with huge eyes.

A video appears on the screen of an upscale restaurant in Chicago. The camera looks like it was set up on the ceiling in the corner of the room. Nothing distinct in the video can be heard over the chatter of the restaurant. All of a sudden, an explosion happens, sending the entire restaurant up in flames, and the video goes black.

"Oh, my God," I whisper. "That's terrible."

# CHAPTER
# THIRTY-FIVE

*James*

A VISE SQUEEZES MY CHEST AND THROAT. I CAN'T breathe.

The news station is playing the video of the explosion on a top-floor Chicago restaurant. Sitting in the middle of the frame near a set of windows is a table with a man in a suit and an empty seat across from him.

Even though this video is about a decade old, it's pretty clear. The faces are easily recognized. And there he sits—Dennis Moore, a senator of Illinois. Unless a person was paying close attention, no one would be able to tell he's irritated and anxious. My eyes don't stray from that table, though. He glances at his watch and looks around the room, his eyes fixating on the elevator while his leg bounces and fingers drum on the table.

And just as quickly as the flames engulf the restaurant, the feed goes black.

My eyes are still seeing the flames taking over everything, leaving people to burn alive on the top floor of one of Chicago's skyscrapers, where a senator sat waiting for someone.

Waiting for me.

I shove off from the couch, my heart racing out of my chest and panic clawing up my throat. Tatum needs to get out of here. I can't even look at her right now. She'll ask too many questions I can't answer.

"I need to get ready for work," I grumble, picking up my coffee cup and snatching hers out of her hands.

A surprised gasp leaves her mouth.

"You should go," I say, walking away.

"Are you kicking me out?"

I don't turn around. "I need to get ready, Tatum." Moving toward my bedroom, I head into the bathroom, closing the door.

"James?" she asks through the door.

I close my eyes, hating the hurt in her voice, but this is something I can't handle right now. I feel like I'm crawling out of my skin. Turning the knob to open the door a crack, I lean out, placing a quick kiss on her lips. "I'll call you. I need to leave quickly. See you later," I say before closing the door, effectively kicking her out.

A moment later, I hear the front door close. Shaking my head, unable to process the emotion I saw in her eyes, I leave the bathroom and walk to the front of the house, checking to make sure she's gone before I lock the door and head into my room again walking straight into my closet and through a door hidden behind my clothes.

I cover my mouth with my hand and take a few breaths before bringing the monitors of my computer alive.

In the past several years, I've taught myself how to hack, code, and gather information I need without being detected. Before I left Chicago, Luca talked about bringing the mafia online, modernizing the game. When I successfully found and hacked into the system he created, I made it a habit to check weekly, if not daily, for any mention of my name. I skim and ignore any business dealings, that's shit I don't need to know.

I only look for my name and Callan's. Reading information about him is the only way I know he's safe.

The monitors light up the dark room. My fingers fall on the keys of the keyboard. I grit my teeth as I get down to work.

I need to know if my time is up.

# CHAPTER
## THIRTY-SIX

*Tatum*

**B**USY.

That's the only word I've heard from James in a week. My texts and calls went unanswered until I stopped texting and calling—when I finally got the point he was trying to make.

He's done.

He's done with me.

I'm not going to walk out on a limb and embarrass myself even more. I know he's said from the beginning that this can't last, that this will eventually be over. One word, though. I didn't think it would end with one word and then nothing.

I thought he'd at least talk to me, try to stay friends for the sake of the rest of the group. The group I'm supposed to meet up with tonight. There's no way that's happening. I can't see him right now.

I can't hear in front of the group how or why he's done with me. Things changed between us after the gala and now this? It's over this quickly? He's removed me from his life that easily?

I've broken down several times this week, but I'm trying to stop. I read too much into his words and situations. It wasn't going anywhere. I force myself to replay the way he kicked me out of his house while barely even looking at me.

That's what I need to focus on.

Not the way he held me.

Not the way he kissed me.

Not the way he said this was more.

No, the cold, aloof James is back. The James I didn't like. The James that annoyed me. Our physical therapy sessions are done, so I don't have to see him. If I want to see the girls, I can call them, have a strict girls' night, no boys allowed.

It's not only James that I miss. I miss Sirius, too. Does James realize when he cut me out, he was cutting me off from him, too? The dog that we found together? The one he's keeping only at my insistence?

If I ignore the gaping hole in my chest, it will go away. Right?

I message Savannah to let her know that I won't make it tonight. She doesn't need to know why, only that I won't be there.

While James has successfully avoided me through the week, I've been avoiding Simon until today.

"Tate."

My head pops up from the patient chart I'm working on. I'm in the break room at one of the lunch tables. Simon is at the table opposite me, leaning down on it.

"Simon," I mutter, my eyes falling back to the chart as I continue making notes and trying to ignore his presence. We haven't spoken in a long time. I don't know why he's trying to talk to me now.

"What time are you getting off?" His tone is friendly and open as if we gab with each other all the time.

"After my last appointment," I retort, not bothering to look his way.

"What time?" he asks again, an irritated tone replacing

the friendly one he used only moments earlier.

"I'm working after hours, so no telling." I shrug.

"I'll see you later," he says. "I want to apologize and be friends."

My hands start trembling from rage. The pen scrapes across the chart, marking through some of my notes. "Simon," I say as firmly as I can manage. "We'll never be friends. You reported me because I turned you down for a date. If you need to speak to me about a patient, fine. Anything else, don't bother. I don't want to talk to you."

Simon spins on his heel and stomps off. How could he think anything else would happen besides that? Did he think I'd leave James and jump into his arms after he reported me?

I take my phone out of my pocket to call James. It rings twice before going to voicemail. When the tone sounds prompting me to leave a message, I open my mouth to ask him to call me. To tell him Simon approached me. Anything. I want to hear his voice and feel his warm hand cupping my cheek. I want to watch his smile light up his entire face, transforming him into something entirely too beautiful.

Instead, I take the hint. I release a breath, snap my mouth shut, and hang up.

The rest of my day is spent in a state of annoyance. I feel like a stretching band that has been pulled too tight and is starting to fray. By the time I leave work, my patience is worn so thin, I worry I'll snap at the next person that even tries to speak to me.

Maybe I should go to The Cellar tonight and enjoy the company of friends. I could show James I'm not hurting. It'd be a total lie, but I could pretend. If I could, I'd strut into The Cellar and take out all my frustration on him, but I can't do that.

Most likely I'd walk in, his gorgeous gray eyes would lock on mine, and I'd fall apart right there. In the middle of a bar. In front of everyone.

So, no. Not going.

Instead I head to one of my favorite restaurants. It's cozy in the bar area with large, cushy, leather chairs in front of fireplaces, which is perfect for the weather outside. Each day is getting cooler and cooler. I've started to break out my scarves and boots.

"Just one?" the hostess asks when I step up.

*Just one.* That's me. One. Singular. Alone. Lonely.

"Yes. In the bar, please, if there's room."

"Right this way."

I follow the hostess through the large entry to the bar area. She walks me toward two inviting chairs facing a fireplace. It's perfect. Secluded and alone, just what I need for tonight. I don't need to share this crazy mood with anyone.

I watch the flames dance as I think about James. I don't know what happened or what went wrong. From the beginning, we agreed this wouldn't last, but I thought that had changed. It's definitely changed. At least for me, it has. Wrapped up in James's strong hold is my favorite place in the world to be.

The waiter interrupts my thoughts when he approaches. I quickly order an entrée and a glass of wine. When he returns with my wine, I take a large sip, relishing the warmth as it flows through me.

"I ordered a bottle of wine. I'd love to split it with a beautiful woman," I hear from next to me.

I flick my eyes up to the man intruding on my alone time. "No, thanks." My gaze moves back to the fire in front of me.

The man sits in the chair beside me, placing the bottle on the table. The annoyance from my day rises to irritation. "That wasn't an invitation."

"Someone as beautiful as you needs company. I'm

Calvin." He smiles showing off perfect white teeth.

"I don't need company. I'm trying to enjoy a nice evening alone." I readjust in my chair, cutting him off with my back turned slightly toward him.

Calvin goes for another attempt, not understanding that he's not being charming, only frustrating. A voice from behind interrupts him—"Get lost."

Relief courses through my system. I turn around to see my brother, and a grin spreads across my face.

Calvin raises his hands in surrender and slinks away. Hammond watches him go with his jaw locked before lowering himself into the seat next to mine.

"Hey, sis," he greets with a smile.

"Hey," I say, trying to force some cheer into my voice, but it falls flat.

"What's going on?" His smile slides away, morphing into a frown.

I start to say 'nothing,' but stop when tears flood my eyes, and I find myself confessing all to my brother. Between my rants, he supplies me with alcohol, listening to everything I say intently without giving much feedback.

A few hours later, all the air leaves my lungs when I'm lifted from the bed.

# CHAPTER
# THIRTY-SEVEN

## *James*

M Y HEART STOPS BEATING WHEN HAMMOND'S name shows on the screen of my phone. It's late. Tatum didn't show at The Cellar tonight. Images of Savannah stabbed and bloody flash in my mind. Harper crying as everything was taken from her. I can't watch someone else I care about get hurt. Fuck.

"What happened to Tatum?" I say in lieu of a greeting.

"That guy she works with broke into her house," Hammond says.

"On my way. She's coming with me," I growl, hanging up and running to my SUV to get my girl.

---

Tatum's eyes fly open when I lift her from the bed. Fear and surprise shine through until she realizes it's just me.

"James," she says in a surprised voice. She blinks rapidly staring at my face as if I'm about to disappear.

"Sunshine," I greet, bringing her tighter to my chest.

She sputters, looking around, searching for something to say.

"We'll talk when we get home, Tatum," I whisper, kissing her cheek. Her eyes widen again when my lips press to her skin. Fuck. I hate what I've done to her this week. I missed her.

"I can walk," she says, crossing her arms over her chest and wiggling to get out of my hold.

My grip tightens even further. "Nope. I just found out some lunatic broke into your house. I'm keeping you right here."

"What?" The word comes out on a shocked gasp.

"Hammond called me," I say as I stop walking and stare at her.

"Someone broke into my house?" she asks, baffled. Her hand comes up to clutch her throat and her eyes widen. "How do you know? What happened?"

"About that," Hammond says, grinning broadly and leaning against the wall at the end of the hallway. "I lied."

"You lied," Tatum repeats, staring at her brother from my arms. She tries to drop again, but my fingers dig into her skin, keeping her body pressed into my chest where I can feel every inch of her and smell her scent.

"Yep," Hammond responds. "Y'all need to talk. I like y'all together. Figured if he thought you were in danger, he'd get here as fast as possible. And if he didn't, then he definitely wouldn't be worth more tears. It's also hunting season, Pop Pop and I would've dragged him into the woods."

My eyes fly to Tatum at the mention of her tears. My stomach turns, knowing I did that to her, made her feel that way.

"Simon didn't break into your house?" A humorless chuckle leaves my mouth as I ask my question.

"Uh, no," Tatum says, glaring at her brother.

"Right," I respond, hustling out the door before Tatum can start arguing about it.

"Thanks a lot," she hisses sarcastically when we pass her brother. She's no longer struggling in my arms, but she's avoiding my eyes.

"What are brothers for, besides getting you rip-roaring drunk and reuniting you with your boyfriend? You'll thank me later. A good scotch will do the trick."

"I'll be paying you back for this," she says over my shoulder as I walk through the door. "It won't be in scotch, though."

Hammond laughs, closing the door right as I walk through it.

I dump Tatum in the front seat of the car, closing her door, and going to the driver's side. We're quiet on the short drive to my house. Tatum is fiddling with the ring on her finger and playing with the vents, unable to sit still. When we pull up to my house, she turns to me. "I'll walk myself inside."

I chuckle, shaking my head. "Walk straight to bed."

"I'm not getting in bed with you," she says, rearing her head back. She's pissed I even suggested it.

"Why not?"

"One word. That's all I've heard from you in a week. And you show up like some white knight? No, absolutely not. Does Uber come this far?"

"Let's go inside," I say, hopping out of the SUV and walking her to the door. Tatum glares at me as she passes by me and takes a seat on the couch, cocking her eyebrow in a challenge.

The couch works just fine. I can hold her on the couch. That's why I wanted her in my bed, I want to hold her to know that she's okay. When Hammond called, something in me snapped. I can't avoid what's happening between us. With Tatum in my life there may be more added danger or unknowns, but I'll do anything to keep her safe.

I sit next to her inching closer to her until our bodies are flush. My arm glides along the soft leather until it's fully behind Tatum.

"Tell me what happened," she demands, crossing her arms over her chest and trying to move away from me. She's pinned between me and the armrest, so there's nowhere for her to go.

I don't answer, and Tatum's eyes search mine before filling with tears. I wrap my arms around her, holding her to my chest. "I got you."

She cries harder, clutching my shirt, and I repeat myself. "I'm sorry, sunshine."

"Why didn't you call me?" she asks with a bite in her tone, releasing my shirt from her hands, and lifting her head from my chest.

I brush her hair from her face, wanting to kick my own ass for being so wrapped up in my past that I froze her out. "I'm sorry for being a dick to you."

She scoffs. "That doesn't answer my question."

"Tatum," I say, urging her to look at me. "Seeing Chicago on the news brought up some stuff I didn't want to deal with. I acted like an ass. I'm so sorry. I missed you this week."

"I missed you, too," Tatum admits reluctantly. She lays her head on my shoulder, wrapping her arms around me. "I'm still mad at you, but I'm tired and I missed being right here. It's the only reason I'm resting on your chest. I didn't understand what happened. I thought it was your way of breaking up with me."

"Fuck," I groan, swiping my hand down my face. I fucked up so bad. "I've never had this. I'm used to being alone. I'm sorry I made you question things. I should've told you I had my mind on other stuff and needed a few days to sort my shit. I'll make it up to you, sunshine."

"What were you thinking about?" Her quiet question makes my throat close.

"Another night." My arms band around her tighter,

worried she'll get up since I'm not telling her right now. I fear I'll have to eventually. I don't know what that will mean for her safety.

"Do you promise?" One of her arms drops from my waist as she lays a hand on my thigh, drawing patterns.

"Yes," I reply, hoping I'm not lying to her.

"If you want this to end, you need to tell me. The waiting for your call or text and the blatant rejection is what hurt the most. Maybe I shouldn't, because as you know, I let Patrick walk all over me, but I want to forgive you. Please don't make me regret it."

I kiss the top of her head. "Fuck, I don't want this to end. What the hell did I do to deserve you? You won't regret it, sunshine. I'll never make you regret giving me another chance. I hate that I hurt you."

She nods, nuzzling deeper into my shoulder.

I slide my arm under her knees, lifting her off the couch to bring her to bed. I hold her close to me, nuzzling her neck and kissing the soft skin there. "I've never felt the way I did when Hammond called to tell me Simon broke into your house. I needed to see you with my own eyes, touch you myself, to make sure you're okay."

She turns so she's facing me, her delicate fingers brushing over my cheek. I tilt my head into her palm, savoring her touch.

"It didn't happen. I'm here now," she whispers, reassuring me. I swallow, hating myself just a bit more. I'm the one who fucked up and now I have her in my arms and she's comforting me. Her heart is huge and welcoming, forgiving me without a big fight. I'll cherish this until I stop breathing, no matter where I end up.

"I know. I won't let it happen. You're safe with me, Tatum. I got you."

# CHAPTER
# THIRTY-EIGHT

*Tatum*

"**A**RE YOU SURE YOU DON'T WANT TO COME?" James asks.

"Yeah," I say, smiling. "You've been a maniac since finishing PT. I definitely don't want to run or work out with you."

He winks. "Unless it's in bed?"

"Exactly," I say, shivering as I remember the night before. James's eyes turn molten, holding me to my spot as I stand in his room wearing only his shirt.

He groans.

"Go. You really need to. You got soft with all that time off," I say, smirking as I rub my hand down his abs. "You went from what? An eight-pack to a six-pack?"

He leans into me, my back arching to get closer. The deep rumble of his laugh sends vibrations through my body, making me want him more. His hand slides into my hair as he kisses me, his tongue tangling with mine, sending goosebumps all over my body.

"I'm going to spend time with Sirius," I say. "I missed him."

"Did you miss me?" James asks, rubbing his nose

against mine.

"Nope. You pissed me off. I was mad at you."

"You missed me," he whispers, kissing me hard one last time before leaving.

I sit on the bed, watching him through the window as he jogs up the small hill behind his house. Damn fine view.

After I grab my tablet from my bag, I head into the kitchen with Sirius trotting next to me. He sits next to his food bowl, looking at me expectantly with his little tail wagging so hard, his entire backside is shaking. I chuckle while measuring his food and giving him fresh water. I sit at the table with my mug of coffee, putting my feet on the chair next to me and opening up the romantic thriller I'm reading.

I'm so engrossed in the novel that I don't pay attention to anything until I hear a slight tear of fabric. I look around the room, seeing nothing, but when my eyes fall to the ground, I start cracking up.

Sirius has one of James's shoes in his mouth. It's bigger than he is, but he's not letting that stop him as he shakes it from side to side and gnaws on the edge. "No," I say through giggles. I don't think it's as effective when I'm laughing, though. "Put it down, Sirius."

I get up from the chair and walk toward him, making him wag his tail even harder. He thinks I'm playing with him. When I get close, he tries to take off down the hall, but he stumbles over the big shoe.

I nab it from him before he can get his little teeth on it again, bringing it to the closet. I freeze when I get there. I was much more invested in my book than I thought. Sirius has been ripping and chewing on anything he could. It's a mess in here.

I look over my shoulder, glaring at him, but the sight of his tongue hanging out and the tiny smile on his face saves him from my anger. No one can be mad at a face that stinking cute and sweet. Hopefully James feels the same way.

Falling to my knees, I sort through his damage. Most of James's shoes are okay, except for some tiny teeth punctures, but there are papers that are torn to bits, and the strap of one of his duffle bags is completely chewed through.

When I try to lift it, I groan from the effort. What the hell does he have in this thing? I try again, putting a little more effort into it by bending my knees and pulling. I fall back into the wall, becoming entangled in his shirts. There's a soft click against my back right before I fall.

Only my legs are still in James's closet. From the waist up, I'm in a completely different room. *What the hell?* Slowly standing, I'm unable to take my eyes away from everything in the small room. There are four linked-metal storage lockers on one wall showcasing guns of all sizes and varieties. On the back wall are so many computer screens with feeds showing James's property and some blank screens. The other wall has a pile of duffle bags. I know I shouldn't look…

Terrified, I slowly walk toward the bags, barely unzipping one and peeking inside. Cash. The bags are filled to the brim with stacks of cash wrapped in paper holders.

I need to get out of here. I stand up, spinning to run out of the room. When I'm a couple feet away, James appears in the doorway.

"What the fuck are you doing in here?" James roars.

"What is all this?" I ask, waving my arm around the room, fresh tears springing to my eyes. I don't know if it's the thriller I was reading or just my overactive imagination, but so many scenarios are running through my head. *Is he in the CIA? Is he on the run? Is he a hitman? Who the hell is he?*

"Get the fuck out of here," James says menacingly.

I tread carefully around him, leaving the room and exiting the closet. He slams both doors, hot on my heels. "Why are you snooping through my shit, Tatum?"

I whip around, staring him in the eyes. "I wasn't. It was an accident," I retort.

"An accident? You just happened to stumble into a hidden fucking room?"

"Actually…yes." I lick my lips and inhale through my nose.

He glares at me, grabbing my arm lightly, pulling me toward him. "Stop bullshitting me, Tatum."

"You stop bullshitting me," I yell. "Who are you?" I ask in a much softer tone.

He sucks in a sharp breath, his eyes flitting all over my face. "What kind of question is that?" His voice is rough and ragged.

"What is all that, James?" I ask, placing my fists on his naked, sweaty chest.

"Nothing," he says. "It doesn't concern you."

I nod slowly, running my tongue over my teeth before I let out a disbelieving laugh. "It doesn't concern me? Are you joking right now? Last night you dragged me from my brother's house to bring me here because my brother lied to you and told you Simon broke into my house. The threat of something happening—just the threat made you ask me to stay with you. You turned back into the James I'm really starting to care about. You promised I wouldn't regret forgiving you. You promised you would talk to me. So, you can barge your way into my life making demands, but I accidentally find something, and I can't question you?"

"No," he says firmly, releasing me and walking away.

I stand there, completely stunned by the finality of his words. He's opened up to me and given me so much, but he's still keeping himself under wraps. Each day, I'm getting closer to falling completely in love with him, but I can't do that for a man who won't share anything with me.

I grab my purse from the kitchen counter and head for

the door. James's hand pushes the door closed when I open it. "Where the hell do you think you're going?"

"Anywhere but here," I bite out.

"No," James growls, clamping down on my waist. "You're staying here."

"No, I'm not." I try to pull the door open again, but James's hand doesn't budge.

"You're staying here."

"No, I'm not," I argue.

"He didn't break in, but what if he does?" James's voice lowers and his hand spasms against me.

"That's not going to happen," I reply angrily, rolling my eyes. He's taking this way too far.

"You don't know that," he hisses, stepping into my space and forcing me to take a step back.

"I'll take my chances," I say, even though I know that is the *wrong* thing to say.

"Don't you dare risk your safety," he replies angrily.

"Why do you care?" I snap back.

"Don't do that, Tatum. You know I care. You're my friend."

I snort. Right. Friend. "That's bullshit, James. We're in a relationship. That's what this is. We care about each other. We have sex. We spend as much time together as possible. Whether you want to admit it or not, *we are in a relationship*. We agreed this is more."

I feel when it hits him that I'm right. I'm still facing the door, but I feel his body jerk slightly at the revelation.

"I'm leaving, I'm not staying here. You promise to talk, but you won't. You keep saying I'm safe with you, but I'm not." At least my heart isn't safe near James. Every moment I'm near him, I want more. I'm consumed by him; I won't ever get enough.

James leans in, putting his head next to mine. "What do

I have to do to get you to stay?"

"Be honest with me."

"Fuck," James mutters. He's silent for so long, I think he's going to deny me until he squeezes my waist. "Fine."

I turn my head, looking into his eyes. For the first time since I've known James, he looks frightened. He keeps his eyes on mine as he gulps. I turn toward him. His hand is braced on the door above me, and other is on my hip. He brings his forehead to mine.

"Don't go," he whispers.

"I won't," I promise. "You can trust me."

He breathes deeply, closing his eyes.

"James," I say softly, bringing my hand up to cup his face. He turns his head, kissing my palm before his anguished eyes lock on mine again.

"I guess that's the first thing I should be honest about. My name isn't James."

# CHAPTER
# THIRTY-NINE

*James*

T ATUM BLINKS RAPIDLY, PROCESSING WHAT I JUST TOLD
her. I could've started smaller, but if she's determined
to know, then I can't go easy. Nothing about my life is
fucking easy. How in the hell did I end up in this position?
I've worked my ass off to stay out of things like this, to keep
a distance, so I could take all my secrets to my grave. I only
hoped that grave would be a long time off. If I tell her, I risk
it becoming an early grave.

Tatum and I can't last, even if I want it to. The day that
I will have to see her with another man, maybe even a kid,
will fucking ruin me. That will be the day I move from Texas
and settle somewhere else. I can't lose her yet, though. I want
every second I can steal from her. If I could choose, have
that type of future, it'd be with her.

"Come on," I say. "Let's sit and have a drink. We'll both
need it."

I gently help Tatum sit on the couch; she looks like she's
in shock, staring off into space, still blinking like a crazy person. I pour us each a glass of whiskey, bringing the bottle
and some waters to the coffee table. It's not even noon, but I
need to break out the fucking hard liquor for this shit.

"Tatum?"

Her eyes slowly come to mine. "Your name isn't James?"

I release a long sigh, freeing something that's been sitting on my chest for a long time. "No."

"What's your name?"

"Connor is the name on my birth certificate. Connor died a long time ago, Tatum. I'd never respond to anything except for James. James is my name in every way that matters."

She shrugs, biting her lip. "Why did you change it?"

I take a large gulp of the whiskey. "The first name on my birth certificate was 'Baby Boy.' My mom was a heroin addict. She tossed me in a dumpster where some homeless person found me and brought me to the hospital. I was premature, close to death, fighting to stay alive. No sense in naming a kid that might die," I say wryly, taking another long drink.

Tatum starts crying, pressing her face into my shoulder. "Baby," she whispers.

"I guess I lied. I'll respond to that, if it's you saying it."

This makes her cry harder and grab onto my shirt. We're just getting started. The faster I get this done, the better it will be for both of us.

"Eventually, a nurse named me Connor. After that, my birth certificate was updated with that name. I was well enough to go home, except I didn't have a home. I had to wait for a foster home with availability. Not every foster house will accept a newborn with addiction issues."

"It wasn't your fault," she says outraged, swiping at her eyes. An angry blush is taking over her face.

"It is what it is. I was kicked from foster home to foster home, none of them good. I was called whatever they wanted to call me. By the time I reached kindergarten, I was already behind in school and confused by what my name was."

"I want to travel back in time and rescue you." My throat closes as I stare at her. My fierce girl.

"Sunshine," I say hoarsely. She doesn't understand what she's already given to me.

"Were you close with anyone?"

I smirk, remembering the boys I hung around with. "Yeah. I had a few friends. One really good friend. He and his baby sister bounced in and out of homes. Sometimes they would be back with their mom, which was even worse than the fosters we experienced. We shared a foster house twice. Don't get me wrong, not all foster homes are bad." I shrug. "Just never experienced a good one myself. Closest I came was when I was almost adopted."

"He's the one you mentioned while we were dancing?" Her fingers lace together in her lap as she processes. "Do you ever talk to him?"

"He thinks I'm dead."

"What?" she gasps, turning to face me completely. She whispers her next words with tears in her eyes. "Dead? What do you mean?"

"We'll get there," I say, running my hand through my hair. "So, Callan was my only really good friend, my best friend. We protected his sister as much as we could. She was a lot younger, only a toddler when we were teenagers, but we did what we could. When we were kicked out of the system, we got a place together. Callan fought like hell to get his sister out of foster care and home with his mom. If she was there, then we could watch over her better."

She chuckles. "Two men and a baby."

I grunt. "Something like that."

She picks up her glass of whiskey, turning sideways on the couch and putting her legs over my mine. I wrap a hand around one of her thighs, keeping her anchored against me.

"Then what?" She swirls the liquid amber around the

glass before taking a small sip.

"We needed money. Hell, we always needed money." I pause, not wanting to go on. I fear that if I even say the words out loud, my worst nightmares will come true. I shake my head. "Fuck. Tatum. This may not be a good idea."

"What? You were trusting me. What happened?"

"If I tell you everything, then you're at risk." I squeeze her thigh, pleading with her to understand.

"You wouldn't let anything happen to me." Her fingers brush over my cheek. She's gazing at me in that way she does, with tender affection and more trust than I've ever experienced. My chest expands. She's right. I'd do anything to protect her, sacrifice anything. I'd lay down my life if it meant I could honor her life.

"No, I wouldn't," I vow to her. "I'd never let anything touch you."

"I know, so keep going," Tatum urges.

My head falls to the back of the couch, staring at the ceiling as I weigh my options. Whether Tatum knows about my past or not, she's possibly in danger just by being near me. If I don't tell her, she'll leave, walk right out the door. My heart jerks in my chest in protest. I lift my head and toss the rest of my whiskey to the back of my throat.

"At some point, we got tangled up with this kid we went to school with. It started small and then got bigger and bigger. That kid was the son of a man in the mafia," I admit.

"The mafia?" Tatum gasps.

"Yeah, the mafia," I say.

"The real mafia?"

I grin. "The real mafia. It's Chicago, Tatum. There are lots of old Italian families."

"You were in the mafia?" she asks, her eyes wide and disbelieving.

"No. I'm not Italian, or at least I can't prove that I'm Italian, so I technically can't be in the mafia."

"But, you…worked with them?"

"Yeah, I was an associate. Really, I was an errand boy, and so was Callan. It kept us protected, gave us money, and made us feel like we belonged to something." I laugh humorlessly. "My entire life I wanted to be honorable and loyal and worthy. Men in the mafia are sometimes called men of honor, or *uomo d'onore*. But it was while working for them I knew I was going down the wrong path. I hated what I was doing, but I barely graduated high school, I had nothing to my name, no prospects. The jobs they gave us slowly started to get bigger. If I was caught, no one would come vouch for me; it'd be my ass sitting in that jail cell."

"What do you mean by 'jobs'?"

*Fuck.* My hand pinches the bridge of my nose as I inhale deeply. "It started out as selling small amounts of drugs or collecting money from the dealers. I never had enough on me to land a felony."

"James," Tatum says softly, leaning her head against my shoulder. "I hate thinking about you in a position like that."

"Me, too. I wanted out, but I didn't know how. I couldn't actually voice that. I'd be as good as dead before the words finished leaving my mouth." I pour a bit more whiskey, throwing it back in one swallow. This is where I lay out the biggest secret of all.

"I got a call for a job one day. I was supposed to bring a duffle bag filled with cash to a restaurant and exchange it with a senator who would give me a duffle bag of drugs. It was a test, a ploy to make sure they had the senator in their pocket. I didn't want to do it. Getting caught with that would mean I'd spend most of my life in jail. I didn't have a goddamn thing to my name, but I didn't want to lose my life. I spent my life shackled to horrible situations because I didn't have a family; I didn't want to spend the next part of my life shackled in a cell."

"Did you have to take the job?"

"If I wanted to live, I had no choice" I say. "The restaurant was on the top floor of a building. The guys hacked in and cut the security cameras for the whole building, that way there'd be none of that evidence. I stood in the lobby, late for the appointment. I was having so much trouble making myself do it. It's not who I was, it's not who I wanted to be. There wasn't another choice, though. Right before I hit the elevator call button, the whole building shook."

Tatum stares at me, taking in each word, each syllable.

"Remember the news report last week? When I started acting like a dick?"

Tatum gasps. "Yes."

"I should have been in there. The video showed the man I was supposed to meet waiting for me. If they've seen it, they know I didn't show. I can only hope they still think I died in the explosion, just wasn't at the table yet."

"Oh, my God," she breathes.

"The entire lobby shook with the force of that explosion. I stood there confused when people started running out of the stairwells and alarms started going off. I fled the building in a sea of other people—with a duffle bag of cash. I found a motel that night and watched the news. They said there were no survivors inside the restaurant. 'I could run' popped into my mind. The mafia would think I was dead, and I had money to start over. It took two more nights in that motel, watching the news, making sure I could do it. Then I took off."

"Oh, my God," she repeats on a whisper.

"I took a bus to a few different states, getting fake documents. I didn't want to do it all in one place. The first thing I got was a fake ID. I was barely twenty."

"How'd you know where to go?"

I shrug. "Guess that's one thing the mafia taught me, how to find other shady people."

"Wow."

"Finally, I made it down to Texas. I wanted to be in a city and just blend in. I bought my land with cash, my gym with cash. Since I started making money, I've replaced every dollar I spent from that stolen money. I've added interest, just in case."

"I saw the money," she whispers.

"I have more money down there than just for that. If I ever need to run quickly, I don't have to worry about a bank. I have an account for the gym and to keep up appearances, but other than that, I like to operate with cash."

"What about the guns?"

"Protection," I say. "If they ever find me, I won't go down without a fight."

Tatum looks terrified at the prospect.

"It's been a long time, Tatum. I play everything cautious, but I don't think they'll ever find out."

"How did they have the video if the cameras were cut?" She asks after a moment of silence.

"Phillip McKay Junior, the son of the Texas senator," I say. She nods her head as I continue. "He's been traveling around the country for years setting fires. A senator always dies in one of them. Before he starts the fire, he sets up cameras inside so he can watch until the fire kills the feed. The man I was meeting at the restaurant was an Illinois senator, he was the intended target that day. I was just in the wrong place at the wrong time. Or I would've been, I guess, if I actually got on the elevator. It's just a fucking coincidence that I chose the city where the arsonist lives and even worse coincidence that he was at the same event we were at."

"I don't want to lose you. I don't want them to find you." Tatum looks at her hands in her lap as she speaks quietly.

"With all the computers down there, I keep track of them from afar in the only way I know how. I monitor the chatter. When I said I barely graduated high school, it wasn't due to my intelligence—just a failing school and school system in general, and I missed a lot of class. When I settled here, I taught myself some things, just enough to be able to stay informed."

"What do you mean, 'chatter'?"

"The mafia families in the States are branches under the Italian mafia. They still report to them, like managers reporting to a franchise owner. I monitor that. I've never been brought up. Not too surprising since I was an errand boy, but I did take off with a lot of money. The only other thing that interests me is Callan and his sister, Braelyn. A couple years ago, I found out he was applying for a scholarship for Braelyn to attend a private school. I created a scholarship and awarded it to her anonymously. Callan is my one regret. He was the closest thing to family I had."

My head drops to my hands as I suck in oxygen. Tatum's hand curls around my neck, rubbing her thumb below my ear. I look up at her and continue telling her about Callan. "I've been thinking for ways to get him out for over a decade, I'd have to reveal I'm alive though. And then, we'd both be dead, or worse, they would use Braelyn to get Callan to do something to me."

"We have to think of something," she states firmly. "For both of them."

I nod my head, but I know it's futile.

We stay silent for long moments. "Now you know everything."

"You're still the best man I know, James. Even with everything from your past."

"I should go to the gym and work today, but I want to stay here with you and just be with you all day," I say honestly.

Tatum doesn't answer. Instead, she curls into my side as I wrap an arm around her, breathing easier than I have my entire life.

# CHAPTER
## FORTY

*Tatum*

I LAY DOWN ON THE WEIGHT BENCH I JUST DISINFECTED, throwing my arm over my eyes and grumbling. "This isn't fun."

"I didn't say it would be fun," James chuckles. I've cleaned three benches in the time James has wiped down almost half of the equipment in the gym. After each one I've done, I've collapsed onto the bench in exhaustion. I really don't like mornings.

"It's too early," I complain.

"Tate," James muses. My nickname sends a flutter through my belly. Since he confessed everything, he's let the nickname slip a few times. I love when he says it in gruff voice, but I love sunshine and my full name from him even more. He's the only one to call me Tatum and that feels special. "I tried to let you sleep in on your day off, you wanted to see what it's like to open the gym."

"Why does Sirius get to sleep?" I mutter. We took Sirius with us to Raise the Bar. He's curled up sleeping in James's office. There's a little over an hour until the gym opens. It's just the two of us and Sirius.

"He doesn't have opposable thumbs. He can't get the

gym ready," James says much closer than he was. I take my arm off my face and open my eyes. He's standing above me smiling with his hands on his hips. "Do I need to entice you to work?"

My breath hitches wondering if he'll entice me in a fun way. James's pupils dilate as he stares at me and a low rumble begins in his chest before he bends in half claiming my mouth. He moves to the front of the weight bench, dropping to his knees without breaking our connection.

I slide forward to the edge of the bench, spreading my legs, allowing his body to come in between them. His hands land on my knees and coast up my thighs to my waist and stop just below my breasts. I moan into his mouth when his thumbs rub over my extended nipples.

James breaks our kiss, breathing raggedly. "Take off your clothes."

I whip my shirt and sports bra over my head. James ducks his head, pulling a nipple into his mouth, sucking hard. I cry out as I weave my fingers into his short hair. He takes his mouth away and tugs on my shorts and panties. I lift my butt from the bench, helping him get rid of the material. I toe off my sandals, kicking them away.

"Wider," James growls. I'm sitting in front of him completely naked while he's still clothed. I spread my legs wider, but reach forward and yank on his shirt. When his shirt is next to my clothes on the ground, he leans forward touching our torsos together. James sighs when our skin connects and he wraps me tightly in his arms as his head sinks into my neck. He breathes deeply and kisses my pulse point.

I wrap my legs around his body and tuck my face into his neck, holding him to me. When James leans back, I lift my head, and move to kiss him. His tongue invades my mouth sending me on the path of destruction with only his kiss.

I whimper as his mouth starts to move down my body,

driving me crazy while he avoids every part I want him to touch. He hovers over my wet core, looking up at me with bright silver eyes. "Watch in the mirror, Tatum."

My eyes leave his, looking behind him at the wall of mirrors. My gasp turns into a moan when he sucks my clit hard. His big, rough hands glide up my body until they reach my breasts. He tugs on my nipples as he plunges his tongue inside of me.

James's back muscles ripple with each of his movements. My chest is heaving and I can see that the blue of my eyes is flaming brighter.

"James," I chant his name, rolling my hips to meet his mouth. His scruff scrapes against the inside of my thighs as he devours me, groaning as I start to convulse around him.

"Please. I…I…Jam—Yes. James," I cry out as I explode into a million pieces. James stands pushing down his basketball shorts and ripping off his shoes. I'm trembling on the bench, the aftershocks still rolling through me. James's eyes are on mine.

"Fuck," he grinds out. "So fucking beautiful."

He lifts me and sits on the edge of the bench and bringing me onto his lap. I collapse on him, leaning my back against his chest. James spreads my legs, making them fall over his muscular thighs. His thick, hard cock is between my legs. I reach down, wrapping my hand around him. A deep groan leaves his lips as he kisses along my neck.

My fist tightens around him, sliding up and down his shaft. Wetness floods my core again as I watch us in the mirror. His face is tucked into my neck kissing me.

"James," I call. "Baby."

He meets my eyes in the mirror.

"Yes," I hiss, jerking him faster. He tugs my hand away, and uses my hip to lift me slightly. "No condom," I breathe.

He nods his head in agreement then urges me down

on him. I sink onto him slowly, letting him fill me inch by inch while our eyes stay connected in the mirror. One of his hands skates over my stomach, up past my breasts, and rests at my throat, turning my face toward his.

"Kiss me," he demands

My lips land on his, sucking his bottom lip into my mouth and grazing my teeth across it. James pulls back looking into my eyes. His hips are rolling slowly as he makes love to me. My breathing is erratic as I watch James's gray eyes moves all over my face lovingly. The grip he has on my neck gets tighter.

"You're mine." His breath skates over my skin as he speaks.

"You've owned me since our first kiss," I admit.

"I'll fall to my knees and sacrifice everything for one minute with you. I can't give you up. You belong to me. I've never belonged to anyone before, but I'm yours, just as much as you're mine."

Unshed tears fill my eyes. "I'm keeping you, James Harris. I don't care what I have to do or who I have to fight. The mafia. You. It doesn't matter. I'm keeping you."

"Christ," he mutters, bringing my lips to his in a deep, wet, passionate kiss. I sink everything I am and everything I feel into that kiss. He starts bucking into me faster, taking his mouth from me, and leans his forehead against mine. "Turn your eyes to the mirror, sunshine. Watch me fuck you. Let me see you come all over my cock. You're the most beautiful thing I've ever seen, see what I see."

I turn my head toward the mirror and watch him power into me until we're spent and calling out each other's name. In that moment, I know what he sees when he looks at me. A woman insanely in love and he's right, it's fucking beautiful.

# CHAPTER
# FORTY-ONE

## James

LIFT THE BAR OVER MY HEAD, HOLDING FOR A COUPLE seconds before lowering, and repeating the process. I can feel each movement in my muscles and it still feels so good. I've been out of physical therapy for weeks, but still haven't adjusted to the fact that I can do this.

"I don't think I can take you seriously with that dog," Corbin says. He's standing behind the bench, spotting me as I lift the weights. He's almost done with his physical therapy and should be able to play by the championship game next month.

I glance down at Sirius, chuckling. He's on my stomach. Each time I raise the bar over my head, he stands, and when I lower it to my chest, he lays down. He's doing his own form of a workout. His tongue is poking out of his mouth and he wags his tail when he notices me watching him.

I've never had a pet, wasn't sure I ever wanted one, but I really enjoy Sirius running and sliding across my wood floors when I get home. He's entertaining and cute. Over the past couple months, he's become my constant companion.

"He's badass," I say.

Corbin hoots before doubling over and cracking up. I

meet Sirius's eyes, he wags his tail and cocks his head to the side. I smile, lifting the bar again and feel Sirius stand on my stomach and lower as I bring down the bar.

"How many dogs do you know that can do that?" I ask.

"But, he's so small. He's a girly dog, like in movies when girl's carry their dogs in purses."

"Sirius is *not* going in a purse," I assert. "He may be small, but he's a badass."

"Whatever you say," Corbin laughs.

I place the bar on the rack, use my hand to hold Sirius, and sit up. I move Sirius to my shoulder, his favorite place to perch. Corbin hands me a towel to wipe off the sweat. He has the disinfectant and paper towels in his hand.

It's something small, but it's respect for the equipment, the gym, and me. "Thanks, man," I say. As I stand, he begins to wipe the bench and bar.

Corbin nods, pausing mid-stroke, and clears his throat. "James?"

His hands are still frozen on the bench, but the one holding the towel is grasping it tightly, letting the paper crumble under his fist. When his eyes don't meet mine, I crouch down, setting Sirius at my feet and tell him to stay.

"What's up?" I keep my tone light. His face is still hidden from view, but there's tension radiating off of him.

"If…if I play in the championship game, will you come?" I pat his hand a couple of times before pulling it away.

"Even if you can't play and you're on the bench, I'll be there," I promise.

His head whips up and searches my face for a lie he won't find. Corbin swallows and nods his head once, looking back down. "That'd be cool," he says.

"What would be cool?" Tatum asks rubbing her eyes. I stand from my crouched position as she gets closer. She's been sleeping on the couch in my office since I opened the gym. She stumbles into me, burrowing her head in my chest, and wrapping her arms around my waist.

"James said he's going to the championship game," Corbin responds. His tone is nonchalant, but he rolls forward on the balls of his feet and his lips are twitching.

"We're both going," Tatum says.

"Really?" Corbin asks in wonder, rocking back.

"Yeah, definitely. I'm going to make a sign and everything."

Corbin shakes his head. "Don't do that, it'll be embarrassing."

Tatum shrugs and I feel her cheeks move against my chest, so I know she's smiling. "What are you doing for Thanksgiving next week, Corbin?"

His hand releases the bottle of cleaning fluid and scratches the backside of his neck. "No plans. My fosters are going to visit family, so it'll just be me."

Tatum tenses in my arms. "You're coming with us to my parent's house."

Corbin opens his mouth to argue and I grin when Tatum slices her hand through the air, cutting him off. "No arguments. It's settled."

She picks up Sirius and walks back to my office. I turn to Corbin. His eyes are huge as he stares after her. "It's best not to argue," I say honestly. "She'll get her way in the end."

# CHAPTER
# FORTY-TWO

## James

"**J**-MAN," CORBIN CALLS FROM THE BACKSEAT.

"Don't call me that," I mutter.

Last week when Tatum and I found out that Corbin was spending Thanksgiving alone, Tatum stepped in, insisting he come to her parents' house with us. His foster family is spending the holiday with their family. They don't bring any of the foster kids. The other children in the house are spending the day with some friends, but Corbin planned to be alone.

I could tell when we picked Corbin up that he was nervous. Those nerves only grew when we pulled up to her parents' house, but the moment he heard her grandfather cursing up a storm, he relaxed. That's what did it for me when I met them, too. That crazy old man. The rest of the day was spent laughing and having a good time.

"Since I beat you in pool, I think I should get a reward."

Tatum laughs next to me, bringing her hand down on my arm and squeezing.

"Reward?" I ask.

"Yeah, like a prize."

"There's no prize for winning a game of pool. I let you win."

I didn't. That kid swindled me. When I glance in the rearview mirror, Corbin's head is thrown back, clutching his stomach, as he laughs. "Whatever you need to tell yourself, J-man."

"Don't call me that."

"Okay, J-man."

I glance at Tate, smirking. She's beaming. Her hand slides down my arm, linking our fingers together and resting our hands on my thigh. I release her hand when my phone starts ringing from the cup holder.

*Unknown.* My thumb hesitates for a split second over the screen, my gut clenching. It's been a good day. I brace myself for something to come crashing down and ruining the day. That's the way it works.

I answer the call. "Yeah?"

"Connor. Long time, no talk, brother."

My veins fill with ice. An anvil drops in my stomach, stealing the air from my lungs. The dark road in front of me turns blurry as I process whose voice I'm hearing. Callan.

Fuck.

No.

This can't fucking be possible. He's still speaking, but I can't hear a fucking word he's saying. A small hand squeezes my clenched thigh.

Tatum.

Fuck. My focus returns, and I glance at her. Her eyebrows are drawn in with her head tilted. The stunning blue of her eyes grounds me.

Tatum.

I have to get her home. And, Corbin. I need to get him home, too. Fuck.

My eyes swing back to the dark road, and I pay attention to every word Callan is saying.

"Happy Thanksgiving, brother. You remember the last

Thanksgiving before you *died*? We rented that shitty-ass motel room because it had that little kitchenette. Our oven was
fucked, and I wanted to give Braelyn a nice holiday feast.
The kind of shit neither of us had. We bought that turkey,"
he laughs.

We didn't buy the turkey. We stole the turkey. Who
knew a fucking turkey could be so damn expensive? Braelyn
was barely old enough to remember anything, but we did
want to give her something. If this was a different life, I'd be
laughing with him. If I didn't have so much on the line, I'd
be laughing with him. But, I'm not. Not even fucking close.

I've pretty much stalked Callan online from the moment
I left. He and his baby sister are the only things I miss from
that old life. I can't laugh about that fucking turkey because
of the person sitting next to me. This can't touch Tatum.

"We thought it would be so easy to cook. All those rec-
ipes you found at the library made it sound so damn easy.
Our potatoes were bricks, the turkey was black. We ordered
Chinese food. I fucking missed you, man."

He laughs again, but it's not a happy laugh. It's dark and
angry. "I got some shit to say. First, fuck you, Connor. James.
Whatever the fuck your name is."

I swing my SUV around a turn, pointing it toward
Tatum's. "James?" she asks softly. I can't bring her back to
my place. I need to get her home right now.

"Fifteen minutes," I manage to say. My voice is so low, I
wonder if he even heard me before I hang up.

"Who was that?" Tatum asks.

"Wrong number," I reply, not looking at her. Anger and
panic flood my system, neither knowing which should take
precedent. My mind is racing with possibilities and plans. I
can't think with Tatum's jasmine scent next to me. Her safety
is the only goal.

Tatum opens her mouth to reply, but I shake my head

once, clutching the wheel with both hands. Corbin is completely silent in the backseat. My eyes meet his in the rearview mirror. He swallows thickly, noticing the rising tension.

"Stay in the car," I say to Corbin when I pull up in front of her place.

"Bye, Tate," he mumbles. "Thank you for today."

"Anytime you want to go over and shoot pool with Pop Pop, I know he'd love to have you," Tatum says with a forced smile, turned in her seat so she's facing him. Her hand reaches through the seats to pat his leg. She winks at him. "See you later."

I step out of the car without meeting her eyes, and when she gets out of the car and stands next to me on the sidewalk, I grab her hand and go to the front door at a clipped pace.

"James, what's going on?"

"Headache," I lie.

She opens her mouth, but I crash my lips to hers, cutting off her words. Tatum lets me take complete control, resisting fighting me, like I know she's itching to do. I banked on her not doing it while Corbin is waiting in the car.

I hold her to me as tightly as I possibly can, running my hands up and down her sides, relishing the feel of her beneath my palms. "Tatum," I whisper, savoring every syllable of her name. "Tatum."

My lips land on her neck, sucking hard and marking a piece of her. I want so much more. If my life was different, if I had a different past, if I wouldn't be looking over my shoulder until my dying breath, I'd give this girl everything. Every worldly possession. Every piece of me. Heart. Body. Soul. Every damn fucking thing. I'd sign over my fucking life to her if it meant I could keep her for just five more minutes.

The only thing she'd have to give me is herself. That's all I want. It's all I need.

I can't keep her, though. Not even for five more minutes.

Not even for thirty more seconds.

The fifteen minutes I demanded sits like a guillotine above my head, sliding closer to end me with each passing second.

"Bye, sunshine."

# CHAPTER
# FORTY-THREE

*James*

CORBIN IS IN THE FRONT WHEN I SLIDE BEHIND THE wheel. I step on the gas, racing down the street toward his house. He's staring at his hands. They're fisted in his lap, and breaths are coming out heavy. Kid is too observant for his age. I know what's coming before he even opens his mouth.

"Are you leaving?"

I release a heavy, pent-up sigh, my shoulders sagging from the fucking weight of that question. Am I leaving? Yeah. Just don't know if it will be on my own or in a fucking body bag. Either way, I won't be around this kid the way I should. Another disappointment for him.

I grit my teeth. "Corbin, Listen to me."

He nods, his face turned toward me. When we pass under a street light, I glance at him, noticing a glassy sheen in his eyes.

"You have four more years in a broken system. I know the neighborhood you're in, it's all too fucking easy to fall into gang life. Working your ass off for a scholarship won't be the easy way out, but it will be worth it. Don't stop. Not even for a second. Rise and grind every damn day. You want out of that life? Work for it. It's not going to fall from the sky and land in your lap. The world doesn't care if you have a heart of gold. You have to work and earn everything you have."

"Will I see you again?"

"You will if it's up to me, kid," I say right as I pull up to his darkened house.

"Stay safe," he whispers, getting out the car and hiding his tears.

I roll down the window and call his name. His face turns but doesn't face me all the way. A giant fist is squeezing the organ in my chest. "I'm proud of you. Don't forget that. You're not going to get rid of Tatum now. Let her be good to you."

With a slight nod and a hand covering his eyes, he heaves a breath before taking off for the front door. As soon as I'm on the street heading for my house, the phone rings right as the fifteenth minute is up.

I don't look at the screen as I slide my thumb across. "You always did like to be on time," I say.

"You're lucky I gave those minutes to you. There's not a lot of time."

"It's a holiday."

"Yeah, Luca thought the family coming after you on a family holiday would be poetic or some shit," he muses.

"Why?" I ask. That single word holds so many questions. *Why now? Why are you doing this? Why are you still part of this shit? Why are you calling?* "How?" I tack on for good measure. *How did you fucking find me?*

"You know the why, asshole." Then he mutters, "Not that you fucking care." He's wrong. Callan and Braelyn are the only things I couldn't let go. One thing I've never told anyone, except for Tatum, is that I risked it all for Braelyn.

"Braelyn," I whisper.

"Don't say her name," he threatens.

I take my hand from the wheel, rubbing it across my forehead. "I tried."

"You didn't fucking try. You left us. I thought you were dead. Dead. Fucking burned alive in the top floor of a god damn restaurant doing something you didn't want to do. I know you wanted out of this life. I wanted it, too. You knew that. You left. You left with a fucking pile of money and left Brae and I in Chicago."

"I sat in a motel room in Chicago for days, thinking of ways for all three of us to leave. After I left, I thought about how to get you out. I didn't know how. I didn't have the fucking answers," I yell into the phone. "Braelyn was a kid, man. Just a kid. Two teenagers in ratty ass clothes with a kid on a bus. We wouldn't have made it out of the city. We'd all three be dead."

I pull into my driveway with my heart pounding, throwing the car in park right in front of the front door, not bothering with the garage. I won't be here for long.

"Don't know why I'm doing this," Callan mutters. I hear the click of a lighter. Callan never smoked when we were kids, but he loved playing with lighters. The click and small flame soothed him and could calm his racing mind.

"Doing what?"

"I fucked up on a drug run. Got short-changed and I didn't notice because I didn't count." Callan is speaking low, lost in a memory I wasn't part of. "Brae had a recital. I finally had the money to pay for dance lessons. I didn't count the money. Luca threatened her. She's under their protection now."

"Fuck," I mutter. If she's under their "protection," Callan may as well have a gun to his head for the rest of his life. They'll make him keep working, and if he stops or screws up, Braelyn will be the price to pay.

"The only reason you're getting this call is because you were once like a brother to me."

"You're still like a brother to me," I declare.

"Fuck you," he seethes. I can feel the fury rolling off of him. He can't see past the abandonment.

"How did you find me?" I finally get out of my car, walking inside my house toward my room. Sirius hops up from his bed, chasing after me on his short legs.

"That fucking guy who blew up the restaurant was from Austin. We all thought it was weird when you weren't at the table with the senator, but didn't think you would be *alive*. Luca wanted to know more about the arsonist, wanted to see if we could get money from him somehow. One of the guys started to learn everything about him." Callan chuckles darkly.

I place the phone between my shoulder and ear, picking up the bags of money I've stored for so long.

"It's almost funny how something so simple is bringing you down," he finally says.

"Spit it out," I say, throwing each bag into the trunk of my SUV.

"A Google alert. Luca's computer guy set up Google alerts for that guy, his family, and closest acquaintances. I never thought I'd see your face again and especially in a country club newsletter."

My hand rakes over my hair before landing on my neck and squeezing. I can picture it so perfectly. Tatum looking fucking delectable in her dress pressed against my body, and a photographer taking our picture. I meant to search him out, but got distracted by the rest of the night.

"He recognized you. We've been watching and collecting information. Tatum sure is a cute girl. She's got a great ass on her and looks fucking hot in those scrubs she wears for work."

"Don't you dare bring her into this," I hiss, clutching my phone in a death grip.

"Relax. Luca's not interested in bringing anyone else into this shitstorm. I've been on her. I wouldn't hurt her." The last sentence is uttered so quietly, it would've been easy to miss if I didn't know Callan so well. His next sentence is said with nothing but pure hatred. "I'm not you."

"I didn't hurt Braelyn," I insist. "I wouldn't. Fuck you for even saying that."

"You left."

"I've been watching since I left. That nice scholarship she was awarded to the all-girls' school by the anonymous donor? It's me. I left because I had to. I didn't come back because I couldn't. I never fucking forgot."

A choking noise comes over the line.

"She doesn't deserve the shitty schools we went to," I state. Callan speaks before I can continue and changes the subject.

"Luca is landing in Austin now. Run. We will find you at some point, and when we do, I'll have no other choice. You'll be on the other side of my gun."

# CHAPTER
# FORTY-FOUR

*Tatum*

J AMES'S WORDS ARE ON REPLAY IN MY MIND. *Bye, sunshine.*

I knew he lied about the phone call. It wasn't a wrong number. He stayed on the phone and then said fifteen minutes. I didn't want to argue with him in front of Corbin; that wouldn't be fair to him. From the moment he took the jerky turn toward my house, James knew I wouldn't protest the change of plans.

Corbin shut down after that phone call, too. What the hell is happening? James surprised me by dropping me off at my place, even before he took Corbin home. I knew this was intentional. My place was out of the way. He walked me to the door, barely saying a word before he gave me a soul-searing kiss.

*Bye, sunshine.*

My feet are wearing a path in the carpet in front of my bed. I'm staring at my phone, begging for it to ring with a call from him or, a text. An e-mail. Something. Any form of communication. A freaking carrier pigeon. Anything to clue me in to what is happening. Something isn't right. James is the most honorable and honest man I know. He doesn't spare feelings. He's unfailingly honest.

And he lied to me.

He lied.

Since he hung up that call, something shifted between us. The tension in the car grew thicker and thicker. We've stayed most nights together since this began, but today he dropped me off.

*Bye, sunshine.*

Not see you tomorrow. Not I'll call you. Not later.

*Bye, sunshine.*

Part of me thinks he wouldn't leave without saying good-bye, a real goodbye. That part hopes he'd tell me that he's leaving, even ask me to come with him. The other part of me knows he's done it before. Took off. Barely looked back.

I didn't even think dropping me off would be an option. I assumed I would go home with him, and we'd spend the rest of the holiday weekend wrapped in each other. James closed the gym for the weekend for the first time ever so we could spend time together.

And then he drops me off?

*Bye, sunshine.*

Something is seriously not right. I call his number, but it goes straight to voice mail.

*Bye, sunshine.*

My heart gets caught in my throat as I try to suck in air. My lungs feel like they're collapsing. His deep, sexy voice repeats his goodbye to me and every word before that. I won't let him do this.

I don't waste time changing out of my dress. I grab my keys, heading out to James's place for some answers. We are past this bullshit. He's going to talk to me. I don't care what I have to do. I want him. He wants me. I know he does. Just last week, we admitted we belong to each other. I'm in love with him.

I *love* him.

*Bye, sunshine.*

That can't be the end.

I grip the steering wheel as tightly as I can as I speed down the highway. My stomach is twisting in knots, an impending doom running through me.

I bang on the door while ringing the doorbell. James throws open the door with a scowl on his face.

"What are you doing here, Tatum?" James's question comes out as a demand.

"What's happening?"

"Nothing. Wanted a night alone. Headache."

"James," I say, stepping toward him, but he steps back. I freeze before shouldering my way inside his house. "Talk to me."

"Tatum," he says, rubbing his hand over his face. "This is getting really intense between us. I don't want that. I need some space."

"Space?" I ask on an empty laugh, repeating his words in my mind while my heart squeezes painfully. This isn't happening. This can't be happening. My eyes snag on a bag next to the door. "Are you going somewhere?"

"Go home, Tatum," James growls.

"No," I insist. "Not until you tell me what the hell happened and not until you stop lying. You spent the day with my family. We were good all day."

"I'm not lying."

"Yes, you freaking are." I step toward him, poking my finger in his chest before wrapping his shirt in my fist, trying to pull him closer. No one has ever fought for him. Not as a kid. Not as an adult. I will. I will fight for him, I'll fight for us. The way he looks at me, the way my heart beats for him is worth it. We're worth it.

"I can't do this anymore, Tatum. This arrangement is over."

"This hasn't been an *arrangement* in a long time."

"It's always been that to me."

"You're lying. I belong to you, remember?"

He steps back, removing my hands from him. "Tate," he says, blowing out a breath.

"Tatum," I correct. I've always been Tatum to him. I want to be Tatum when I'm with him and Tate with everyone else. "I belong to you," I repeat.

James's eyes slowly close and he mutters. "Got caught up in a moment."

"Liar," I spit out.

My eyes catch the piece of luggage again. "Are you going somewhere?" I ask again, biting my tongue to stop the sting of tears. I will not cry.

"Yes," he says.

"Where?"

"Leave, Tatum," he growls.

"No." I bite my tongue to stop the flow of tears. "Something happened. Be honest with me."

"You want fucking honesty?"

"Yes."

"That phone call was my old friend, Callan. Remember him? Mafia friend. They know you exist. They know your name. The fucking mafia knows *you* exist. They know I'm alive. They're coming after me. I'm leaving. I can't take the chance with you being here. They'll chase me and be far away from you. You will *always* belong to me and I can't let them fucking touch you."

I stop breathing, terror seeping into me. James steps closer, cupping my face. "I did lie. This is more." He drops a quick kiss to my lips, stroking his thumbs across my cheeks. "I will protect you. They will *not* come for you. Go to Roman's. Tell him everything. Let him protect you. He will."

"James, you can't leave. You can't," I beg. "We'll figure

this out together."

"I have to."

"No, we'll figure this out," I say again.

"Take Sirius with you. Do not *ever* come back here," James demands. Each time he speaks, it's a bit more frantic. He's trying to rush me out of here and away from him.

"You're not coming back?" I ask.

"No."

"Ever?"

"I don't know." He picks up his bag and turns away from me. "Go to Roman's. Now."

James starts moving faster after looking at the time on his phone.

"Why?" I ask. "We can both go."

"Roman and Kiernan have dealt with shit like this before. They're both trained in more than you can even imagine. He'll know what to do for you. Go. Now. Leave now, Tatum."

"Wait," I yell as he keeps moving farther away from me, the tears falling too rapidly to stop them. "I love you. Stay. Please stay. I know you love me, too. I know you do. Stay. We will figure this out."

"Fuck," he mutters. "You can't, sunshine." He walks to me, cupping my face between his hands. He kisses my mouth lightly over and over. "You can't love me. You have to let me go. It's the only way you're safe, the only way Savannah, Harper, Hudson, all of you are safe. If I could, if I had a different life, I'd never leave your side. Go. Now, Tatum." James releases me and walks out the door to his SUV, jumps in, and drives away from me. I'm frozen in place long after his brake lights fade.

⚜

When I pull into Roman and Harper's driveway, they're not home. I remember they went to Liam and Savannah's for Thanksgiving, so I head over there, not willing to wait a minute longer. James needs his friends. I refuse to leave him alone in this.

Liam swings open the door with a boyish grin on his handsome face. "Hey, we were hoping y'all would stop by. Left a message with James a while ago. Where is he?" Liam looks past me into the dark night then back to my face and to the tiny dog in my hands. His head tilts as he watches me. "Tate?"

A sob breaks free from my throat. Liam pulls me inside the house. "What's wrong? Is everything okay?"

"No," I say with a trembling voice, running a hand through my hair and taking a deep breath. I forcefully stop my tears and straighten my spine, ready to do whatever I need to do. "Is Roman here?"

"Yeah," Liam says, looking concerned. He guides me toward their living room where Harper, Savannah, Liam, Roman, Kiernan, and Hudson are sitting. The only ones missing are Valerie and Gabe. Hudson jumps to his feet first when he sees me, followed by a very pregnant Harper and Savannah.

"Tate?" Hudson asks, bringing his hands to my shoulders. "What's going on? Where's James?"

I ignore his questions, my eyes finding Roman's. "Can I talk to you? Privately."

Roman glances at the others. "Sure."

I bend to put Sirius on the ground, not caring that I forgot my manners and didn't even bother asking if I could put him on the floor.

Roman guides me to Liam's study, sitting on the edge of Liam's desk while I take one of the chairs in front of it. "What's wrong?"

I take in a deep breath, deciding to lay out the facts as quickly as possible. It took me almost thirty minutes from when James left to arrive here. Roman and whoever else need to leave now and find him. Time is moving too quickly. "James is in trouble. He left. He needs help. He told me to come to you to ask if I can stay with y'all to make sure I'm safe."

"Of course, you can stay."

"I don't care about that," I say, slashing my hand through the air. "He's going somewhere. I don't know where, and he's going up against people determined to kill him. He said he's leaving to get them away from me."

"Who?" Roman asks.

My shaking hands press against my heart as I try to center my breathing, unable to comprehend that the man I'm in love with just took off without a backward glance to fight the freaking mafia. Six months ago before I met James, the most dangerous part of my life was going to a midnight movie by myself.

"The mafia." My voice cracks. I want to curl up and cry and worry and beg for James to be okay. That's not how he'll get out of this unharmed, though. The only way is for me to keep going, keep pushing, and fighting for us. I won't stop until I get that growly giant to confess his love for me.

"Did you just say the mafia?"

"Yes."

"I'm getting the other guys," Roman declares before marching out of the room. A minute later, Liam, Kiernan, and Hudson file into the room. "Start from the beginning," Roman demands.

I tell them almost everything. I leave out the private details of James's childhood, but I tell them about the money, the mafia, and finally the phone call from his long-lost friend.

"I don't know what he said," I say, twisting my hands. "Just know that he called, and they talked."

"Fuck," Roman hisses.

Hudson looks shell-shocked. "Shit. That's what he's been running from all these years? I always knew he was running from something. Didn't think it would be this."

I nod.

"Why didn't he tell me?"

I shrug. "To protect you. To keep the seal on his old life as tight as possible."

"Hudson, Liam," Kiernan says, transforming from the goofy guy I've come to know to a man who will take no arguments. "You stay with the girls. Here. Roman and I will do some digging and get James's stubborn ass back here."

"Go to the living room, sweetheart," Roman says softly.

"But—"

"No, I'm guessing since those girls like you so much, you're probably a lot like them. If you're in here and know even a fraction of what we plan, you'd try to come along. And, that's not fucking happening."

"Jamesy boy wouldn't like that," Kiernan says.

"Don't tell Savannah and Harper what's going on," Liam requests.

I nod, staring at each of these men, knowing there's no arguing or pleading for them to let me come. As long as they help James and bring him back in one piece, I'll try to do whatever they ask. My heart is begging for me to go chasing James, though.

# CHAPTER
# FORTY-FIVE

## James

I PARK BEHIND THE GYM, GOING IN THROUGH MY SECRET entrance—the door I had installed for this very reason. They found me. After all these years of living out of their reach, they found me. One slip up and mistake, a moment of weakness allowed this to happen. I got so caught up in Tatum and those damn blue eyes that I forgot to follow through on something so simple. A picture in a country club newsletter.

I don't believe in fate, but if it exists, it's a real fucking bitch. Years ago I chose Austin to escape to, to live a new life. Years and years of thinking the restaurant explosion was an accident, but it was someone from Austin.

Someone who ran in the same circles as the girl that ripped the heart from my chest, claiming it as hers. Tatum arrived in my life so quickly, I didn't stand a chance against her.

Tatum's broken sob plays over and over in my mind. I lied to her, but I'll never be able to tell her the truth. I love her. I love her with every broken and battered piece of me. She's the temptation I couldn't ignore or resist.

She felt like a reward for my years of silence. A reward for the life I lived. She felt like an angel sent to me, but instead,

I think the devil sent her, tempting me with the most beautiful girl and the brightest light.

Someone who has only lived in darkness can't resist a light like hers. I'd give anything to spend my life making her light shine even brighter while selfishly basking in her sunshine. She knocked me on my ass with her attitude and made herself the center of my universe. Now I have to walk away from that, from her.

I have to willingly walk back into the darkness.

Her terrified and forlorn face will greet me every time I close my eyes. I did that. I made that look cross her face; I caused that pain. My chest tightens from the agony of knowing I hurt her by walking away. Every mile I drove away from her caused more and more pain. I could hardly breathe by the time I made it here. I wanted to turn around, gather her in my arms, and take off running. A life of looking over your shoulder, a life of uncertain death, and a life without her family isn't fair. I know she would've gotten in my passenger seat if I asked.

I couldn't do that to her.

My trunk is filled with cash, guns, laptops, and enough clothes to get by on. I have more cash and guns at the gym. I'm not willing to leave them here when I know I won't be back.

I walk out of my office to stand in the middle of the gym. With my hands tucked in my pockets, I look around. One phone call is taking everything away from me. I'm willingly giving it up to keep Tatum safe.

If I didn't have her, if they didn't know about her, I wouldn't go anywhere. If I received that phone call pre-Tatum, I'd have sat my ass on my porch waiting for them with a gun in my hand. Sure, I've kept everything as easy as possible to escape since I arrived in Texas, but the minute I started owning things—the gym, my car, my house—I knew

I'd never run. I'd fight for them until the bitter end.

I'm not running now. I just want to get out of this town for when the dramatic showdown happens. Showdowns with the mafia are always dramatic. *Anything* with the mafia is always dramatic. I want this shit to happen so far from Tatum, they can't get to her. If I could hide her on the moon, I would. Roman will keep her safe. Kiernan will help him track the threat and know when it's over. I'll either be dead or moving on to another city.

The front door of the gym flies open.

I grab the gun from the waistband of my jeans.

Two dark figures walk in. With all the lights off, I can't see who they are.

"A couple months ago, we took down a cartel king. Now we're going to face the mafia. This will be fun, boys," Kiernan says, striding closer to where I can see his grinning face.

I swear, only this knucklehead would be grinning when thinking about going toe to toe with the mafia. Roman is just a couple feet behind him, silently assessing me.

Hot fury pumps through me. "What the fuck are you doing here?"

"Helping you," Roman returns, rolling his eyes.

"I needed your help keeping Tatum safe. I was fucking trusting you."

"She's safe," Kiernan assures me.

"She's with Harper," Roman states. "I wouldn't leave my pregnant fiancée without protection."

"We're helping, even if you grumble the entire time," Kiernan says, clapping me on the back. "The mafia? Sure were keeping a lot under wraps, huh?"

I grunt, shrugging his hand off my shoulder.

"It's happening here," Roman says.

"Absolutely not," I say through gritted teeth. "Too close."

"This is your turf. This is the best shot we have," Roman

declares. "Don't do it somewhere they could surprise you. This place is the best bet."

*Shit.* He's right.

"Do you have that guy's number?" Kiernan asks. "What did he say when he called? Tatum didn't really know."

"No, Callan called from an unknown number. He gave me a warning, even though he'd be dead if they knew. Said he'll see me soon and I'd be on the other end of his gun."

"Damn," Kiernan says, taking his phone out of his pocket and bring it to his ear. "I'm going to find his number. Full name?"

"Callan Fox."

A few minutes later, Kiernan hangs up with his and Roman's security firm and rattles off the number as I dial. Each ring makes my heart pound harder and faster.

"Should I call you Connor? Or James?" Callan answers.

"Doesn't matter. Let's meet. I'm guessing your boss arrived safely, and you've been in town, probably raiding a vending machine at some motel."

"Fuck you," Callan says. I have to smother my laugh when I hear the crinkle of wrappers in the background.

"Raise the Bar gym. Come. I don't think we finished our conversation from earlier."

Callan hangs up.

"ETA?" Roman asks. He's primed and ready for a mission.

"Didn't say," I respond. "Imagine it will be soon. Armed?"

Kiernan huffs, insulted by the question. I walk outside, grabbing a few duffle bags of money—money that I've counted hundreds of times. Obsessively counted. I place them in the gym—hidden from sight, but near enough to grab when that time comes. This showdown could go in so many ways, just depending on who shows up with Callan and Luca. I wasn't important enough for any large player in the mafia to think about—until I took their money. I just hope my bargaining tool works.

Callan doesn't disappoint. He shows up in under an hour. Five men walk into my gym. Luca Mancini is leading them in a crisp suit, Callan flanking one side, along with the others I don't recognize.

"Well, well, well. Look who it is in the flesh. You've grown, Connor. Or is it James?"

"James," I grunt. My eyes lock on my childhood best friend. Anger, betrayal, and confusion are flashing hot in his eyes. "Callan," I greet.

He raises an eyebrow. "You look good for a dead dude."

Callan looks mostly the same, only older, a little bigger. The one major difference is the darkness hanging over him like a cloud. His eyes are still eerie against his tan skin. They're the lightest blue I've ever seen. He breaks our stare, his lips curling in disgust as he shakes his head.

They span out, lining up in front of us. The man standing on Luca's right pulls a gun from behind his back pointing it at me.

"Mother fucker," Kiernan grumbles, grabbing his gun from his holster pointing it right between the eyes of the man aiming his gun at me. His gun switches targets and moves to Kiernan.

In the next second, each man in the room has a gun out. My gun is aimed at Luca. Kiernan and Roman have theirs trained on the men flanking him. Not one of us is free from the barrel of a gun. No one speaks as the heavy breaths echo in the empty gym.

"What've you been up to?" Luca asks with a smile.

"This and that," I answer casually with a small shrug, as if we were talking over a cup of coffee.

"Callan," Luca says. "Get it done."

Callan steps closer to me with his gun raised, aiming

between my eyes. The gun wavers in his hands slightly. He tightens his grip as his eyebrows pull in. I hear him release a breath as his shoulders pull back and he purses his lips.

"Callan," I say calmly, keeping my gun pointed toward Luca.

"James," Callan spits out, the gun wavering off center again. It's been a long time since I've seen him, but when I knew him, he had a sure and steady shot. The gun range was where we released our anger at the world. Callan could go round and round while keeping the gun in his hands steady and aimed true.

"I'm sorry," I say, seeing the betrayal in his eyes. He's wondering why I left him in that life and took off. The conversation earlier didn't answer enough of his questions, and the last piece of information I gave him probably left him with more. He didn't expect to hear I've been paying for his sister's school. I didn't get to apologize, either. Apologizing isn't something I do often, but I've waited a long time to say those two words to my friend. "Didn't think I had a choice at the time."

Callan stares at me, the gun continuing to tremble. He shakes his head slightly, closing his eyes tightly before they open and land on me. He breathes deeply through his nose.

"Don't do this, Callan. We can figure this out. You want out, I'll help."

"You'll be dead," Luca says. His gun is gone, and he's inspecting his nails like he's bored out of his mind. He's completely unperturbed, as usual. Since Callan and I met him and he brought us into his crazy world, he's wanted to keep his hands clean while his thugs do all the work. He's bored easily. His father—one of the higher-ups in the chain—is ruthless, but as long as Luca is making money and he can do as he pleases, he doesn't give much of a shit about anything.

Earlier, Callan said this showdown with me on a holiday

is poetic justice. Along with Luca's easy demeanor, I know he's slightly entertained, wondering how this will go down.

I'm about to propose a trade when the door opens. My heart stops and every ounce of oxygen leaves my lungs as I hear Tatum's sweet voice call my name.

Callan cuts his panicked eyes to Tatum and back to me. I step toward her, but I'm stopped by a gun to my chest and forehead. One of the goons is sweating and grinning. He's older than the others, probably one of Luca's father's men. The other is younger and patiently waiting for instruction as his gun is pressed into my chest.

"Tatum," I say, hoping she'll understand my plea for her to turn her ass around and get the fuck out of here. What the hell is she doing here?

Luca's gun is back out, pointing at Tatum. My eyes flick to Luca. There's a spark in his eyes. Fuck. My gaze swings back to Tatum. I can't risk looking at Roman or Kiernan, but I trust them to have a gun trained on Luca.

"Leave," I hiss. "Go. Go. Right now."

Tatum is frozen, her terrified eyes flitting from gun to gun to gun.

"I...I...."

"Sunshine," I plead. "Go."

"Don't leave. This is just starting to be fun. If you take one step toward that door, I will kill you *and* him."

Tatum gulps, her fearful eyes meeting mine. She knew something was happening. Why the fuck did she come? "It's okay, Tatum. Come to me. Slowly." I don't let my voice show my anger.

Our eye contact only breaks when Luca moves toward her with his gun aimed at her head, and Callan steps in front of him, blocking Tatum completely.

Luca laughs. "Another interesting turn of events. Truly I'd like to get this done quickly, though. I'm going to need you to move, Callan."

"She's innocent," Callan says calmly. His head turns the slightest amount addressing Tatum. "Follow my steps. Stay behind me."

Callan starts to move closer to me, shielding Tatum the entire way. Luca glares daggers at him. "You're lucky I hate cleaning up dead bodies. I might make an exception for you and your sister, though. Remember who is protecting her."

"She's innocent," Callan repeats angrily, swallowing thickly and cutting his eyes to me.

*What the fuck is happening?* Callan is openly defying Luca.

"I protect my sister," Callan whispers furiously, spittle flying through his teeth.

Luca glares at Callan, his eyes narrowing. "Luck runs out."

Once Tatum is close enough, Kiernan grabs her from behind Callan, shoving her behind the three of us. We gather closer together, blocking her from view. The calm man with his gun trained on me backs away while the other keeps it against my forehead, licking his teeth and smiling sinisterly.

Callan turns his gun on me again, backing away and moving to Luca's side. "Thank you," I say. Callan grinds his teeth, and his eyes flash angrily.

As we stare at each other, he's unable to hide the emotion in his eyes. He doesn't want to do this. Every waver of the gun and shift of his feet tells me that. He said he wanted out of this life. If Luca hadn't held Braelyn over his head all this time, he wouldn't be doing this. It's exactly how I felt when I took off with the bag of money. I didn't want to do the task I was assigned, but I also didn't want to die.

"This is taking too long," the goon with his gun on me says. "If Callan won't do it, I will."

"Step back," Luca says, his gun back in its holster. "This

is Callan's job."

The man grumbles but moves back.

"Let's make a trade," I say.

"What kind of trade?" Luca perks up, his lips tilting slightly. He moves from bored to amused so easily. He likes to do the least amount of work while collecting the largest amount of money he can. Hopefully I can sway him.

"Let's end this," the goon says as he wipes a shaking hand over his sweaty brow. I ignore him, keeping my focus on Luca. Luca doesn't respond to him or give any orders. The goon impatiently groans. "Let me do it, boss."

I open my mouth to offer the deal, but I stop when a gun cocks and movement from the side catches my attention. I barely register the movement when Callan springs into action, launching himself in front of me to block me.

The crack of the gun firing echoes throughout the gym.

"No," Callan roars, barely heard over the echoes of the gun, his body jerking back, slamming into me. The impatient goon fired his shot intended for me, hitting Callan in the shoulder. I steady him, helping him stay on his feet while adjusting my aim at the fucker who fired.

Luca remains still, completely unruffled. He sighs, rolling his eyes. The thug keeps his gun trained toward me and Callan; he's not moving a muscle.

I hear Tatum's shocked breaths behind me, but I can't risk turning my head. Callan is leaning against me, and I'm propping him up. The coppery scent of his blood is filling my nostrils. Sweat starts rolling down my back. Every man in the room is sweating, the smell filling the space and mixing with Callan's blood.

My arm is over Callan's chest; his heart is beating rapidly beneath my arm. His breathing is ragged, but he's still alert and focused on the men in front of us. The men he came with. The men he just betrayed for me. His sister's life is definitely on the line, now.

The tension in the air fills me with adrenaline, pumping through my veins and readying me for action. I register the placement of every gun in the room. Two trained on me and one pointing toward Kiernan and Roman. They've remained my silent sentries at my side, but I can feel the need for action rolling off each of them. Battle and anticipation are nothing new for them.

Luca's gun is still in his suit; he starts picking lint off of his suit, but I see the muscle popping from his clenched jaw. The goon who shot Callan is drenched in sweat, his eyes casting from us to Luca. His hands around the gun are wobbling as his whole body leans forward and is vibrating with energy. He wants to shoot again. The other two calmly wait for instruction, their clenched jaws the only sign of tension.

Tatum is shivering against my back, the fear seeping from her and into me. She fists the back of my shirt, her head resting between my shoulder blades. Her tears soaking through my shirt are urging me into action. I *will* protect her. I won't allow any of this to touch her, Roman, Kiernan, or Callan.

White, hot fury is filling me, each ragged breath from Callan spurring my anger. Luca's eyes are downcast, looking at himself. I need to take control of this situation right the fuck now.

"I have a trade," I growl. I've spent years thinking about what I'm about to offer him. The fact that it's Luca here and not someone else is the best possible chance I have.

His greed and laziness may work for me. I've saved for this moment I hoped, begged, and prayed would never come.

"What kind of trade?" Luca repeats, examining his nails.

"I have your money," I say. "All that I took plus double your standard interest."

Luca raises his eyebrows, calculating that amount in his head. I know this greedy fucker will keep most of it for himself. "Really?"

I nod. "I'll make it triple if Callan is dismissed as an associate." I won't let Callan go back to that life, not after his show of support toward me. Even if the offer is accepted, his days could be numbered. Callan and Braelyn will get out of this, I'll do whatever it takes. I've looked for a solution since I left, but never found one. That won't happen now.

"Interesting," Luca says, swiping his thumb along his lips.

"Quadruple," Callan says ruggedly, breaking free from my hold and trying to stand straight. I reach out to balance him, but he shoves me off.

"Quadruple?" Luca's eyes light up, excitement showing.

"How do you know I have that?" I ask quietly.

"I still know you. You have it, fucker," Callan answers roughly. He holds a hand over the wound on his shoulder, straightening his spine as much as possible. "Plus, the information I have that would send every head boss in the organization to prison. It's yours. Here's a small freebie of the information I've collected—the dickwad who just shot me is sleeping with your wife and stealing a thousand dollars a week from your restaurant."

Surprise rocks through me. Callan has always been scrappy and will do damn near anything for his sister, but collecting information on the mafia? He'd be buried alive in a grave before he knew what was happening if they caught wind of it.

My hand tightens on my gun, keeping my aim on the guy itching to shoot someone again. His face is red from anger. He's definitely more loyal to Luca's father than Luca. Luca can be swayed with the right amount of money; his father has ordered enough hits to fill multiple cemeteries.

This fucker is itching for a bloodbath, especially now that this secret is on display. Out of the corner of my eye, I see Luca look toward the man in question.

"Is it true?" Luca asks. I reach one of my hands back, squeezing Tatum's hip and pushing her slightly away from my body, but close enough that she's hidden from view. My hand goes back to my gun. That touch was too short, but it will have to get me through this.

The man sputters, outraged, searching for an answer.

Luca takes a step back, contemplating. "So it is true."

"He's lying," the man protests.

Luca stares at him then turns his attention to us, rubbing his hand along his jaw then through his hair. He looks back to the man accused of stealing and sleeping with his wife. The other goons tense and stand straighter, waiting for an order. The entire room pauses, waiting for what will happen.

I shift my aim toward Luca, but not directly on him. Luca slowly pulls his gun from his suit, pointing it to the floor then aims his gun on the traitor. He shoots him in each leg. His pained cries fill the gym as he topples to the floor, his hands covering the gaping and bleeding wounds.

"Shit," Kiernan says under his breath.

My aim is fully on Luca, anticipating his next move. His focus is on the small fleck of blood on his white shirt. "Fucking hate messes. Get him out of here," Luca says calmly to the other two men.

One of them takes off his shirt quickly ripping it and wraps it around the wounds. "Don't want blood in your car, boss."

Luca nods and motions with his hand that they should carry on. The men pick up the injured asshole and carry him out like it's something they do all the time. The only evidence something happened here are the small drops of blood on the floor.

"Always surprises me that some areas of the body don't bleed a lot," Kiernan muses to himself.

Tatum's name chants through my mind. She shouldn't be here. Dammit. I need a way to get her out of this. The anger filling me quickly turns to dread when Luca points his gun toward us swinging it from one side to the other.

"Now what to do with you lot," he mutters.

"There are four guns trained on your head, and you only have one for the four of us. The way I see it, you'd have four bullets in your skull before your finger even hit the trigger," I taunt. "The money I offered you would do you no good if you're dead."

"I'd take the money," Kiernan says. "Bodies are a bitch to clean up."

"The money I took plus quadruple your standard interest," I repeat.

Luca's eyes flare with intrigue.

"And my information," Callan pants, his breathing becoming heavier with each second.

Luca cocks his head, pointing his gun straight at my head then my chest. I stop breathing, moving my finger to the trigger. Luca smirks then lowers his gun. "Bodies are too much trouble. Get me my money," he says.

"Roman, grab the money," I say, since he's closest to the bags. Roman grabs them quickly as Kiernan covers for him, none of us trusting Luca until he's out that door. Roman tosses each bag to Luca, and they each land with a heavy thud. "All the money plus quadruple."

"Empty your gun," Callan demands.

Luca laughs, pulling his phone from his pocket and calling one of the goons back to retrieve the bags. He empties the bullets from the gun, sticking them in his pocket, but hands the gun to his goon. He doesn't take his eyes off us and doesn't speak until the goon is out of the building.

Callan takes a set of keys from his pocket, tossing it to Luca's feet. "Storage unit 1314 at the place by the pier. That information will clean out your rats and make you a wealthier man."

"You have my word," Luca says, pressing a hand over his heart. "James, you are free."

"And, Callan? He's in this deal. Callan is free, too."

His eyes move to Callan's.

Faster than I thought he could move, he pulls another gun from the inside of his suit, and he shoots Callan in the stomach. "If he lives, you can keep him, too."

Callan becomes dead weight in my arms. I lower him to the floor, Kiernan and Roman stepping in front of us with their guns aimed at Luca. "Don't shoot," I demand. If we shoot him, the rest of the mafia would rain down on us faster than we could prepare.

Luca leaves the building without looking back.

"Fuck," I grit out, pressing over the wound on Callan's stomach. "Get an ambulance here!" Tatum hovers next to me, pressing her hands on top of mine.

Callan is gasping for breath and groaning in pain.

"Get...get Brae out of Chicago," he asks, staring into my eyes. "Please."

I nod. "I will. As soon as I can. I'll get her out."

Callan nods, closing his eyes.

"Don't," Tatum says, bringing her hand to his face. "Wake up. You have to stay awake. Braelyn needs you."

His eyes flutter open, locking onto Tatum. His mouth opens slightly, but nothing comes out.

"Cops and ambulance are on the way. I reported a burglary gone wrong. Suspect fled on foot," Roman says.

"Turn off my cameras," I say, not breaking eye contact with Callan. *Fuck.* I should've tried harder to get him out sooner. I shouldn't have left him in Chicago.

"Kiernan's working on it and erasing the footage and stashing the guns."

The few minutes it takes the ambulance to arrive feels like an eternity. Callan's eyes start to shut again.

"Stay awake, Callan. Fuck. Stay awake," I plead.

His lids lift slowly. He coughs once, fighting to keep his eyes open.

"Keep fighting. Braelyn needs you. I need you back in my life. Keep fucking fighting. Don't fucking close your eyes. Dammit. Callan. Stay awake."

When the paramedics burst through the doors, Callan's eyes close and stay shut.

"Dammit, Callan. Fight. Fucking fight."

# CHAPTER
# FORTY-SIX

*Tatum*

"WE HAVE TO FIND BRAELYN," JAMES SAYS, squeezing my hand. Since the ambulance took Callan, James has stayed by my side— holding my hand or with his arm around my shoulders pressing me into his side—not letting me stray farther than an inch. His use of the word *we* and ironclad grip on my hand settles my nerves.

James and I have so much to talk about, but I'm not going to bring it up in a hospital waiting room while his childhood best friend is in surgery.

We answered the police's questions about a burglary gone wrong. Kiernan dove into a story as soon as the police set foot in the building. Callan, a friend visiting from Chicago for the holidays, wanted to see his friend's gym. While most of the group were sitting in the office, Callan was standing at the front of the gym looking at pictures on the wall. A man broke in through the open door. Callan moved to restrain him but was shot in the process before he could reach the suspect. The would-be burglar took off when the rest of us piled out of the office. We corroborated his story, each of us filling in details about the masked man coming to steal from James—a man known to keep cash on hand for any neighborhood families that need some help. Kiernan weaved the story so thoroughly and convincingly, turning to the rest of us at different points to back him up, that I almost believed that's what actually happened.

A tale of a burglar breaking in is easier to believe than we had a showdown with the mafia. The freaking mafia.

"We'll find her," I say, leaning my head on his shoulder. "Do you have any idea where she is?"

"Yeah," James lets go of my hand to wrap his arm around me. He places a kiss on top of my head and breathes in deeply. "I can't stop imagining what could've gone wrong. Can't lose you, sunshine."

I reposition myself, wrapping my arms around his middle, not even paying attention to the metal bar of the chair between us that's digging into my ribs. "You're never losing me, honey."

"So fuckin' glad you're safe."

I squeeze his middle instead of responding. It's been four hours without an update. All of our friends are surrounding us, and my family will be here soon. None of them know Callan, but they know James. Every time his eyes sweep around the room landing on each person that is here for him, he swallows thickly.

I burrow my head deeper into James's shoulder, whispering my confession. "I was so scared."

"What were you doing there tonight?"

"I needed to see you. I couldn't handle thinking I may never see you again, look into your eyes or watch you laugh." My breath hitches, my voice cracking at the end. James smiling and laughing is my favorite sound and sight in the world. I *needed* to see him one more time. "I can't tell you how many books I've read and movies I've watched where the girl goes out putting herself in danger, and I always thought she was just making the situation worse."

James grunts. I poke him in the ribs. "I know," I whisper. "I never thought I'd be *that* girl, but here we are. I'm her. Thing is though, I never understood them, never understood what was really at stake. I'd take on the freaking world, James, I'd take it on, just to see you one more time." I lean my head back, staring up at him.

His gray eyes are filled to the brim with emotion as he stares at me. "I know what I said before I left, but I wouldn't even last a day without you. I would've have found a way to come back and be with you."

I stretch, pressing my lips to his. His hand weaves into my hair at the back of my head, keeping my lips against his until he breaks the kiss.

"How did you sneak out?" There's slight humor mixed in with the exasperation in James's voice.

I roll my lips between my teeth, biting back a smile before making my voice as innocent as possible. "I said I was going to take a shower and left through the window."

James smirks, shaking his head. "I'm so fucking pissed at you."

"Why?" I ask, taken aback.

"You put yourself in danger. I couldn't handle it if something happened to you."

"I'm sorry."

"I am, too." He brushes my hair behind my ear and raises my face to his.

"For what?" I ask.

"Not telling you earlier that I am completely in love with you."

A warmth fills my entire body. There's a part of me that knows he loves, I feel it, I trust it. I still want to hear the words. I want to hear him say it in his deep, husky voice. "You love me?"

"I love you to the depths of my soul, Tatum." James's hand tightens in my hair, bringing my lips to his, and muttering against them, "Depths of my fucking soul."

*I*

*love*

*you*

*to*

*the*

*depths*

*of*

*my*

*soul,*

*Tatum.*

My heart starts pounding, beating to the rhythm of that sentence. I breathe a sigh of relief, luxuriating in the warmth of his love. I close the last millimeter between our lips, kissing him over and over, soft kisses all over his lips as I whisper my love back to him.

We break apart, and my head falls to his massive shoulder. "Can't believe I'm thankful for being shot," James mutters.

I raise an eyebrow. "What?" I ask.

"If I hadn't been shot I wouldn't have met you."

"I don't like thinking about you in pain or shot or losing blood. I have to believe we'd have met another way. Maybe we would've met at the grocery store."

"In your cat pajamas?"

"My kitten pajamas," I correct, the corners of my lips twitching.

"Cutest fucking thing I've ever seen. You in your crazy PJs and polar bear slippers. I wanted to kiss you so bad."

James body stiffens, his spine going straight. I look up at him, but his eyes are on the entrance to the waiting area. My eyes turn to see my parents, brother, and Pop Pop rushing in, looking around. James clasps my hand tighter, standing and pulling me up with him.

My mom throws her arms around me, and my dad wraps the both of us up in a hug, kissing the top of my head. My brother and Pop Pop step up next, neither of my parents letting me go entirely.

"I have a lot to explain," James says. My family's eyes turn toward him. "I owe every one of you an explanation, but know I'd die to keep Tatum safe. I'd walk through a storm of bullets to get to her. My past isn't pretty, but I won't let it touch her. I'll spend the rest of my life making sure her light keeps shining. Making sure she smiles and laughs every day until my final breath."

I stop breathing, staring at him, amazed at the way he put it all out there. My family doesn't know what's going on; I gave a very, *very* skimmed-over version—I told them I'm in a hospital waiting room with James hoping his friend makes it through surgery after being shot.

"This isn't your fault, baby," I say. I know what he's doing; he's taking the blame, stepping in front of it and taking a stand. For me.

"My choices led us here, sunshine."

I shake my head but fall silent. James and I stare at each other. He's begging for forgiveness, and I'm trying to ease his worries. My family may not know what's going on yet, but they will, James will give them that honesty.

He's the best man I know.

And, he's mine.

*Mine.*

Pop Pop breaks the silence, trying to ease the tension that's flowing in our small group. "Sounds like a hell of a story, son" He steps toward James and puts his hands on James's shoulders. "Not a damn doubt that you'll take care of my girl."

The tension radiating off James eases. My mom breaks from me, rushing over to James and nudging Pop Pop out of her way, and throws her arms around him. "We don't walk away when things get tough in this family."

James swings his surprised eyes to me before breaking into a huge smile. It drops just as quickly when a doctor walks through the doors.

"Callan Fox's family?"

"Here," James says stepping up to the doctor. Everyone stands behind him, our friends getting out of their chairs and rushing over to have his back.

"You're family?" The doctor asks.

James stretches to full height as he places his palm on his chest. "He's my brother."

# CHAPTER
# FORTY-SEVEN

*James*

"Go away."

"Nope," I respond dryly.

"Get shot and still can't ever get any fuckin' peace," Callan grumbles, staring up at the ceiling. "What's a man have to do to be left the fuck alone?"

Tatum and I haven't left Callan's side since he woke up after surgery. He'll have to stay in the hospital while he heals from the massive blood loss and internal injuries, but luckily, he'll be okay.

"You stepped in front of a bullet for me, and you think I'm just going to leave your stranded ass here?" I ask gruffly, irritation prickling through my system.

"Done it before," he spits.

I bring Tatum's hand to my lips and kiss her soft skin before I drop it, scooting my chair up to the hospital bed. When I grab Callan's hand, he tries to yank it from my grasp, but I hold on, willing him to look at me. I've spent years wondering how I could honor the friendship Callan gave me as a kid. I searched for other choices, but I never found one. He's out of that life now.

Now I will do everything for him and Braelyn.

"Callan."

Callan doesn't move his gaze from the ceiling. The only acknowledgement I get is his jaw clenching and a muscle jumping in his cheek.

"Look at me," I demand.

Callan's insane turquoise eyes swing my way. Anger and pain are waging a war within them. "What?" His voice is a low growl.

"Brother…"

Callan snorts, shaking his head.

I ignore it and continue, confessing everything I wish I could've since I left Chicago. "I'm sorry. So fuckin' sorry. I tried to find a way to get you and Braelyn here without all of us ending up in a pine box."

Callan swallows hard. His eyes dart to Tatum and back to me.

"Callan, I—"

"Save it. I get it," he mumbles. "I need to get back to Chicago. I need to get Brae."

"We're working on it," Tatum says, scooting her chair forward to join me next to his bed.

"Working on it?" Callan asks skeptically.

"My dad is a partner at a law firm, and while he doesn't practice family law, he has a colleague that does. They have a sister firm in Chicago. We're working on it."

"Not taking a hand out," he grunts.

"Not a hand out," I say, squeezing his hand before releasing it. "Family helping family."

"Brae is my only family."

"Not true," I say with a small tilt of my lips. "Tatum loves me, therefore she loves you. She took you under her wing the minute you stepped in front of her, and she claimed you as part of her family when you stepped in front of a bullet for me. You won't get rid of her now. Trust me, I tried."

Tatum lightly slaps my thigh. "I think I'm the one that tried to get rid of you, not-so-jolly-green-giant."

My eyes find hers, and the warmth shining from them makes my chest tighten. Callan chuckles next to us, and our gaze breaks to look at him.

"I'm too tired to argue about this shit right now. Solving it through lawyers and crap will take too long. I need her here. *Now*. I don't fucking trust Luca. I need her out of that city."

"Kiernan is in Chicago right now, working on it. We're hoping he'll be here by tomorrow."

Callan closes his eyes. "Fuck. She has to be okay."

"She will be," I insist. There's no other option.

"My dad said the best thing is to get her down here as if she's visiting. Doing it legally, that means your mom knowing about it. Once she's here, we'll go from there. Callan, I know you don't know me, but I keep my promises, and I'll work with you and the lawyers until we can get Brae here permanently. You're staying in Texas."

Callan stares at her, gauging every one of her words. Trust doesn't come easily to either one of us. Tatum meets his stare, challenging him to find a lie in her words. He won't. My girl is fierce.

Callan dips his head once—a silent acceptance.

"You have a big family now. Get used to it," Tatum says patting his arm.

Callan raises a brow. "I think I like you."

Tatum grins. "Good."

"How the hell did someone as pretty as you end up with this guy?" Callan asks, matching her grin.

I grunt. Somethings never change. There are brief glimpses that show me the guy I knew is still under the anger, but sometimes when his eyes meet mine, I know he's still pissed off. Not enough to want me dead, seeing as how he stepped in front of a god damned bullet for me.

Tatum shrugs. "He's entertaining. When he gets really mad, he gets bright red. I think it's great, plan on doing that for the rest of my life."

"Definitely like you," Callan says between chuckles.

Tatum leans forward, planting a kiss on Callan's cheek. "Thank you for saving James." I grip her thigh when her voice breaks. "I'll never forget that as long as I live."

"Why?" I ask. That question has been popping in my head since he jumped in front of me.

Callan stares at Tatum. He lifts his hand, brushing a tear off her cheek. "Don't thank me, sweetheart." Callan turns his bright eyes to me, grinding his teeth. "As much as I want to deck you in the face for making me think you were *dead* for damn well near a decade, you're still family. You and Brae. That's it."

"I'll make it right," I vow.

The tense moment is broken by the sharp taps on the big wooden door before it slowly eases open. Tatum gasps when she sees Kiernan coming in with a bright smile.

"Got a surprise for you, man," Kiernan says, stepping aside.

All the air leaves my lungs.

Braelyn.

The last time I saw her, she was about to start kindergarten. It's been almost ten years, but I almost expected to see the same small girl from a long time ago.

I can't believe the teenager standing in front of me is Braelyn. She's tall, thin, and looks exactly like Callan did at that age. Her long dark blonde hair looks a little dirty and her clothes are a bit tattered. The jeans she's wearing a little short.

All of that is going to change.

Turquoise eyes, the same as her brothers, lock on Callan

before she runs into the room, throwing herself on him.

"Callan," she cries. "Oh my god. I was so scared."

He grimaces in pain but wraps his arms around her. Her face is tucked into his neck as she sobs uncontrollably. Callan blinks rapidly, rubbing his palm on the back of her head, whispering to her.

Braelyn lifts her head and stares down at him, wiping the tears from her face. "What's going on? Kiernan wouldn't tell me much. He said I had to hear it from you. What's happening?"

"We'll talk Brae, promise. How was your first flight?"

Braelyn glowers at her brother. "Don't change the subject. I'm not a baby anymore."

"You'll always be one to me," Callan says, tapping her on the nose. "We'll talk. I promise. No bullshit. Say hi first, though."

Braelyn turns her head, looking at Tatum and me. "Connor," she whispers before rounding the bed and hugging me.

"You remember me?" I ask, tentatively wrapping my arms around her slim shoulders.

"Barely," she says, taking a step back. "Lan-lan told me about you, and he has a picture of you. That's how I knew it was you. Kiernan told me you're alive and your name isn't Connor anymore."

"No, Braelyn. I go by James now."

She looks at me with an eyebrow raised and whole lot of teenage attitude. "That's weird. Why? Why did Callan think you were dead?"

"I'll explain later, Brae," Callan says. Brae scoffs before they settle on Tatum. Kiernan chuckles from the doorway.

"Hi," Braelyn says softly.

"Hi, sweetie. I'm Tate. James's girlfriend."

Girlfriend. Christ. I wrap my arm around her shoulder,

silently communicating how good it feels to hear her say that word. Mine. Tatum is mine. Now that my past is officially behind me, there's no way I'm leaving her side. I don't even want her out of my sight for a second. She took twenty years off my life when she walked into the gym. Things could've ended so differently, but they didn't. She's here. She's next to me. She's mine.

"It's good to meet you, Braelyn. We're going to give you some time with your brother," Tatum murmurs, reaching out to grip Braelyn's hand.

"Thanks," Callan says as we walk out of the room with Kiernan.

Once we reach the waiting room, Kiernan stops and turns toward us. "You were right," he says, placing his hands on his hips and his face in an angry scowl. "Their mother is a piece of shit. She signed the paper allowing this visit after I gave her some cash. I took some pictures of the place for the lawyer. It's a fucking sty."

"Fuck," I mutter, rubbing my hand down my face.

"It's okay," Tatum says. "We're going to figure this out for them. My dad's firm is on it. One way or another Callan and Brae are here to stay. For good."

I tuck Tatum under my arm, kissing the top of her head. I love when she becomes protective, and I'll never be able to thank her for wanting to help my family. The family she was born into is amazing, but I had to cobble mine together along the way.

"Money bags over here," Kiernan says, gesturing toward me. "Can just drop some cash on that woman's doorstep, and she'll sign over Brae."

"No," she whispers.

"Yeah." Kiernan runs a hand through his hair. Unfortunately, I know he's right. Kiernan glances at Tate, grinding his teeth before sighing. "You're right. We'll figure this out, help them. Whatever they need."

I clap him on the shoulder. "Thanks for going, man. I owe you."

"You don't owe me anything, but if Tate wants to dress as a candy striper to show me her gratitude, I'll take it."

Tatum laughs, her hand falling on my abs as her head nuzzles in my chest. I can feel her whole body shaking against mine, and it feels damn good. "It's stripper."

"Not the way I'm picture it."

"Not happening," I growl, pushing Kiernan back.

"Worth a shot." He shrugs. "Savannah, Harper, and Val will be here in the morning with food. They don't want Callan to eat hospital food and want Brae to feel welcome."

"Christ. They haven't even met him yet," I mutter.

Tatum smiles. "Big family. I told him he's getting a big family."

"He's going to love them fawning over him. It'll go straight to his head."

Kiernan laughs before saying his goodbyes and taking off.

"Ready to go?" Tatum asks, hugging my waist.

"Yeah, sunshine, let's go home."

She tightens her grip when I say the last word. *Home.*

# CHAPTER
# FORTY-EIGHT

## James

*Three weeks later*

"**I**'M SO EXCITED TO SEE HIM," TATUM SAYS STANDING on her toes looking over the crowd.

"I think they're still in the locker room," Callan says leaning against the fence at the exit of the stadium. "Can't believe this is my first weekend out of the hospital and I'm at a high school football game."

"A *champion's* high school football game," Tatum exclaims. She grabs onto the front of my jacket. "We have to do something for Corbin. He did so great."

"Will I go to this school when I move to Texas?" Braelyn asks. Callan slings his arm over her shoulder.

Callan smiles while looking down at Braelyn. She's been excited at the prospect of moving to Texas. Tatum's father's law firm is doing everything they can to make it happen quickly.

"We'll see," Callan says. "Not sure where we'll find a place yet. For now, we're at Hudson's."

"We can stay there," Braelyn says. "I like it there. My room is huge."

Callan shakes his head. "We're finding a place when I

get some money saved."

"Corbin," Tatum shouts as he makes his way toward us.

When he reaches us, Tatum throws her arms around his neck hugging him tightly. "You did so great, champ. I'm so proud of you. How's the shoulder?"

Corbin grins hugging Tatum back just as tightly. "Great. Didn't hurt at all."

Tatum turns toward me. "I told you I was the best physical therapist."

I kiss the top of her head. "I only doubted you for a couple of weeks," I joke.

Corbin stands in front of me and extends his hand. I push it out of the way, bringing him in for hug. "You're going places, kid."

He makes a fist in the back of my jacket.

"Damn proud of you," I say quietly. He nods his head once, hugging me tighter before letting go.

"Corbin," Tatum starts. "This is Callan and his sister Braelyn. Callan is new to Texas and we're hoping Brae joins us here soon, too."

"Good game," Callan says, but Corbin ignores him and stares at Braelyn. She's gazing back at him, tucking a piece of hair behind her ear.

Tatum bites her lip to stop her grin. "Brae helped me make the posters and she held one up during the game."

Corbin's chest puffs out and he stands taller, beaming. "Hi, Brae."

"Hi." A blush rushes to her cheeks when he uses her nickname. Braelyn bites her lip after she whispers her greeting.

Callan is looking back and forth between the two, pushing off from the fence he's leaning against. "Oh, hell no."

Tatum and I chuckle watching Callan staring down an

oblivious Corbin. He hasn't taken his eyes of Braelyn for even a second.

"This is going to be good," Tatum whispers.

My only response is a kiss to her smiling lips.

# CHAPTER
## FORTY-NINE

*Tatum*
*Two months later*

"J AMES," I CALL BEFORE CLAMPING MY LIPS SHUT, trying not to burst into a fit of laughter. "That branch is way too big for him."

"He can handle it. It's just a stick," James says, shooting me a grin before tossing the stick a few yards in front of him.

Sirius trips over James's foot before taking off after his prize. The stick is longer than Sirius. He manages to pick it up, but stumbles sideways. He turns, trying to run back to James, but he can't quite manage under the weight. Sirius head is cocked, and the branch is getting closer and closer to the ground. It's definitely not a stick, but a branch. At least compared to Sirius's little body.

"He's too small for it," I insist, worrying about my little pup.

"He's fine," James says, calling to him. Sirius's eyes are locked on James as he moves as fast as he can, covering those few yards with his tiny legs.

"I think that branch weighs more than he does."

"Stick, sunshine. It's a stick. Our boy may be small, but he's tough," James says, laughing as the branch touches the ground. But Sirius doesn't stop his mission. He keeps rushing toward James, wagging his tail, as the branch drags along the ground.

"Atta boy," James says picking up Sirius when he finally reaches him and takes the branch from his mouth. I stand watching them, putting my hand along my brow to block out the sun. Sirius launches himself at James's face trying to kiss him, his whole body shaking from the force of his tail. "See? He's proud of himself."

I throw my head back and laugh before stepping up to my two guys. I hug James tightly, kissing his chest.

"Was it weird going back?" I ask, raising a hand to scratch behind Sirius's ear.

"To Chicago?" James asks.

I nod. He just got back from Chicago with Callan. My dad and his colleague, Callan's lawyer, pulled every string, used every favor and connection. They had to move custody proceedings along. Callan and Braelyn's mom didn't even put up a fight when Callan approached her about signing her rights away.

Braelyn hasn't been able to stay in Texas in an official capacity yet, but we've all chipped in and brought her down for visits almost every weekend over the last two months. Callan had to appear in front of a judge in Chicago, and James wouldn't let him go alone.

James also wouldn't let me go with them.

"Yeah, it was strange as hell being back. I'd go on any trip you asked me to, sunshine, but I really hope you never want to go to Chicago."

"I don't want to go there," I mutter. That place holds to many dark memories for James, and I'd be looking over our shoulder the entire time. "I wish you would've let me go with you."

"Fuck no," James hisses. "I don't think Luca will go

back on our deal, but I can't risk that with you. Also couldn't leave Callan alone to face that."

"I know," I whisper. "I want this to be over for them."

"It will be," James says confidently. "Callan is set up here in Texas now. Hudson gave him a good job with great pay and benefits at his construction company, and he's living with Hudson in his monstrosity of a house."

"Dad said he's sure it will go Callan's way," I say.

"Yeah," James says. "Talked to him while we were in Chicago. They think it will be over soon. Callan will probably have to go back one more time."

I nod, knowing that means James will also be going back. If he does, hopefully it's for the last time ever.

"Want to go out to the field?" James asks.

I nod again. He kisses my forehead. "I'll be right back," he says, releasing me and striding toward the house.

A minute later he comes back out without Sirius, but with a blanket. He snags my hand as he passes, pulling me along as we go to our spot in the middle of his field. The grass where we lay has become flat, but it's an easy marker of where we like to be. James spreads out the blanket before getting on and lying on his back.

"Get over here, sunshine," he says, making this bright day even brighter with his grin. I sink down next to him, immediately putting my head on his chest and slinging a leg over his hips. My hand rests over his heart.

James wraps one arm around my back, resting his hand along curve of my ass, while his other hand joins mine on his chest.

"Do you have plans tomorrow?" James asks.

"No," I say.

"Good." He taps his hand on my ass.

I tilt my head back and catch a smug grin slide across his face. "Why?"

"You're movin' in tomorrow."

"What?" I ask, choking on a surprised laugh.

James rolls us so he's on top of me. "I can't lose you."

"Never," I reply. "You will never lose me."

He dips his head, nuzzling my neck before trailing his tongue up its column. James nips his way to my lips, sliding his tongue inside my mouth, tangling it with mine. My hands weave in his hair. He breaks our kiss, staring down at me.

His gray eyes turn molten as a breathtaking smile takes over his face. "Glad you agree."

"I didn't agree," I say, laughing.

"That kiss was your agreement." He kisses me again. "And that one."

"Move in?" I ask.

James pulls back, scanning my face. "Yes. I want you here. I never thought I'd get something like this. My past is behind me. For good. It's done, I can actually move forward. I'm doing that with you."

"I know, James, but—" James cuts me off with another kiss to my lips. He trails his lips over my cheek to my ear.

"I love you," he whispers. "You're mine. You'll always be mine. I can choose my future, and I'm choosing you. Get on board. You're moving in tomorrow."

"Okay," I say, grinning. Questions race through my head as I open my mouth to voice them, but James cuts me off with another kiss.

"We'll figure it out. Your lease. Any other concerns you have, we'll figure it out, but we'll figure it out living together in *our* home."

"Okay," I repeat, pulling James's head down. Full lips mold to mine. I swipe my tongue along the seam of my lips. James opens, plunging his tongue into my mouth, making me moan.

"I could kiss you out here for hours," I say.

"I could kiss you out here forever," James murmurs against my lips.

# EPILOGUE

*Tatum*
*Nine years later*

THE SOUND OF A CELL PHONE BREAKS THE SILENCE IN our room. My head is on James's chest. I don't open my eyes, but I feel him stretch for his ringing phone. My eyes slowly blink open. It's still dark outside.

I glance at the clock on the nightstand. Who could be calling at 2:30 in the morning? I groan, pushing my face deeper into James's chest.

"'Lo?" He greets. His voice is muffled and tired, but when his entire body turns to stone, I wake up.

"Yes," he says, voice serious. I sit up, reaching over him to turn on the lamp. He sits up, too, locking eyes with me and grabbing my hand.

"Boy," he says. "Eight years old. Mother signed away parental rights tonight when she was incarcerated"

Oh my god. He's on the phone with Sabrina, our social worker, about a foster child. I know he's repeating everything she's saying. We haven't had a placement since we adopted our now six-year-old daughter, Delilah, two years ago.

"Do we accept placement?" James asks, squeezing my hand.

"Yes, yes, yes," I rush out. "Of course, we accept."

I place a quick kiss on James's lips and jump out of bed. I grab the yoga pants James tugged off me earlier in the night and drag them up my legs. Half-way up, I freeze. "Oh my god," I say.

"What?" James asks, standing from the bed. He just hung up with the phone with Sabrina.

"I can't meet our foster son going commando," I quietly screech, ripping the pants off legs while running to our dresser. I trip, crashing into the edge.

I stop breathing and listen carefully to see if I woke up either of our kids. "Okay, good," I say opening the drawer, taking out the first pair of panties my fingers touch. "I didn't wake the kids."

"Tatum," James says laying his hands on my shoulder. I whip around, still naked, holding the panties in hands.

"Wait," I say. "Should we wake them?"

"Sunshine," James says patiently. "No, we shouldn't wake our six-year-old and our four-year-old. They need to sleep. Stay calm. He'll be here in an hour."

"What's his name?" I ask, my nose burning. Fostering isn't easy. We've had nine kids over the past seven years. I broke each time one of them left, but prayed for the best. Our oldest daughter, Delilah, was one of our foster children. She became eligible for adoption about eight months after she came to us.

We jumped on the opportunity to keep her with us. Delilah bonded with our youngest, Emery, from the very first day. Emery was only a toddler, but Delilah loved to help me care for her. Emery has James's eyes and my red hair. She's my mini-me, except for the eyes.

Delilah's raven hair and dark eyes come from her birth mother and her creamy white skin comes from her birth father. She looks like Snow White with her light skin and dark hair.

James plasters my front to his. My body starts tingling from feeling his skin against mine. "His name is Connor," James chokes out, unable to hide the emotion in his voice.

My voice trembles when I answer him. "Oh my gosh."

"I know," he says. After a long moment of silence, taking in the craziness that we're bringing in a foster child with James's birth name, James breaks the silence. "We need to get ready, sunshine."

We dress silently and exit our room, heading into one of the rooms we added on to our house. I take off the floral sheets while James grabs a navy set from the closet.

"Oh my god," I whisper as I drop the fitted sheet on the mattress and my hand comes up to cover my mouth. "No. No. No."

I speed walk out of the room, walking as lightly as possible past the girl's rooms and into the kitchen, opening the pantry.

"Tatum," James says. "What's going on? Are you okay?"

I spin around facing him. "This morning Emery knocked over my bag of flour. We're out of flour. I can't make pancakes in the morning. Oh my gosh. We have nothing here to make for him for the morning."

"Sunshine," James whispers pulling me into a hug and kissing the top of my head. "I love you. I love you so much, but you need to calm down."

"I can't be calm. Connor will be here soon. He's our first placement in two years. Do you think the girls are ready? I wanted to make him pancakes in the morning."

James leans back, placing a kiss on my lips. "I'll go to the store early in the morning. The girls are just like you. They're ready for anything."

James's words soothe my soul. "Thank you," I whisper, I kiss the center of his chest. "I love you to the depths of my soul."

"Sunshine," James murmurs.

After we break apart, we finish getting the room ready and wait in the living room for Connor to arrive.

"Remember," I say. "It's not always easy. They don't always like us."

"Tatum," James says with a smile in his voice. "I know the drill. I was a foster kid. We'll find a way to handle this situation and give him the best possible life while he's here."

"Will he be available for adoption?" I whisper.

"I don't know, sunshine, but remember even if he is, we may not be the best placement for him. We'll try to be everything he needs, but it doesn't always work that way."

"I know," I say, feeling my heartbreak already.

Headlights shine through the window as a car approaches the house. James unarms the alarm and we step out onto the porch and wait for our son.

Sabrina gets out of the passenger side and opens the backdoor of the minivan. James clutches my hip tightly as Connor steps out of the car. My hand is fisted in the back of James's shirt. I want to run to him and hug him, but I know he needs to lead this first meeting.

Connor keeps his eyes on his shoes as he approaches us next to Sabrina. His hair is as dark as Delilah's and is sticking up in all directions. It looks like he was woken up suddenly. Sabrina holds a bag with a few of his belongings.

"Connor," Sabrina says. "This is James and Tatum."

Connor finally looks up from his shoes. Light hazel eyes meet mine. And a piece of my heart clicks into place as we stare at each other. It's the same click I felt when we met Delilah for the first time.

I know James feels it too when his fingers press into my hip. James and I sink into a crouch.

"Hi, Connor," I whisper, sticking out my hand. "Do you like pancakes?"

A small smile tugs at the edges of his lips.

*One year later*

Pride fills me as we leave Tatum's parent's house and pass their mailbox. Her mom painted it just for this occasion. Connor grinned when we arrived this morning for brunch before the courthouse and he's grinning now as we pass it.

*Welcome to the family, Connor.* He's been part of our family since day one. Everyone in our lives immediately fell in love with him. It wasn't easy in the beginning, but with therapy, unwavering love, and persistence, he accepted his spot in the family. Today makes it legal.

We're officially adopting Connor today.

When we arrive at the courthouse, everyone is already there. All of our best friends and Tatum's family. We pile into the courtroom waiting for the judge. Connor sits between Tatum and I in his gray suit and navy blue tie that matches mine. The girls, in their blue dresses, are sitting on the other side of Tatum. She's also wearing a blue dress that matches her eyes perfectly.

Our eyes lock over our son's head. Her eyes fill with unshed tears.

"I love you," she mouths.

"To the depths of my soul," I reply.

THE END

Enjoy Vow of Honor?

You can make a huge difference in a book's life!

Reviews encourage other readers to try out a book. They are critically important to getting the word out about a book and mean the world to every author.

I'd love your help in spreading the word about Vow of Honor. If you could take a quick moment to leave a review on your favorite book site, I would be forever grateful. It can be as short or as long as you like. You can do that on your preferred retailer. Or on Goodreads. Or on BookBub. Even better? All three! It's as simple as copying and pasting!

Email me a link to your review at emmarenshaw@outlook.com so I can be sure to thank you. You're wonderful!

# BONUS SCENE

Want a little bit more of James and Tatum? I wasn't quite ready to let them go! By signing up for my newsletter, you'll get this bonus scene plus you'll be the first to see cover reveals, exclusive news, excerpts you won't find anywhere else, and giveaways! Sign up by going to the link below.

www.subscribepage.com/VOH

# ACKNOWLEDGEMENTS

Creating a book from the spark of an idea to the finished product in your hands truly takes a village. I couldn't live this dream of mine without the help of so many around me. Please accept an apology to anyone I may have left out, it wasn't by intention—my sincerest apologies and my deepest gratitude.

My darling husband, I'll spend the rest of my years thanking you for everything you do for me. Your love for me astounds me every day. Thank you for the encouragement, support, and love. I'm grateful for the days when you push me to expand my boundaries and continue in the pursuit of my dreams, for forcing me out of my bed when I want to sleep a little bit longer. You're my shoulder to lean on when I need it and my kick in the ass when I need that, too. Thank you for listening to me talk for hours on end about my books, characters, and the book world. I'm the luckiest girl. Te amo.

Mom, thank you for your unfailing honesty and for traveling to help me through the process of releasing a book. Our two-hour phone calls keep me sane on the hardest days. I love you for all you do and for passing down your creativity to me.

Dad, I'll never be able to tell you how much it meant to me that the first book you read in years was mine. You've spent your life giving everything to mom, my sister, and me. I'm always thankful for that. Your love and support doesn't go unnoticed. I love you!

Sestra, thank you for providing me with a lifetime of material to use for my books. I love you!

My family, Del Pueblo family, and friends, thank you all for every ounce of love and support y'all give me. I feel it so deeply and am truly humbled by everything y'all have done for me. Each of you holds a very special place in my life, I don't know where I would be without y'all in it.

Catherine Cowles, there will never be enough time in the day to thank you for everything. I'm so thankful I met you and have you by side during this journey. Thank you for our chats, listening when I cry, and laughing along with me.

Grahame Claire, thank you so much for your insight and words of encouragement. I love having you in my corner and sharing our triumphs and failures. I'm so glad we're on this crazy ride together!

Traci, you've made me a stronger writer. I love your honest feedback and hilarious comments. You make editing more enjoyable! You're the best!

Bloggers, thank you so much for all the love and support. I've loved connecting with so many of you and hope to meet more of you in the future. Whether I've chatted with you or never spoken to you, I'm incredibly grateful for the hard work and dedication you give to the book community. Thank you so much! I wish I could hug all of you.

Michelle, Jennifer, Amber, Caterina, thank you SO much for helping me find teasers. All of you went above and beyond! It helped me so much and I'm so grateful for each of you.

The ladies of Emma Renshaw's Books and Addicted to Love Stories, y'all are freaking wonderful! Thank you so much for the love and support!

A huge Thank You goes to: Kristen, Hang, Stacey, Becca, Give Me Books girls, and every other person that contributed to this book. It all means so much and each of you deserve so much more than a thank you.

Lastly, thank YOU! I wish I could thank every reader in person, give them a big hug, and a slice of cake! Every time a reader like you picks up my book, my dreams come true. You're magnificent! THANK YOU!

# ABOUT THE AUTHOR

Emma loves to write, just don't ask her to write about herself. If she isn't writing, you can find her lost in a book or trying to get her doggo to take a selfie with her. He usually refuses. At the end of the day, you can find Emma at the closest Mexican restaurant eating queso and sipping on a margarita. She lives in Texas with her husband and dog.

# CONNECT WITH EMMA

You can find Emma in all the book-loving hang outs!

Website: emmarenshaw.com
Facebook: facebook.com/emmarenshawauthor
Instragram: instagram.com/emmarenshawauthor
Goodreads: goodreads.com/emmarenshawauthor
BookBub: bookbub.com/profile/emma-renshaw
Amazon: amazon.com/author/emmarenshaw

Do you love Facebook reader groups? Come hang out with
Emma in these groups!
Emma Renshaw Books:
facebook.com/groups/emmarenshawbooks

Addicted to Love Stories:
facebook.com/groups/addictedtolovestories

Kiss & Tell Romance:
acebook.com/groups/kissandtellromance

# ALSO BY
## EMMA RENSHAW

*Vow of Retribution*

*Vow of Atonement*

*Vow of Honor*

Made in the USA
Columbia, SC
27 May 2022

9